The Ninth Stone
KYLIE FITZPATRICK

Weidenfeld & Nicolson
LONDON

First published in Great Britain in 2007
by Weidenfeld & Nicolson

© Kylie Fitzpatrick 2007

1 3 5 7 9 10 8 6 4 2

A CIP catalogue record for this book
is available from the British Library.

ISBN 978 0 297 85276 6 (HDBK)
ISBN 978 0 297 85301 5 (TPB)

Typeset by Input Data Services Ltd, Frome

Printed in Great Britain by Clays Ltd, St Ives plc

Weidenfeld & Nicolson
The Orion Publishing Group Ltd
An imprint of the Orion Publishing Group
Orion House, 5 Upper St Martin's Lane,
London, WC2H 9EA

www.orionbooks.co.uk

For Nick and Saoirse. We three met in the beginnings of this book and have had great adventures since.

Suspended in the heavens is a net, made entirely of threads of light. The net hangs high above the palace of Indra, king of the gods. At every crossing of Indra's net is a crystal gem, and each is illuminated, not only by its own light, but by the light of every other gem it reflects, and by reflections of reflections, embracing an infinite galaxy. I am one such crystal; I am one, but reflect all. I am often mistaken for the planet Venus, for in the night sky I am the most brilliant of stars. To the Romans I was Amante de Dio, the love of god. In India I am Varga, a name I share with thunderbolt, for we are as powerful as each other. In English, I am Diamond. If you were to examine Indra's net more closely, you would think that its vertical threads run through space, and its horizontal threads through time. The measuring of time is a peculiarly human device, with little to recommend it, so let us for simplicity say that I am situated at the intersection of two threads; I connect time and place. I am their meeting point, their narrator . . .

Uttar Pradesh, Northern India, 1863

On principle, Lord Herbert was content to leave the governing of everyday affairs to his wife. She needed to be kept busy, he felt, and there was simply no use in making the least attempt to thwart her will. If Lady Cynthia wanted to journey by elephant and camel for one hundred miles from one pandemoniac holy city in India to another, then she would do so – with or without him. Were it not for the good company of their extraordinary chaperone, who at the insistence of the Maharajah was to journey with them the entire distance to London, then Charles Herbert was certain he would be entirely vexed by boredom. The long, slow and dusty trek was enlivened only by their escort's superior knowledge of both history and myth, including a rather fanciful intelligence on the Hindu lore of gems. Jewels and mysticism being amongst Cynthia Herbert's favourite amusements, his wife was enthralled, he was entertained, and so the days passed quite pleasantly enough.

The province of Uttar Pradesh, they had learnt, contained more Hindu holy cities than any other in the whole of India. It was also a place of pilgrimage for the wandering Sanyasi ascetics, since this was where the Buddha had taught his first sermon. The province stretched from the Ganges plain all the way to the Tibetan foothills of the Himalayas, and their company had already encountered several weary and threadbare pilgrims between the holy cities of Benares and Ayodhya.

Uttar Pradesh was an unfathomable distance from his favourite cigar divan on Piccadilly, but Lord Herbert was trying hard not to be reminded of such things. Just as he was trying not to be reminded of tigers and bandits, both creatures being native to the high country through which they were passing. Surely, he thought, no self-respecting beast would approach an entourage of twenty-four camels, six elephants whose mahouts were elite hunters, a train of at least three dozen porters (some carrying beds and tables on their heads),

3

and an armed guard of sepoys, although they might be attracted by the small herd of cows, calves and sheep, kept for the provision of fresh meat. In order that the company be comfortable over the journey, which was to last several weeks, the Herbert camp consisted of sundry large canvas tents, complete with Turkish rugs for the floor, table and bed linen, silver and chinaware, candlesticks and ornaments, as Lady Herbert insisted on keeping proper table, even in the wilds. There was port wine and brandy and usually plum cake, but always rice pudding with honey, which she had taught the cook to make from basmati, albeit with yaks' milk.

Now, according to their erudite guide, they were within one day's ride of Ayodhya, the legendary city said to have been built by the gods. They had climbed steadily from the river plain and as the sun hurried to the southern hemisphere behind the distant Himalayas, they were at last nearing their camp. Lady Herbert was listening intently to another of their companion's ubiquity of Hindu fairytales. This time it was about a foolish demon named Bala who went to heaven with the intention of slaying the king of the gods, Indra, but was convinced by Indra to sacrifice himself instead. The gods dismembered the unfortunate Bala, whose body was then transmuted into gemstones. His teeth became pearls, his blood ruby, his bile emerald, his bones diamond, his eyes sapphires, his flesh coral, his skin topaz, his fingernails moonstone and his body fluid beryl.

Nine of the Hindu's most notable gods then claimed a stone as their own, and thereafter the gemstone became representative of both the deity and the planet that deity ruled, as though planet, god and jewel were one and the same. These nine entities were known as the *navaratna*. Charles Herbert had heard the term before, during their stay as guests of the Maharajah in Benares, but had taken little interest in the matter. He knew that the navaratna was something his wife, the Maharajah and their escort treated with the reverence of the Holy Cross, and was therefore inclined to think even less of the idea. The very notion that nine pieces of coloured rock might have magical properties was profane and indecorous. However the story of Bala had conveniently taken up the remainder of the journey to their designated camp, and already there was the usual fuss and clamour to turn the arid wilderness and scorched grass into a temporary scullery, dining room, bed chamber, parlour and stable. Cynthia was being helped from her kneeling camel, her voluminous petticoats quite startling in the eerie twilight. Lord Herbert allowed a porter to pull his own beast to its knees and took a moment to steady his nerves and his legs. He was simply not the intrepid adventurer that his wife wished him to be, and wanted nothing more than to find a tree behind which to relieve himself. After that, he would have his boots removed, his glass charged, and begin the process of dulling his wits.

As he wandered away from the jangle of camel bells and cooking pots, Charles Herbert had the sensation that he was being watched. But this was nothing new – he had become familiar with his own paranoia, and knew that the campsite had been chosen as much for its relative safety as for its scenery. Besides, a small band of sepoys and porters always strode ahead to start a fire and clear the ground and to alert any lurking beast that didn't want its head mounted on the Maharajah's wall. Content in this knowledge, Lord Herbert met his death. As the air in his lungs imploded – forced as it was to remain there by what felt like a silken cord about his throat – he saw the dying rays of the Indian sun glint off a long knife, bright and curved like a new moon. He thought of Bala the demon, whose dismembered limbs had been flung to the gods, whose flesh had been turned into coral and whose blood became rubies . . .

Part ❖ I

I shall never forget you, never. Never forget
Your memory woven about the beautiful things of life.
The sudden thought of your face is like a wound
When it comes unsought
On some scent of jasmine, lilies or pale tuberose,
Any one of the sweet, white fragrant flowers,
Flowers I used to love to lay in your hair.

Adela Florence Corey

❖ 1 ❖

When well wetted and beaten into a pulp and mixed with gum and then boiled in a pipkin, there is simply nothing equal to *The Times* for stopping holes or cracks in one's canoe, which is, as Mr Pepys would say, an excellent thing in a newspaper.

Mary Kingsley

Amen Corner, London, 1864

In the tea room on the third floor of the London *Mercury* building, Sarah O'Reilly rolled her St Bruno's Flake tobacco twig thin, and gazed down through the dusty windowpane to the street. This was her favourite time of day, especially on days such as this when she'd had plenty of errands to run for Septimus Harding. It meant that she had to take her smoke break later than the other compositors, but she had the dingy little room to herself. It was bare except for a copper pail into which the compositors put their tea mugs, a rickety wooden table and some stools. Pinned to the walls were pictures from the more common penny journals: illustrations, yellowed from the sun and all the tobacco smoke, of half-clothed women advertising lacy stays and stockings.

From the third floor, there was a fine view of Paternoster Row and – when the fog lifted – of the eastern end of Fleet Street. On this sharp, spring afternoon, the Row was a spiralling motion of top hats and umbrellas, reminding Sarah of the black wheels of the steam presses in the basement, which in turn reminded her of her good fortune.

The idea of finding work indoors had come to her in the bitter winter of the previous year, as she huddled over one of the vents above the basements of Paternoster Row. Below, the hot engines of the newspaper press made a noise like a steam train, and had set Sarah's mind to thinking how cosy it would be to spend the winter months in the warmth, rather than on the streets selling apples and dried lavender

9

stems so that she and Ellen could stay clear of thieving. If she were earning proper coin, then Ellen could stay off the streets altogether. She could even go to school.

Sarah had already taken to dressing as a boy when some clothes were left behind by a former tenant at the White Hart, the gin mill where she and Ellen now lived in the cellar room. Ruby the landlady said that the boy had died of being a chimney sweep. He'd got stuck up a chimney and no one knew he was there, so when the fire was lit the smoke from below had filled his poor lungs. The breeches were slightly singed, but the boots almost fit, and the cap was large enough to hide half of Sarah's small face.

So, she had called herself Sam, and had talked her way into a job with Septimus Harding, editor of the *London Mercury*, where she was employed to run messages and to deliver documents and manuscripts wrapped in brown paper and string. She had almost lost her position once out of curiosity; she had too much of that for her own good, Pa used to say. But wasn't it just the Irish in her? That's what Pa always said when he got squiffed and took to lamenting over his ancestry.

Pa had been hoping for an easy life once they stepped off the boat from County Wicklow. He'd said London would be a grand old town where the sun shone every day and they'd be welcomed by one and all. But in Devil's Acre there was no way of knowing if the sun was shining, seeing as the alleyways were always in shadow, and as to London people being welcoming, well, aside from Ruby, no one seemed to care about London's new residents either way. Pa thought he'd make his fortune without even trying, and he never tried, that's for sure; not once he saw how things were here. Mam had had to work like the devil when pa was too cockeyed to go out in the herring boats.

It was while exploring the third floor one evening after the compositors had left that Sarah's curiosity got the better of her. As she stood in front of a tray of type blocks, she began to arrange a small word, copied from a draft sheet still pinned to the board. Then a longer word, and then a sentence. By the time the night porter had discovered her, she was entranced and heedless to the jingling keys that signalled his approach. Were it not for the kindly nature of Septimus Harding she would have found herself back on the frozen street. Instead, he arranged that she should earn tuppence ha'penny more, and said they would see how she fared as an apprentice compositor.

It had not taken Septimus Harding long to see through Sarah's disguise – nor the other compositors, all of whom were men – but he was pleased with her work and said he didn't want to see 'her perfectly good wits go to waste'. Nevertheless, Mr Harding remarked that it wouldn't do to have a girl in a newspaper office, so Sarah kept wearing breeches and after a while no one seemed to notice.

She was lucky, she thought, as she wrapped her thin, ink-stained hands around the tin mug and looked down at the street. The owner of the bookstall opposite had put his striped awning up against the threat of rain, and was standing in the doorway in his shirt sleeves, in spite of the late snow that lay melting in sooty patches across the flagstones. The man was pink-cheeked from taking a measure or two of rum with his pork pie. Sarah had seen him do this on more than one occasion in Dolly's Chop house right next door.

Now, two yellow-haired children had stopped at the roasted chestnut barrow outside Dolly's. The woman looking after them was dressed in the stern, navy serge of a governess, and was trying to shoo them along, but the children were rubbing their hands together over the little coal fire and the eldest – a lively, comely boy – was pleading for some of the barrow's delicious fare. His sister watched the unruly behaviour of her brother hopefully, but remained demure, as befitted girls of her class. Not for the first time, Sarah was thankful for her freedom. She had noted, since she'd arrived in London, that girls who were privileged by way of birth and wealth might as well be living in fancy prisons for all the freedom they had. The little girl in the street had a face like a porcelain doll, with springy flaxen ringlets, and she reminded Sarah of Ellen, or of how her little sister might look if you scrubbed the coal dust and river mud from her, untangled her messy blonde hair, and dressed her in pretty clothes.

As the governess finally surrendered and opened her purse, a brightly painted omnibus drawn by four jingling dray horses clattered to a halt, momentarily eclipsing the theatre of the street. When the omnibus rattled away again, Sarah spotted Mrs Korechnya stepping out across the road. She was on her way to visit Septimus Harding, as she had once done every week. They hadn't see Mrs Korechnya much over the winter, on account of Mr Korechnya dying.

Lily Korechnya was an object of great curiosity to Sarah, as she was completely unlike any other lady she knew – not that she could say she knew any *real* ladies, except for the pastor's wife at the Christian Ladies Charity, who didn't count because she had hair on her chin. To begin with, Mrs Korechnya never wore a mantle or a bonnet. Sarah was not especially fond of the season's bonnets. From three floors up, many looked worse than a magpie's nest, with feathers and shining trinkets and coloured ribbons, and a tall gentleman might easily have mistaken them for a sewing basket and been put off proposing marriage. For marriage was what the fancy-bonneted women who promenaded here, and on the Strand and Oxford Street, were primarily concerned with – Sarah knew that much. She believed that Mrs Korechnya wore a hood instead of a bonnet precisely to avoid attracting the attention of gentlemen. Her costume, beneath her hooded cloak, was narrow and understated, not cumbersome and ungainly like the silly crinolines that were, unbelievably, still the fashion. Sarah took an interest in the fashions, though she had less opportunity to observe them now than when she sold apples from a basket at Cathedral Corner.

But it was time to get back to work. Sarah gulped the remains of the thin tea that had been stewing in the great iron pot since morning, put her tin mug in the pail, and returned to the compositing room to collect the trays of copy that had been made ready for downstairs.

The industry of the building reverberated quietly in the large third-floor room. Here the vaulted ceilings were high, and the floors bare wood. Although this room contained none of the latest American machinery for the composing of print type, it had its own sounds: the scraping of stools, the rustle of paper, the pitch of metal against metal as stereographs were etched. The two dozen or so compositors and stereographers were arranged in four rows, waistcoats hunched over easels. They paid no attention to her (they never did), nor to the sleek black rat that she had seen sniffing around the doorway of the tea room. They were devoted to their narrow columns of type: Imperial Parliament and the business of Marlborough Street, shipping news, advertisements and obituaries, reviews and crime reports. Sarah still loved to see the flat trays of type resting on the long benches, and the upright easels with draft sheets pinned to them. She loved the smell of paper and ink. It made her feel proud to be part of such a business.

The space had once been a workroom for 'devotion of another order', as Septimus Harding was fond of saying, for it had been inhabited by the paternosters who made rosary beads for St Paul's Cathedral before it was destroyed by the great fire. Mr Harding said that was why the small triangle of streets had come to be called Amen Corner. Nowadays Paternoster Row was home to the overflow of publishers, stationers and book binders from Fleet Street.

Sarah had been labouring all day over a painstaking assemblage: an advertisement for 'Perry's Cordial Balm of Syriacum'. It was the longest advertisement she had ever been given to set, and she was determined that there should be no errors. As she slowly reread the text, she was again puzzled by the word *'spermatorrhoea'*. Whatever condition this was, it was in urgent need of curing since so many new potions seemed to be devoted to it. A single measure of Perry's would 'enable men at once to fulfil the most sacred obligations of married life, ensuring health, manhood and vigour'. At twelve shillings a dose, it must be some kind of holy potion, Sarah thought, perhaps something to do with God, aiding as it did in sacred obligations . . .

When all of the print trays had been stacked neatly atop each other, the irritating Jack Thistlewite gave her a message for Septimus Harding. He always liked to find fault with the copy as it made him feel clever. Sarah pulled her cap down a little out of habit, and took the back stairwell. She preferred it to the central one because it was barely used by anyone except Nelly the maid, and Sarah often went there to have a quiet smoke when the tea room conversation became too bawdy for her. They sometimes forgot that she was a girl, or maybe they just didn't care.

Septimus Harding's rooms were on the second floor. The first floor was occupied by the clerks and proofreaders, along with the offices of the regular writers and the front desk, manned by the fearful Mr Parsimmons. Mr Parsimmons, the receiving clerk, was in fact harmless and was only frightening because of his appearance and an occasional severity of mood. He was excessively thin and had a hooked nose, the skin on his face was stretched tightly across his skull, and he was scarred from the pox. He had worn a black cravat for more than a year,

13

which meant that he was in mourning for someone who had been very close.

Mourning was an altogether different matter for the Irish. Sarah had seen plenty of dead people; they inhabited the same rooms as the living in the homes of the poor, usually stretched across two chairs since the table top couldn't be spared. Pa had been around for a good week after he passed away, and Ellen had even hidden a dead mouse she wanted to keep under his legs. It meant they had grown used to him being dead before they buried him, which made sense. Same with Mam, and it had been a comfort to have her in the room anyway. Not a day had passed in the whole year since then that Sarah hadn't ached for her mam's touch. Sometimes, especially when Ellen was sad, Sarah felt the absence of their mother like the sting from a raw wound. It seemed uncanny that you could feel the lack of someone even more powerfully than you felt their presence. The baby had died before Mam, but she didn't want him in the room so Ruby had taken him away. It was Ruby who took care of all the bodies in the end. They were buried near the Ropemakers' Fields, at a cemetery where there were no fancy head-stones or pretty stone angels, just rows of wooden crosses, mostly with Irish names carved into them. Three crosses in a row now, each bearing the name O'Reilly. Sarah and Ellen had taken some violets for the graves, but they had wilted by the time they got to the Ropemakers' Fields since it was almost a half day's walk from Devil's Acre.

On the last turn of the darkened stairwell, Sarah could see the corridor that led to the door of Septimus Harding's office. This was where she had her quiet smokes, because she could not be seen, but also because she could see the comings and goings to the editor's rooms. 'Curiosity killed the cat,' Ruby would have said. She often caught Sarah eavesdropping at the White Hart. At this particular moment, Inspector Lark from Marlborough Street was coming, while Mrs Korechnya was going. Mrs Korechnya had left her cloak downstairs, so Sarah got a good look at her gown, which was velvet and the colour of port wine, trimmed with cobwebby mulberry lace at the cuffs and collar. The bodice was heavily embroidered in mauve and silvery green with tiny snowdrop pearls like a garden in spring. Sarah had never seen anything quite like Lily Korechnya's outfits, but she had heard the compositors call her *bohemian*. She knew that Mr Korechnya was from Prague, because all matters pertaining to his wife were discussed at length in the tea room – she was one of the few writers who visited the third floor, and the only woman besides Sarah and Nelly the maid. She also knew that Mrs Korechnya was a friend of the famous Barbara Bodichon, who wrote letters to the *Guardian* newspaper about changing the laws for married ladies and streetwalkers. Mrs Korechnya's black hair was caught at the nape of her white neck by a silver filigree clasp in the shape of a butterfly, with little coloured gemstones on its pretty wings, and she always smelt of rosewater. Sarah noticed that Lily Korechnya did not wear mourning black, even though her husband had died less than a year ago.

Inspector Lark's eyes lingered on Mrs Korechnya's departing figure before he turned and knocked at the door of Septimus Harding's office. Sarah waited on the stair a moment then gave a quiet knock and followed him in. There were two rooms, joined by a great wooden arch, but only the second room was tidy and dust free since this was as close as Nelly dared come to the editor. This second room was where Mr Harding had meetings with the sub-editors. They would sit around the low table on green leather chairs, talking about print runs and sales figures and what the other broadsides were publishing. The office where Septimus Harding sat was lined from floor to ceiling with cluttered shelves, heaving with books and binders. She had never seen so many books in one place, not even in the bookstalls of Fleet Street or Charing Cross Road.

'Hmmph, Sarah,' Septimus Harding mumbled as she entered. He was looking at her over the top of his half-moon spectacles, and there was ash from his pipe on his not-so-white cravat. The cravat was wrapped about his neck in a manner that made him look like a cler-gyman, and there was ink on his shirtsleeves. Sarah noted that a button on his waistcoat, which had been straining for weeks, had finally popped off. The editor was always dishevelled, just like his desk and his office, but there was nothing untidy about his mind. Sarah thought that he talked as if he were running red ink through lines of bad copy. He didn't like cumbersome writing, or speech, and if he could make do with a word rather than a sentence, or a grunt rather than a word, then he would.

Inspector Lark was standing – for he never sat – warming his back at the grate. He dressed like a gentleman, though there was nothing of the dandy about him. He was dark of hair, eye and skin, but certainly not handsome; in fact at times he looked decidedly ugly. His coat was well-cut, though not in the current fashion, and his whiskers were neatly trimmed. Most intriguingly, his boots were always clean. Considering the filth on the streets that he frequented, Sarah found the matter of the inspector's boots fascinating. He lit a cheroot while she placed the trays of type on the editor's desk. The room was smoky from burning coal and pipe tobacco, and was much warmer than the third floor.

'Very good, very good,' said Septimus Harding, chewing on the end of his pipe and casting his eyes over the trays. 'Something else, Sarah?'

She had not turned to go, and had taken off her cap.

'Messages from above, is it?' His blue eyes were twinkling as he looked at her from beneath the enormous black tufts of his eyebrows.

'Yes sir. Mr Thistlewite says the copy from the shipping clerk is bollocks.'

She heard Inspector Lark chuckle.

'Does he? What do you think?'

She shrugged. 'Don't know, sir. Shipping don't interest me.'

'And what *does* interest you Sarah?' This from Lark.

'*Me*? When Mr Melville writes that Devil's Acre is an open sewer, with all kinds of *nocturnal vermin*, that's what interests me sir. That's real bollocks that is!'

'You're familiar with Devil's Acre then?'

'I live there sir, and I know what all them words mean.' She was proud of this, and wouldn't tell the Inspector anything but the truth, him being a policeman.

'I have heard that you know your letters, and I hold you in the highest regard: a true lady of the press.'

Not in half as much regard as he holds Mrs Korechnya, Sarah thought. 'Thank you very much, sir.' She hesitated a moment, then turned back to the editor. 'What is spermatorrhoea, Mr Harding?'

Septimus Harding coughed on his pipe, and Lark guffawed.

'Blast,' said the editor. 'Who gave you the Perry's advertisement to set?'

'You did yourself, sir.'

'Damn! Entirely forget that you're a girl sometimes. Off you go. I have an important matter to discuss with Mr Lark.

'Yes sir. Is it a murder?'

Lark looked like he was investigating a murder; she had seen this look before, when two prostitutes had their throats slit in St Giles.

'It is.'

She put her cap on reluctantly and, deciding that this was the wrong time to question Mr Harding further on the sacred nature of spermatorrhoea, she turned to go. She was instantly forgotten, for Septimus Harding's attention was firmly fixed on what the policeman had to tell him. Sarah did not shut the door completely behind her and stood in the hallway, listening intently.

'They're little girls Septimus, and they parade along Betty Street between midnight and dawn. Their mothers put them up to it – those who have mothers . . .'

'I know, I know, John. It's a damned filthy business. Was she raped?'

Lark nodded and lit another cheroot. 'Tell Melville to be sparing with the melodrama will you? I don't want your readers to think we're running a circus instead of protecting them. Protection? Hah! The very idea of it is quite impossible. But the public must at least believe that we are doing our best.'

Inspector Lark threw the stub of his cheroot into the fire, put on his hat and bade good-day to the editor. He left so quickly that Sarah only just had time to scamper up the stairs and hide in the shadows.

'Good-day Sarah,' he added as he strode briskly away along the corridor.

As she walked home in the early evening, Sarah thought about the child brothels on Betty Street and on Dock Street, closer to Devil's Acre. She thought about how close she had come to joining the parade between Piccadilly Circus and Waterloo Place; she knew exactly what price was fetched for a virgin, it was something she'd 'overheard' in the bar at the White Hart. When the cholera took her mam and their baby brother, she and Ellen had been left to live by whatever means they could, and the prospects were grim. She'd seen match-factory girls whose jaws had been eaten away by phosphorous. Some had even died from it. Mam had always said she'd rather die than go to the workhouse, and when her illness became grave, she made Sarah promise never to let Ellen be taken there either. Mam knew Sarah could look after herself, but she was always worrying about Ellen, as the child trusted everyone and had some peculiar ways. Mam had taken in more sewing after the whiskey got the better of Pa. In the fashionable season, between April and July, she would sit at the table from six in the morning to midnight; stitching a velvet collar to a candy-striped taffeta gown, or tiny satin buttons to cotton gloves. Mam was no seamstress, but could turn her hand to a rosette or a pleat or a row of lace to make an old gown look fresh and fashionable. Sometimes she would put a dress on Sarah to see how it was coming along, and Ellen would giggle at her sister looking so fancy.

The picture Sarah had when she thought of her mother was of her sitting at the table with some fine cloth bunched up around her, looking anxiously at the tallow from time to time, worrying that there would not be enough to last the job. The basement room was always dark, save for a slant of light from a tiny window that led onto the alley above. Mam's fuzzy, copper hair would fall in little wisps around her face, and stick to her forehead in the summer, or when she was poorly. She had been poorly much of the time that last year. By the time Sarah turned fourteen, Mam planned to have saved the twenty pounds for her to go and live with a Cheapside tailor, to be trained as a proper seamstress. She would receive no wage, only food and board, and would be expected to work day and night and only go home one Sunday in a month. She would have done it too, but that was all in the past, and Sarah's fourteenth birthday had been and gone. By the time she died, Mam had only managed to save seven pounds and six pence, and this was what Sarah and Ellen had lived off until Septimus Harding took her on.

These thoughts occupied Sarah as far as Puddle Dock, from where she took the route home along the river. From Amen Corner there were many ways to reach the infamous Westminster rookeries known as Devil's Acre. When she had errands to run, Sarah walked along Fleet Street and the Strand because she liked the commotion and the way the streets were lit by gas lanterns at night. She also enjoyed looking in all the shop windows; at the clothiers and haberdashery and milliners, the glittery crystalware from Bohemia and delicate Chinese porcelain. She particularly liked the look of the sugared plums in the square-paned window of the confectioner's, and meant to buy one for Ellen one day. She watched how the shop men would run out into the street in their aprons to open the door of a liveried carriage and fuss over a lady, putting a sack down on the dirty flagstones so that her silk boots were not sullied. Here, according to Mr Melville's brand of newspaper writing, 'the cunning and nimble-fingered profit by any means that their wits can contrive'. Sarah supposed that the 'cunning and nimble-fingered' described the likes of Ellen's friend Holy Joe and the barefoot urchins with running sores who hung around the docks. She would never describe Holy Joe as cunning, but he was a thief, no two ways about it.

The river was the fastest route to Devil's Acre. When the water level was low, as it was now, the stench was acrid, and there was always the danger of being robbed between Puddle Dock and Temple Lane, even in full daylight. Closer to the West End and Westminster, the back lane taverns served as a meeting place for the class of criminal who fancied themselves above the unskilled crimes of the East End: safe-breakers, coiners and forgerers, and the cleverest of pickpockets who would not look twice to see if you were wearing new shoe leather. The new boots she'd bought for Ellen were thieved only last week, stolen off her little feet by a gang of urchins from the East End. Just as well Ellen didn't like wearing boots, even in winter. Without them, she could easily walk into the water to get something that caught her eye, a bottle or a paper flower from a lady's hat that the wind had blown in. She was usually covered in mud up to her knees, and Pa used to call her his little mermaid. Sarah thought this was why Ellen stayed close to the river now; she had always liked watching Pa go out in the boat. Ellen was too young to be angry like Sarah was about the drinking and about Mam having to work so hard. Ellen and Pa had been inseparable, and she still cried for him in her sleep.

And there they were now, Ellen and Holy Joe, sitting on Whitehall Stairs with a small band of ragged children and that stick-legged Indian boy that Ellen had befriended. Sarah couldn't remember his name; it was a funny, foreign one. They were all taking pot shots at a passing steamboat with Holy Joe's slingshot. They made an odd couple: little blonde, eight-year-old Ellen and big, blundering Holy Joe, who had the eyes of a child and the strength of a dray horse. He was more than thirty and less than forty, Ruby said, but he couldn't remember his age, and nor could anyone else.

As Sarah approached, Ellen took aim and a small stone knocked the top hat off a gentleman passenger. Holy Joe laughed so much that he almost fell off the stair. The unfortunate gentleman could only watch as his hat spun away on the current of brown water.

When Holy Joe caught sight of Sarah he clapped his hands. He was a simpleton and could barely speak, although he had not always been this way. Joe had once been a preacher, Ruby said, and was as sensible and as clever as you like, until he was hit on the head by a chamber pot. It seemed that whoever was tossing the contents of the pot out of the window had slippery hands, and had let the whole thing fly. It had fallen right on Holy Joe's poor head and knocked the sense clean out of him.

Ellen looked up guiltily, not sure how much of their sport her sister had witnessed. Sarah pretended not to notice; she was more surprised by Ellen's marksmanship than anything else. The slingshot was Joe's prize possession – he'd made it himself, and had even carved his name into it. It was all right to go shooting at pigeons since they could be eaten, but not at posh folk who might make trouble for them. Sarah held out her hand to Ellen. 'Come on, Trub, lets go have our tea. Phew! You smell bad, Elly, where you been?'

Ellen shrugged and said nothing. She kissed Holy Joe on the cheek, and then after a moment, she kissed the Indian too before slipping her small grubby paw into Sarah's inky one.

They walked for a while in silence, along the embankment and past the herring wharves where some scrawny kittens were picking over a pile of fish bones. Ellen made little mewing noises, and tugged at Sarah's hand, but her sister held firm, pulling the child quickly past them. There were enough fleas in their bed straw already.

'What's his name again – the darkie?' Sarah kept her voice light, because if Ellen detected a note of criticism, she would clam right up. Recently she'd been talking less and less, although perhaps this was from spending her days with Holy Joe. It wasn't that Sarah disapproved of her keeping company with darkies, but that Ellen collected odd people, or rather, they were drawn to her. Sarah was always surprised by the number of people in the street who greeted her sister: footpads and sailors, prostitutes and swells, and one day on Waterloo Bridge a cross-eyed gypsy crone had called out to her by name.

"Is name's Victor,' said Ellen.

'Victor! Not much of a name for a darkie, is it?'

Ellen shrugged and kicked a stone.

'Pretty good with that slingshot, aren't ya, Trub?'

'Holy Joe taught me.'

'Holy Joe been teaching you anything else?'

Ellen didn't answer, but skipped ahead through the doorway of the White Hart. Sarah sighed. By the end of summer they'd have the coin for new boots, a wool pinafore and chalk and slate; then it'd be school by day.

The White Hart gin house was one of the cleaner establishments in Devil's Acre, but the building dated back to the time of Queen Anne, so it was damp and smelt of hops and bodies that hadn't seen a bath since summer. There were rooms upstairs for threepenny lodgers, with a proper bed, and a chair. As was usual at this time of night, Ruby's front room was full of dockworkers seated around the long table; they were from the coal barges so had skin the colour of soot, and were warming their aching limbs with a jar of stout. Two card games had begun, and the street girls were sitting around watching, hoping for a taker. Ruby wore a black ribbon around her freckled neck, and a pink dress with a dirty frill at the bust. She was a good forty years of age, Sarah reckoned, or maybe more considering the number of teeth she had missing. The landlady was behind the bar surrounded by her admirers. The rabbit catcher was there again and as Sarah and Ellen walked through the room, he kicked at a dog that was sniffing around his brace of rabbits that lay pink and dead on the stone floor. Just like he's sniffing around Ruby, Sarah thought.

"Lo girls!' Ruby called, and blew Ellen a kiss. Ellen blew one right back, and the men at the bar roared with laughter. At this, Ellen poked her tongue out at them and disappeared down the cellar stairs.

'You tell 'em, girlie,' Ruby called after her. 'Gotta watch that one, she's well too brave,' she said to Sarah.

'Know that all right, Ruby. School soon, though.'

The cellar housed Ruby's copper for doing laundry, two enormous wooden ale vats with brass taps, and the casks and pails for gin making.

The room the O'Reillys rented was on the side by the main alley. Behind the White Hart there was an even narrower lane, and a row of dilapidated hovels, all crushed together and made from bits of old crates and stones with no mortar. Most of the lanes and alleyways of Devil's Acre looked like this.

Ellen was busy emptying the pocket of her apron as Sarah closed the door behind them. It wasn't as cold as it might be here, on account of all the fermenting in the air – it warmed the cellar, Pa had said. He never went for gin himself; not enough fire in it.

'Any treasures, Elly? Where you been today?'

'All over.'

She knelt on the floor, carefully arranging some pieces of coloured glass, two pretty oyster shells, a dead beetle and a shiny jet button.

'What did Holy Joe find then?'

'A book.'

'A book? What sort of book?'

Ellen shrugged. 'Picture book.'

'Where?'

'Fleet Street.'

'Holy Joe's thieving on Fleet Street now?'

'Not thieving Sarah, he found it. He don't steal when I'm with him, you told him not to, so he don't. Truly honestly.'

Ellen was holding a piece of Bristol glass up to the candle flame and making the blue star dance across the table on to the broadsheet Sarah was reading. It was last Saturday's *Mercury* – Mr Parsimmons gave her his old copies. She was looking for Lily Korechnya's column, which was published under the name of Mr Evans. The compositors said Mrs Korechnya had chosen this name because the writer Marianne Evans called herself George Elliot. It was curious, Sarah thought; when she wrote a penny novel one day, she'd be sure to call herself Sarah O'Reilly, and not some man's name.

Her thin blackened forefinger stopped at a column: 'Exceptional Women, by Mr Evans, An Essay on George Sand'. The George that Mr Evans (Mrs Korechnya) wrote of was a peculiar French woman who wore riding breeches and smoked cigars, and who wrote poetry and love letters to men thirty years her junior. How did Mrs Korechnya know these things?

Sarah wondered if Mrs Korechnya knew anything about Ireland; how it was greener than green, with fields and stone walls and old, old trees. Perhaps, Sarah thought, she might even go back there one day. But Sarah was London Irish now, and she was beginning to like it that way.

✢ 2 ✢

Waterloo, London,
27 April, 1864

Dear Barbara,

I sit in my front room with my coffee, and am shamed to say that I am still wearing my robe. Lately I am disposed to begin my working day thus, and seem to be bothering less to dress, unless of course I go to the market or to the newspaper office.

The fog is still thick, making shadowy forms of the street vendors of Waterloo. I have been watching the morning street closely these last weeks, for it is a theatre, and I have observed that the attention of the boy who sells jellied eels is regularly captured by a certain milkmaid. The girl passes always at the same time, returning home to her farm after her rounds. Her empty wooden buckets swing from the yoke across her shoulders, and her wide hips sway from side to side. I believe that the jellied eels boy is making a habit of standing by his station outside my window at precisely this hour each morning.

This is no longer the respectable address that it was before Waterloo Station was built, Barbara, but I like it all the more for its lack of respectability. Have you heard that Waterloo Street is now referred to as the 'new Haymarket'! Indeed, I am neighbour to some of the finest whorehouses in London; they open their drawing rooms so that the courtesans from St John's Wood can drink champagne and eat oysters discreetly with their gentleman patrons. Were I writing the Imperial Parliament column, I would report that far more intriguing parliamentarian activity may be found on Waterloo Street after midnight than in Whitehall by day!

If we are to believe the figure published recently in The Lancet, *there are some 80,000 prostitutes now working in London, which means that one in every sixteen women is earning her keep on the streets. One in sixteen! And this does not include the children. I cannot help but think* that the moralising coming from the press, and from the pulpit, is more in horror of female emancipation than the tarnishing of our immortal souls. Do not misunderstand me, for I know that women turn to prostitution not through choice but necessity, and that for many it is dangerous to their health and an unhappy trade. But if some good may be found in this, then it is that the work enables many to improve their circumstances, to educate themselves and to invest in a more respectable trade. Are you horrified at my libertinism?

My good mother was horrified, upon visiting me last week, to observe men in shirt sleeves smoking tobacco on the street. I could not prevent her visit, much as I tried. Fear not, I was dressed, though not to her approval. She lives in Christian terror that I am being disrespectful to the dead by not attiring myself in mourning cloth. In fact, she is habitually embarrassed by my unfashionable presentation, as you know. I will not wear black, for Franz preferred colour always. Colour and light. He would say of this fog 'the light is not fit to paint by', but still he would be in his studio, drawing down the sun to his canvas with oils and powders, his smock covered in paint and his pale hair falling across his eyes.

I am preparing myself to visit Franz's studio in Kensington; I have put it off for long enough and it would be foolish to keep paying the rent there. I must clear it out, and how I dread that moment.

I thank you for your words of consolation, my dear; your letters are like lanterns, helping to light my way through the darkness of grief. I thank you also for not deigning to offer a solution to the same. Mother suggested that laudanum might ease my heart, since she uses it regularly herself for melancholy and anxiety. I will not take it, for I have observed how it dulls the mind and fatigues the limbs. Yet she wonders why I avoid the company of my father, when it is he who administers her poison, and believes, as do all respectable physicians, that a woman is not well unless she is submissive, and if necessary, sedated. I have in my locket a coil of Franz's hair – this is my heart's ease.

Do not fear that I am too much alone in an empty house with only the society of Mrs Vesper. My housekeeper is as silent as you remember, but I am never displeased by her manner, though visitors sometimes find her peculiar. There have, in fact, been few visitors besides Mother, for I have presently no interest in the salons that Franz and I once so loved. The gaiety and liveliness of these occasions seem to belong to a different life altogether, though it was not so very long ago. I am told that the sadness will lessen, little by little, with time.

Yet I do not dip my quill in ink to spread my melancholy, so I shall tell you of a meeting I had recently with Miss Herbert, the sister-in-law of Lady Cynthia Herbert who will shortly return from India. You will surely have heard of Cynthia Herbert, for she was once doyenne of the Chelsea and Hampstead ladies of the brush. There was a time when she collected lady artistes like butterflies, pinning them through their bright wings and covering the walls of her drawing room. She is terribly wealthy and has been patroness to Lizzie Siddal, and to the photographer Julia Margaret Cameron. But onwards, to my meeting. You may or may not know that Cynthia Herbert has a famed collection of jewels. She has fine taste, and the purse to support it, and is reputedly well known to the Gold and Silversmiths' Company on Regent Street. I am informed that she is particularly concerned for her collection, for she is ailing in her grief, and has not been the same since the recent death of her husband, Lord Herbert. They spent two years together in India before his sudden passing, and between you and me, when I spoke to Lord Herbert's sister, I gained the impression that there was some strangeness about his death, which she masked rather too carefully. She did not give details, but I gathered that she could not bring herself to recall the horror of it.

It seems that Cynthia Herbert wrote to her sister-in-law from India after Lord Herbert's demise, to ask her if she knew of a lady who might undertake some specialised clerical work for her, pertaining in particular to her jewellery. As we know, it is not uncommon for a lady such as Cynthia Herbert to amass property in this form, since any other holdings become part of her husband's estate on the day she weds, but is it not a little unusual that she should become concerned with it so soon after his death? Still, it was kind of Miss Herbert to think of me, knowing of my recent loss and presuming that I might need to find employment. In fact, Barbara, Franz's family have provided for me most generously, since I, of course, refused my father's request that I return to his home as a respectable widow might!

Lady Herbert is to arrive in London next week, and Miss Herbert suggests that we might take tea together once she has recovered from her voyage. She has also said that we may each find some comfort in the company of one who has shared the same loss. I had not thought to take *on any new endeavour, other than my regular contribution to the* Mercury *and my essays for the* Englishwoman's Journal, *but even Mrs Vesper has an opinion on my spending so much time in the front room. She has actually offered to help me dress, which is not like her at all, since when I first employed her services as housekeeper she made it clear that she was not a lady's maid. I, in turn, assured her that I had no need of one! In truth, Mrs Vesper has been much more than a housekeeper, especially while I was ill, and I have come to rely upon her companionship and sound judgement.*

Septimus Harding would like me to continue with my essays on exceptional women, in spite of my recent absence from the pages of the Mercury. *He says that the* Guardian *publishes reviews on women, and so must we. And so I am seeking subjects, and have decided to contact Julia Margaret Cameron. And should I write of you? The famous Barbara Bodichon, not only painter and patroness of education and the arts, but defender of our sex?*

I trust that all is hale with your many endeavours my dear, and shall write again.

In fond friendship,
Lily

÷ 3 ÷

We cannot tear out a single page of our life, but we can throw the whole book in the fire.

George Sand, 1837

At Temple Pier, at the end of Strand Lane, the embankment of the Thames River was almost deserted. Here were small cargo docks and a brood of ramshackle port offices. On a spring evening such as this, when the smells of the river and the refinery and the brickworks were not clinging to cold fog, the dockworkers and shipping clerks were settled in their respective taverns just as soon as the sun set, taking a jar or two.

Herbert Peasey, junior shipping clerk, had not yet gone to the Anchor because the paperwork had got the better of him that day. He was weary from checking crates of tea, sacks of grain and dark, oily coffee beans, and choked with the dust of them. As he looked about him in the holding shed, he remembered what had happened here the previous week, and he shivered. The small vessel *Lakshmi* had arrived at Temple Pier just as he was about to have his dinner, and there had been a fuss, as there always was when a cargo from Bombay docked. *Lakshmi* was officially a passenger vessel, but one that carried only a small number of 'select' passengers, meaning those who were prepared to pay for a suite rather than a cabin on one of the larger liners. *Lakshmi* therefore had room in its hold for exclusive cargo.

There had been contraband on board; Herbert could read all of the signs now. Most of the smaller Indian merchant boats shipped items privately, and this meant there would be a couple of extra hands on the crew; dark-skinned and dangerous looking natives who worked their passage to London. They came into the city with their belongings knotted into cotton bundles that could have contained anything: gemstones, sandalwood ornaments, opium in particular. Some of the couriers were no more than boys, but even so, they had a certain look about them and Herbert always gave them a wide berth. There had been a courier on board the *Lakshmi* that day, Herbert was certain, a small bandy-legged man who stood out from the others.

There had been the normal commotion when *Lakshmi* finally docked and while the cargoes were being unloaded, but as usual it was a woman who made things more difficult for Herbert than they needed to be. By her costume and the way she bore herself she was clearly a figure of some social standing, and she was also in mourning. She waited on the docks – unusual behaviour for someone of her station – in a state of agitation, for it seemed that the captain of the ship was refusing to release some of her possessions. When Herbert reluctantly approached the lady she was winnowing herself with an oriental fan with such rapidity that her bonnet was lifting from her ringlets to quite comical effect.

He gathered, upon interviewing the woman, that her manservant and the captain had disappeared into one of the holding sheds some time ago with her jewels. They had been in the ship's safe, but when she sent her man to retrieve them, the captain had turned nasty, insisting on a higher payment than was previously agreed. She implored Herbert to go after them, and unable to refuse without appearing a coward, he could only pray that the matter had been resolved by the time he arrived.

He supposed they had chosen the holding shed because it was dark, and because you could hear the approach of boots on the rotting floorboards. However, they hadn't heard Herbert, because the burly, turban-wearing captain was shouting loudly at the other Indian, who was fairer of skin and taller, and who was standing quite still and silent. There, on top of a crate, was a piece of silk and even the gloomy light from the small, dirty window was enough to cause the gemstones lying upon it to wink and flicker. Herbert gazed in awe – he'd seen plenty of sparklers, but nothing like these. They could only be diamonds by the way they shimmered, but he had never witnessed diamonds of such breathtaking colours.

From what he could gather, the captain was demanding an astronomical fee for the safe passage of the sparklers, and as Herbert approached hesitantly from the shadows, the man put his meaty hand on his wide leather belt. In fact, his hand rested on the hilt of an excessively large blade, judging by the size of its ornamental scabbard. Herbert Peasey was not a brave man, and he could not say what lent him the boldness to step forward. It could only have been the diamonds, for he felt curiously overcome by them. He was more than polite as he introduced himself to both men as an agent of Her Majesty's Shipping and Customs, and enquired if he might be of some assistance. He edged as close to the gems as he dared. The stones were even more splendid than he had imagined, even though they were uniformly only slightly larger than a boot button. Amongst them, impossibly, was a diamond the colour of blood.

Peasey was by now accustomed to seeing Indian diamonds, identifiable by what the Hatton Garden carriers called 'rose cut'. It was a mode of faceting that fashioned large planes across the stone, rather than the many tiny, glinting facets of the so-called 'brilliant' cut that was preferred by the London ladies. Herbert stepped closer, despite himself, and was barely aware that he had reached out his hand to touch the red diamond. He could hardly explain it, but he had felt as if the scarlet crystal were beckoning to him, and that when he had touched it, he was no longer a humble clerk but a man of substance.

What happened next was so swift that Herbert might have missed it had he blinked. The captain drew his weapon but was instantly disarmed, his knife falling to the floor with a clang. Suddenly he was in the grip of the silent Indian. It looked, from where Herbert was standing, as if the other man had the length of a silk handkerchief about the captain's neck, allowing only enough slack so that the man could beg for mercy. Finally he let the captain stagger away, rubbing his neck and cursing. Herbert must have made a noise then, for the Indian took a step towards him. Herbert muttered an apology, although it was not he who was trespassing, and backed away so quickly that he toppled over several crates of china. The Indian bundled up the precious stones, then followed the captain out at a more leisurely pace. Only when they were both out of sight did Herbert himself stagger away, trying not to upset any more crates as he leant on them to steady himself. Then he caught sight of the small, bandy-legged Indian he had noticed earlier, darting out through the holding shed door. Had he also witnessed the scene? Perhaps he was simply hoping to steal a handful of rice as so many of the sailors did when they docked.

When Herbert came back out into the daylight, the captain had already vanished – presumably below deck on the *Lakshmi* – and his assailant had joined the lady in black on the docks. A moment later they both disappeared into a waiting carriage. The sensation that the Indian's eyes lingered on him still, looking into his very soul, condemning him even, had made Herbert feel cold for the rest of the day.

Herbert had spent two years in the shipping business now, and he meant to go to sea, in another two years by his reckoning. The English sailors who came and went at Temple Pier were rougher than he, and Herbert was not of the disposition to be bothered with physical labour, rather, he planned to become a seafaring merchant and to make his fortune in the East. He had seen many such gentlemen, and they were of all persuasions, not just the ones who were born lucky.

The Strand was only a stroll from the docks and his damp little office, where a foul smelling gas lantern burned above the table over which he hunched almost all day long. As he locked up for the evening, Herbert imagined himself as a successful merchant, walking from his boat along the lane to the Strand. He would have several fashionable shops, selling finery from the lands he visited. Then his girl would wear a brooch with diamonds, like the brilliants he had seen in Regent Street.

He had devised a rather clever means of keeping his books, although in truth it was Georgina's idea. It was also easier on his conscience if he thought of her as the mastermind behind their scheme. She had been watching him early one evening, waiting impatiently, because she had it in her head that they were off to the music hall. She had asked what would happen if he didn't list everything, and when he'd explained that then there would be no tax charged for the cargo, she'd said, 'Well, they'd like that, wouldn't they, all those sailor swells who fancy themselves gennelmen. Bet they'd rather pay you less than the tax for your trouble.' He agreed that they might, but reminded her that he worked for the Ministry of Shipping, and that some guv at Whitehall would have his breeches if he didn't complete the work as he should. 'And how would *they* know?' Georgie had said, and gave him that sassy smile that always made him want to hitch up her skirts. After the music hall that night, they drank some gin and made plans.

Tonight, Herbert Peasey was abroad later than usual. He was going to have one ale at the Anchor as he always did, and then go home to

Georgina. Things were progressing well, and now and then he took a little extra tax: a handful of coffee beans, or a yard of silk, or some trinket for Georgie. He had even turned a blind eye to cargo he knew should not be coming in at Temple Pier; it was just the same, he'd decided, as 'not noticing' the Indian couriers with their cotton bundles. He had thus far overlooked the necessity to record several crates of sandalwood, ivory and a quantity of semi-precious gems. He had lowered himself and he knew it, but by now these small misdemeanours seemed perfectly normal and he was becoming more brazen. And why shouldn't he look after himself? Wasn't that what all the guvs at Whitehall did?

The alleyway leading to Strand Lane, where the Anchor was situated, was always in shadow and when the sun disappeared, it was damned dark. There were storehouses made of old stone on either side that had partly been destroyed by fire and never rebuilt. In the ruins lived a few ailing vagabonds and some local thieves. It was a desolate part of the wharves, but not dangerous to the dockworkers and sailors who had right of passage due to their size and street fighting ability. Shipping clerks such as Herbert did not fall into this category, but he hadn't been mugged yet, since there was usually a great deal of activity in the alleyway when he passed. Tonight however, at this late hour, it was deserted, and so dark that Herbert wished he'd brought his lantern. It made him nervous, the darkness that fell close to the water; it seemed somehow blacker, denser. Only the pale crescent of the moon allowed him to see the shadowy walls of the storehouses and a rat or two scurrying about. In the holding sheds at the wharf, rats were a problem as they chewed through the sacks of grain and spices. Tonight, in the absence of even a street urchin, the rodents were welcome companions.

When Herbert Peasey was struck practically senseless, his first thought was that he had collided with a tree trunk. But there were no trees to be seen; in fact, the closest trees were a mile away, at Watergate Gardens. He was certain that he was now lying on the ground, and his eyes must be closed, because everything was black. And there was a smell; a musky perfume that he had smelt before, though he could not remember where. For a moment the scent was so pleasant and calming that Herbert could think only of having a cut of mutton for his tea, and of Georgie's lovely, lovely legs.

Soon enough there was a presence with the smell. Although he could not see anyone, a breath of air had touched his face, so slight that it was as though someone had thrown a cloak open nearby. Herbert no longer felt calm, because now his eyes were half-open, and the darkness was shifting above him. He could not tell if there was more than one shadow because his vision was impaired by the loudness of the drums. At least, it sounded like drums. Then one of the shadows moved directly above him, and was leaning closer, and Herbert could smell the odour again; so familiar, what was it ... ? The drums grew louder, and the pressure from the excess of blood in his skull made him fear that he should not have taken taxation into his own hands, for the lord of darkness had come for him.

Herbert could no longer breathe. It was as though his throat had closed in on itself; and his heart was beating so fast that it was keeping rhythm with the drums. Was there someone above him? On top of him? He could not say. Perhaps it was an angel, come to escort him to heaven; perhaps he had been forgiven after all. In the end, before he died, Herbert Peasey imagined himself upon a ship, sailing to the East, with the sun and the wind at his face, and a fine lady called Georgina by his side. Instead of waves breaking across the prow of his ship, there was an ocean of many-coloured diamonds, all casting rainbows of light into the sky, winking at him as if they knew his secret.

⁘ 4 ⁘

I am tolerably well-convinced that I shall never marry at all. Reason
tells me so, and I am not so utterly the slave of feeling but that I can
occasionally hear her voice.

Charlotte Brontë

Detective Inspector Lark looked uncommonly ugly as Sarah collected
a parcel from the editor's offices. Neither he nor Septimus Harding
seemed to notice that she had not yet left the room – she had bent to
tie her bootlace before reaching the door – for they were talking as if
she was not there.

'It is, as yet, impossible to ascertain the mode of death. It is a most
unusual case, and as I've said, best to keep the report brief and *without*
sensation. I'd like to have a word with Melville myself, if I may.'

'By all means, by all means,' Septimus Harding chuckled. Then he
became serious again. 'But you must have some notion of the cause of
death, man! That is your business isn't it? Death?'

'I am not an undertaker, Septimus. I have, as yet, no opinion on the
case; I have never seen anything like it before.'

Mr Harding was right, Sarah thought. Lark was a policeman, he
should know these things. How else was he to protect the likes of Ellen
and the girls on Betty Street? The Inspector turned towards the fire,
and proceeded to gaze into it. Sarah backed slowly towards the door.

'He was not strangled, there were no marks on the neck, but his
windpipe was completely crushed. There was also a nasty bruise right
between his eyes.'

'Any motive in sight?'

'Any number – the victim worked at Temple Pier.'

Sarah had reached the door to the hall, and was turning the handle
slowly and quietly, when there was a sharp knock from the other side
and the door opened with some force, throwing her to the floor. Gregory

34

Melville stepped over her and approached the editor's desk. She could tell it was him by the way he smelt; like a brew house.

'What in tarnation are you doing on the floor Sarah? I thought you had an errand to run for me?'

'Yes sir. I was just looking for something down here, a block I dropped. Can't find it though, so best be delivering that parcel, sir.' She quickly closed the door behind her. Shame Melville had to interrupt. He was a nasty piece that one, and she'd thought so even before he wrote that shite about Devil's Acre. She'd give a penny to hear what Lark had to say to him; she liked it when the inspector got riled, but she'd already been in enough trouble for one day.

The delivery address was to be had from Mr Parsimmons, who was picking his teeth behind the front desk. His teeth were pointy and as yellow as the piano keys at the Christian Ladies' Hall.

'Waterloo Street, thank you, Sam.' He gave her a calling card from his ledger. Mr Parsimmons always called her Sam; Sarah wasn't even sure if he knew she was a girl, but it made no difference to him, as long as the work was done.

On the card was printed, in curling letters, the name and address of Lily Korechnya. Sarah went via the docks to Waterloo Bridge, since the pathway along the river was quicker than going along Fleet Street and the Strand where they were too many distractions. She'd stop to look at boxes of penny novels in a bookstall, and she'd forget herself, and then she'd have to tell Mr Parsimmons she'd got lost. He'd never believe her; she knew every street, lane and alley all right, from going out nights looking for Pa. Not that she'd want to delay today, not for anything, because she was carrying a parcel for Lily Korechnya. Until now, she'd never actually spoken to Mrs Korechnya other than to say good morning or good afternoon.

Along the embankment, the wharves were a clamour of mud larks and urchins and fish vendors, with a band of sailors from the Queen Mary merrily making their way to the nearest tavern. As she approached Temple Pier, Sarah remembered that this was where the murder had taken place; she would tell Ellen not to come along the river past Waterloo Bridge. Maybe the murderer was a madman – there seemed enough of them about, according to Melville. But then, she'd always imagined that a madman would commit a much more bloody murder than the one Inspector Lark had described. Maybe it wasn't a murder at all, but an accident? She wondered if he had considered this. Most probably he had, him being a policeman, but there wouldn't be any harm in asking if she got the chance.

The usually constant stream of motion across Waterloo Bridge was at a standstill, a tangle of horses and carriages. The resigned drivers sat on their hammercloths looking at the river, or placating flustered passengers. Some gypsy boys were turning cartwheels between the buggies and hansoms, begging for coppers, and there were street vendors hawking peanuts in paper cones at the windows of an omnibus. Sarah weaved in and out of the commotion, dodging piles of dung. It was a fine spring day, and she loved being out in the open air. To her right were the houses of Parliament and the spire of Westminster Cathedral, which soared above the slate green pall from hundreds of chimney stacks. To the left, all the way to London Bridge, there were steamboats and ships and barges on the river.

As Sarah came to the other side of Waterloo Bridge, she found the reason for all the congestion. At the junction there was a funeral procession of at least a dozen ebony wood carriages, each drawn by four jet horses with inky plumes at their forelock. Sarah stopped to look at the spectacle, a little startled by the presence of death on a day so potent with life. Death was ever present, she knew that much, and even when she forgot about Mam and Pa for a time, she was always reminded by something, if not by a funeral procession, then by a face in the street. Still, there was no use in feeling sorry for herself, and besides, death called frequently on the poor.

Lily Korechnya lived in a surprisingly unrefined area of London. Sarah had imagined her in Chelsea or Hampstead with a house full of servants and a garden, not in a terrace with the noise and hurly-burly of the street right outside her door. The brick-dust seller and chair mender were trying to outdo each other shouting 'sharpen them knives, penny a quart' and 'chairs to mend', and a boy with a pail full of stinking bullocks' liver and tripe was also competing for customers, though he was no match for the men. His wares were meant to be sold as dog food, but Sarah knew they'd end up boiled and stewed on a pauper's table that night.

The door to Mrs Korechnya's home was painted emerald green, and there was a shiny brass knocker, but before she had even touched her hand to the cold metal, the door opened and a woman who could have been Mr Parsimmons' sister appeared.

'Good afternoon, Miss. You've something for the mistress? From the newspaper, is it?'

Sarah had never been called Miss before, and she was surprised as she liked to think that she was, to all observers, an errand boy and apprentice compositor. She had not given much thought to what would happen when she could no longer pretend. She knew that her body would betray her sooner or later, but so far she hadn't even got the curse, and she was thin and small for her age, like Ellen. Pa had said they'd be great strapping lasses if they'd grown up in the special air of Ireland, that is, before the famine of course. But she didn't believe Pa's tales, and besides, she'd noticed that Ireland became ever more wondrous a place as the level in the whiskey bottle got lower.

'I'll take the parcel, Miss. You can be sure that the lady will have it just as soon as she walks in the door.'

Sarah raised her chin slightly to get a good look at the woman from beneath the brim of her cap. She was a puzzle, for although angular and severe in appearance and dressed in plain brown without a frill or flounce in sight, she seemed soft as well.

'You her maid?'

'Good Lord! I'm no *maid* child. Mrs Korechnya doesn't have a maid, for she's perfectly capable of attending to herself.'

She held out her hand for the parcel, but Sarah hesitated. She was sorely disappointed that she would not get to meet Mrs Korechnya herself. 'I'm meant to give it to her direct,' she mumbled, saying the first thing that came into her head. But instead of telling her not to be foolish and to hand over her parcel, the female Mr Parsimmons smiled.

'Very well, you'll find Mrs Korechnya in Kensington. If you'll step into the hall, I'll get the address.'

The hall was vast, Sarah thought, for a room with no purpose other than comings and goings. It was bigger than the cellar room her entire family had lived in – when there were five of them. There was patterned linoleum on the floor, and an enormous painting on the wall. She took a step closer to the painting while the woman went over to a pretty mahogany table.

'That's the master's work.'

Sarah hadn't heard her come back, and looked down to see if maybe she wasn't wearing any shoes, but she was – and sturdy lace-up boots at that.

The painting was of a woman in a gown made of fabric Sarah had never seen the like of before, all silver, like a spider's web caught in the sun. Her raven hair was loose about her shoulders and she wore a wreath of white flowers wound through it. The woman had dark, almond-shaped eyes and skin like fresh cream, and a wide, handsome mouth. She looked like Mrs Korechnya, Sarah thought.

'Venus, that's the lady's name,' said Quiet Boots. 'Painting's called *The Venus of Waterloo*.'

'The painter's dead, ain't he?'

'Lung fever carried him away in the winter. In body, of course, only in body. It's a long walk to Kensington, and I dare say you'll be expected back at your work. We'll have to find you a driver.'

'A cab? Me? Never.' Sarah laughed at the idea; she'd never been in a cabriolet, or any kind of carriage for that matter: it was a luxury of the highest order. But already the woman had disappeared into the street and was conversing with the dark-skinned driver of a shabby hansom. She gave him some coin from her pocket, and beckoned to Sarah, smiling as she gave the girl's cap a little tug. Sarah climbed in and Quiet Boots vanished into the house, closing the emerald green door behind her.

The cab that carried Sarah from Waterloo Street to Kensington smelt of hair oil and horse leather, and there was a draft of damp air trickling through the varnished floorboards. The Strand looked like a carnival from this perch, all bright spinning crinolines and parasols, though it was only May and the sun barely warm. An organ grinder with his scraggly monkey was pursuing a group of clergymen, and the sun glinted off the shop windows. It was a fine day all right, Sarah thought, and here she was, taking a ride in a cab along the Strand. Wait till she told Ellen and Holy Joe about *this*. As they passed the gates of Buckingham Palace, Sarah settled back into her seat and wondered what Quiet Boots had meant when she said that Mr Korechnya was dead only 'in body'. Dead was dead, unless you believed in heaven, and she wasn't sure if she did, although she liked to think of Mam and Pa and the baby being there.

Finally they arrived at a place where there were fewer gates and walls, but a field or two, and groves of fruit trees. The building the driver pointed to was all grown over with briar and ivy, and there were crumbling stone statues of beasts at the gate. The great front doors did not seem to be in use, since the ivy almost covered them, so Sarah walked through an arbour of blossoming branches towards two long glass doors that opened, just like windows, on to the garden.

And there she was, Lily Korechnya, sitting at a table in a large room which had no other furnishing apart from something that looked like a bed with an arm and a cushion at one end. Lily seemed completely lost in what she was writing, and Sarah walked into the room without knocking, not wanting to interrupt her. Mrs Korechnya did not look up from her writing, and this gave Sarah time to get a good look at her. Her gown was ivy green and made from Indian cotton. Mam had said it was a fine cloth and had liked sewing it. The narrow sleeve of Mrs Korechnya's dress was embroidered with a white flower, graceful as a swan's wing, that looked exactly like the flower the woman in the Venus painting wore in her hair. Whatever Mrs Korechnya was writing was making her sad; she wasn't crying, but her left hand swept across her brow, and every now and then she breathed a deep sigh. Against the walls there were numerous paintings without frames, more than Sarah could count, and on the floor by the table was a large blue hatbox. When Sarah looked at Lily again, the lady was looking straight back at her, a small smile playing on her lips.

'Good afternoon, Sarah.' Lily Korechnya put some blotting paper over what she had been writing, folded the fine parchment carefully, then put it in the hatbox.

That evening Sarah told Ellen and Holy Joe about her time in 'Franz's studio', as Lily had called it. Mrs Korechnya had talked of things no one else had ever spoken to her about; like schooling and paintings and the Greeks, who had more than one god, and some of them were women. One god was more than enough trouble, Sarah had said, and that made Lily laugh. She'd found out that Venus was one of the Greek gods, and that Quiet Boots's real name was Mrs Vesper, and that there wasn't a Mr Vesper because he'd died of typhoid.

Holy Joe and Ellen had spent the day rag picking, selling bits of cuff lace and silver buttons to a mud lark at Whitehall Stairs. Just for a few coppers, but every little helped, and Ellen liked to help. Ellen and Holy Joe were now playing a game with stones and coloured glass on the stone floor. Joe was just as trusting as Ellen, which worried Sarah, but he had a nose for danger and was strong, although not much of a fighter. Sarah shuddered again at the memory of Inspector Lark's description of the murder by Temple Pier. Perhaps she would find out more tomorrow.

'Where's that book you found, Joe? The one from Fleet Street?'

Holy Joe beamed, and reached a broad hand into his coat pocket.

'It's a picture book,' he said, his grin lighting up his face so that Sarah couldn't blame him, no matter how he came about the book. He meant no harm, he just took what he liked when he came across it; and he was good at it too. It made Sarah wonder if he already had the skill when he was a preacher, before he was hit on the head by the chamber pot. Holy Joe held out the book to her; it was small, with a thick cover, and as dirty and yellow as Mr Parsimmons' teeth.

'What does it say? Can you read it?' Ellen was as bright eyed as Holy Joe.

Sarah opened the cover to a brittle page that was covered with small stains from where the rain had fallen on it.

'"The Little Mermaid, by Hans Christian Anderson",' she read.

Ellen clapped her hands. 'That's me! I'm the little mermaid, ain't I, Joe!'

Holy Joe clapped his hands too, and the pair of them moved a little closer to Sarah, their faces glowing with expectancy. Sarah sat up straight, and held the book open with both hands. She had a queer fluttering in her stomach, like she used to get when she'd find herself at night in a part of the city that was unfamiliar, looking for Pa. She took a deep breath and cleared her throat, like Septimus Harding did when was about to read something important.

⁘ 5 ⁘

Waterloo,
12 May, 1864

Dear Barbara,

I must tell you of my meeting yesterday with Lady Cynthia Herbert at the Chapter Coffee House on Paternoster Row. It is an establishment I would not normally enter, as you know, for there one is likely to encounter editors and other gentlemen of the press who forsake the very idea of an astute female! The room was filled almost entirely with the smell of men, cigar smoke and of lately ground coffee. I was quite relieved when I spotted Lady Herbert at her table in the corner of the room, away from all the yellow gas flames dancing in their pretty lanterns. She rose to meet me, her black silhouette rather striking against the rosy blush of the wallpaper.

As I had dreaded, a circular table by the window was attended by a group of straight-backed editors from Rivington, the theological publishers. Their table was scattered with loose papers and in its centre was a thick, foreboding manuscript still tied with string. I tried not to imagine what might be contained in such a commodious theological work. Since it was necessary that I pass their table, I nodded courteously towards the grey whiskers and rimless spectacles of the younger Rivington, who is a retired physician and one-time colleague of my father. He did seem surprised to see me, and I'm certain even more astonished when Lady Herbert arrived at my side, and tucked my arm beneath her black taffeta pagoda sleeve. She propelled me to a table laden with sufficient dainty cakes for a tea party, and I could feel the gaze of the Rivingtons upon us, no doubt wondering what Dr Hall's daughter might be doing meeting with such an iconoclast.

'A timely rescue' she said to me, sotto voce. 'It is alarming, is it not, when one considers that gentlemen such as these are busily weaving the moral fibre of our middle classes. Tea?'

I replied that I would prefer a glass of coffee and she wrinkled her heavily powdered nose, saying that the stuff was too astringent for her delicate constitution. She was attired in inky black from the lace mantle on her ringleted head to her jet silk boots, and she looked weary, as though troubles and cares had worn her to her very marrow. Gone are the days when Lady Cynthia Herbert surrounded herself with a stable of bright minds and aesthetic souls. She has become reclusive and, I believe, irritable with polite society, no doubt as a result of her recent bereavement. But oh, the jewel against her dark bodice contained all of the life that seemed to have drained from this once magnificent woman, who not so very long ago had all of London's young bohemians at her feet. The jewel hung from the end of a gold chain, and was a single stone the size of a sovereign that flared with refracted light. When Lady Herbert noticed that I was taken with it (in fact, I was quite mesmerised, and fancied for a moment that it winked at me mischievously) she seemed most pleased.

'It is a diamond, Mrs Korechnya, a stone that in different ages has been both feared and coveted. It must be kept close to the heart in order to make one invincible. I am glad that you are also an advocate; I look forward so very much to showing you my collection. But my dear, you simply must attend the Royal Academy, for I was privileged to bring with me from India some unusual diamonds which remain the property of the Maharajah of Benares. They have now been recut by Voorsanger, whom you will no doubt have heard of.'

I had not, and said so. I thereupon learnt that Voorsanger is a master diamond cutter from Amsterdam, most famed for recutting the Koh-i-noor. Even I have heard of the giant blue diamond that was so disputatiously presented to Queen Victoria by the East India Company. It seems that Voorsanger's artistry in combination with the Maharajah's unusual diamonds have given rise to something of a public spectacle, for the jewels are now on display at the Royal Academy. I had not the heart to admit to Lady Herbert that I am not, after all, an advocate of diamonds and gemstones and wear little jewellery but my locket. But I did promise to visit these stones, not least because I have become increasingly aware that solitude is a refuge and that, if I do not resume contact with society soon, I may lose interest in it entirely. In fact, there is an unusual young Irish woman, rather a tomboy really, who is intriguingly employed as an apprentice compositor at the London Mercury. I should very much like to encourage

42

her, for I suspect that she is bright and wonder if she might not be the ideal companion for such an outing.

By Lady Herbert's account, the Maharajah of Benares is a cultured man and a great enthusiast of the European painters, and would certainly admire the work of Franz Korechnya. It surprised me that she knew of my husband's work and I discovered that she had visited Prague before the revolution that brought Franz and his merchant family to London. She said that she had noticed his talent when he was little more than a student, and informed me that Prague, like Benares, was a special place; a 'city of light'. I am to understand that these cities are amongst the locations considered holy by the mystics: the borderlands between the living and the dead. She added that, should I wish, I would be most welcome to attend her circle. I ought not have been surprised that my companion was a devotee of spiritualism, for she exhibited all of the symptoms of one made vulnerable by her loss. I declined as graciously as possible.

When I informed her that I still have many of Franz's paintings in my possession, she appeared most interested. In fact, she said it was an outrage that as a Jew he was refused admission to the Royal Academy. 'Contrary to the opinion of the gentry, an artist need not be Christian to be gifted,' she said. 'Nor pale of skin. Why, my Indian manservant has more talent with a pencil than some of the artists lauded by the Academy.' I have promised to select some canvases for her to view, for I am determined that in death Franz should receive the recognition that he was denied in life.

We agreed that we would resume our meeting at Herbert House on an afternoon to be arranged, for she was becoming agitated and uncommonly watchful. She remarked, 'I thought it best that we meet first in public, but now that I have seen you, I am calmed.' I would guess that Lady Herbert's calmative is, in fact, an opiate, for I have observed the same particular effects in my mother. To convince me further, beside us two gentlemen were discussing the virtues of esparato grass, and its economic superiority over wood-pulp in the making of paper. They were engrossed, and paying the conversation at our table no heed whatsoever. Yet Lady Herbert glanced nervously at them several times, and seemed watchful even of the waiter, who was hovering at attendance. I noticed that she kept nervously fingering the large white diamond at her breast with her black gloved fingers. In an attempt to make light of her own discomfort, she told me that she had once dined in the company of Charles Tiffany, of Tiffany and Company in New

York, who informed her of a medieval superstition about diamonds. It seems that they were once believed to protect against spirits. 'What rubbish,' Lady Herbert said to him, 'I have found quite the opposite to be true. Indeed, they attract spirits!'

I am now more intrigued than ever by the enigmatic personage of Cynthia Herbert, and look forward to keeping company with her. I shall tell you more of our meetings anon!

In friendship,
Lily

❖ 6 ❖

You cannot hope to bribe or twist, thank God!
the British journalist. But, seeing what the
man will do unbribed, there's no occasion to.

Humbert Wolf

At the sight of Gregory Melville coming through the doorway to the
back stairwell, Sarah's attention was easily diverted from the advertisement for Keating's Pale Newfoundland Cod Liver Oil: AN EXCEP-
TION IN RESPECT OF PURITY FROM MANY OF THE OILS SO
ABUNDANTLY ADVERTISED. She was in a perfect position to observe
any visitors to the third floor, since her easel was at the back of the
room and close by the door. She didn't like Melville using this stair,
since she considered it the exclusive territory of herself and Nelly, and
Gregory Melville was always creeping about.

He reminded her of a tom cat, stalking a dove in an alley.

Mr Melville was always impeccably attired, though in her opinion
his taste was better suited to a rarefied swell than to a gentleman of
the press. He might almost be called handsome, but for his greasy
complexion and the waxy pallor that identified those of his profession
on account of the drink and all the hours spent indoors. Melville had a
sheet of copy in his hands and a smug look about him, as if he'd caught
his dove and was about to devour it.

Sarah pulled her cap down a little so that she could still keep an eye
on him and appear to be attending to her advertisement. It was a fact
that cod liver oils were abundantly advertised, and in truth she was a
little weary of reading the same old malarkey over and over, of how
Doctor Ricord's Essence of Life would restore manhood, how effective
a remedy Lambert's Asthmatic Balm was. Pa had always said that
everything in the penny press was malarkey, and she wondered what he
would think if he knew that his own daughter was now working for a

45

newspaper. He hadn't been one for books either; it was Mam who'd made sure Sarah did her reading, often out of *Mrs Beeton's Dictionary of Everyday Cooking* which Ruby kept in her kitchen because she thought every respectable household ought to have a copy, even though she couldn't read it herself. Mam had only one book of her own which she had brought over from Ireland, stories from the Bible and about the saints, with a frayed green cloth cover. They used to read it every single night until Pa sold it off for a bit of drink. That was when Sarah realised he was lost, since he knew how much that book had meant to Mam. Their wedding rings had gone long before, to buy flour and tea and boots for the winter, and she remembered how sad they both had been about that. Ellen wanted to go and visit Pa and Mam soon, and Sarah had promised they would, even though the little field full of wooden crosses and weeds behind the Ropemakers' made her heart as heavy as stone.

Melville's gaze fell briefly on Sarah as he passed, but flicked away again, as though she was not worthy of his interest. He had never paid her much attention, which she was thankful for. He stopped at Jack Thistlewite's easel and they conferred over whatever new mischief Mr Melville was designing. Sarah wished Mr Harding wouldn't let him get away with the rot that he wrote in his crime column – sometimes the editor didn't even want to read it – and she reckoned Septimus Harding hated having to dirty up his pages with such scandal-mongering and gossip. But she'd heard him say to Inspector Lark that he had to 'wash his hands' of certain reportage, since it sold papers, and the *Mercury* couldn't afford not to be selling papers.

Melville was good at stirring up trouble; he knew how to make people want 'justice' after a particularly villainous crime. It was a fact that a prostitute or some poor sod could be beaten black and blue within a breath of dying, and the villain would do just a month or two in Westminster Bridewell, but if the same punter had his property damaged or stolen, then there'd be a hanging for sure. Sarah knew where Melville found his stories; how he toured the taverns around St Giles and Cheapside, meeting with the most prosperous of London's mobsmen and sneak thieves and forgerers, buying the dirty tattle he needed. Melville never came into the White Hart when he was writing the filth about Devil's Acre, since Ruby'd never let his sort drink in her front room. Instead he'd called at some of the less reputable ale houses and gin palaces around Westminster, sniffing out his regular informers so he could present what he called a 'true account' of a particular crime. Jack Thistlewite usually set Melville's column, and Sarah would always hear about it at tea time, when the cards got going, fuelled by a sneaky nip or two from someone's flask. Then the men would begin to brag about how well-informed they were, on account of the stories they were compositing.

It seemed that Mr Melville's latest sensation was a lead on the murder of Herbert Peasey, the unfortunate shipping clerk from Temple Pier who'd been done in two weeks since. He'd been cooking the books, Jack said, and turning a blind eye to some particularly choice comings and goings. *Gregory* – he said, since he liked to call his superiors by their first names in front of the other compositors, though he hadn't yet dared call Mr Harding *Septimus* – was going to get to the bottom of it, and it was going to be a *big* story. It was always going to be a big story; anything Jack touched had to be and in truth he wasn't much better than Melville. Both of them liked stirring up trouble and you could tell by the way Mr Melville wore his trousers tight and put so much oil in his hair, that he was hoping to become a swain to the ladies on account of his bravery in chasing villains until they were locked up in Bridewell or Newgate. There was nothing any of the compositors liked better than a good hanging; they'd go to Newgate prison with the rest of the punters, even taking a little pride in the spectacle, since it was newspaper men like themselves who helped bring the fiend to justice.

Sarah didn't like hangings so she stayed well clear of the Old Bailey on hanging Mondays. The crowd would start gathering on the Sunday, when the long wagon with all the scaffolds rolled up outside the stone walls of the prison. It stopped by the black door from which the shackled prisoner would emerge, head bent woefully, the following morning. A hanging was as much of a sporting event and as festive as a day at the dogs or a good cock fight. Mr Harding said the only thing that was different about a hanging was that no one took out any bets since the outcome was already decided.

Jack went on about the Peasey murder all afternoon, breaking the customary silence of the compositing room and making Sarah wish she were a man so she could tell him to shut it. He said that *Gregory* was writing an important piece on the fat profits made by London merchants who received precious cargoes from the East; sandalwood, opium and jewels that never made it into the log books of the port authorities. He said that Mr Melville was just a concerned citizen who was morally opposed to those profiteering in such a way. This seemed unlikely to Sarah, but no one was interested in her opinion. When the second visitor to the third floor that afternoon appeared, Jack started to boast all the more.

Mrs Korechnya had rarely been seen in the compositing room since her husband's death and her column, 'Exceptional Women', had not been printed in the *Mercury* the whole winter long. Sarah thought Lily Korechnya was more exceptional than any of the women she had read about in 'Mr Evans' column; more than the sickly poetess Elizabeth Barrett, or Christina Rossetti, or the painter called Lizzie something.

Lily came in through the main door wearing the kind of fine gown – ivory merino with a bodice of brightly coloured needlework flowers – that caused the compositors to watch her slyly as she walked. Lily Korechnya had a fine walk, Sarah thought, as if she were queen of her own mind, even when she was as sad as Mary Magdalene must have been when Jesus was crucified on the cross. That was in Mam's book of Bible stories and saints; not that Mary Magdalene was any saint. In fact, to Sarah it sounded like she was a street walker, since Mam had called her 'fallen'.

Mrs Korechnya couldn't help but hear Jack going on about Melville's *big* story, and she stopped politely in the middle of the floor to listen. As she did so, Jack self-consciously smoothed his hair, and Sarah believed the lady noticed too, since she smiled a little as if she knew she had the upper hand. When he was done preening, Mrs Korechnya said, in a most kindly and ladylike way, 'It is quite as you say Mr Thistlewite; the city of London is full of marksmen and thieves, but consider also the land from which the smuggled cargoes are plundered. Children are sent down into the belly of the earth to break their backs so that a fine lady in London might wear pretty baubles. Did you know, Mr Thistlewite, that in India under British rule, as many children starve to death in one day, as in the East End in an entire year?'

That shut Jack's trap. Not that he cared about the starving children, but he didn't like it that Mrs Korechnya had a better knowledge of words than he did, and Sarah could tell that he felt stupid. He thought a good deal too much of himself already.

Then, to Sarah's great surprise, Lily walked right over to her easel and looked at what she was doing. She was so close that Sarah could see the silver gilt buttons that fastened her waisting and showed how narrow she was about the middle. Sarah put her head down and rummaged amongst the print blocks in her tray, suddenly feeling shy and awkward though she couldn't say why, since Mrs Korechnya was always sweet natured with her. She could smell the rose water in Lily's thick black hair.

Mrs Korechnya was looking at the advertisement for Keating's, and Sarah could tell that that she was still amused by Jack's foolishness, since there was a hint of a smile on her wide, handsome mouth. Sarah raised an inky finger and tilted her cap. She was not mistaken – above her were two laughing eyes, the colouring of which was a great curiosity; green, then blue, like the picture of the sunlit sea on Ruby's whiskey bottles.

'How fares your young sister Ellen since last we met?'

Once she'd shared her plans for Ellen's schooling, Sarah felt braver. 'My spelling's all right, ain't it?'

'Indeed. I think we must talk to Mr Harding about giving you some more instructive tasks than aiding in the sales of cod liver oil! Besides, Sarah, it is a vile medicine – even the smell of it makes me feel quite ill. I wonder ...' And she paused for a moment and looked at Sarah questioningly. 'How would you like to accompany me to the Royal Academy this Saturday? There is an exhibition of diamonds I would rather like to see and I would be delighted to have your company.'

Sarah's heart skipped a beat or two and her eyes widened with surprise. She could not fathom why Lily Korechnya would choose the society of a scruffy Irish lass in breeches, but she was thrilled nonetheless.

'Oh yes, I would like it. Very much, please.' She lowered her voice. 'Don't pay no attention to Jack, Mrs Korechnya, he's too big for his boots by a mile. Him and Mr Melville think they're on the way to another hanging, that's why he's crowing.'

At this, Lily's eyes stopped twinkling and she lowered her voice. 'I am less disturbed by Mr Thistlewite's arrogance than by his politics,

Sarah. I am not in agreement with public hangings; nor with any hangings, in fact'.

'Me neither' said Sarah, and she felt proud of having the same opinion as someone as clever as Mrs Korechnya.

'Well then, Sarah, I shall expect you at my house on Saturday morning. Shall we say eleven o'clock?'

Sarah nodded and gave Lily a bright smile. No one but Ruby had paid her much attention since Mam's death and she couldn't remember the last time she'd had a day out. She didn't know anything much about diamonds either, but already she felt a fizz of anticipation. She hardly dared hope that Lily Korechnya might want to be her friend, but at least she'd be able to tell Ellen and Holy Joe about the fancy places that gentrified folk disappeared into.

⁘ 7 ⁘

Waterloo,
29 May, 1864

Dear Barbara,

It does seem that I am presently writing of diamonds a great deal. None-theless, I must tell you of a recent excursion I made to the Royal Academy. It was the first real outing I have taken to any place other than the Waterloo Market and Paternoster Row since Franz died, and I shall now admit to myself that I have not wanted the world to seem the same without him. The very idea of this occasion made me nervous, though my uncertainly was not over how I might fare without my husband by my side, but rather with whom I should share the event, when you, my dear friend, are in Hastings over the summer months.

I chose well, for my companion was young Sarah O'Reilly, the appren-tice compositor at the London Mercury and a young woman who has lost most of her family, yet whose very aliveness fills me with hope. I believe the arrangement suited us both admirably, since Sarah, under normal circumstances, would no more enter a building as imposing the Royal Academy than wear a pinafore. The disapproving glances we received as an unfashionable woman with neither hat nor chaperone accompanied by an urchin were as entertaining to me as they were unap-parent to Sarah. So spellbound was she by the cherubs and nudes on the domed ceilings and with the grandness of the marble stair and the gilt-framed paintings, that she seemed almost disappointed when we came to our destination: a small glass cabinet upon a faux-Corinthian pedestal.

I must admit to being as captivated by the brilliance of the diamonds – nine in total and each a different colour – as the rest of the crowd that had gathered around them. Sarah uttered not a word until we left the building, and then said only that she thought the stones were odd and that they gave her the jitters, for they were nothing more than rocks after all, but wasn't it as though they were alive? And it was. It was just as if each contained within it a furnace whose blazing light and energy shot through the eyes to the very heart of the observer. Each was displayed on its own mount of black velveteen, and of all, the red diamond was the most magnificent. You will think me fey, but this stone had about it a most unearthly quality, almost as though it were daring me to covet it. A plaque beneath the cabinet told that these were rare stones, collected over many years by the Maharajah, resident in Benares, of the Indian province of Uttar Pradesh. I could not help but wonder for what reason an Indian Prince came to entrust such treasures to Lady Cynthia Herbert.

I must tell you that only yesterday I kept my appointment to take tea at Herbert House. I was collected at three by a handsome landau carriage with the Herbert livery monogrammed in gold and white upon its door, and a driver dressed in a dark claret swain coat with a pea-green waistcoat beneath. If Lady Herbert must wear black, then her servants, it seems, provide her with a palette of colour. I chose my own costume with some care, and decided upon the gown the colour of dark moss in the gothic style that Mr William Morris has revived; it has lilies embroidered on the sleeves, and I find myself increasingly drawn to the motif, for Franz made a habit of painting it. The lily, he told me, is the most sacred of flowers: to the Romans it was a symbol of hope, to Christians the flower of Mary and of motherhood, and, at the same time, the flower of death and the white star of resurrection. Christina Rossetti says that in the language of the poets a lily stem speaks the return of happiness, so I shall continue to wear my namesake until mine returns. I have become sentimental, Barbara, and you will forgive me, but now that he is gone the symbols and reminders of our love are most precious to me.

The journey to Hampstead was nothing less than luxurious in Lady Herbert's landau, for the cushions were covered with velvet, and also monogrammed, which I found a little daunting. Lady Herbert is a peculiar concoction of grandness and rebel spirit, and I find her character per-plexing. In Hampstead all was clean and quiet, with evergreen branches dipping across the newly paved road (although I found the hush pleasant, still I prefer the commotion of Waterloo Street – particularly in these days when I would keep my mind from straying too much into silence). There was a young man at the gate of Herbert House, dressed smartly in the same colours as the driver, and as he unfastened the iron bolts the gate swung open and I beheld grounds the likes of which I have never seen in London before. I knew instantly that this Elysium was modelled on an eastern garden, for there were glossy, flowering plants I did not recognise, statues of exotic deities with multiple arms, and a pond afloat with water lilies. The largeness of the house was imposing, but it had an elegant symmetry: pure white, with four Roman columns of pale marble framing its gleaming black doors.

I was shown by an ancient butler into Lady Herbert's expansive drawing room, which, as you know, contains little furniture and an inordinate number of paintings. In fact, there is little clear wall to be seen. I was delighted by the gallery; nudes beside demons, and Hindu goddesses amidst Dutch masters. All the while there was an Indian man, sans the Herbert livery, standing still and watchful by the door like a statue carved of wood.

Lady Herbert rose from her white divan as I entered, and the Siamese cat that was perched on her lap leapt gracefully to the floor. A regal creature, I thought, that seemed irritated by my presence. About Lady Herbert's neck were beads made of large, pink gemstones which caught the light in such a way that I enquired if they might be diamonds. She seemed pleased that I had once again noticed her jewels. She nodded and replied, somewhat cryptically, 'The evil eye shall have no power to harm, him that wear the diamond as a charm – no monarch shall attempt to thwart his will, and e'en the gods his wishes shall fulfil.' These, I was informed, were the words of an anonymous poet, a Roman of the second century. I was beginning to wonder if Lady Herbert's interest in gems was based entirely on superstition, and thought this an opportune moment to enquire after the nature of my prospective duties. Lady Herbert told me that she would like a catalogue made of her jewellery and gemstones. She expressly does not want a solicitor, insurer or jeweller to undertake the task, for she trusts few, as I have noted. In fact, she said that this must be undertaken by a woman, since just as women are partial to gems, so do the stones themselves prefer the fairer sex!

She tinkled a small crystal bell, and her elderly butler appeared with tea. The service was silver and crystal, there were small spiced cakes and an exotic sweetmeat in rose syrup, and the tea was flavoured with cinnamon and clove. We were accompanied for the duration by the Indian, whom she called Govinda. I imagined he may be more than a servant to *her, but this could be mere fancy. He was fairer of skin than many of his countrymen, and taller, and he had a peculiar way about him that I find difficult to describe to you: at the same time courteous and watchful; innocent in appearance, but with eyes that guard secrets.*

Lady Herbert enquired some more after Franz's paintings, and I agreed to bring a selection of canvases for her perusal. She alluded that she might raise some interest in their purchase, since her friend the Maharajah of Benares was a dilettante, and, as she had mentioned before, partial to the works of European painters. She would be visiting him again the following spring, she informed me, though she said it in such a way that I almost felt as though she were attempting to convince herself rather than me. It is my understanding that the diamonds at the Royal Academy are thence to be returned. I felt cheered by Lady Herbert's suggestion that the Maharajah might patronise Franz's paintings, for it is my greatest wish that he continue to be remembered as a gifted Romantic. There are certain pieces which I know to be more than competent, in particular the Venus in the hall, for which I sat.

When we had finished our tea, I was led up a wide central stair of black marble, and as we climbed I recognised landscapes by both Turner and Constable adorning the walls. Govinda followed silently behind, which I found disconcerting, though my hostess barely seemed to notice his presence. We ascended another flight of marble stairs after the first landing, and then another, until we were at the top of the house. Then Govinda took from his waistcoat pocket a brass key, with which he unlocked one of the doors off the landing. The room was small, and without paper on the walls, which were instead painted the amethyst blue of Moroccan courtyards – a colour I have never before seen on the interior walls of a London house. Against each of these walls was a tall Indian chest with many small drawers, each with a keyhole.

Throughout the afternoon, Lady Herbert took from the drawers one exquisite piece after another as Govinda, as inscrutable as ever, stood to attention, by the door. There were bouquets of turquoise and seed pearls, roses carved of the finest coral and set amongst leaves of jade; there were necklaces of cascading yellow diamonds and bracelets of mosaic rubies and emeralds set in weighty gold. There were aquamarine sapphire earrings; gilt and obsidian brooches, and strings of large, oyster-grey pearls. I could barely take it all in. And then there were the stones; some still rough, for I learnt that the Indian and Persian rulers admire uncut gems, and there is not the expertise in the East to cut the fifty and more facets that cause a diamond to catch and splinter light as it does.

By the end I was dazzled and could no longer exclaim, since each piece seemed more remarkable than its predecessor. Of course, I delight in the aesthetic of gems, like most of our sex, but I have never felt the potency of desire that Cynthia Herbert displays, nor the yearning to have them glittering about me. Indeed, I believe I would find it most distracting!

When each small drawer had been opened and its contents displayed to me, Lady Herbert reached across and took my locket in her hand. 'He gave this to you?' she asked quietly, and I could only nod.

I opened it so that she could see the lock of white hair I keep coiled within, and she examined it at length, as though considering something quite carefully.

'Why not have the hair made into a proper mourning piece, my dear, for it is not good to keep the spirit of the dead locked away.'

'It is only my husband's hair,' I replied, 'not his spirit.'

'But you are mistaken, Mrs Korechnya, for the very essence of life is contained within our hair, as it is in the marrow of our bones. If you will allow me for a moment to use the rather inelegant language of science, hair contains carbon, the same indestructible property that is found in all organic matter. Diamonds, as you will know, are pure carbon and therefore capture energy and store it. Because all gemstones are formed deep in the underworld, nurtured like seeds by the earth and the stars, they embody the purest of celestial powers and have many mysterious properties.'

I thought it typical of Lady Herbert that she should endorse both science and metaphysics in almost the same breath. I am no stranger to the unworldly, sharing a house with Mrs Vesper, and Franz often told me tales of witchcraft in Prague before the revolution. King Wenseslas himself once employed a court magician and astrologer to advise him and even the name of the city means 'the gateway between worlds'. Like Cynthia Herbert, Franz believed that such places existed and we agreed, light-heartedly, that should we ever be parted, we would meet at one such gateway. It was a romantic sentiment, but Barbara, if only I had known then how deeply I would long for that meeting.

'The powers contained in gemstones,' my hostess insisted, 'are largely dependent upon the intention, the strength of will and the character of the person wearing the stone. In India, the diamond and its deity rule over the planet Venus, whose domain is the heart and its desires.'

She then went on to tell me that the wearer of a diamond, through purity of heart, might attain a higher knowledge. Diamonds, in this rather extraordinary philosophy, were potentially an elixir, providing wisdom, psychic clarity and good health. However, should an immoral desire overcome the bearer, such as a lust for power, then demons would break loose and grave ills befall them.

Lady Herbert did not appear to have benefited from the diamond's mystical powers herself, for she had become lethargic and appeared to be thoroughly exhausted. I had noticed as the afternoon progressed that her breathing had become more laboured, and often it required some effort for her to speak. I had noted also that Govinda was paying her much closer attention. I had several times seen her sip from a small vial of coloured glass: laudanum, the physician's cure-all for the nervous disorders of the female. I am inclined to think that the multiplicity of nervous disorders my father and his associates ascribe to women are in fact nothing other than subdued intelligence and frustration.

But as usual, I digress. Suffice to say that I think it a tragedy that a once strong and spirited woman like Cynthia Herbert should become languid, and I cannot help but wonder if some other force besides her grief is stealing her spirit away. I have but one further observation to make on the subject of my time at Herbert House, and it concerns the enigmatic Mr Govinda. He uttered barely a word the entire afternoon but as I rose to take my leave, he asked me what I had thought of the Maharajah's diamonds. I replied that I thought them very beautiful but that I was not amongst those who idolise the stone. He raised an eyebrow and for a moment I thought that he did not believe me. 'Then you have no desire for diamonds, Mrs Korechnya?' He asked in his lilting accent, and when I replied that I had not, he nodded his head rather thoughtfully, and caught Lady Herbert's eye.

And so I give you another lengthy chronicle of my interior hills and dales. I should love to hear more of your plans for the new school for ragged children in Westminster, and did I not even yet say how wonderful an achievement? By coincidence, the girl Sarah O'Reilly, whom I have *mentioned above, has a young sister who will be attending when classes begin, so I shall be able to report to you personally on how one small life is affected by your generosity and hard work.*

In fondest friendship,
Lily

When I am dead my dearest,
Sing no sad songs for me;
Plant thou no roses at my head,
Nor shady cypress tree;
Be the green grass above me
With showers and dew drops wet;
And if thou wilt remember,
And if thou wilt, forget.

Christina Rossetti

More than a week passed before Sarah was able to take Ellen to the Ropemakers' Fields, and it was on a Monday. Mornings were the best time to go to the graveyard for the poor; the light did something special then, and it didn't seem such a sad place. Mr Harding had said she could have the time off, since she'd worked the Sunday on account of a special edition of the newspaper coming out.

Sarah had forgotten about Mondays at Newgate, and they were almost upon the Old Bailey when she remembered why there was such a big crowd in the street. At first she'd thought that it was a little early in the day for a travelling showman to be drawing so many punters, or a Punch and Judy, but it didn't take long for her to realise that what was causing all the fuss and the air of morbid festivity was a hanging. There was a press of spectators between the scaffold outside the prison and the end of the street where Sarah and Ellen were trying to make their way through the crowds. Then, as one, the great volume of bodies closed in and no one was moving anymore, because the black door in the tall stone wall had opened.

Sarah couldn't see the prisoner, or much else apart from the beam above the death trap, and the rope hanging from it made of gallow grass. That's what Pa called the special hemp that made strong rope, rope that wouldn't break with a dead weight strung on the end of it. Fishermen used the same rope to moor their boats. Sarah looked down to check on Ellen, who was staring wide-eyed and holding on tightly to her hand. Ellen only reached up to Sarah's ribs, so she wouldn't be able to see much more than trousers and aprons. Ellen could sense it though, the excitement and expectancy that had taken hold of the crowds, and she was coming over all strange.

Mam had said that Ellen had a bit of the sight. Their Grandmam – who'd wasted away from hunger before she could get in the boat for London – had had it, and she could look clear through you, Mam said. But having the sight wasn't much help to Ellen as far as Sarah could see, it just made her stare into the corner of a room as if she were someplace else entirely. Sometimes in the night Sarah would wake and find her little sister sitting at the table in the dark, just sitting and staring. She'd been doing that since Mam passed and she'd kept on talking to Pa for ages after he'd gone, as if he were still there with them in the room, making them laugh. Then after a time, Ellen had stopped talking to him, and Sarah thought that was when Pa had really left them.

Sarah didn't like it when Ellen went all silent and faraway, in part because it made her feel lonely and in part because she was afraid that her sister's spirit might one day wander off and never return. Sometimes, if she couldn't sleep, Ellen would go upstairs at night and sit by the fire in Ruby's kitchen. Sarah had gone looking for her more than once, but now she didn't bother, since the landlady's kitchen was the warmest place to be in the White Hart at night. Ellen was only part earth child, Ruby reckoned, and the other part she didn't know what.

Ellen was doing it now, staring straight ahead of her, as a great hush descended on the waiting crowd. If she could have moved, Sarah would have pulled Ellen as far away from the hanging as she could. The thing was, they couldn't budge an inch, for they had been swallowed by the mob. The horde of spectators seemed to be panting like a great bloodthirsty beast. It was over quickly, and the crowd knew it because a great roar went up only moments later, and before long the vendors and hawkers were back to shouting about hot pies and lemonade.

Sarah gave Ellen's hand a little shake. 'Come on, Trub, this is no place for us today, let's go to the field.'

'He's dead, ain't he?'

'Sure is. Dead as that rat you found in Ruby's kitchen. Come on.'

'We gotta meet Holy Joe, Sarah, we promised.'

'Well, we will. Don't get all fussed. He's having a jar at the Stag. I'm not going to leave without him, silly.'

The Stag was an alehouse and Sarah didn't like it one bit. In fact, the whole row along Lime Burner was a sorry mess of slums and brothels. Mam always reckoned the people walking about in this part of the city had lost their souls to Lucifer. It wasn't one of Holy Joe's normal haunts, but on occasion he'd meet with some of the footpads he knew who had 'contacts' and could sell on anything Joe might have found or pinched. Sarah guessed that was what he was doing at the Stag today. Sometimes Holy Joe puzzled her, since for a trusting, simple-minded giant he always knew how to cut a sharp deal in the business of 'transient property', as Septimus Harding called it.

Holy Joe was waiting outside the Stag, which was a relief, since Sarah didn't want to go inside. She knew what it would be like in there; the smell of stale sweat, old clothes and hops, and a few greasy candles burning low on sticky tables. Joe wasn't alone; that Indian with the funny name was hovering beside him. Ellen let go of Sarah's hand when she saw the two of them and went running to throw her arms around Joe's legs. He patted her hair, but was fixated on the Indian boy who was talking to him. As they drew closer and she got a good look at the darkie, Sarah heard Joe use his name. It wasn't Victor at all, but something that sounded more like *Vikram*. She also realised that he wasn't a boy, but a slight young man with a feathery moustache. She couldn't make out what he was saying, but he seemed to think Holy Joe had all his wits about him and they were conversing in earnest. Joe lost interest soon enough though, since Ellen started to search through the pockets of his sailor's coat for new treasures, and his face immediately reverted to its open, childlike expression. The darkie slunk away, but not before Ellen had given him one of her finest smiles, the kind she reserved for people she especially liked. Sarah repressed a sigh; Ellen did befriend the strangest folk.

'C'mon you two, we're off to the Ropemakers'. Reckon we'll have to go by Ludgate Hill, since there'll be some merrymaking round the Old Bailey after the hanging.'

The Ropemakers' Fields were a good few miles' walk: right to the end of Cheapside, which was quiet on account of the hanging, and then across Commercial Street where the night trade had given way to closed shutters, and only a sleepy street sweeper or two crossed their path. Then they had to walk almost as far as Whitechapel before cutting across Spitalfields to the small, disused plot which was the graveyard for the poor.

The field was a riot of wild flowers, and the weeds had grown so high since they were last there that you could hardly see the row of simple crosses that marked the place where more than half of the O'Reilly family rested. Ellen tugged away from Holy Joe's hand as soon as they opened the gate. She was getting bigger, Sarah thought, though she was still direfully thin. The wool pinafore she used to wear was so ragged by the end of the winter that it had just about dropped right off her, and the red cotton smock Ellen now wore came from the Christian Ladies. Sarah didn't like going there much, since she had to mind how she talked, and the dull matrons were always praying and asking the lord to forgive children like her and Ellen as though the O'Reilly girls couldn't possibly be getting by without sinning. Still, there was always a cup of tea and a bun going in the church hall, and they needed the clothes all right. The pastor's wife usually tried to get Sarah into a dress, but so far she'd got away with choosing breeches instead. Ellen's pale hair was shining brightly in the morning sun, and she'd stopped to pick some daisies to put on the graves. She wouldn't wear boots even if she had them now that it was summer, and her little feet were covered in dirt and scratches. It'd soon be time to get Ruby's laundry soap to her again.

Once they'd pulled up all of the weeds, Ellen put a few daisies down on the earth at the foot of each small cross. Then they sat for a while, just she and Ellen, since Joe was off with his slingshot chasing a rabbit.

'Tell me more about the darkie, Trub. You seen much of him lately?'

Ellen shrugged and was silent for such a long time that Sarah thought she wasn't going to answer. When she did, it was such nonsense that Sarah wished she'd never asked. 'He lives in a castle across the seas, just like the little mermaid's prince, and he's here cos he's been sent by an Indian princess!'

'But does he do honest work, Elly? Or does he earn his coin the same way as Joe?'

'Oh no, Sarah, he works. He delivers little packages to posh folk.'

Sarah was intrigued. 'What's in the packages?'

'Medicines,' said Ellen importantly.

They were interrupted by Holy Joe, who came back swinging a dead rabbit by the hind legs and wearing his silly grin. Ellen ignored them both and started telling Pa all about how Sarah was reading her a story called 'The Little Mermaid', and wasn't it funny, since that was just what Pa used to call her? At that, Joe pulled the picture book out of one of his pockets and handed it over to Sarah while Ellen looked up at her with pleading, blue eyes. Sarah opened it up to where she'd marked the page with a scrap of newsprint. She sat the book in her lap and took a deep breath. She read about how the old queen set a white garland of lilies in the little mermaid's hair, and how the sun had only just set when she raised her head above the waves, but all the clouds glowed rosy and golden and the evening star gleamed clear and bright. Then the little mermaid swam right up to a ship and saw that of all the men on board, the most handsome was the young prince with the great dark eyes. Ellen was enchanted, and so was Holy Joe. Both begged for more when Sarah closed the book.

'I'm going to visit the little mermaid and see her palace under the sea,' said Ellen decisively.

'Don't be silly, Trub. She's just part of the story, and there's nothing at the bottom of the sea but fishes and mud.'

Ellen wasn't having any of that. 'Well, if it's writ in a book then it must be true!'

'Not everything that's writ is true, Elly. Why, even what's in the broadsheets ain't ... true half the time.' She handed the picture book back to Joe, who looked as indignant as Ellen that she'd dared to question the Little Mermaid's existence. Sarah felt a little stab of fear. 'Don't you go out in the river on your own, Trub, you hear me? If you want to, we'll go down to the water together and wait till she comes up looking for that prince with the great dark eyes.'

'Victor's got dark eyes too, ain't he?'

Sarah didn't answer; it hadn't occurred to her before that Ellen might be sweet on the Indian. She'd have to keep an eye on the darkie, for she wasn't sure if he could be trusted.

❖ 9 ❖

My Love,

This is only the second time I have been able to summon the courage to bring myself to the place where your presence still lingers. Is it not strange that although I long for you so that it is an affliction of body and soul, I have not, these past few months, been able to enter the room where I knew I would find you? I write because in this place I feel closer to you than I have felt since you left my side, and because there are still subjects of which I can speak to no other.

At first, I would not believe that you were gone, then I was angry at the cruelty of the forces that took you away from me so suddenly. After this I cannot say what came over me, but I do not remember the days passing, and throughout the winter I could barely rise from my bed. I have not entered our room since they bore you from there, and have passed many a lonely night in the blue room since then.

Not once did Martha Vesper urge me to rise, nor to speak, for she could see that it was taking all of my strength merely to face the dawn of another day without you. She would stay with me, attending to some needlework, until I made a show of taking my breakfast. Septimus Harding has been equally forgiving of my wretchedness, and I read in the London Mercury *that Mr Evans was unable to contribute his regular essay, due to illness. I have since returned to the offices and Mr Evans is once more on the hunt for his exceptional women.*

Around me, stacked against the walls, are your canvases – some unfinished – and on the shelf, jars of tinctures and powders and linseed, boxes of hog hair and sable brushes. It seems that if I touch them I will burn my fingers, though really the scald will be to my heart, for how can I hold the objects through which your own heart whispered its secrets? I sit at the table by the window, where I used to work whilst you painted. The chaise longue is behind me, and I can barely rest my eyes upon it, for it bears memories too affecting; memories I dare not stir, for fear that they might overcome me.

Now I can feel the strength returning to my limbs, if not to my heart, and so I have taken the first steps, Franz, into a world you no longer occupy. I have in fact been employed to undertake some clerical work by a lady who believes in the existence of a spirit world. Peculiarly, I am comforted for the first time by the thought that so many share her conviction that such a place exists. I can understand now why the widows of the war in the Crimea and the India mutiny attend these circles, they who had so little time with their young husbands.

When last I visited Hampstead, I brought with me several of your canvases, for Lady Herbert has the idea that her friend the Maharajah of Uttar Pradesh might like to purchase certain of your paintings. According to my hostess, he is a collector and enthusiast of the European Romantics. She was genuinely thrilled by what she saw, and then proposed something which, for a moment, rendered me speechless. She suggests, Franz, that I travel to Benares with your paintings and present them in person to the Prince! I understand that her Indian attendant, a gentleman by the name of Govinda, has offered to accompany me, for he must soon return to the employ of the Maharajah.

I remain undecided upon this matter, and have resolved to make no decision until my next visit to Herbert House. Would that you were here to advise me, my love! Perhaps I must put to trial the very superstition which has been my constant companion since I first met with Lady Cynthia Herbert; that diamonds are not only harbingers to desire and thieves of the heart, they are also conductors of spirit matter. Dear Lady Herbert believes that with these stones, she might contact the dead. Would you be drawn back to me by a diamond, my love? If only it were so.

Yours for ever,
Lily

⁜ 10 ⁜

I shall not see the shadows,
I shall not feel the rain;
I shall not hear the nightingale
Sing on as if in pain:
And dreaming through the twilight
That dost not rise nor set,
Haply may I remember,
And haply may forget.

Christina Rossetti

Martha Vesper hailed from a family of cotton millers in Manchester, and had had little experience of domestic service. Still, she had taken to the profession of housekeeping naturally, being practical and hard-working by nature, and by gender predisposed to the finer details of the domestic arts. As before, she had posted an advertisement in *The Times*, since this was where a respectable householder in need of her services was best served to look. She was aware that there were many women who were more qualified than she for such a post, women who had character assurances from the most reputable London households. This did not deter Martha, however, for she was of the opinion that a house chooses its inhabitants, right down to the servants, though she preferred to think of herself as staff. A house, she believed, had its own requirements quite aside from those of its master and mistress, and whispered these from its shadows, cupboards and hallways. Martha was sensitive to such things.

The Korechnya residence on Waterloo Street was certainly the most unusual household she entered in her search for a new position as housekeeper. Martha felt at ease with the Korechnyas, because she knew that she would be left to get on with her work without interference. On the occasion of her interview, she had looked around the bohemian parlour and declared, 'It feels like a friendly house, if a little colourful, and if you don't mind my saying so, I should work very well in such a place.' Mrs Korechnya hadn't appeared to mind her saying so, since she'd proclaimed that she was delighted by Martha Vesper's plain speaking. She'd said that she was weary of the thinly disguised disapproval for her unorthodox tastes that the more experienced candidates had displayed. Martha was not perturbed by the unconventional, for she did not take much interest in the fashions, and from what she could observe, nor did her young mistress.

Mornings at Waterloo Street were quite unlike mornings in any of the other households that had employed Martha Vesper. When the master, Mr Korechnya, was alive, he did not take breakfast, but had only a cup of chocolate in the kitchen, warming the seat of his trousers by the range. He would buy his dark bread from the German baker at Waterloo market on his way to the studio, and was gone long before his wife came downstairs. Now when she heard the cloth of Lily's gown whispering on the stair, Martha was relieved, for during the winter there had been many weeks when her mistress could not rise from her bed. Then, the tray of coffee and freshly baked rolls would remain untouched on the bedside table in the blue room, and Mrs Korechnya might have passed to the other side herself, so still and lifeless she seemed. Her lovely hair lost its gloss entirely, and threads of silver began to appear though Lily was but eight and twenty. The master would have wept to see her, for her skin became sallow, her eyes darkened, and there was no meat on her bones, so that her white bedgown hung in loose folds about her shrunken bosom. Martha Vesper was not a woman easily given to sentiment, but she had to bite her lip many times in those weeks to keep from shedding a tear.

She did not worry for the master himself, of course, nor did his passing take her completely by surprise. She had seen the death wraith around him and had tried to will it away, but she was no match for the undertow from the other side. In the end she could only induce him – for he feigned robustness to the last – to take some brewed lungwort and coltsfoot. When she washed the linen and saw the spots of blood on his handkerchiefs, she knew how it would end.

Martha often saw his apparition in the bedroom those first weeks, when she went in to take the curtains and linen, to black the grate and fire irons, and to put away his fine clothes. He was looking for Lily and seemed bewildered, standing by their empty bed. Then, early one morning in the sixth week, when Martha was in the blue room sitting by her sleeping mistress with her needlework, she saw Franz one last time.

Lily had passed a restless night, so that her sobs and groans had woken the housekeeper, who, like a mother, smoothed Lily's hair from her damp forehead and made her sip some poppy and valerian, (she had thrown the laudanum from Doctor Hall out of the window, for she believed it did more harm than good). When Lily finally slept, Martha stayed, looking up from her embroidery frame at intervals to check that her mistress was not tormented by her dreams. And there was Mr Korechnya, his white hair untied and falling to his shoulders. He had not died an old man as such hair might imply, though he was some years older than his wife. No, his hair was white from his nervous disposition, Martha believed, though his skin was still smooth and the colour of pale walnut. His tall frame leant over his wife's sleeping form, and he kissed her on the mouth and whispered in her ear; then he was gone and all that remained was the slightest smile on Lily's pale lips. Martha knew that she would begin to improve now, for the ghost of Franz Korechnya had found his wife at last and said goodbye. Sure enough, when Lily woke that morning, she ate almost her entire breakfast, and even enquired after the newspapers.

Martha bought the *London Mercury* and the *Guardian* each day when she heard the paper boy calling out, even in the weeks when she knew that the expenditure was wasted. But now Mrs Korechnya had resumed passing her mornings in the library, dressed in one of her strange, oriental house gowns, her hair loose, her notebooks and papers scattered in a muddle across the desk. Her mistress would not touch the post until she had completed her morning's inspection of the London press. Lily read selectively, Martha Vesper noticed now that she watched more closely, and she wrote pages and pages of heaven-knows-what in her notebooks. The reading of broadsheets and the writing of notes were not habits common to the ladies she had served. Most ladies, Martha had observed, read only *Pears'*, and the *Ladies' Pictorial*, and jewellers' catalogues. Martha Vesper had no time for journals and newsprint, though she could read and write, and at first she thought it imprudent that her mistress spent two pennies a day on the papers. But now she admired Lily, for she was most certainly her own person, and had been even before her husband died.

Since Franz Korechyna's death, the housekeeper had made a habit of dusting and polishing more regularly in the front rooms, and kept the fire built if there was a chill, so that the place was always comfortable and cheerful, and so that she was near at hand. She did this unobtrusively, taking care not to disturb her mistress, who occasionally looked up from the page and stared out of the window. She had lately been taking more of an interest in the street vendors – goodness knew why. As Martha cleared the breakfast tray from the table, Mrs Korechnya was reading from the *London Mercury* and had two fine creases between her dark eyebrows.

'Mr Melville is making such a fuss over this business of smuggling. If we were to believe him, then all of the world's shadows are gathering over London.' She sighed and looked up at Martha. 'The revolution of the press may be a good thing, but I fear the editors are often too profligate with the truth. They are creating an illusory London, and I am not certain that I think it wise, for it fills idle minds with fears and imaginings. Even Septimus Harding, who is an honourable man, will print what he believes his readers prefer to pay their penny for.'

Martha Vesper nodded her head thoughtfully and carried the tray to the scullery. She didn't mind it when the mistress shared her worldly concerns; Mrs Korechnya needed to think as sure as she needed to breathe. As Martha saw it, the world was just as it should be, and if any shadows were gathering over the city of London, then it only meant the light was hidden for a time. And there was light in the most unexpected places if you could see clearly; creeping down a filthy alley early in the morning or falling across the window seat in the disused parlour. The parlour was on the opposite side of the reception hall to the library where Mrs Korechnya now spent her evenings as well as her mornings, and the mistress now tended to avoid it as assuredly as she avoided the upstairs bedroom where her marriage bed lay cold and empty.

Martha returned to the library to dust bookshelves that were dustless, and polish the coloured glass panels of the lampshade she had polished only yesterday. As she wiped the curved surface of the globe, which stood three feet high on slender mahogany legs, it spun on its axis. She placed a hand on the sphere to still it, and polished the brass meridian around its girth. She was aware that Lily was watching her as she lifted her hand from the map, and looked to see which land it had been resting on. It was a game they sometimes played.

'Which nation have you landed upon today Martha?'

'Why, it is India, madam. Fancy that.'

'India!' For a moment the mistress looked as though she might confide something, but then thought better of it. 'Do you know, it was some-where Franz always wanted to visit, though I have never craved colour and light as much as he did; it suits me just as well to see misty forms through the fog, for then I can imagine all manner of ... what is it Martha?'

Martha Vesper was having one of her 'feelings', and it had something to do with the locket that Lily always wore at her bosom. Usually it was hidden inside her gown, but this morning it sat atop the embroidered red, pink and orange poppies of her bodice.

'Have you moved the hair from your locket, madam?' She was more outspoken now, since she had nursed Lily through her grief; although she had never been one to mince her words.

'Why, no, Martha. I couldn't bear not to have it about me.'

Martha's feeling was stronger now, though she could not put a finger on why she was so uneasy, but that premonition had something to do with the master, or maybe just his hair. Most peculiar. At that moment, the door knocker sounded, and Martha left the room. It was the child again; the tomboy from the newspaper office, standing there with that impish grin on her freckled face and a few blades of red hair poking out from under her oversized woollen cap. She'd love to get some soap to those breeches and that shirt.

'Well, good morning, miss. No package today?'

'No, missus. I've a letter for Mrs Korechnya from Mr Harding.'

'A letter is it? Well then, you'd better come in and give it to her yourself.'

The girl's face split into a huge grin, so that Martha couldn't help but smile herself. She showed her into the parlour, after the girl had paused in the hall to remove her cap and attempt to smooth her hair, which would not be smoothed but stuck up at the front like the comb of a rooster. She was a strange little thing with her rough Irish talk and her quick blue eyes that tried to see everything all at once. Clever as you like, this one, but good hearted with it, Martha thought.

'Good morning Sarah, what an unexpected pleasure!' Lily rose from her chair and extended her hand to the girl, who didn't shake it but kissed it, so that both Martha and Lily had to hide their amusement.

'Sit down child, and give the mistress her letter while I get you a cup of chocolate.'

In the kitchen, Martha went looking for the hunk of dark chocolate, which she hadn't made use of since the master died. Lily was not one for sweets and it was no wonder she was slender as a maypole, although she was getting more fleshed out now that Martha made certain she ate proper meals. The gentle bullying was another liberty Martha had earned during those dark weeks. If left to her own devices, Mrs Korechnya would get all caught up with her words and books, sitting in that library for hours on end, not dressing unless she went to the market, and that was a precious rarity still. And now the boss was sending messages so that she would not even have to attend the newspaper office! He seemed a kindly soul and certainly meant well, but she'd send her own letter back, Martha decided, letting him know what she thought was best for her mistress.

The chocolate should have been in the cool larder wrapped in a cheese cloth, but it was nowhere to be found. It was neither amongst the cake hoops and sugar cutters, nor hidden in a preserving pot, nor in the empty stone flasks for making elderflower wine. Martha sighed with exasperation and sat on her stool by the range, as this was where she did her best thinking. Suddenly she knew what had happened to the chocolate, and she smiled, chiding herself for not having thought of it before. Of course *he* would have moved it! But where would he put it? There was only one place: a large cupboard in the scullery where he kept some of his things; rolls of Irish linen, for he had stretched his own canvases, pots of coloured powder and jars of amber linseed oil. This was also where his paintings were now stored, the ones that Lily had brought back from Kensington.

Neither the mistress nor Martha had been able to take a proper look at the paintings yet, nor did they know what to do with them. It was fine work, anyone could see that, though the paintings would never be accepted by the Royal Academy because Franz was a Jew. The portraits of London's wealthy Jewesses had all been returned by Lily to their sitters – even the unfinished ones – but she had refused payment. What was left were pictures like the one in the hall, of women who looked as if they came from times long past, from worlds distant or merely imagined. And there was the chocolate, wrapped in a cheese cloth with a string around it, nestling amongst the pots and jars.

Lily and Sarah were so deep in conversation when Martha returned to the parlour, that they barely noticed her.

'. . . History is full of women who dared to claim the freedom that is the birthright of men and achieved greatness, even as military leaders. Have you not heard of Queen Boadicea, or Joan of Arc?'

Sarah shook her head, and then frowned. 'And I s'pose Queen Victoria must be a woman, though I never thought of her as one.'

When Martha set the tray on the table, the child just stared at the pretty china cup steaming with dark chocolate, and at the plate of knead cakes and fresh butter. Martha had supposed she didn't get much to eat; she had that look about her.

'Sarah and I were discussing the fundamental differences between men and women, Martha. Would you agree that these exist?'

'That I would, for they're a breed apart madam, no two ways about it.'

'But what would you say that they were, if you had to think of their very essence, Martha?'

'If it's essence you want, then the man of our time is made up of three parts: desiring, doing and talking about doing.'

This made her mistress laugh delightedly. The child was good for her, Martha thought.

'And the woman? What say you of the woman of our time Mrs Vesper?'

'Another three parts: thinking, feeling, working. But all six parts fit together, don't they madam?'

'Indeed.'

Sarah had not missed any of this. The child's eyes were darting between Lily and the housekeeper as she sipped her chocolate. The first sip was a sight to behold, for her thin face seemed almost shocked at the deliciousness of the creamy liquid. The girl wiped some butter from her chin with a man's handkerchief, and put down her cup.

'I best be goin', Mrs Korechnya. Mr Harding will have my breeches if I'm not back with a reply by dinner.'

'Of course, Sarah, but you needn't worry, for I will tell Mr Harding that I detained you in considering my response. In fact, with your leave, I should like to propose that I borrow you for an afternoon, to accompany me to Kensington. We might even see if the morrow is suitable for our appointment. What do you say?'

Martha found herself smiling again. Mrs Korechnya looked just as pleased by the arrangement as the child, but the housekeeper knew that she was asking as much out of loneliness as for the pleasure of Sarah's company. The morrow was in fact the anniversary of her marriage.

'I shall pen this now, agreeing to his proposal that I write a piece on Julia Margaret Cameron, although he seems to have forgotten it was my idea!'

'Is she one of them *exceptional* women?'

'She is indeed. Mrs Cameron is the first woman to have become a commercial photographer, and she has taken portraits of Mr Tennyson and Mr Dickens and of George Eliot.'

'George the *lady*?'

Lily laughed. 'That's right, George the lady.'

While her mistress described to the child just how clever and brave George the lady was, Martha slipped out of the room to write her own letter to Septimus Harding. This she put into Sarah's hands at the front door, where her mistress could not see.

⁘ 11 ⁘

Sarah was full up with ideas and questions by the time she met Lily Korechnya the following day. She had begun to feel alive in a peculiar way since she'd met Mrs Korechnya and she couldn't make anything of it, except that she hadn't felt so safe since before Mam died. Mr Harding had always been kind, and Ruby was too in her straight-speaking way, but with them Sarah felt like she had to be all grown-up, her being the head of the family and all. With Lily she could be who she really was, which was only half grown-up. Whatever was happening, the world seemed suddenly to be lit up by grace. 'The grace of the maker,' Mam would have said, although Sarah had her own ideas about the maker now, since she'd lost half her family.

When Sarah had arrived back at the newspaper after visiting Waterloo Street the previous day, the editor had had his topsy-turvy office to himself, which wasn't always the case. Inspector Lark was inclined to drop in most days and Sarah reckoned this was as much for the company and friendship of Mr Harding as for the business of reporting crime. Around Septimus Harding were towers of paper, stacks of binders and ledgers and notebooks, a dish full of pipe ash, a sherry glass and a teacup. Nelly had once moved some books to dust and hadn't put them back in the same place. Mr Harding had made such a fuss when he couldn't find the book he wanted that the maid was now completely terrified of him.

When Sarah told him that she had a letter from Mrs Korechnya's housekeeper as well as one from the lady herself, the editor's bushy eyebrows had tilted upwards.

'A letter from Mrs Korechnya's *housekeeper* Sarah? Do you think she wants a job too?'

'Shouldn't think so, sir. She don't seem the type.'

'And what type would you say she is, this Mrs Vesper?'

'Well sir, she looks like Mr Parsimmons, but she's not unhappy like he is. I'd say she's clever, but not Mrs Korechnya's kind of clever. She seems content just to be looking after her mistress, sir.'

Septimus Harding had broken the seal on the housekeeper's letter first, and was reading it and listening to Sarah at the same time. 'There is one quality that you have missed out Sarah, for it seems that our Mrs Vesper is also bold! She asks me please not to make it so convenient for her mistress to work at home, and that Lily Korechnya needs to be *more* acquainted with the society of her colleagues, not less. Well, well, women are bossy creatures, aren't they? I suppose you'll be bossy too one of these days.'

Sarah was horrified; 'No sir, I won't,' and she meant it.

'We'll see, we'll see.' For an instant, the editor's expression became solemn. 'If you want to make something of yourself, Sarah, you stay clear of husbands, for there are few who would let a woman apply her mind, and yours is a good one.'

This piece of advice had stayed with Sarah all afternoon, and was with her still. Next Mr Harding had broken the seal on Lily Korechnya's letter. He had agreed to allow Sarah to accompany Mrs Korechnya to Kensington, since he'd been instructed to protect the interests of the lady, and, he said, it would do Sarah good to be in the company of 'one of this city's most distinguished female minds'.

'Are they different then, sir, female minds?'

'Indeed, Sarah. In my opinion, certain female minds have a capacity for sensitivity and objectivity that many great men lack. This is not something to go bandying about, you understand, since the newspaper establishment of this city has been built upon the wits and industry of men, and an idle woman is sometimes the showpiece of a successful man.'

As Sarah crossed Waterloo Bridge, the sky darkened and a chill rose from the river. She felt a shiver down her neck and looked towards Temple Pier. The little port was as busy as ever, in spite of the murder only a few weeks before. There was a colourful foreign vessel moored against the end of the longest wharf. Its bow was pointed towards the bridge and at its prow was an enormous, beautiful lady whose skin was dark wood and whose robes were painted gold. On its decks were dark-skinned sailors, and docks' workers were milling about on the wharf. Sarah knew from the shipping news that Temple Pier was where the foreign cargoes came in, and for a minute she wondered what forbidden treasures Herbert Peasey might have died for. That was what Mr Melville was saying now: that he was a bad man, and was done over by some other bad men.

When Sarah arrived at Lily Korechnya's emerald green door, she reminded herself of what Septimus Harding had said: that she had a good mind, and he knew all about minds. It made her feel more confident about seeing Mrs Korechnya, since she certainly didn't want to appear witless. Mr Harding needn't have told her about staying clear of husbands, she thought as she banged on the door with the brass knocker, she'd already figured that one for herself. She wondered what Mrs Korechnya's husband had been like, he must have been different; and Mr Harding, he had a wife too. So maybe there were men who didn't mind a woman with a mind, not like Jack Thistlewite who pretended he knew most everything, even when he didn't.

Mrs Vesper answered the door and then Mrs Korechnya appeared, wearing her dark, velvet cloak. It wasn't really cold enough for a cloak, despite the darkening sky, but Sarah had already noted that Mrs Korechnya liked to keep herself hidden from the world. It was a shame, since she had the most intriguing costumes Sarah had ever seen.

As they rode through the streets in the carriage, Mrs Korechnya started writing something in a notebook and Sarah craned her neck to see what it was. She tried hard to imagine Oxford Street as 'an artery that flows between the east and west of London, from where the city traders practise their alchemy; transforming female boredom and desire into gold'. She knew that an artery had something to do with the blood running like a river through the body; she'd read that in a copy of The Lancet, although she'd always thought it was much too clever a journal for the likes of her. Mr Harding kept copies of the publication in one of the piles on his floor, and she'd looked at it once or twice when she was waiting for him to finish with a meeting. Sarah didn't know what alchemy was, though, so she added it to her list of questions for Mrs Korechnya.

'Here also,' Lily was writing quickly and in a fine copperplate, '*in the shadow of the parade of shining cloth, the liveries and jewels, are the colourless, threadbare rags of beggars, and unshod children with barrows and basket wares.*'

Sarah was perplexed that one of the city's most distinguished female minds was writing about street urchins, since she wouldn't have thought in a hundred years that that it might be something the gentry would fancy reading.

'That something for the *Mercury*, Mrs Korechnya?'

'Perhaps not, no. Sometimes I write purely to empty my mind, and at times it makes me feel less alone. Otherwise I find that all becomes a tangle of imaginings and memories.'

Then Sarah told Mrs Korechnya about how all the reading of old newspapers and the thinking she was doing was making her head so hopping busy that some nights she couldn't sleep.

'Then you must write, Sarah!' the lady said after listening to her quietly. That made Sarah laugh; *her* be a writer? That was just a dream.

They arrived at the old house in no time at all, and as Mrs Korechnya was searching through her carpet bag for a great brass key, the rain came on. Above the glass doors hung a large briar rose whose blooms were plump and glistening with water, and which dripped on to them as they entered the house. It smelt so sweet after the dirty air of Waterloo, and the paving stones outside the doors were covered in pale pink petals, like a velveteen carpet. There were fewer paintings against the walls than there had been the last time Sarah saw this room and in the dark stormy light, Franz Korechnya's studio seemed most eerie. Lily shivered slightly beneath her damp cloak.

'We must light a fire,' she said, and disappeared through a door in the far wall. Sarah followed her, and saw that it was one of four opening on to a long corridor. At the end of the corridor was a wide staircase, leading both upstairs and down.

Once they had brought wood up from the cellar and Sarah had made the fire, the studio seemed a little warmer and less unearthly. Mrs Korechnya busied herself lifting the lids from boxes and opening the doors of a book cupboard. It hadn't seemed that there was anyone else living here, and Sarah was beginning to wonder about the house.

When Lily came out of the book cupboard carrying a blue hat box, she asked: 'Are all them other rooms empty?'

'There were other painters here once, but Franz was alone last winter ... before he passed away. It can be very cold here during the dark months, but my husband paid such things no heed. He would still be painting now, in this weather, in spite of the darkness and the rain. The doors to the garden were always open, for Franz did not believe that London was cold – not like Prague in the winter. Often when I visited, I could barely speak as my teeth were clattering so. Then he would close the door and remember to build the fire.'

She looked different when she talked about Mr Korechnya, as if she had returned to the time before he was gone. Sarah's curiosity was nagging at her, and she wondered if it was proper to enquire about days gone by.

'He must have been the sort that liked a woman with a good mind,' she said, recalling her talk with Mr Harding and thinking this a harmless remark.

'Indeed. If I close my eyes I can almost see ... Oh Sarah, forgive me. You are too young to hear of romantic tragedy.'

'Was he handsome, Mr Korechnya?'

'Oh yes. His hair was moonlit white, and reached right to his cravat, which was always of patterned silk.'

'And did you meet him in London?'

'Franz and I met at a salon – do you know what that is?'

Sarah shook her head.

'It is a meeting of sorts; a gathering of people who want to talk about philosophy and art and the peculiar ways of the century we inhabit. This salon was a little special though; it was held in the home of Gabriel Rossetti, who is a painter. The gathering was in memory of Lizzie Siddal, Rossetti's wife and model, and a painter also, who had recently died from an overdose of laudanum.'

'You wrote about her!'

'I did. It was not as sombre an occasion as it might have been, since the author Wilkie Collins attended, and he had passed the day in a gin shop, so was quite in his cups! He had perhaps been as much in love with Lizzie Siddal as half the men at her wake. The group of painters –

they called themselves the brotherhood – believed they had created a new religion; a religion of beauty, and that was what the author Mr Collins was telling Franz Korechnya when I first saw him. "But beauty is not to be equated with pureness of heart," I heard Franz reply. And then he said that artists could be forgiven their romantic idylls, when their landscape was so darkened by soot and poverty.

'Mr Collins caught me listening, and paid me a compliment of sorts. I took the opportunity to ask him why he had allowed the character of Walter Hartwright in his novel *The Woman in White* to become enamoured of the faint-hearted Miss Fairlie, rather than the spirited Miss Halcombe. To this, the author replied icily, "I am inclined to agree with Mr Ruskin; a true wife in her husband's house is his servant, it is in his heart that she is queen." When I heard Franz Korechnya mumble something in defence of our sex, I became all the more intrigued by him.

'I watched him as he walked over to a wall to examine one of Rossetti's paintings. Lizzie appeared in it, as she did in so many of the brotherhood's paintings. Her famous hair glowed like new copper, and her eyes like beryl. I wondered as I watched Franz, if he too had been in love with her. But then he turned and looked across the room to where I sat, and his eyes held mine as though by some thread of light. It is not something that I can easily describe to you, Sarah, this meeting of ours, for it was as if our very souls wished each other well.

'At supper, he contrived to sit beside me, and we talked all the night, about Prague and the salons of Berlin where there is not the stifling segregation that one finds in London. There, Jews and Christians, men and women, the nobility and the middle classes all meet as intellectual equals. His was not the kind of interest that I was accustomed to from men ...'

Mrs Korechnya stopped talking and gazed into the fire. The flames burnished the deep mulberry cords of her poplin gown, and her lovely pale face. She has been made sad by her memories, Sarah thought, and it seemed as if she had forgotten where she was.

'Did he ask you to marry him that night?'

Lily laughed. 'Not quite. The next day I heard the echo of his voice; the strange accents he placed on otherwise commonplace words. I saw the shape of his lips when he smiled. He came to visit me that afternoon, and when he said that I was an unconventional woman, I asked if he found this unattractive. It was then that he asked if I would marry him.'

Lily stood up and ran her fingers through her dark hair, looking a little confused. She anxiously touched the locket at her neck, a gesture Sarah had noticed her making several times that afternoon.

'Today is the anniversary of our wedding you see. Forgive me, for it has made me sentimental, and I did not wish to burden you.'

'You haven't, I'm not burdened, honest. Not a bit!'

Lily smiled gratefully at Sarah, then looked around the room, suddenly brisk and without a trace of her former sadness.

'Now, I should like to take the last of these canvases back to Waterloo Street, for I have made the acquaintance of a distinguished lady who has already seen some of Franz's paintings and would like to view more of my husband's work.'

❖ 12 ❖

Dear Barbara,

I have now paid several visits to Herbert House, and have begun to make a catalogue as agreed. I had wondered how I might overcome any ignorance on my part of the names of particular gemstones, but I need not have worried, for I am accompanied at all times by the man Govinda. His knowledge of such things is immense, though he speaks only if I ask a question. I have become more accustomed to his silent presence, and where previously I imagined him uneducated, now I think differently. He is watching and listening always, though his expression remains unreadable. When I ask about a stone, he will not only tell me its name, but also its purpose, for I have discovered that in his country, each gem has some transcendental property. For instance, red stones such as coral, carnelian, ruby and garnet, stimulate the blood and are generally empowering to the whole person. Unless, and this Govinda stressed, that person is unbalanced. In such a case, the 'heat' of a red stone can be dangerous and cause aggression. Green stones on the other hand, such as emerald and jade, are considered calming and restorative, like a walk through a forest with the light descending through the green leaves above.

Cynthia Herbert has told me that Govinda is a special guard from an order of Hindu warriors who are employed to protect the Maharajas. The Maharajas hire such men because they are trained to kill, and think nothing of doing so, should a thief or bandit threaten the prince, his palace or his jewels. In India, she said, the wealth of kingdoms is contained not in the vaults of banks but in caskets stored deep within the stone vaults of palaces.

When the day's task is complete in the amethyst chamber, I take tea with Lady Herbert in the drawing room, surrounded by her extraordinary gallery of paintings. Sometimes her sister-in-law, Miss Herbert, joins us for she also lives at Herbert House, but she is rather timid, and I believe a devout Christian, so the two Herbert ladies have little in common. When last we met, I brought with me more canvases from Franz's studio, and I was inconceivably nervous as she unfurled each one, attempting to see Franz's work through another's eyes. I could not, for each painting is far too familiar to me, and all I could do was watch her face and hope that she was as moved by my husband's work as I. She gave nothing away until the end, and only when the last canvas lay flat on her drawing room floor did she speak.

'These are fine indeed, and I should like to purchase several myself. The others you must transport to India, Mrs Korechnya, for I am certain that my friend the Maharajah of Benares would be delighted to take delivery of a small collection by such an accomplished painter. We must now discuss payment for your assistance in cataloguing my collection.'

'It is enough,' I said, 'that you take an interest in my husband's work. I could not possibly accept payment ...'

'Tosh!' she said scornfully. 'My proposal is this: I am aggrieved that you keep your husband's hair locked away thus,' and she reached across and tapped the locket about my neck. 'I should like to have it made into a proper mourning piece, so that, in time, his spirit will release you. But it will not do so if you lock it away from the daylight!' Lady Herbert then cast a glance at Govinda. 'Govinda is in fact a fine draftsman and, when I discussed the matter with him, he suggested that he might design something appropriate. He has already commenced with the arrangement for the Maharajah's diamonds.'

I was surprised that the nine diamonds I had seen on display at the Royal Academy were to be made into a jewel, and said so.

'But of course! It was the foremost condition of the diamonds leaving India, for I know of a fine jeweller in Hatton Garden. Pray let me bring him the lock of your husband's hair, for then he can make both the Maharajah's jewel and your mourning piece. Though, you must tell no one that the diamonds are destined for the jeweller's bench; the Maharajah's piece must remain our secret!'

I remain strangely reluctant to participate in this superstition, but Lady Herbert has been generous in her offer to afford my husband the acknowledgement he did not enjoy in life and I have therefore agreed to *have a mourning piece made from the lock of his hair. I admit that I am intrigued to see what Govinda will design for me. Until then I wait anxiously to have Franz's 'spirit' returned to me.*

In fondest friendship,
Lily

❖ 13 ❖

I had heard that diamond merchants cast freshly flayed sheep into
the valley of diamonds, the meat being sticky, jewels cling to it; then
vultures and eagles swoop and carry the meat to the mountain tops
where the merchants scare them and collect the jewels.

'The Legend of Sinbad', from *The Thousand and One Nights*

Hatton Garden caught the overflow from Fleet Street and the Strand,
and was therefore considered a fashionable enough area in which to be
seen shopping, particularly since retail there was of a more specialised
nature and, Joshua Finkelstein believed, more *important*, for he took
his business very seriously indeed. That is why he was still working on
a late summer's evening, a concession he made only for his most valued
clients. By definition, these were clients who valued him in turn, and
were willing to demonstrate their appreciation in pecuniary form.

Throughout the spring, from the small window of his basement
workshop, Joshua had watched as the hems of lady's dresses changed
from merino to muslin, and their boot leather from black to ivory. This
was the only part of the street that Joshua had a good view of from the
basement, but sometimes it was a very fine view indeed, for on a windy
day a crinoline could be taken by a gust and rise too swiftly for anything
to be done. Then he had a delectable eyeful of stockings and lace and
bloomers. Joshua Finkelstein was no longer a young man, but neither
had he been cursed with the slowness of his advancing years. He was
proud that his virility had been preserved, in spite of the trouble it had
caused him in the past.

When the shop bell rang, he would have his leather apron off and be
up the stairs and into his shop as quick as a fox, for he didn't yet trust
young Davey with the customers. There was just enough room in the
shop for two ladies and two gentlemen, or for three ladies, but certainly
not for four – not until the fashions changed. Business had been good,
particularly since Lady Cynthia Herbert had become a client. He was

surprised when first she called, she being a regular customer at Garrard's, the Crown Jewellers. The problem with Garrard's, he thought, was that there were so many smiths and apprentices and shop assistants it was impossible for one's business to remain discreet. At Finkelstein's, there was only Joshua and the young apprentice, Davey. Davey had just the right measure, for Finkelstein's purpose, of untrained youth and unfledged dodger. He wasn't beyond occasionally collecting his master's tax-free sparklers from Temple Pier, provided there was a regular bonus of two shillings for his trouble. With this, a young man could buy himself a warm bath in Whitechapel, or make a half-payment on a new linsey waistcoat. Joshua Finkelstein did not make a habit of discriminating between stones that came to him through the proper channels and those that did not. There was too much money to be lost if one was unerringly scrupulous.

He'd let Davey off early today, since he was determined to finish the Herbert job that evening, and his apprentice was showing altogether too much interest in the unusual commission. After all, the peculiar Indian charm was supposed to be kept a secret, though the diamonds themselves had certainly caused a commotion at the Royal Academy. Davey hadn't liked being sent away since he'd taken a shine to the red stone, as had Joshua himself, and had been itching to see the finished piece.

Joshua Finkelstein rarely set stones himself these days; more usually, he carried out repairs and bought pieces for his shop, mostly from the East, as the 'exotic' was now the fashion. And since he had been the first jeweller on Hatton Garden to stock Burmese ruby brooches, Tibetan turquoise earrings, traditional Rajasthani choker necklaces and even gold-tipped tiger's claw brooches from Ceylon, he had acquired a certain reputation, (there was nothing like acquiring a reputation, Joshua always said). His reputation was precisely what had led the famous Lady Cynthia Herbert to visit him just over a week ago, on a fine summer's day. That, and her clear anxiety that the commission remain discreet, for the diamonds were now the public's fancy, and she said that she was concerned for their safety.

Joshua had agreed to Lady Herbert's request – even though he made it clear to her that he was not strictly a maker of jewellery any more – because she was offering a preposterously generous fee, and because the design was vaguely familiar to him. He had seen one of these Indian amulets before, in the form of a ring on the finger of a merchant who had sold him some large, teardrop emeralds from Jaipur. It was a disc containing eight precious and semi-precious stones arranged in a circle around a ruby. When Joshua had enquired after the unusual design of the piece, the merchant had said that he wore it for protection, and that it bore with it the blessing of the gods. It surprised Joshua that Lady Cynthia Herbert would be taken with such a trinket; there was something a little too primitive about it, he thought, with all those unmatched stones. He didn't even like the phylactery of his own faith, and charms for love and prosperity made him feel unquiet – *heathen* was the word that came to mind. He was a Jew, as were many of his customers, and he shouldn't be paying attention to the superstitions of another creed, it was bad for business. As for love, he, like many of his faith, had married for love, but that was long ago.

Lady Herbert had been accompanied by an Indian, a manservant he presumed – though one without the appropriate air of servitude, Joshua felt. Indeed it was the Indian who had carried the little velveteen pouch lined with quilted satin, but before Lady Herbert would let Joshua see what was inside it, she had asked if he could put his shutters down and lock the door so that they could not be disturbed. He had done as she asked because his curiosity was immense. Cynthia Herbert's jewellery and gem collection was legendary, and he had a feeling she was going to show him something very fine indeed. And Joshua had not been disappointed, for what spilled out of the little pouch on to the glass counter were treasures such as he had never seen before; not in eight years with the Gold and Silversmiths' Company on Regent Street, no in the almost twenty years that he had run his own establishment. There were nine gems in all and although Joshua had heard that these colours did occur in diamonds, he still could not quite believe what he was witnessing. However there was no mistaking a diamond; the particular crystalline growth within the stone occurred in no other gem and made them sparkle with an intense, dazzling light. Joshua had seen pale pink and lightish blue and yellow diamonds, but never emerald green, deep sapphire nor bright copper, nor, most rare of all, fiery red. The red diamond was particularly remarkable, and it blazed so that he imagined it might scorch him if he touched it. But touch it he must, and when he held the stone in his hand, it was as if the fire in the belly of the diamond heated up the blood in his hand, and then in his arm and his chest, so that he quickly had to put it down.

Each stone was cut exquisitely and Joshua could see the work of the master; the Dutchman Voorsanger had a sixth sense for precisely where to cleave a diamond, and his skill at cutting was unsurpassed. The stones were uniformly between ten and twelve carats in weight and, to the naked eye, unflawed. Later, under his eyeglass, Joshua saw that all of the diamonds were indeed flawless. The red diamond perplexed him, frightened him almost, for the stone flared even when he blacked the lanterns and blew out the candles. It seemed to have an interior light that reminded Joshua of the luminous heart of Jesus in a painting that he had seen on the parlour wall of a Catholic household. And there was something else that disturbed him about the stone, for as soon as it was in his keeping, he was again stirred by the dangerous desires he had landed him in so much trouble as a young man and that he had fought so hard to contain: the fervour in his loins, the whores, and the pictures his wife had found that had caused her to visit her sister in the north, never to return. Joshua was an old man now, content to gaze up skirts and look slyly down a lady's décolletage as she bent down to look at the exquisite jewellery he deliberately kept beneath the front counter, but the jewel had rekindled his old yearnings.

Lady Herbert had stayed only long enough to make it clear that he must treat the commission with the utmost secrecy. He was almost relieved when she left his shop, for she was as nervous as a rabbit and had insisted on seeing his vault before she departed. She had once been far more handsome – buxom as he remembered – but she seemed to have shrunk since returning from the Orient, and there was a paleness in her eye where once there had been a sparkle.

The Indian had not left with her. He produced some detailed drawings on a scroll of draft paper, the quality of which was uncommonly fine. It was obviously foreign as there was decorative Sanskrit writing around the pictures. Joshua had asked what the writings meant but the Indian was dismissive; 'It is not important. You can see from the drawing that the red stone must be central, and the others arranged around it, *exactly* as shown.' Then he drew the jeweller's attention to the second part of the commission, which by comparison was relatively straightforward:

the hairwork lilies, arranged on a large oval of jet. Whilst Joshua examined the drawings closely, the Indian man had stood in silence. He wore a turban and pale, baggy trousers and a long tunic made of something coarse but soft; raw silk perhaps. Against his brown skin, the effect was rather striking. He also wore a ring, which was unusual for a servant. Joshua appraised the jewel with a swift glance. The stone was a ruby, and was worn on the middle finger of the man's left hand. The setting and cut of the stone and the gold were Indian, but the ruby was sizeable and would still be valuable if re-cut. The man caught Joshua looking at his ring.

'Red stones contain the energies of the sun; giver of life.'

For some reason this unsolicited information made Joshua feel uneasy. Still, he could not stop himself from enquiring; 'The red diamond in the charm . . .' but he did not proceed beyond this, because the man held up his hand.

'Be careful, it is dangerous . . .' His eyes were suddenly caught by a movement at the top of the stairs, and Finkelstein followed his gaze. It was Davey, whose sly curiosity had got the better of him. But he was brazen enough to step forward rather than remain skulking in the shadows, and he made some excuse about needing another of the fine-tooth saws used for cutting silver. These were kept in a drawer behind the counter and he seemed to make rather a habit of breaking them. When he had got his saw and had had a good, sideways look at both the drawing and the Indian, he returned to the basement. The Indian then left the shop, taking his scroll of parchment with him and without offering further explanation for his mistress's odd request. The jeweller was obviously expected to work from memory, such was the secretive nature of the task. Quite absurd.

Joshua Finkelstein had not done the hairwork himself, but had sent little parcels of the hair out to the daughters of the draper on Holborn. Like their embroidery, their weaving was impossibly delicate, and he had seen some fine miniatures produced by their nimble little fingers: forget-me-nots woven from the gossamer hair of a dead child and fixed to an ivory cameo; a graveyard scene with a tiny, flaxen weeping willow leaning over a tombstone. When he had visited Holborn to collect the hairwork earlier that day, the draper's two daughters were seated on their stools as usual, their heads bent over needlework frames, their graceful white necks made rosy from the heat of the hearth. Joshua was captivated by their loveliness, which only served to remind him of his past sins. The girls had transformed the coil of white hair into Lilliputian flowers. Joshua left without looking again at the beauties by the fire, who were oblivious to the quickenings they aroused.

For the entirety of the time that the red diamond had lain in his vault, Joshua had been unable to contain his desires and had been lured back into the arms of the Haymarket whores. It was all most peculiar, he thought, most peculiar. He had tried to keep his frolics from Davey, although he still kept the basement workshop free for the occasional 'private consultation' with certain customers; he did not like to call them courtesans, for he considered the word vulgar. Now that the charm was made and he was no longer required to handle the 'dangerous' diamond, Joshua had touched neither breast nor buttock for days, and was starting to feel that he might again be able to enter the synagogue and show his face to his God. The serene Indian with the penetrating gaze would collect it on the morrow, and he had been rather pleased with himself when all the bezels were fast and the charm lay on his bench, its nine eyes winking. He was equally proud of the large oval of jet upon which was fastened the delicate wreath of white lilies. Now he needed only to varnish the lilies and fix the glass, then to file a little here and polish a little there. He was certain that each piece looked identical to the drawings.

The bell in the shop trilled as Joshua leaned intently over the shank of a ring he was enlarging for a dowager whose fingers had thickened. It was the most piffling of all his common tasks, and irritating because he did not feel that he could impose a fee upon a loyal customer for such a small job. If more gold was needed, then of course he would charge for the metal, but if the ring was just to be stretched, then the service was gratis.

Joshua made certain that he was smiling brightly as he reached the top of the narrow stone stairs which led to the shop. It was uncommon that he receive callers at this hour, although anyone could see from the street that his basement lamp was lit. He was nettled when he saw that his caller was only Davey. The boy's waxy skin and dark eyes were infused with an unearthly shine from the gas light of the street lamps. Did he looked nervous? Joshua wondered. He undid the chain and fumbled with the large brass key before it turned in the latch with a satisfying click.

'I beg your pardon for calling so late, Guv, but I've left me new tartan waistcoat in the cupboard, and I'm off to the penny gaff.'

He shimmied past Joshua before the jeweller could object, and darted downstairs in an instant. He was back before his master could follow and make sure that his true purpose was not to have one last gloat at the Herbert job, which lay all but finished on the bench, waiting for its final buff.

'Fanks, Guv. I 'spect Mr Turban's back tomorrow for that queer particular.' Davey shuddered melodramatically. 'He gave me the dithers.' Then the boy disappeared off into the shadows in search of the evening's entertainment.

When he was finally ready to retire, Joshua Finkelstein's only regret was that he had worked well past the hour that the taverns closed. He could not be done with walking home in the night fog, not when his eyes and neck ached from bending over his table, painting lacquer on the minuscule lilies with his impeccably steady hands. When he laid down his tools, the strain of keeping his hands from shaking when his heart was beating fast and his brow sweating caused Joshua to take a measure of brandy with him to the divan in the corner of his workshop. There was another reason why he would not venture home at this late hour. He was afraid. Handling the Indian jewel again had unnerved him. It was all hocus pocus, of course, and he felt like a fool. Still, he made certain that the door of the shop was locked, and he took a second measure of brandy to help him sleep, confident that he would wake with the sun as he always did. Then the manservant would call, and once Davey had taken over he would spend his dinner hour at Haymarket, he decided, one last time, because the sight of the draper's daughters had been too much for him. A man could not be expected to resist all temptations, was his consoling thought as he drifted into sleep. But it seemed that no sooner had this thought formed, than he was awakened by a sharp rapping at the door upstairs.

Surely it was barely first light, thought Joshua irritably as he climbed the stairs to the shop, still not fully awake. The darkness outside was not night, but heavy cloud he realised, as he opened the shutters, expecting to see the tall Indian. But there was no one in the street.

Perhaps it had taken him so long to raise himself, that the man had walked a short distance along Hatton Garden? Joshua unlocked the door and stepped out to survey the darkened street. The gloom was caused by a fog as green and as thick as pea soup, though it smelt much worse. Some rotting matter, and the acrid smoke from the chimney stacks on the river, no doubt. Joshua was confused, in his sleepy state, by a shadowy form that stood shrouded in fog. It was still, but appeared to be fluid, as though it were swathed in a great, dark cloak.

For no reason at all, Joshua Finkelstein was suddenly wide awake, and the fear from the previous evening returned, though this time it was more acute. Bile ascended from the pit of his stomach to his throat. He sensed that the danger he had felt whilst working in his basement was now only feet away from him, and he was unprotected. Joshua backed away slowly from the formless presence in the fog, until he was upon the doorstep of his shop. He proceeded no further than this, for there was a blinding pain right between his eyes, like a sharp blow. It knocked him sideways from the doorstep and he fell, smashing his head against the cobblestones of the street. From here he could see the apparition move towards him; or were there two? The air became spiced by a smoky sweetness as two great black wings enfolded him. He could no longer breathe, though he was not certain if this was because the chill dread had frozen his throat, or there was some other impediment. He was suddenly aware of the preciousness of breath; breath that gave life, and took life away; like the god of the sun; like the troublesome red stone. But he should not be thinking of heathen charms, and so he tried to imagine his David's star, which he had once worn beneath his shirt, but no longer did, since he had come to feel unworthy of its beauty. There was a searing heat behind his eyes that exploded into crystalline shards; like fire, like blood-red diamonds.

⁜ 14 ⁜

A cynical, mercenary corrupt press will produce in time a people as base as itself.

Joseph Pulitzer

Sarah was abroad early the morning after the second murder was reported. Her curiosity had directed her north of Fleet Street, towards Holborn and Hatton Garden. She hadn't been to Hatton Garden before, since there were no pubs that sold Irish whiskey in these parts. The jeweller who'd got himself killed was called Finkelstein, this much Sarah knew. She walked along the road, looking at all the pretty shops: jewellers and watchmakers, milliners and boot makers. The shops were not open yet, and there was almost no one else on the street. Maybe people were scared of the murderer now. She did not have to look too hard for Finkelstein's shop though, because first she saw Inspector Lark. He was standing outside the panelled glass of the shop looking in, and with him was a young policeman. Sarah knew he was a plucky one, because he was wearing the black wool trousers and short coat of the Bow Street boys; these were the officers who did the Westminster beat, though you never saw them in the rookeries. According to Ruby, certain Bow Street boys got paid twice; once by the guvs at Whitehall and once by the street girls, so they wouldn't be locked up.

Sarah was still far enough away from Finkelstein's for Lark not to have seen her, but he would any minute, as he had eyes like a bird of prey. There weren't many places she could hide, so she walked back a little way and crossed the road. Now she was on the same side as Lark and the policeman, and there were two trees that were big enough for her to hide behind. This she did immediately because the two men were beginning to walk towards her. It was just as well there was no one else on the street, Sarah thought.

Soon she could hear Lark's voice and smell his cheroot.

'I want to know about his clients, and any connections he might have with the black market. Something stinks here, Gerard. There is more than a passing similarity in the way the jeweller and Peasey died, and it seems that the Jew had some connections with the Temple Pier wharf.'

'With respect sir, most of the jewellers in London have such connections.'

'I realise that, Gerard, but Finkelstein was known as an importer of Indian jewellery. I also want to know what his last commissions were, if there is evidence of him having anything of excessive value in his shop at the time of death.'

'Nothing we've found . . .'

'I realise that nothing has been found, man, no actual jewels, but I want to see his paperwork. Get in there and box up all of his ledgers and anything else that might be of interest. You know, letters, bills, drawings, whatever is on his bench. As soon as possible.'

'Yes sir.'

'And Gerard . . .'

'Yes sir.'

'Find me that boy, his apprentice. I want to know why he didn't show up for work yesterday or today. Either he was involved in the crime, or we might be looking for another body . . .'

By this time they had passed Sarah, who had edged round to the other side of the tree as they walked towards her was now watching their backs. The policeman, Gerard, was younger than she had at first thought and had closely shorn fair hair. She hadn't got a good look at his face, but he sounded an all right sort. Not one to make a street girl pay him off, but then you just never knew, and that was the truth. Lark was looking like he hadn't slept in a good while, and his white shirt was slightly crumpled beneath his waistcoat. Still, his boots were clean as ever. He didn't have a wife, Sarah had decided, since he seemed an honourable man, and no honourable man would look at Lily Korechnya the way Lark did if he were married.

When Sarah next saw Inspector Lark he was in the editor's office, and so was Gregory Melville. Another day had passed since the murder and the broadsheets were desperate to make the crime seem even dirtier. In the absence of facts there was always hearsay, or invention. Sarah thought that she'd never seen the policeman look quite so ugly, nor Melville so smug. Septimus Harding was just plain irritated. It seemed that she had mistaken his grunt, which she had thought meant 'enter', for one of his 'don't interrupt' noises. Gregory Melville was seated opposite Mr Harding, and Lark was pacing about the room. She could tell that Melville had the upper hand because he had a sly smile on his greasy face. As usual, he had too much hair oil on his side whiskers and it had stained his cravat. The collar of Melville's bold-check short coat was turned up and his trousers were as tight as ever.

'Not now, Sarah, come back after dinner.'

She was dismissed before she'd even opened her mouth, but she wasn't going to miss this, not for anything. Outside in the hallway Sarah put her ear to the keyhole, for she dared not take the risk of leaving the door open a crack; not with Mr Harding in such a dark mood.

'There is no *evidence* to suggest that the murders at Temple Pier and Hatton Garden are connected, nor that Finkelstein was in possession of the Royal Academy diamonds. I must insist that you revise your column to that effect.'

'Codswallop, Inspector. The victims had identical bruises on their foreheads and, according to the morgue report on the first death, there was suspicion of strangulation. If I'm not wrong, Finkelstein was also strangled.'

'The windpipes of both men were crushed, but there were no marks on the throat, Melville, which is technically not death by strangulation. And I would thank you not to approach the morgue without consulting me first. I can only guess what underhand means you have employed to obtain your information, and I don't like it, man. This is police business ...'

'Police business! Pah! The business of the police is to prevent crime, not to hide it from the good citizens of London. How are they to keep themselves safe if we do not inform them of the danger on the streets? Why do you suppose Joshua Finkelstein, a *jeweller*, was killed? I have it from respectable sources that he was involved in black marketeering.

He had connections with Temple Pier. I also have it that the very method of murder which killed both men is exclusive to the Indian assassins known as thuggees, and that the jeweller's apprentice is missing. Of course, if you have anything enlightening to add to my column, I would be only too happy to include your professional opinion, but until then, sir, I must continue doing *my* job.'

'Your thuggees are entirely fictitious; the bandits are no longer active in India, let alone in London. The boy Davey might be a petty criminal but this was no petty crime, *sir*. I can guess the identity of your "respectable" sources, Melville, and I look forward to seeing them locked up in Bridewell.'

Sarah had to make a run for it then, because there was the sound of a chair being scraped back, and the next moment, Melville came through the door and took the stairs two at a time, brushing past her as though she was as unapparent as a street beggar. She heard him stride furiously along the hallway above and knew that he was on his way to see Jack Thistlewite. She crept back to the editor's door, which was now open a crack. Lark had his back to her and Mr Harding was looking at him as though waiting for an answer. After a moment, Lark nodded his head slowly.

'I had heard the same rumour and I see now that I was a fool to think the cheap press and the likes of Melville would not pounce on it like the filthy magpies they are. There is a strong possibility that the tattle from the street originated with Davey the apprentice, and that the nine Indian diamonds Voorsanger cut have indeed been stolen. They were certainly not on the premises. I have this morning been at Herbert House, hoping for verification, but Lady Herbert would not receive me. Indeed, there is something peculiar going on there, for the curtains were drawn and the butler looked as if he had not slept in days. I intend to call again before sunset.'

Lark threw his half-smoked cheroot into the fire, a sign that he was soon to depart. Sarah climbed the back stairs to the third floor, thinking about what she had heard. Perhaps Melville had his facts right for a change and the diamonds had been stolen? She knew enough about the newspaper business to know that this was a big story, and she supposed that by now Jack Thistlewite would have been appraised.

The compositing room was empty, and the men who hadn't gone home for their dinner were playing a game of cards in the tea room. Sarah poured herself some of the disagreeable brew, and went to the window. She took her tin from her shirt pocket and was about to roll herself a fag, when she saw Inspector Lark leave the building and walk briskly away in the direction of Holborn. He'd be going to Hatton Garden, she'd wager, and then perhaps back to Herbert House. She could tell by the set of his shoulders that he was as angry as Melville, and she had a feeling he was going to make the reporter pay for his insults. Sarah felt sorry for the policeman, and suddenly thought of the story of St George from Mam's book. Lark was like St George, and the streets of London were his dragon.

'Been running errands for the boss 'av yer Sam?' It was the weasly Thistlewite, bored with the slowness of the game and fixing to stir up trouble.

'I have Jack, and I've business in his office directly.' Sarah liked to appear busy, it was the only protection she had against the irritating superiority of the compositors.

'What business is that then?' Jack was pretending to be unconcerned, but Sarah knew that he was busting to know if she had any inside information.

'Nothin' as you'd like to know, just business.'

Jack Thistlewite gave a certain look to the other card players, and they all sniggered knowingly, which made her bristle and want to say something to impress them.

'I've been off visiting with Mrs Korechnya.' At this there was a lull in the game, as the compositors imagined Lily, all rose-scented and corset-free.

'Mrs Korechnya is it? Well.'

'She's writing a piece on a lady photographer.'

The men around the table laughed uproariously at this. 'Photography don't get done by *ladies* Sam, you'd best make certain that your Mrs Korechnya isn't makin' that up!'

'Well, she just isn't, and the editor has asked her. So.'

'Is that right? *Well.*' More laughter.

Sarah crossed the room and stubbed out her fag in the tin on the table, not looking at Jack or the others. She hated their leering grins and their small minds. She could tell Melville had been talking to them, since Jack Thistlewite was even more self-satisfied than normal. At least she'd seen the diamonds, which was more than any of the compositors could boast. She could always tell them that, she supposed, but something stopped her. When she thought about the sparklers she had to admit that she felt a little uneasy, and the idea that they were loose on the streets of London made her feel queer.

Sarah was glad to leave the compositing room at the end of the day, which wasn't usually the way for her. Even though she was becoming bored of all the advertisements for tonics and balms and potions to make men into better husbands (there was nothing, she'd noticed, to make women into better wives, but then maybe women didn't need it so much), she still liked being part of the business. There was something about words in print that gave Sarah a thrill, even if the words were sometimes foolish or a blooming waste of good paper.

Ellen and Holy Joe weren't by the river and Sarah hoped she wouldn't find them at Holy Joe's doss house. She'd told Ellen not to go there for it was filled with all manner of low life. Not as bad as his previous lodgings – the place in St Giles that ran a school for child pickpockets in the kitchen – but there were bugs everywhere and they'd got into Ellen's clothes and hair the last time. Ruby had had to scrub her from top to toe with laundry soap so she wouldn't infest the basement. Bugs were bad for gin making, Ruby said.

The narrow passage leading to Holy Joe's doss house contained some of the worst slums in Devil's Acre, and the ground was littered with excrement and rubbish thrown down from the tenements above. Sarah hated going there, for more than anywhere else in London, it reminded her of how bad life was for some. Mostly she wouldn't let herself think about the people she knew who had gone to the workhouse or whose lives were as miserable as sin through sickness and hunger and poverty. She'd seen a dead body or two down this passage, left there like a pile of stinking rags for the rats to pick over.

She reached the door of the doss house – which had once been a normal house with six rooms but now slept thirty to a room and sometimes even four or five to a bed – but she didn't go in. Instead she whistled, for this was her signal to Ellen and Holy Joe. A moment later, Holy Joe's head stuck out of one of the windows, his silly grin showing the few teeth he had left.

'Ellen there with you, Joe?'

Holy Joe shook his head and shrugged his shoulders, looking bewildered. 'No Ellen.'

Sarah's heart missed a beat. 'You mean you haven't seen Ellen today, Joe?'

Holy Joe nodded his head and shrugged his shoulders again. 'No Ellen. Lonely Joe.'

'She isn't at the White Hart?'

Joe shook his head sadly.

'You come right down here, Joe. I don't know why I think you're able to look after her just because you're big. Come down here now, we're going to find that little piece of trouble.'

Sarah felt like crying, but that wouldn't solve anything. Holy Joe appeared beside her, looking ashamed. He was wearing his sailor's coat; he never took it off, not even in the summer, for he kept all of his belongings in its pockets.

'Maybe she's with that darkie. You seen that Victor around, Joe?'

Holy Joe shook his head and his great shoulders shuddered with sobs.

'Jesus, Mary and Joseph, don't cry, you'll start me and then we'll both be useless. Come on Joe, help me think where she might be.'

They went to the herring wharves first, since this was where Ellen always used to come with Pa. After that, Whitehall Stairs, and then all the way past Waterloo Bridge to Puddle Dock. It was getting dark by the time they'd walked back along the embankment to Westminster Cathedral. Ellen had friends who sold basketwares here, but none of them had seen her. Sarah was beginning to get a sick feeling in her gut, but she kept her fears to herself.

'Let's go back to the White Hart Joe, maybe she's home now. If she ain't, then maybe Ruby's got some ideas'.

Ruby was behind the bar, and laughing her loud, bosomy laugh, since the Rabbit catcher was there and she'd had a few. "Lo Sarah, Holy Joe. Where's the little un then?'

Sarah's gut clenched tighter. 'Hoped she might be here, Ruby. Joe hasn't seen her all day. Do you recall seeing her any time?'

'Can't say as I have. But that one slips past yer like a shadow.'

'I'm going back out then. Any chance of giving Holy Joe a jar, Ruby? I'm going down to get my waistcoat.' She'd best put her coins in the tin too, Sarah thought, since she'd been paid today and there was good chance of being robbed in the alleyways by night.

There was a tallow burning low on the table in the cellar room, and there was Ellen, curled up on the mat in the corner, fast asleep. Sarah felt weak at the knees all of a sudden, like laughing and crying at the same time. Then she got angry, at herself, at Ellen, at Joe, for no particular reason except that for a while she thought she'd lost her little sister, and she was supposed to be looking out for her. She'd promised Mam. And without Ellen, she'd be all alone in the world.

She went to get the tin, moving a broken brick behind the door to retrieve it from its hiding place. It was getting heavy, and now more than ever she wanted Ellen to be in school. The next thing was to convince her to go, and then to keep her there. She got the shock of her life when she opened the lid, because there amongst the coppers and shillings was a shiny gold sovereign. Ellen must have been woken by the sound of the jingling coins, because suddenly she was standing right behind Sarah, making her jump.

'Blimey, Trub, don't creep up on me like that! Where have you been all day, Elly? Why didn't you meet Holy Joe like you're supposed to? Do you know how afraid I was? There's bad men out there. Don't *never* do that again, you hear? *Never.*'

Ellen's lower lip was trembling, her little, heart-shaped face was deathly white, and there were blue shadows like bruises beneath her eyes.

'What is it Elly? You poorly?'

Ellen shook her head and a coil or two of dirty blonde hair fell into her eyes. 'Just been playing. Didn't mean to make you 'fraid Sarah. Please don't be angry.'

'You been playing with Victor?'

Ellen paused, then nodded.

'I ain't angry no more, Trub, you just worried me sick is all.' Sarah reached over and pushed the stray locks out of her little sister's eyes, then pulled her close and squeezed her tight. She wondered if Ellen had been as pale yesterday and the day before, and she just hadn't noticed. The girl didn't sleep at all some nights, and on occasion, Ellen had had her boots on when she woke up, like she'd been out in the night. She'd pay more attention now, Sarah promised herself, she wouldn't let her little sister get ill. 'Now how 'bout if I go get Joe and we ask him if we can read some more of his picture book about that little mermaid?'

At this Ellen's face brightened, but still there was something not right with her Sarah thought. 'Where'd that sovereign come from Trub?'

'Found it.'

'Found it where?'

Ellen shrugged and looked at her feet. She was playing with something about her neck; some beads.

'What's that you got there, Trub?'

'Beads. From Victor.'

'What sort of beads are those?'

'Sandals.'

'Sandals?'

Ellen nodded. 'Sandals wood.'

'Elly, Victor's not in with any bad men is he, you've never been thieving with him, have you?'

Ellen shook her head solemnly. 'No, he's all right. He don't know London so well and I've just been helping him is all, Sarah. Really truly.'

When Sarah came back with Holy Joe and a meat pie from Ruby, it was as if the pair of them had been parted for years instead of hours. Joe lifted the child right up above his head and showered her with kisses. After both had emptied their pockets, showing the day's findings of boot laces and bits of pretty china and a snuff tin, they ate Ruby's pork pie. Ellen didn't eat much Sarah noticed, and gave most of her portion to Joe, who could have eaten the whole pie himself. Then Holy Joe got the picture book out of his pocket and handed it solemnly to her.

'Do you remember where we left off the story, Trub? I forget.'

Sarah hadn't really forgotten, she just wanted Ellen to think about books, and to like them so that she would want to go to school.

'The little mermaid was going to the sea witch for a spell so's she could get an immortal soul and make the prince love her. What's an immortal soul, Sarah?'

'It's what you get when you die.'

'Is that what Pa's got?'

'Suppose so, though I pity the angels if they have to go off lookin' for him all over heaven.'

❖ 15 ❖

But bring me poppies brimmed with sleepy death
And ivy choking what it garlandeth
And primroses that open to the moon

Christina Rossetti

Every morning Martha Vesper listened out for the paper boys so that she could buy the broadsheets for Mrs Korechnya. The lads cried all the louder when there was some bloody news, and they had been shouting at the tops of their lungs of late: *'There's nothing beats a stunning good murder'*, and *'Royal Injin diamonds stole!'* Martha liked to stay clear of talk, and did not partake in idle yatter with the washerwomen or street vendors, but she couldn't help but know about these murders. Still, she had too much to do to be wasting her time thinking of such things. At this very moment there were two knead cakes in the oven, and the iron was almost hot enough for the linen. The silver was still only half polished, and there was a leg of mutton to be broiled with sage for supper, since the herb was good for cleansing the body of spirit matter. Martha was of the opinion that the spirits of the deceased cling to the very bodies of those who grieve, and not until the body was free of the troublesome attachment, could the living be at peace. She did not discuss these convictions with her mistress, although she'd gathered that Mrs Korechnya was liberal of mind.

When she'd discovered that her new housekeeper was given to sensing the presence of 'others', the mistress had seemed more fascinated than disturbed. It had proved impossible to keep this matter from her employer, since to Martha the spirits were as extant as the living. Thus she might be seen talking to the air or chastising an empty space for shifting things around in the parlour. All that Mrs Korechnya objected to, in regard to what she called *spiritualism*, was the 'unscientific' nature of disembodiment. Yet the current fashion in ectoplasm and table-tipping was a means of employment for women and a comfort for the bereaved, and as these were both worthy causes, Mrs Korechyna said that she could not fully disapprove.

Despite herself, Martha Vesper's thoughts turned once more to the matter of the broadsheets; something about these particular crimes made her uneasy. The second victim was a Jew, but since the first had been a Christian, death by the hand of one intolerant to a particular faith had been ruled out. The Jew had been in the business of jewellery, and now the entire, unpleasant business was being whipped up into an exotic tale of smuggled gems. It was just the kind of tommyrot that made it seem wasteful to give even a copper to the papers and she couldn't be done with filling her head with such nonsense. Yet Martha had one of her *feelings* about these deaths, which meant that their shadow was somehow close. She didn't like that one bit. 'Anuvva dark, evil def!' the paperboys cried, and for once, Martha agreed with them.

Martha collected the silver candlesticks from the parlour and straightened the curtains as she passed. It was a shame not to use this room, for more than any other in the house, the parlour was a testament to Mrs Korechnya's artistry. The walls were papered in one of Mr William Morris's more exotic fancies, with peacocks fanning their bright tails under trees laden with pears. The curtains were sapphire blue Indian silk shot with gold thread, and the divan was from Prague, its legs carved to resemble the sinewed haunches and feet of a mountain lion. Across its scarlet brocade back was a brightly embroidered shawl. Once the divan would have been scattered with leather-bound notebooks and broadsheets. Once the piano would have been played here every evening, and Martha Vesper would listen, seated by the range in the kitchen with her needlework. There had been times in this house when there had been little need of her industry, for when both master and mistress were in the house the lower floors were often still and empty. Then Martha would go upstairs only when both had risen, to change the linen and the water.

Now Mrs Korechnya was in the library and her notebooks and inkstand were untouched. Ever since the mistress had given Lady Herbert the hair from the locket, there had been a chill breath upon the air. Martha could only presume that the master did not approve.

The door knocker sounded. Martha put the silver candlesticks down on the hall table and adjusted the pins that kept her linen cap in place. It would be the tomboy she'd warrant, cooking up some new excuse for a visit. In fact, it wasn't Sarah on her doorstep, but a gentleman she'd not seen before.

'Good afternoon,' he said, 'I believe this is the residence of Mrs Korechnya?'

'It is, sir. And who might I tell my mistress is calling?'

'Detective Inspector Lark from Marlborough Street, if you would be so kind.'

Inspector Lark was a distinctive gentleman in appearance, although his frock coat was in need of a hot iron, she noticed, and his whiskers of a blade. His brow was gleaming with sweat, and his thick black hair was damp at the temples, for it was a steamy afternoon. Otherwise he was perfectly composed. All in all, Martha's impression of Inspector Lark was favourable, even though his dark, hooded eyes and vaguely foreign complexion lent him a nefarious look.

'If you'll step in, I'll inform Mrs Korechnya that you're here, sir.'

Martha left him stroking his chin as though he'd just realised that he should have stopped at a shaver before calling on a lady.

Mrs Korechnya was at the table, and behind her the window was open, but there was no breeze to move the closeness of the air. She had taken off her waisted blouse and so wore only a front-laced, sleeveless undergarment, and her silk shawl had been discarded on the chair back. She had that faraway look and Martha had to repeat herself twice before her mistress was roused.

'There's an Inspector Lark here, madam, from Marlborough Street, who says he'd like a word.'

Lily raised her eyebrows and a shadow passed across her face. 'What could he want with me, Martha? It is nothing inauspicious, I hope?'

'I couldn't say.'

'Perhaps it is merely some newspaper business. Detective Lark is an associate of Septimus Harding . . . I suppose I must see him.'

'Your shawl, Madam.'

Lily had not noticed. 'Yes, quite so. Thank you, Martha.'

When she returned to the hall, the Inspector was gazing at the Venus painting, and Martha thought his expression had softened.

'Mrs Korechnya is in the library, sir. Follow me.'

The mistress had arranged her shawl so that her shoulders and bodice were covered, and she was standing by the window.

'Good afternoon, Detective Lark.'

'Good afternoon, Mrs Korechnya.'

'Would some iced tea be a satisfactory refreshment, since it is too balmy an afternoon for a hot beverage?'

'Iced tea would be more than satisfactory.'

Martha nodded, and left the room to fetch some lemon mint from the kitchen garden. She was not one to pry, but she was most curious to know the policeman's business with Lily Korechnya.

When the housekeeper returned with a pitcher of mint tea and the good crystal tumblers on a lacquered tray, Lily was seated once more, and her shawl had slipped from her shoulders. She seemed unaware that she was half-dressed, and her face wore an expression of disbelief. Lark was asking questions about Lady Herbert's jewellery, and his eyes were trained on the face of his interviewee, as if he were making an enormous effort to keep them from the chiselled curve of her white shoulders and the lacing at her bosom. In Martha's estimation, this manner of restraint only confirmed what she had first surmised; that the inspector was a gentleman. Her mistress's answers were composed with care and, Martha thought, with a degree of caution. Yes, Mrs Korechnya said, she had been engaged to make a catalogue of Lady Herbert's jewellery, but the task was incomplete, and so she could not say that she would notice if any item were missing, were she to view the collection again.

'It would be impossible, sir, for Lady Herbert's jewels are contained within a small room, not within a jewellery casket. I am not an expert on such things, and since all of Lady Herbert's jewels are exceptional, no item stood out as being any more remarkable than another.'

Lark only nodded gravely, then asked for the precise date upon which she had last visited Herbert House, and if the nine diamonds that had been on display at the Royal Academy were in Cynthia Herbert's possession at that time. To this, Mrs Korechnya looked surprised and replied that, since she had not seen the diamonds in any other location than on public display, she could not say. Martha noted that she hesitated before answering, and the inspector must also have noticed.

'What I would like to discuss with you, Mrs Korechnya, is a matter of some gravity, and also, secrecy.' He did not need to say anything more than this for Martha to know that she was being asked leave the room. She turned.

'No, wait Martha. I would prefer it if my housekeeper stayed, Inspector Lark. Indeed you will not find a soul more honest and discreet.'

'Very well,' said the inspector. He took a tattered notebook from his pocket. 'Please forgive me, but I am obliged by the code of my profession to make a record of . . . interviews.'

Lily caught her eye, and Martha saw that her mistress was not nearly as calm on the inside as she outwardly appeared. She wondered what indelicate news Detective Lark had conveyed in her absence. In turn, the housekeeper indicated silently that the shawl had been forgotten, and Lily gathered it again around her without altering her expression. Martha took a step closer, as a gesture of solidarity.

'I have recently verified that the jeweller Finkelstein was in possession of Lady Herbert's diamonds at the time of his death.' At this, Lily's hand flew to her mouth, and Martha's sense of foreboding intensified. Lark's expression had darkened. 'Unfortunately, what started as a rumour reached the insatiable appetites of the gutter press before my officers could confirm it, but I can see that you were not aware of this connection.'

'I do not read crime reportage, Inspector, for it belies my faith in human decency.'

'Quite so. It is possible that this intelligence might have originated with either the jeweller's missing apprentice or the thief, allowing of course that they could be one and the same, and the diamonds may already be circulating on the black market. I admit to being perplexed, for I cannot see how the crime was committed . . . I must now ask you again, Mrs Korechnya if, when last you viewed Lady Herbert's collection, there was anything which might have led you to believe the Lady was intending to deliver the diamonds to a goldsmith?'

Lily sighed. 'There was. I was asked not to divulge it . . . forgive me. I understand that the stones, which as you must know belong to the Maharajah of Benares, were to be made into a jewel of some kind.'

Lark only nodded and reached into his pocket. 'My apologies, I should have presented you with this immediately.' He handed her a small, brown parcel, and continued whilst she unwrapped it. 'I have recently interviewed Mr Govinda at Herbert House, and he told me little, but said that the diamonds had not been retrieved from Finkelstein's. He informed me this was yours. My sergeant found it on the jeweller's bench.'

Lily now held in her hand a large pendant that resembled a cameo. Its facade was a thick oval of jet, and the intricate white hairwork, fashioned into a wreath of lilies, was raised from it in delicate contrast. Her head was bent over the piece as though examining it, but Martha knew that she was hiding her tears.

'It was to be a gift from Lady Herbert – a means of payment for the assistance I lent her . . . I understand that it might seem insignificant in the scheme of things, but to me it is beyond value . . . Thank you, Inspector.'

Martha was perplexed. Why did the police not ask Lady Herbert about the diamonds directly? Surely Lark did not suspect her of being involved in the murders! The inspector now had his guard about him again, and his face was its former, unreadable mask. He inclined his head towards Lily and turned on his heel to leave. Martha bustled after him, glancing swiftly at her mistress who now looked looked deathly pale. It struck Martha, as she showed the inspector to the door, that it appeared as though the burden of his profession was tiring his very soul. She had already noted his sensitivity, and it was a rare quality in a man, rarer still in a policeman.

In the library, Lily stood by the window and watched Lark's retreat along Waterloo Street. She turned when the housekeeper entered, and Martha felt a chill from the base of her neck to the bottom of her spine. The room seemed suddenly without light, as though a portly cloud had drifted before the sun. The shadows that gathered in the room were noisome, and it was all Martha could do to not tell them to hush so that she could think, for they imparted a message as clear as a crystal bell.

'Is something amiss, Martha?'

'You should not wear it, Madam.'

'Oh Martha. There is no need to be superstitious. It has been a day of ill tidings, that is all.' She passed her hand across her brow.

'Certainly. I fail to see why the detective could not ask Lady Herbert the very questions he has troubled you with, madam.'

'Lady Herbert is dead, Martha. She died last night, perhaps by her own hand.'

'Heavens! It is the diamonds, madam, there is some evil guiding them, I'm certain of it now.'

Lily sat heavily, clasping her hand to her breast. 'But how could such a thing be true? They are only carbon after all, they have no life.'

'Oh, but they have life, diamonds have. They steal it from the living.' Martha regretted her words as soon as they were spoken, for the mistress looked all the more shaken.

'I pray that you are mistaken, Martha, yet I can scarce believe that such a vigorous spirit was defeated by grief alone . . .'

Martha could not reply, for she felt a cold certainty that Lady Herbert's death was an ill omen indeed.

❖ 16 ❖

Kensington,
23 September, 1864

My Darling Franz,

It is long past midsummer and the days gradually shorten. So, it seems, does memory also fade, and the short distance that we journeyed together. In only three years I feel that I have lived my entire life. Kind people, who bother to imagine how it must be for one bereaved, say that with time the wound of grief heals, and then with more time, the world will once again seem populated and as full of possibility as the map of an unknown land. I admit to becoming accustomed to your absence, though I am far from daring to imagine a future without you.

Since I last wrote, there has been much that is perplexing and worrisome in my once-quiet world. First was the murder of Lady Herbert's jeweller, followed by her own death only last week. And then the occurrence of a visit from a senior officer of the Westminster constabulary; a kind but rather brooding detective inspector by the name of Lark. During this visit, Inspector Lark disclosed to me that the rare and precious diamonds that belong to an Indian Maharajah and were in her custody have been stolen! Indeed Londoners appear to have adopted the theft as a personal affront, for the gems were on display for a time and have powers of seduction that would rival Homer's sirens!

More recently, indeed, only yesterday, I had two more visitors. The first was young Sarah O'Reilly, in whose company I have often found myself of late. She has about her a vibrancy and luminosity that defy her past and her station in life and I admit that I have become rather fond of her. Not long after Sarah's arrival, who came with the pretext of delivering some post to me, the doorbell sounded yet again. This time it was Inspector Lark's sergeant, a charming and fresh-faced young man by the name of Gerard. He had come, he said, to deliver an item of paperwork that makes official the delivery of my pendant by Inspector Lark. I wear it now, my love, and I feel that you have returned to me. The hairwork is very fine and is displayed on a convex oval of jet, mounted on a solid-gold backing. The lilies are exquisite and form a ring around its edge, with one larger flower in the centre. It is my guess that Govinda, whose design it was, took the idea of a wreath of lilies from your painting, The Venus of Waterloo. The painting still hangs in our reception hall, but I carried it with me once on a visit to Herbert House to show to Lady Herbert. I am as yet undecided if it will form part of the collection that I shall take with me to Benares.

For yes, I have decided to go there, my love, and told Lady Herbert so just before she died. I know how you longed to go to India yourself, Franz, and that you believed that it would be a land I would fall in love with, in spite of all my worst imaginings about mosquitoes and heat and the absence of water closets. At first I rejected Lady Herbert's proposal, believing it to be no more than the ramblings of an ailing spirit. But then, I began to dwell more on the notion of travelling to a land where all is unfamiliar, from the heat of the sun and colour of the sky, to the perfume from the gardens.

So, I have decided to sail to Bombay, and from there to journey by train to Benares. Lady Herbert immediately sent a letter of introduction to the Maharajah, so confident was she that I would undertake the journey. I cannot pretend that I am unaffected by the belief in Hindu mysticism that Benares is a city such as you believed Prague to be; a place where one may stand at the gateway between the worlds of the spirits and of mortals. Do you remember how we pledged, jokingly, that should we be parted, we would meet in such a place? If only it could be so.

But back to my young visitors, who stayed with me and took tea, and talked to me of the strange disappearance of Lady Herbert's diamonds. I have learnt from Sarah that the crime writer from the Mercury, Mr Melville, will soon publish more of his 'findings' with regard to the two murders and how they are linked to the missing diamonds. I am afraid this is not good news, for everything he touches is stained with gossip. Like many of his profession, he delights in spectacle and sensation. From Mr Gerard I discovered only that the constabulary have been unable to locate the jeweller's apprentice, who is now their prime suspect. He was unable to divulge any details of the case, this being the ethic of his profession, and

I was therefore unable to ask him if they had learnt anything from the impenetrable Mr Govinda, either about Lady Herbert's death or the diamonds.

I was intrigued to observe a vague discomfort between Sarah and Sergeant Gerard, for in age there could not be more than three years betwixt them, and I could tell that in each there was a recognition of the other's intelligence. Perhaps they are kindred spirits?

Here in your studio I am comforted by the knowledge that this was where your heart and soul found expression. It is now late afternoon, and I will come here only once more to shut the house. I shall miss it dearly, but none of your former colleagues use it any longer, for they find it run down and too cold in the winter. Were it my house, I should tend the garden and fix the swinging seat beneath the magnolia tree. I would repair the walls where the draft and damp enter and mend the holes in the floor, but the landlord has clearly no interest in the preservation of an old building.

It is only one month before I shall depart for Benares, and there is much for me to do. You are with me always, as long as I wear this pendant about my neck, even if I must leave this place where I have found some solace since we parted.

Yours for ever,
Lily.

She studies her reflection in a jewel, knits her brow, and oh so
tenderly touches her lip.

Vidyapati, 15th century

Devil's Acre was the place Vikram had first encountered the underbelly
of London, and now, as he walked along the embankment towards
Westminster, he realised that he knew its maze of tenements and dingy
taverns and whorehouses almost as well as he knew the warren of
alleyways in Benares. The initial shock had worn off over the weeks
since he'd stepped off *Lakshmi*, though he had been stunned to discover
that the type of clean, impeccably attired Britisher he had met whilst
in the employment of the Maharajah of Benares made up only a small
proportion of the population of this island. There was, in fact, poverty
and crime here on a par with the most squalid slums of Calcutta and
Bombay.

The Maharajah was not in London this season, since he, like Vikram,
was besotted with the rarefied loveliness of a village girl he could not
hope to present at Buckingham Palace. Not that Vikram could see why
the Britishers made such a fuss over their monarch; she was a squat,
drab woman, who wore only black. What's more, she had designs on
being empress of his country, which was a notion he found both absurd
and insulting. Queen Victoria had never even visited India, and he
hoped that if ever she did, she might at least wear some colour. How
he missed the colours of his country; the ladies in their bright saris,
their shining silks. He missed yellow in particular, since this was the
colour his beloved always wore. She had paid him little attention since
she graduated from dancing girl to concubine, in fact, she treated
Vikram with disdain, because even as a member of the Maharajah's
special guard, he was now beneath her in station. She'd treat him better
once she discovered that he was a true warrior of Kali.

Vikram kept reminding himself that when the red diamond left the palace vault, he had been the one sent to retrieve it. Everyone knew that the Maharajah would make a navaratna charm once he had his nine diamonds; this obsession of the Prince's was by now common knowledge as he had searched far and wide to find his coloured diamonds, though who would ever have thought a red diamond would be found, *and* discovered in such a manner? The traditional navaratna gemstones were sacred: sapphire, ruby, emerald and pearl, beryl and moonstone, coral, topaz and, of course, one diamond. They should not, under any circumstances, be replaced entirely by diamonds. It was small wonder no jeweller in India would make the charm. Of course, Govinda had recognised Vikram on the boat, but that didn't matter, since he was known to be the Maharajah's opium runner, and everyone knew that there was a market for the drug in London.

Vikram sighed and shook his head. He was almost in Devil's Acre now, and he was keeping a lookout for Ellen along the river bank. They had initially met by chance; she had been with the simpleton Holy Joe the day Vikram got lost in Devil's Acre. It was Ellen who had offered to walk with him to Horseferry Road, asking him all manner of questions along the way. When he said he'd come by boat, she said she had too, and she wanted to know everything about the land he had sailed from. Her blue eyes had lit up when he told her about the palaces along the banks of the Ganges, and how when people died, their bodies were burned on the wide stone steps along the banks of the river instead of being buried. He had been surprised by her courage, and her acceptance of him, when so many of the Londoners he'd encountered looked straight through him. Vikram had quickly realised that Ellen could help him; the opium deliveries were taking three times as long as they should because he kept getting lost.

Although there was much about London that still enticed Vikram, he was beginning to tire of Londoners, who clearly had no respect for the sacred. He had only to look around him, at the intricate workings of the largest and most prosperous city in Europe, to know this. There was more gold here now than there had ever been in Constantinople, or in Delhi under the rule of the Mughal empire. The difference was that in this city it was being turned into grotesque, noisome factories, and machines that belched filthy smoke, rather than into golden statues and gilded palatial domes and marble paving.

He had been sleeping in the stables of the London residence of the Maharajah, which was in the vicinity of Hyde Park. This grand old house was perfectly suited to the display of riches and glamour that secured the respectability of the Maharajah and his wives. Wife was a word used only in the singular by the Britisher, but in India wives were purchased in a far less subtle manner. Vikram did not think much of his customers there: the young Prince of Jodhpur, and the Nawab of Bahawalpur, who were were spending the season at the Maharajah's residence playing cards and polo and keeping the company of duchesses and baronesses.

Now, whenever Vikram walked along the muddy Thames embankment with its smell of rotting fish and sewage, he longed for the sacred waters of the river Ganges and for the untamed gardens on its banks. He dreamed of ferns and blossoming orange trees, and the shining domes of stupas, the small garden temples where the devout prayed and left offerings. He dreamed of returning to Benares with the red diamond and finally winning the affection of his beloved, though he knew in his heart that she would never leave the palace. The Maharajah was showering her with jewels, dressing her in spun gold, and feeding her on arrowroot halwa and sweetmeats dripping with rose syrup.

Vikram was hoping to see Ellen by the river to give her another sovereign, as they had agreed. But Ellen was nowhere to be seen. She was probably off with that band of urchins who hung about the banks, chasing pigeons for their supper, or getting up to some other mischief. It was easy to forget that she was just a child; she had the ways of someone much older.

By the time he reached Devil's Acre it was almost dark, and the alleyways were in deep shadow from the tenements on the western side of the cathedral. Vikram never went to the White Hart, since the landlady there was one of those who looked straight through you. Ellen's sister was strange with him too, not because she was afraid of him but because she clearly thought he was up to no good. He always took extra care to be charming to her, but she was clever, like Ellen, and he knew she didn't trust him.

The best thing would be to go to Holy Joe's doss house, since the smiling giant of a man would tell him anything he wanted to know, including the whereabouts of his young guide. Vikram had already acquired some very useful information from Holy Joe and had now sold most of his sandalwood beads to merchants who asked no questions about taxes and duties. Maybe Ellen was there with him, or maybe she was hiding as she sometimes did, and would jump out of the shadows to surprise him. He hoped not, since he was already feeling skittish. He didn't much like the alleyways around the doss house, as they were some of the worst in Devil's Acre, and it was coming to the time of day when the most desperate and crafty were abroad. Not that Vikram was afraid of them, since he was trained to fight, and he was more agile than most of the criminal element of London. He didn't touch the opium he sold, and he didn't drink, for both clouded the mind and slowed the body.

When he felt a presence behind him, he thought he was prepared, but just as an arm went around his neck, he was knocked to the ground by a sharp blow right between the eyes. Vikram was more surprised than afraid, and then he was confused; not just because the blow caused a pain that split his mind open like a coconut, spilling all of his hopes and desires on to the musky earth where he lay, but because *he* wasn't supposed to be a victim.

There was just enough light for Vikram to see the ground into which his face was now pressed, and to smell its dank odour. In a moment he would be able to raise his head, but not yet, since the pain was making him dizzy, and besides, there was a small and mangy brown rat only inches from his face, and he needed to keep an eye on it. He had always been suspicious of rats, since they were not discriminating in their eating habits, and if hungry enough would venture forth to gnaw on a sleeve if its inhabitant lay prone for long enough. There wasn't much time to think of anything else, because just as the rat looked at him and registered that he had been lying still for long enough to be a potential food source, his attacker was once more upon him, forcing the breath from his lungs as though they were bellows. Again, Vikram was surprised by the familiarity, and it was this that told him he was dying, if not already dead. It didn't matter, since either way he would soon be a true warrior of Kali, victorious on the battlefields of Indra's palace. As he watched his earthly dreams trickle away, his final thought was that his love would never know how he had died, and worse, what if she believed he had taken the diamonds for himself?

❖ 18 ❖

The Press is an invention for the development of original sin.

David Urquart, 1860

Sarah no longer felt safe in the shadowy lanes of Devil's Acre, not since a darkie had been done in only a stone's throw from the White Hart. It wasn't so bad when the violent crimes had been further along the river, but this one was far too close to home. Sarah knew about the killing before the news got out to the public, because Inspector Lark had been with Septimus Harding all day yesterday, and had made the editor promise that Melville wouldn't get wind of the third murder until the police were good and ready to tell the story. Their story.

Now it was Tuesday morning, and two days since the darkie had been found face down in an alleyway with his windpipe crushed. He'd had the same bruise as the other two, although this time it was not so neatly between the eyes. All of this Sarah knew from listening at the door of the editor's rooms when she should have been upstairs with her type blocks, compositing an advertisement for some lotion or potion; she could not remember which. They'd found a weapon too, but she didn't hear what it was and she was busting to know.

The Strand was alive at this hour, with maids, tinkers, paperboys and beggars all out conducting the day's business. Sarah cherished the time she had walking to work and home as it gave her room to think. Sometimes she wondered what the future held for her. Lately she'd been wishing she could do what the penny-a-liners did, go to the streets and mouse out a story for the papers — not the brand of flashy, rotten journalism touted by Mr Melville and his like, but something altogether more heroic and accountable. Mostly, however, she'd been thinking about Ellen starting school next week, and being with children her own age instead of Holy Joe. Mrs Korechnya said the school for poor children who lived around Westminster was run by Barbara Bodichon, the woman the newspaper writers and compositors loved to ridicule more than any other. Sarah wouldn't have minded going to a school like that, where girls learnt as much as boys about why steam trains got to travel so fast and all Mr Darwin's malarkey (that's what Pa said it was), but she was the breadwinner now. She still reckoned she was lucky, since she had the newspaper and Mrs Korechnya to learn from. The school would cost a penny a week, but there was enough in the tin now, even after she'd bought Ellen shiny new boots, a sharp pencil and a book to write her letters and sums in.

Sarah hadn't seen Mrs Korechnya for a while, since Mr Harding had been taking her housekeeper's advice and had not been sending 'Mr Evans' so much correspondence. However this had not encouraged Lily to visit the offices of the *London Mercury* more frequently, as Mrs Vesper had hoped. Sarah had knocked on the emerald green door on a few occasions because she was close by, running an errand to Battersea or the bookstall at Waterloo Station. Then she would have some of Mrs Vesper's bittersweet lemonade. Mrs Korechnya was always attentive and charming, but she had a look about her as if she were trying to see something a great distance away. Sarah thought maybe it was because of the wedding anniversary, though that had been some time ago now. Still, she was going with Lily to the big house in Kensington tomorrow. She liked the old place since it was quiet, there were birds in the garden, and big rooms with high ceilings and a fireplace in every one. There was an attic as well as a cellar, she was certain, though she hadn't had a chance to explore properly. She imagined you could get a grand view of Kensington from up there, with fields and farms and maybe more than one church spire.

When Sarah arrived, Lark was in with the editor again, and Melville was there too, which meant that the murder would be in the papers tomorrow. Sarah had too much to do upstairs to keep an ear to the door of Septimus Harding's rooms, since she'd got behind yesterday doing just that, and she didn't hear the full story until later in the smoking room. Jack Thistlewite was all puffed up and regaled the other compositors with the story *Gregory* had told him when he came stalking around the third floor: how the murder of the Indian was the latest in a series of 'mysterious and gruesome executions', as if there would be more of them and people should latch their doors and windows. According to Melville, the Indian had been on the same boat from Bombay as Lady Herbert, whose diamonds had been filched, and the shipping clerk and the jeweller had both tried to get the sparklers for themselves, which was why they'd been murdered. It was all the doing of the jeweller's apprentice, Jack said, and the mob he was working for.

Later, when the other compositors went for their afternoon smoke, Sarah took a look at the copy pinned to Jack's easel. She didn't like what she read one bit. The murdered Indian had been a small man, who looked like a boy. Her stomach gave a flip, since how many small Indians frequented Devil's Acre? According to Melville's 'sources' the darkie who had been killed was a smuggler and opium runner. Sarah thought Inspector Lark wouldn't like what Melville had written next; that the London Police were now entirely baffled. She felt a little sick. What if it was Ellen's new friend who was dead? And not just dead, but killed dead. Her little sister had had too much death in her short life, and so had Sarah.

As she got to the sunless lane that led from the river into Devil's Acre that evening, Sarah felt afraid. Usually, she walked right past the narrow alley where the darkie had been killed but now she took the long way around, past Holy Joe's doss house. There was some sort of commotion outside the door and, from a distance, Sarah thought it was just the drunken inmates, who were regularly thrown out into the street by the landlord to sober up. But then Sarah saw Inspector Lark with Holy Joe, and then she saw Ellen.

Ellen was as white beneath her dirty cheeks as Sarah had ever seen her, and her eyes were so wide that they looked like they might pop right out. There were some Bow Street boys with Lark, and it looked to Sarah as if Holy Joe was being nicked. Probably he'd been caught stealing and, if he had, then chances were that Ellen had been with him too. No one was paying any attention to her little sister though; Ellen stood huddled in the doorway of the doss house, as if she were being held upright by the door. Sarah started running just as Ellen's legs gave way.

Everything that happened next seemed like a dream. The Bow Street boys took Holy Joe away with his wrists tied up tight in a leather strap, while Sarah held Ellen tight against her so that she wouldn't fall down like a cloth doll. Joe looked like a startled rabbit, and the fear in his eyes almost made Sarah weep. Lark stayed behind, and when he noticed Sarah and Ellen, he came over and asked them if they knew the prisoner.

'He's all right,' Sarah replied. 'He don't have all his wits 'bout him much, but he's good hearted. I suppose he's been thieving?'

'No Sarah, we're arresting him on suspicion of murder.'

It was all she could do to keep her own knees from buckling under her. In fact, Sarah was so dazed she could barely speak. Lark said he would accompany her and Ellen to the White Hart, and ended up carrying Ellen the last bit, since she wasn't looking too good by then.

When Ellen had gone inside, Sarah finally mustered the courage to speak her mind.

'Why do you think it was Holy Joe that done the murder? I know he's pinched a few things, but he wouldn't hurt a fly. He's been good to me and Ellen.'

Lark sighed deeply and regarded her with a kindness she had not seen before. 'We found a slingshot with his name carved into it, Sarah. It was on the ground right next to the body when one of our boys arrived at the scene.'

They'd discovered only that the Indian's name was Vikram, Lark said, and that he was found by a resident who couldn't get in his door because the body was in the way. Sarah was muddled and sickened and shocked. Her fears about the victim being Ellen's friend were correct, for she remembered that Victor's proper name was Vikram. She also knew damn well that Holy Joe was incapable of murder, and she was certain the police wouldn't hold him once they'd realised the same. Maybe Joe had dropped his slingshot in the alley before Vikram died, since if he'd dropped it after, he'd have surely seen the body . . . Or what if Joe had seen the body, and got frightened, and that was how he came to drop his slingshot? He never let it out of his sight, so it wasn't as if he'd leave it lying around. The more she thought about it, the more confused Sarah became.

That night she lay awake, watching Ellen sleep, thinking and thinking. When tiredness finally overcame her, her dreams carried her along the dark, shadowy alleys of Devil's Acre. She awoke feeling cold and afraid. Ellen was not beside her and that didn't help. Then Sarah realised that the sun was higher than it should be, which meant she was late. Who was going to keep an eye on Ellen while she was at the newspaper now that Holy Joe was in the lock up? Ruby was too busy to be minding children, and she opened her bar at midday.

She found Ellen up in Ruby's kitchen, getting the kettle ready for making tea. She was sitting on a stool by the fire, where a rabbit hung, skinned and ready to put in a pot. Ruby was peeling potatoes and chattering away to Ellen about how fine a day it was, and the neighbour's puny crop of cabbages. Ellen might have been listening and she might not. She was swinging her legs and humming a little tune while she watched the steam rise from the kettle.

Sarah said 'Morning' to Ruby and went over to Ellen. 'Come on Trub, let's have some bread and tea and then I've got to go. I'm late enough as it is.'

Ellen didn't appear to hear her. She kept on humming and watching the kettle, as if it were going to do something other than get hotter. Then, out of nowhere, she said 'It's Victor that's dead.'

Sarah didn't need to ask how Ellen knew that. Probably there had been talk of the murder when Joe was being arrested last night.

'That's right, it is.'

Ruby had stopped chattering, and was watching Ellen closely.

'What's gonna happen to Holy Joe?'

'Oh I 'spect they'll let him go today or tomorrow, Elly, once they figure it couldn't have been him done anything that bad.'

'It was very bad, wasn't it?'

'Aye. But it's done now, and we've got to keep on living like always. Come on Trub, look sharp. I only just remembered that I'm off to Kensington with Mrs Korechnya today, and there's nothing for it but for you to come along too.'

All the way along the embankment, Ellen was behaving strangely, like she did at night when she stared into corners. She kept wanting to stop and look at the river, probably hoping to see the little mermaid, Sarah thought. She practically had to pull her sister along, and it was only when they got to Waterloo Bridge and away from the water that Ellen picked up her feet.

When Mrs Vesper opened the door and saw Ellen, she raised her eyebrows, but said only, 'Good day to you both. The mistress will be down directly, and I've made some fresh lemonade. Follow me.'

Mrs Vesper's kitchen was not at all like Ruby's; for a start it was clean, and there was light coming in the window. The kitchen door was open and Sarah could see a small garden, surrounded by a stone wall. It was full of rows of little bushes, all different shades of green. Herbs, she supposed. Ellen didn't like Mrs Vesper's lemonade, since it was more bitter than the stuff they bought for a treat at Piccadilly. She pulled a face when she tried it and Mrs Vesper laughed and set about making some chocolate. She put some creamy milk in a pan on the range, and then she grated some chocolate from a great hunk which looked just like dried mud. This she tipped into the milk pan, and then mixed with some brown sugar and stirred. Ellen's face was a sight when she tried it, and she smiled so wide that they all laughed.

Mrs Korechnya came into the kitchen, then and spied the tangle-haired urchin with chocolate around her mouth. She asked no questions but put out her hand and said, 'You must be Ellen!'

The three of them travelled in the carriage over Waterloo Bridge and past Hyde Park and Buckingham Palace. Along the way, Ellen wouldn't take her eyes from the window, or answer anything that was said to her. When the three of them got to the old house, she jumped straight out and ran into the garden.

Mr Korechnya's studio was empty now; all the paintings and easels had gone and the strange one-armed chair. All that remained was Lily's little writing desk by the window, and next to it the blue hatbox in which she kept her papers.

'Is there an attic here?' Sarah asked.

'I believe there is. Shall we find Ellen and explore?'

Ellen didn't want to come inside since the sun was shining in the big, overgrown garden and she was looking for four-leaf clovers. Mrs Korechnya could tell that something was up and that Sarah didn't want to leave her alone. 'She's safe here, Sarah, and she's happy. Come on, let's find the attic shall we?'

They looked in all the rooms on the top floor of the house before they found the hatch to the attic, with a ladder up against it, in a dressing room.

'You go up first, Sarah. I wish I had breeches like yours. They really are a most practical costume.'

'I wouldn't know what to do with a skirt, but I like the way they swish, and you always look very fine, Mrs Korechnya.'

'I think you must call me Lily now, since we are friends, are we not?'

Sarah felt foolish about the prickle in her eyes and the way her throat became tight for a minute. She was all emotion today. Just as well Lily kept talking from below while she climbed the ladder and blinked hard to stop the tears. When she got to the top of the ladder, there was an attic all right, but there was nothing in it. She'd imagined that attics were always full of broken furniture and crates of rags and empty jars and bottles; that they held the promise of discovery. This one was a big room, with two windows in the eaves and bare wood floors. It was dusty up here, and the corners were choked up with cobwebs, but the view from the eaves made up for the lack of hidden whatnots. There were church spires just like she had imagined, and a distant forest, and the river like a silver ribbon unwinding across the land. As Lily joined her, and they both stood looking out across the green and yellow fields, Sarah sensed that she had say something important to say. She had been biting her lip, and then took a deep breath.

'I am to go abroad, Sarah. I have some business in India.'

It was all Sarah could do to keep back the tears that had been threatening all day. 'You going for ever?' she whispered.

'Heavens no, but it is a long journey and I expect to be gone for some months.'

'Is it newspaper business?'

'No. Another matter.'

'Does Mr Harding know?'

'Not yet. You seem troubled today, Sarah.'

How could she tell Mrs Korechnya that this news, on top of Vikram's murder and Joe's arrest was almost too much of a load for her narrow shoulders? She could not begin to explain how Lily's precious friendship and company had made her feel less worried about Ellen and even more determined to make something of herself. She only hoped that one day she might become a little bit like Lily Korechnya herself, though she supposed she'd have to stop cursing and lay aside her breeches first. Sarah sighed deeply, but resolved that this sad news would not spoil their day together. At least she could tell Lily some of what was troubling her.

'They've taken Holy Joe to the lock-up for killing that darkie. But I just know he didn't do those murders – he's not a bad man. He had a knock on the head, see; he used to be a preacher and he only thieves 'cause he's poor, not 'cause he's bad.'

When Mrs Korechnya asked who Holy Joe was, and Sarah said he was Ellen's friend, just like the darkie who'd been killed was, she nodded her head and looked thoughtful.

'Then we must speak to Inspector Lark again and make certain that he knows how good Holy Joe has been to Ellen. Sometimes, if it can be proven that a prisoner is of good character, then the law is kinder.' Mrs Korechnya looked at Sarah gravely. 'We must also make certain that the school teacher knows that Ellen has lost both of her friends, and that she needs particular kindness.'

For the first time that day, Sarah began to feel better. Lily would tell the policeman that he'd made a mistake and they'd let Joe go and everything would be like it was before, except better because Ellen would be in school. They went back downstairs, and Lily stood in the centre of the studio, looking around at the bare walls. Then she went to her little table by the window and lifted the hatbox. She was speaking almost to herself as she opened its lid and gazed upon its contents. 'I suppose I must take it with me, for it contains writings I could not bear to be parted from . . .'

Sarah could only nod. Ellen came in all pink-cheeked with a posy of sweet pea blossoms in her hand and a crooked daisy chain on her head. She gave the sweet peas to Lily and then ran out again. Lily looked at Sarah and smiled her lovely smile.

'Don't be sad, Sarah, for whatever happens, remember that we are friends.'

⁂ 19 ⁂

Waterloo,
3 October, 1864

My Dear Barbara,

I have received a compliment from a gentleman, and I barely knew which way to look, unaccustomed as I have become to such attentions. It must be the thought of sailing far from these shores as winter approaches that has returned to my cheeks their 'bloom' and to my eyes their 'sparkle', for this is how each was described to me by Inspector Lark. We both happened to be waiting for Septimus Harding in the editor's offices, and the inspector kindly remarked that he was happy to observe my improved health. Our conversation then turned to a matter of common interest; that is, the prolonged incarceration of the simpleton, Holy Joe. John Lark told me that he has noted the benign character of the prisoner, and has fought for his release on these grounds; also those of insufficient evidence. Yet so intent is the entire city of London, from the presses to the courts, to convict a murderer, that he is helpless.

The other matter I raised with Inspector Lark was that of the welfare of the O'Reilly girls. I have come to feel a maternal urge towards these orphans, and do so enjoy the companionship of Sarah, who, I am beginning to suspect, has the makings of a writer. I do not regret not having children of my own, dear Barbara, since a family was something neither Franz nor I longed for. Unlike some married couples, we were both more than content in the company of each other. Inspector Lark has also observed the special situation of the two girls, and remarked upon how he admires Sarah, for he said that hardship can often have the opposite effect, and that it is down to Sarah's strength of character that the girls have managed to stay away from crime and the workhouse.

Thank you for keeping me abreast of Ellen O'Reilly's progress at the Westminster school, and for instructing the head teacher there to treat her with special care. Sarah has already told me that she suspects little Ellen might not be attending class regularly, and that when she does, she is not paying sufficient attention. It seems that her notebook remains empty of lessons, but is filled instead with drawings of castles and mermaids. I am inclined to agree with your colleagues that the child is troubled, if indeed she talks to herself rather than to the other children. Children are not sympathetic creatures largely, and they conform too much to acceptable behaviour, as do their elders. I believe there has been more grief in Ellen's short life than her receptive nature can withstand, and I worry that it is having an effect on her health. The trouble with the business of education is that each small person has a certain nature, and I am concerned that someone with Ellen's peculiarity might attract the wrong kind of attention from visiting inspectors. There are some terrible institutions in London for children who do not conform to the acceptable model, and we must be sure to protect her from them.

I am to be accompanied abroad by the Indian, Govinda, who was once always by Lady Herbert's side. I had at first thought that he was her servant, but discovered that he is, in fact, in the employ of the Maharajah. I long to ask him about the diamonds that were stolen at the time of the murder of the Hatton Garden jeweller. I believe they remain the property of the Maharajah, who surely must be expecting them to be returned, crafted into whatever jewel he and Lady Herbert agreed upon. I cannot help but wonder what the Maharajah will think when he learns of their theft. Surely he will be enraged and Govinda will be blamed? After all, he was clearly the guardian of the stones and, according to Cynthia Herbert, the architect of their design, along with that of my pendant. I wear the pendant containing Franz's hair always, and feel that somehow, he gives me strength through it. It is a striking and exquisitely crafted piece, in spite of Mrs Vesper's misgivings.

There has as yet been no opportunity to converse with Mr Govinda at length, for he has called but once to confirm my passage, and would not step into the house. I understand that he has already been questioned by Inspector Lark, for he must surely be under suspicion himself, and so the matter is rather too delicate to raise. For myself, I have no fears as I have come to the respect this quiet man and can see no evil in him.

But I am in haste, my dear, for already it is time for luncheon (Martha *will not permit me to miss a meal) and there suddenly seems too much to be done in one morning, let alone in one day. I shall be certain to write in detail of all that I encounter in my travels.*

In friendship, as always,
Lily

⁖ 20 ⁖

She sat by the fire in a beautiful black satin gown, with a green
shaded lamp on the table beside her, where I saw German books
lying and pamphlets and ivory paper cutters.

George Eliot

Mrs Vesper lit the fire and drew the parlour curtains against the Waterloo
Street gas lamps. The bright tails of the peacocks on the wallpaper
shimmered by the light from the hearth. She had bought Madonna lilies
at the Waterloo market, and placed them in the powder-blue Wedgwood
vase on the pianoforte. There had not been lilies in the house since the
master passed away, but before he had a fondness for them and their
sweet balm had often lingered in the parlour in the summer months.
The flowers were the first thing that the mistress noticed upon entering
the room.

'I thought that vase was broken, Martha. I have not seen it in some
time.'

'No, madam, it had merely been misplaced.'

There was no need to explain that the blue vase had in fact disappeared not long after Mr Korechnya's death, and that Martha had
found it hidden in the master's cupboard in the scullery. He had never
liked English ceramics, for he believed all such objects to be inferior to
those from Bohemia. Although she had not see his spirit since he'd
kissed the mistress goodbye, Martha would be relieved when the
master's spirit finally detached itself from the house, for only then could
she be certain that certain objects would be found where she had left
them.

Lily was still holding her cloak and was stroking the black fur around
its hood as though it were a cat. She was nervous to be in the parlour,
Martha could see this clearly. She took a step into the room and
shivered, although it was barely yet cool enough in the evenings for a

fire to be lit. Martha had built it, and bought the flowers, because this was the mistress's last night at Waterloo Street before she set sail for India, and all the rooms would feel cold and empty soon enough. Martha had a feeling, and she couldn't say what it meant; she knew only that something would change in this house after Mrs Korechnya was gone. She adjusted the pins in her linen cap, as she did when she was in a certain mood, and her mistress knew her well enough now to read every twitch.

'I shall miss you, Martha. I have written to the bank and to my solicitor to inform them that you have power of attorney until my return. I can't bear the thought of my father meddling, and I know that you will keep my affairs and this house in order in my absence.'

'That I will, and I shall be happy to see you return to us, madam.' Martha adjusted her cap some more and poked at the fire.

'I have something more to ask of you. I have told Sarah O'Reilly that she may come to you if she, or her sister, have any troubles. Ellen has become more withdrawn the longer they keep Holy Joe in prison. At least they have not hanged him yet. I believe Inspector Lark is doing his best to keep Bow Street away from him, although he has opined that if they interview him again, Joe will admit to anything, since he weeps like a baby every time they come near him.'

'It is a nasty business to be sure, madam.'

'It does seem that their only evidence is the slingshot. All three victims had the same mark on their foreheads, and the police say that it was caused by a stone from a slingshot. This was intended to stun the victim, I suppose, to make it easier to crush the windpipe. It is too horrid to think that the real culprits might still be on the streets.'

'Then you don't believe it was the simpleton and apprentice who committed the murders together and stole the jewels, Madam?'

'No, I don't, and neither does Inspector Lark. The matter of the stolen diamonds is almost entirely sensation, and I know exactly how it came to be bandied about. Why, who is to say that Lady Herbert had not already collected the diamonds, or perhaps the jewel they were fashioned into? Although the diamonds have not been located, they were not reported as stolen by Lady Herbert before her death, which could mean that she had already sent them back to India or deposited them somewhere else for safekeeping. I believe the inspector knows a murderer and a clever thief when he sees one, and from what Sarah has told me, their "dangerous" suspect is nothing but a gentle idiot.'

When her mistress had calmly revealed that she was to go to India and that Lady Herbert's man was to accompany her aboard the first-class vessel *Kenyon*, Martha had had mixed feelings. It seemed to her that Mr Govinda must have had some knowledge of his princely master's diamonds, but why hadn't he reported them stolen? If indeed he was in the employ of the very same Maharajah whose jewels had gone missing, then wouldn't he be concerned about their whereabouts? Martha did not doubt that Inspector Lark had interviewed the man thoroughly, and could only surmise that the Indian was innocent. Or perhaps, too clever to be proven guilty. She had tried, when he stood on her doorstep, to assess his character, but he was impenetrable. It was a quality she had rarely encountered.

When the housekeeper had enquired if Mrs Korechnya meant to keep the house open while she was away, she had seemed shocked.

'Oh Martha! If you mean do I still require your service, then yes. I shall not be gone for longer than the autumn and winter months and I should like you to look after the house until my return.'

She was right, Martha thought, a house needed to be warmed by life and laughter, or it would become an inhospitable place to all but the spirits. If her mistress wanted her to remain at Waterloo Street, then Martha would gladly stay. And if the O'Reilly girls wanted to visit her, all the better, since someone needed to be watching out for them, especially the little one. She was as sensitive as they come – missing a layer of skin was what they called people like Ellen, and Martha believed the child saw the others, though she was not yet certain.

'Well, I will gladly look out for the girls, madam,' Martha said, answering her earlier question, 'and as they have both developed a taste for chocolate, I am convinced that I shall see them from time to time. You can be assured that all will be well here.'

'I have no doubt about that, Martha. And now I must retire, for I rise early to board the *Kenyon* at St Katherine's Pier.'

There was a moment then when the housekeeper caught her mistress's shadow, and she thought she saw there, along with the certainty of safe passage, a flicker of danger.

'Be careful, madam, for it is a land of peculiar faith, and I hear that a woman alone is not safe.'

'A woman alone is not safe anywhere in the world of men! But do not fear – I shall be guarded by Govinda, whom I am certain will keep me safe. Good night, Martha, you need not rise to see me away.'

'I shall be awake before dawn, madam, for I cannot have you leaving without your breakfast!'

As Lily turned to leave the parlour, the door knocker sounded. She looked at Martha, frowning.

'Who could be calling at this late hour?'

Martha Vesper wondered the same herself, until she unlatched the door and beheld the inspector from Marlborough Street. He had shaved, was wearing a new coat, and had about him his usual air of detachment, though also tonight, a distinct melancholy.

'I apologise for the unsociable hour, Mrs Vesper, but it is imperative that I speak with your mistress before she departs.'

The hour was indeed unsociable, and Martha might have turned away any other gentleman calling upon a widow after nine o'clock. But since it appeared that the inspector was here on police business, she nodded and showed him into the parlour. Here Lark apologised again, after bidding Lily good evening. Martha Vesper hovered by the door. It was only prudent, she thought. By firelight, the policeman appeared almost handsome, since the imperfections to which daylight was unkind, were softened by shadow. He took in the rich colours and fine cloths of the candlelit parlour, and seemed somewhat calmed by its elegance.

'I shall not keep you long, Mrs Korechnya. I am calling at this late hour to inform you of a development in the case of the accused, Holy Joe. It is not good news, but I thought it better that you hear it from me than by any other means. I have come directly from the prisoner's cell at Newgate, where he has confessed to committing murder on three counts. Under these circumstances, it is no longer in my power to defend his innocence and unless, by some miracle, we find the true fiend, he will hang on Monday next.'

❖ 21 ❖

Good society has its claret and its velvet carpets, its dinner engagements six weeks deep, its opera and its faery ball rooms ... how should it have need of belief and emphasis?

George Eliot

Sarah knew that she would never forget that day, though it had begun the same as any other. She'd taken Ellen to school, and waited by the freshly painted wooden gate until the prim lady teacher took her little sister by the hand and led her into the neat, one-room building. She'd waved goodbye, pretending not to see the mournful expression in Ellen's round blue eyes, then walked quickly along the Strand to Paternoster Row, fretting over whether little Trub would stay in school all day. Sometimes she did, other times she didn't. Sarah rarely took the path along the river any more, not since all the murders. Besides, the water also reminded her of the fright she'd had that night not so long ago, thinking Ellen had waded right in looking for the Little Mermaid.

As Sarah walked, she also thought about Mrs Korechnya and how she must be out at sea by now as her ship had set sail early that morning. What must it be like, she wondered, to be on a ship bound for a distant land? Sarah couldn't get used to the idea that Lily Korechnya was no longer at Waterloo Street, since she'd taken to visiting almost every time she had an errand to run across the river. Her thoughts turned to her newest and most treasured of possessions. After that last day in Kensington, Lily had presented her with a small parcel, and Sarah had spent that evening back at the White Hart smoothing and running her hand over the silky sheets of her first ever, proper gift. The parchment smelt different to the esparato grass paper that the *London Mercury* was printed on; it had a clean smell all of its own. The pot of ink and two pretty quills with silver nibs and ebony wood were almost too precious to touch. Sarah was not yet fully acquainted with the use of the quill, since she'd only had a pencil to write with before, or Ellen's chalk and slate from school. She'd been practising her hand on old newsprint before she dared to mark the unsullied parchment and write her first inked characters.

Sarah arrived at the newspaper at the same time as Inspector Lark, who was in such a hurry that he didn't see her until she said 'Good morning, sir.'

'Good morning, Sarah.'

'Everything fine with you, sir?' She tried not to ask the same question every time she saw the policeman, since he'd promised he'd tell her just as soon as he heard any news about Holy Joe.

'I've been wanting to speak with you.'

That must mean bad news, since if it was good tidings, he would have told her straightaway. Sarah didn't reply.

'Come with me, I am visiting Mr Harding.'

Mr Harding had a white napkin at his collar, and was eating a pork pie. He looked as if he had been at his desk the entire night, since his chin was unshaven and his whiskers were standing out in tufts. The gas lanterns were lit at dusk and burned at the *London Mercury* until morning, but it was unusual for the editor to stay with the night printers and writers.

'Good morning, good morning. Sarah. John.' He took another bite of his pie and gestured them in towards the dying embers of his fire.

'It has become autumnal suddenly, hasn't it?' This was directed at Sarah, who was warming her breeches by the coals.

'Aye sir, it has.' Sarah knew they were definitely going to tell her something bad then, since both Septimus Harding and Inspector Lark were making small talk, and neither could look her in the eye. Usually they just ignored her and talked over each other. 'They're going to hang Holy Joe, aren't they?'

Lark released a sigh that made his shoulders shudder, and the editor pushed away his half-eaten pie and removed his napkin.

'Yes,' said Lark.

'But he didn't do it!' Sarah could feel the panic rising and spreading across her chest like poison.

'There was nothing we could do,' said the editor.

'You let Mr Melville write those lies, sir.'

There was a shocked silence. Sarah didn't care, it was the truth.

'The *London Mercury* does not print lies.' Septimus Harding was white about the gills as he spoke, but his voice was even. 'Mr Melville is a senior writer for this paper, and although I admit that his prose is ... colourful, it is not by the hand of the press that any prisoner is accused and tried.'

Lark took a step towards her and put his hand on her shoulder. 'Holy Joe has admitted to the murders, Sarah.'

That did it. 'No! You're lying! He never!' She jumped up and ran out of the room and out of the building. Mr Parsimmons called out to her as she passed his desk, but she didn't stop, not until she got across Waterloo Bridge. She wasn't even aware of where she was going until she remembered that Lily Korechnya was no longer at Waterloo Street. She felt all the worse for Lily's absence, and almost turned around, but she didn't know where else to go.

Mrs Vesper looked pleased to see her, which was a relief since she had wondered if she'd become a nuisance with all of her visiting. This time instead of showing her into the library, Mrs Vesper took Sarah down to the kitchen where a big copper for washing linen was boiling away on the range. The housekeeper didn't ask any questions, she just put the milk pan on and set about making some chocolate. When she spoke, it was to enquire after Ellen.

'She don't talk much, so I have to read her face, but she's up a lot in the night.'

'She's not a sleeper then, the little one?'

'She's always been a bit queer, but more of late.'

'You best be bringing her to see me then. I'll need something to fill the time now that the mistress is gone, and I'd say you could both use a good meal now and again. Those breeches of yours get more ragged every time I see them!'

Sarah had to smile at this. Then she remembered what had brought her there.

'They're going to hang Joe.'

The housekeeper only nodded and stirred the chocolate.

'You knew?'

'That policeman visited last night and told Mrs Korechnya before she left.'

Sarah bowed her head and stared at the dust on her boots. That meant Joe would probably be drawing the crowds to Newgate the very next Monday. Sarah felt the sickness spread to the pit of her stomach.

'Ellen don't know.'

'Ah. Then we must find the time and place to tell her gently, and be certain that she is nowhere near Newgate on the day of the hanging. I would say that this kitchen is the place, this very evening after a hot supper. Before we hear the paper boys crying about it on the street tomorrow.'

When Sarah got back to Paternoster Row, she went upstairs by the main stair to avoid having to pass the editor's rooms. She knew in her heart that really there was nothing either Mr Harding or Lark could have done to save Joe, but she still felt angry and betrayed, and there was no one else for her to blame. As she passed Mr Parsimmons he looked up and instead of reprimanding her, as was his custom, he gave her a broad smile, putting his rotten teeth on display. Mr Harding must have told him not to scold her, which was something. The third floor was less sympathetic, although Sarah had made sure that none of the compositors knew that Holy Joe was her friend. They'd find out sooner or later, since nothing stayed a secret for long when you worked for a newspaper.

As she'd dreaded, the news of Holy Joe's confession and the date for the hanging would appear in the next edition of the *London Mercury*. It was all she could do to get through the day without punching Jack Thistlewite on the nose, since he said he'd known all along that Joe was a dangerous fiend and he couldn't wait to see him hang. More than anything, she wanted to walk right up to Jack's easel and rip the draft of Melville's story to shreds. She almost did; she imagined how good it would feel, and the look on his face when he saw that his 'sensational' story wouldn't make it into the next day's paper. But then she imagined Mr Harding's face, telling her she couldn't work for the newspaper any more, and she remembered how he'd given her a chance to get off the streets. She expected she'd be hearing from him soon anyway, over her behaviour that morning.

The editor didn't call her down all day, and she was rolling a fag for the walk home when his rotund form appeared in the compositing room doorway. There was dead silence when the compositors saw him.

'Good evening, gentlemen.'

A chorus of 'good evening, sir'.

'Ah, there you are Sarah. Come down to my office, would you?'

She nodded and followed him between the easels and down the stairs. Mr Harding didn't speak until they were in his rooms with the door closed behind them.

'Never fear, I'm not going to lecture you on your disappearance this morning, since the circumstances were ... exceptional.'

'I'm not feared Mr Harding.'

'No, I'm certain you aren't ... though I'm less certain that is always such a good thing.' He paused, and narrowed his eyes as though he were trying to read her. 'I'm more than happy with your work, and on the recommendation of Mrs Korechnya I have been considering allowing you to compose some more ... earnest print.'

Sarah's heart lifted. 'I'd like that, sir.'

Mr Harding cleared his throat and rubbed at the ink stain on his forefinger. 'I hope that you will not think ill of the newspaper business over this matter, for you may one day discover that it has something worthwhile to offer you.'

'No sir, I don't.'

Septimus Harding looked at her long and hard. 'Good girl. Well, then I shall tell you why I have called you. This afternoon I received a letter, delivered by hand, from Mrs Korechnya's housekeeper, who as we know is not afraid to speak her mind. She has asked that I allow you a day's leave on Monday, for ...' he faltered.

'For the hanging sir.'

'Yes. For the hanging. I have replied that you shall be free to spend that day as she sees fit. I may as well tell you that Mrs Vesper has also sent a letter to Inspector Lark, requesting that he call on her at his earliest convenience. I should not expect she will see him before the hanging though, Sarah, for this confounded business is keeping him terribly busy. Am I to understand that your young sister is poorly?'

'Not exactly poorly, Mr Harding, but she's not right neither.'

'Well, you must look after her. You are lucky to have such women as Mrs Korechnya and Mrs Vesper taking an interest in you.'

'I always say that I am, sir.' Sarah hadn't been feeling so lucky lately, and she had to keep reminding herself that she had a roof over her head and food and a job to go to. Still, every time she thought about Holy Joe alone in his cell, waiting to die, she felt her stomach turn over and she wanted to weep. She dreaded having to tell Ellen the news that evening.

When she returned to the White Hart, Ellen wasn't in Ruby's kitchen, so Sarah went down to the herring docks and there she was, sitting on a flat stone watching some ragamuffin boys skipping stones across the water. One of them had a slingshot and was eyeing up a gull that was picking at some herring bones. It made Sarah think that any one of them might have been playing in the alleyways with Joe's slingshot the night Vikram was killed, since he was always letting children play with whatever they could find in his pockets. And it would be just like him to take the blame, not realising the kind of trouble it could get him into. While Sarah watched, Ellen jumped up and ran at the gull so that it flew off before the boy could take aim.

Later, as they walked across Waterloo Bridge, Ellen seemed pleased to be out, and she even smiled when a tinker lifted his hat to her. It was Sarah who couldn't enjoy the walk, in spite of the sky being pink and gold with the sunset. Her mind kept skipping urgently from one thing to another, so that if Ellen hadn't warned her, she would have put her boot straight into some fresh horse manure. By the time they sat down at the kitchen table in Waterloo Street, Sarah was feeling so queasy that she could hardly even taste the pork chops, peas and suet pudding on her plate. There were dumplings too – Mrs Vesper said they were just the thing to fatten the two of them up. As the housekeeper lifted a steaming cherry pie from the oven, the door knocker went. It was Inspector Lark. Sarah didn't think she'd be pleased to see him again after running out on him that morning, but she was. Maybe he could still help Joe after all.

Lark sat down next to Ellen and ate a piece of cherry pie while Martha Vesper busied herself clearing plates. Ellen hadn't taken her eyes off the policeman since he'd walked into the kitchen, and when he'd finished his pie and complimented Mrs Vesper on it, she said, 'They ain't going to let Joe out, are they?'

Sarah dropped her fork on the floor, but Lark continued to dust the pie crumbs from his waistcoat for a moment.

'Why do you think that, Ellen?'

"'Cause you're sad, and so's Sarah, and nobody has said anything about Joe, and that's why you're here, ain't it?'

Lark talked to them both in his deep, steady voice and explained how it was; once the accused had admitted to a crime, then there was nothing to be done, since nobody was going to try and prove the prisoner wrong.

'But he *is* wrong!' said Sarah, feeling the panic rise to her throat all over again and trying not to show it in front of Ellen. Ellen had a terrible calm about her which was worse than if she'd started shouting or crying. Often when she was troubled, she just got quieter and further away.

As Lark walked them home, Ellen slipped her hand into his, and Sarah noticed that at first this seemed to make him uncomfortable, but then he looked pleased. On Waterloo Bridge they stopped to look down at the fishing boats going out with their lanterns lit. Sarah told the Inspector what she thought about the slingshot and the urchins, and said maybe he should come down to the river and talk to them himself. He said he would, but in her heart she knew it was probably too late. Ellen knew it too; she had that funny look, like she'd had the sight.

Lark seemed to guess what she was thinking. 'I'm sorry,' he said, and she could tell that he meant it.

'But why would Holy Joe say he done it when he didn't?'

'He might have been made too scared to tell the truth Sarah. Sometimes people like Joe are too trusting. They become the pawns of more dangerous criminals. Joe might not even have known he was doing something wrong.'

'Holy Joe wasn't that slow-witted. You didn't know him – he knew right from wrong.'

'But he was a thief, Sarah.'

'Thieving ain't the same as killing. Anyway, better to steal a crust of bread than watch your family starve. I was lucky I never had to, but not everyone's so lucky. Looks like Joe's luck's finally gone and run out.' Sarah bit her lip hard and looked away so that Lark wouldn't see she was weeping.

·⚬ 22 ⚬·

My Dear Barbara,

Already we have been at sea more than two weeks and it is the first day
that I can hold my hand steady to write. I am thankful for the privacy of a
single cabin, since the motion of the sea and the tilting of the vessel have
made me quite unwell.

Before I had even accepted her proposal, I received what has proven to
be invaluable counsel from Lady Herbert. She provided me with a list of a
lady's requirements for the journey and most welcome amongst the pro-
visions I saw fit to include have been two tins of plain arrowroot biscuits.
I have been able to stomach little else, for the ship's biscuits are hard and
dry and altogether unpalatable. On Lady Herbert's recommendation also,
I packed some flavoured tea, a spirit lamp with which to brew it, and some
brandy I foresee shall become useful once my nausea abates!

My cabin is no more than a cupboard, with room for little other than
my portmanteau (upon which I rest my inkstand), a cot and the bucket of
fresh water that is my daily ration. It is barely sufficient for washing after
I have taken aside a portion for drinking, and I have quickly learnt to be
frugal. I also have Lady Herbert to thank for suggesting I bring with me
my oldest undergarments and petticoats, which I throw out of my porthole
when they would otherwise need laundering, since the business of laundry
is rather perplexing at sea.

I am told that we have had fair weather, though it has oft seemed violent
from where I lay on my cot, watching the small, round window of my cabin
display sea, then sky, then sea again . . . I gather that the south Atlantic is
infamous for its contrary gusts and intemperate climate, and the captain
delights in telling tales of less fortunate vessels which have been blown off
course as far as the South Americas. This is by far a more attractive disaster

than being dashed against the rocky shores of Africa, where, according to my questionable source, survivors might be captured and transported to slave markets! The captain, who seemed such a gentleman when I met him at St Katherine's Pier, has been transformed beyond recognition since we set sail. Indeed, he acquired a hardness and ill temper from the very moment the mooring ropes were loosed. I have encountered him on several occasions, and have overheard him remark (and I shall not repeat his words verbatim) on the folly of allowing women aboard ship. Already there have been complaints of the coarse language and heavy drinking of the Bristol sailors, but I have noted that such prudishness does nothing to sweeten the captain's temper.

I have kept to myself by and large, and so have the few other passengers well enough to take some air on deck. Perhaps when we become hardier sailors we will be less unsociable, for the greater part of the journey still lies ahead of us. I have thus far had the inclination to converse only with my unusual companion, Mr Govinda. He has endeared himself to me by taking notice of my ailment and proffering a lump of ginger, which he instructed I should cut a small piece from and steep it in boiling water, then sip the concoction to ease the nausea. I found it a most pleasant and curative tonic. I believe Govinda sleeps with the ship's company in one of the hammocks that are strung up on the starboard side at nightfall, and he spends his days reading from the same large book, seated cross-legged in a quiet nook by the prow. I have not yet glimpsed a page of this book, since he closes it whenever I approach, and there is no title stamped on its cloth jacket. The binding is in fact very beautiful, being scarlet silk embroidered in gold with oriental characters and designs. I shall ask him what it is he reads when we are better acquainted, yet I wonder if I shall ever really become acquainted with Lady Herbert's man, since he does not find it necessary to mark silence with words, and is refreshingly not given to idle repartee.

21 November, 1864

A further week has passed, and we are sailing at fair speed, or knots as sailors call the measurement of nautical miles and the time it takes to span them. It is accountable by the divisions tied in a great rope which is flung over the side with a weight at its end. When the ship has her sails full, the rope slips ever faster from the deck. There is much to know about the business of keeping a vessel afloat and pointed against the wind, and with each day that passes I have more respect for the ship's crew. Any ship on the sea is a veritable floating island of men, and to watch their care for her – the polishing of brass and oiling and mending of sails – one might think that even the roughest and most barnacled of the opposite sex takes pleasure in domesticity. The decks are washed down several times a day, but I have discovered that this is to prevent the planks shrinking with the heat rather than for any concern over cleanliness.

We crossed the equator at Gabon, and the temperature has soared to unimaginable heights. I, who have experienced no greater heat than Italy and Spain in the summer months, could never have imagined the fierceness of the mistral wind of north Africa, nor the baking sun of the southern hemisphere. I wear only cotton gowns and foresee that I must purchase another, in a light colour, when we dock at Simonstown in the Cape of Good Hope.

I have recovered my health sufficiently to enjoy the sea air, and have recently met with several women whose cabins are close by mine. My neighbours have proven to be a gaggle of lady missionaries headed for the very same destination as I: Benares. Three of their company are named Mary, which at times confuses our conversations in the most delightful way. Benares, I am informed, is the holiest place of the Hindu faith, and it is from here that these god-fearing women intend to convert the entire nation to Christianity. It is an ambitious plan, and one must admire the stalwartness of their faith if not their narrow-mindedness. Their society is docile but not entirely dull, although I am more than a little perturbed by their clear disrespect for the ancient religion of Hindu. Indeed, when I referred to it as such, one of the Marys seemed horrified that I thought there could be any 'religion' but that of the Christian Bible.

I have progressed in becoming acquainted with Govinda, and have learnt that the book he reads from is, in fact, the most sacred of Hindu scriptures – the Bhagavad Gita. I have asked him to explain how his faith differs to me, as I cannot read the text written in Sanskrit. Firstly, he says, I must understand that Brahma is the 'divine reality' which exists in all things, and that everything in the world, every wave upon the sea, every breeze and creature and plant is a manifestation of Brahma, and therefore contains an element of the divine. It becomes complex almost immediately hereafter, for there are a multiplicity of gods and goddesses. Amongst them though, is a trio of three central gods: Brahma, Shiva and Vishnu. Each of these deities has a female consort, and I am delighted to inform you that all three derive their power from their goddess companion! I shall here list these ladies for you, since it will aid my memory to write their names down, and because I have much time at hand for detail. Brahma, the creator, is betrothed to the goddess Sarasvati. This lady presides over the domain of wisdom, spiritual knowledge, creativity and the arts. She dresses only in yellow, and sits upon a throne which is a water lily. I am most taken with Sarasvati above the other two goddesses, not least because she favours the lily. Lakshmi is consort to the Lord Vishnu and is lady of fortune and prosperity, and the beautiful Parvati keeps sweet the temper of Shiva, known also as the Destroyer.

There is one other goddess, Kali, whom I find most intriguing. My curiosity is only heightened by Govinda's reluctance to call this goddess by her name, and by the fact that Kali alone amongst the goddesses of the Hindu has no male consort. It is this fearsome deity that inspires the dangerous cult of the thuggee, whose followers have been known to kill, offering their victims to the goddess in sacrifice.

The watery panorama whose vastness and moodiness I at first found quite alarming is now an object of complete fascination. I have seen the ocean look as cold and as foreboding as a sheet of steel, or as luminous as a cloth of gold when the sun rises and sets, spilling its molten light across the water. At these times I have felt closer to the grace of a divine being than I ever have in a chapel or cathedral, and I begin to understand the allure of the sea.

I have only once had occasion to venture below deck, in an endeavour to obtain some clean water from the galley (the bucket delivered to my cabin that morning being the colour of weak tea). I shall not do so again, for it was made clear that this is strictly the domain of the cook and his men, and I hereby retract any favourable observation hitherto made on the domestic prowess of their sex. The belly of the ship is an unpleasant place quite aside from the squalor of the ship's kitchen. Here there is a press of unhappy passengers who cannot afford lodgings on deck, their only privacy being a curtain strung across a beam. The stench alone is oppressive, since close by the human accommodation there are livestock pens, into which ducks and chickens, cows and pigs are crowded so densely that the poor beasts can barely move as they await their encounter with the cook's knife. There are horses also, for I heard them snorting and stamping, and I discovered that they are bound for a regiment in Bombay.

Simonstown, Africa,
16 December, 1864

We have tied up at Simonstown, and I write from a table by the sea in a pretty, sleepy fishing village. I cannot describe the simple pleasure of walking upon the motionless earth, and have taken off my shoes to feel the sand beneath my feet.

The three Marys and company have hired a carriage to see the sights at Constantia and I was invited to join them, but in truth I welcome the opportunity to escape their company. Instead I shall tell you of a recent conversation I had with Govinda one night whilst we sat on the deck watching the copper disc of the sun dipping into the sea. When it had disappeared, the water shimmered like a bowl of silver pearls, and a pod of indigo porpoises appeared at the stern and travelled for a spell alongside the ship's hull. They seemed such happy, playful creatures that it was impossible not to laugh as they jumped and dived.

Foremost in my mind on this night was the matter of the missing diamond jewel. In fact, there have been several occasions when I have considered enquiring after it, and I had secretly hoped Govinda might offer some clue as to its whereabouts. With the ocean glittering around us it seemed an opportune time to broach the subject, so I asked Govinda about the significance of the charm which Lady Herbert was to have made for the Maharajah. I did not broach the subject of its disappearance or suspected theft, for I thought the matter too indelicate. The habitual serenity of his face remained unchanged but for the slightest tightening about his mouth. Only from this could I guess that he knew something more of the jewel than he might have disclosed to Inspector Lark.

After a short silence, Govinda quietly informed me that the charm was an 'astrological talisman' and that in its unorthodox composition, the jewel was potentially a danger to anyone who might seek to use it. I asked him to explain this to me, since I am quite baffled by the idea that a particular gemstone (or nine) could affect the very fibre of existence. All Govinda would tell me was that Lady Herbert believed that by being in possession of the charm she might make contact with the spirit world, and specifically with her dead husband. He seemed troubled, and when I finally, and rather cautiously, suggested that the theft of the diamonds might cause the Maharajah great distress, he appeared to not have heard me.

The village of Simonstown is hot and dry, and the sun has a strength of light I have never before encountered. Franz would have loved to see this landscape; he would have exclaimed over the way flowers and cloth and the strange fruits in the marketplace are lit by its brilliance. The buildings are freshly painted timber bungalows, and the African women wear radiant, flowing robes, as though they are clothed in rainbows. The Dutch settlers here are notable by the whiteness of both their skin and clothing, and by their broad straw hats, but they have not attempted to change this place; not by culture or design. I wonder how much of England I will find in India, for I fear the British are less sensitive to indigenous custom.

Having reached the southern tip of Africa, half the journey is now complete, and so my thoughts turn more and more to what awaits me. In part I am intoxicated by the unknown, and in part quite overcome by nerves. I have happily become acquainted with other passengers besides my crusading neighbours, and so am refreshed by the company of a variety of people. There is an official of the East India company and his wife, a pastor and his wife, and a band of military men who are bound for a hill station in the north of the country. There are also several women, like myself without chaperones; one is joining her family in Bombay after attending Queen's College in London, another is a nanny with a post in Delhi, and another is engaged to an Indian man. This lady intrigues me most of all, for soon she will wear the veil with which Muslim women must cover their hair and part of their face. She seems unperturbed by the prospect, for she is clearly in love, and so all the world is full of possibility.

Bombay,
18 January, 1864

We have reached Bombay where we will pass three nights before boarding the train for Benares. I understand that this journey will take one week, and can only hope that the company of missionaries have a different travelling schedule to my own!

The pages I wrote in the last weeks at sea were spoiled when the *weather suddenly turned stormy and tipped an entire pot of tea across my portmanteau. Thankfully, the liquid did not seep into the chest, since it would certainly have ruined all of the white cotton I purchased in Simonstown. The latter part of the voyage, aside from this occurrence, was without incident, and by the time we were in sight of land, I almost longed for a pirate ship to break the monotony.*

The first sighting of the west coast of India was a more welcome vision than I can describe. As we approached the port of Bombay, passengers were crowded on the deck leaning on the railings, and there was an elevation of spirit one and all. My first impression of this city, and of this land, was its white shores, delicately fringed with forests of palm. My second impression; its very distinctive smell. Were I a perfumer, I might attempt to identify the particular fragrances – there is the pungency of mysterious tobaccos and spices, sweet-smelling incense and jasmine, and the earthy smell of animals. Here cows walk the streets quite confident that the path they tread is sacred. Also to be seen are camels, dogs, elephants, horses, monkeys, and in the bazaar I saw even a chained cheetah!

The Taj Hotel, where I am most comfortably accommodated for two nights, has a striking view of the Port of Bombay. The buildings along the promenade were built by the East India company, and so bear the mark of European settlement. White stone pillars and Romanesque grandeur are nothing less than striking beneath the glare of the burning sun and against a sky of cornflower blue, although they are surrounded by pukha bungalows and mud brick huts with roofs made from coconut palm. In the harbour, great ships and brightly painted passenger vessels and long, narrow fishing boats are all moored together in a great tangle. On the shore, barrels and crates and sacks are daily loaded and unloaded by more bodies than I have ever seen in one place. Dark-skinned fishermen sit on the sand wearing only a loin cloth and mending their nets, while women in lime green and cherry pink saris pass with fresh flowers in their hair, or carrying baskets laden with fruit or palm leaves on their head.

I am struck by the great number of men who have no more pressing task than to pass the entire day squatting on the ground chewing betel tobacco and spitting streams of bright red liquid into the dust. These men are openly inquisitive, and I have felt the gaze of many. It is as though time has a less structured form here, for there is nothing of that bustle and affected importance of employment that characterises the city of London.

Now it is nearly dark. The sea breeze is warm, the white muslin curtains float upon it, and the smells from the street are carried upwards to my balcony. I am enthralled by so much that is foreign and unusual, and already I feel new strength, for here there is no reminder of my former life.

I shall ensure that this letter boards the very next boat to London from Bombay, and all being well, it shall reach you as spring buds appear in your garden. I trust that all is well with you, and it is perhaps as well that the pages I spoiled are missing, for this has proven a lengthy chronicle. For all of its rambling, the writing of a letter to an absent friend has been my best company, and it bears with it my fondest regards.

Lily

⁃ 23 ⁃

Laugh and the world laughs with you,
Weep and you weep alone,
For this sad old earth must borrow its mirth,
It has trouble enough of its own

Ella Wilcox

Martha Vesper had repeated everything that the property agent had told her when she wrote to Mrs Korechnya. She could tell he was honest, and since that was an uncommon trait in his profession, she had taken the liberty of consulting the mistress's friend Mrs Bodichon when she came calling at Christmas. With Barbara Bodichon's blessing, Martha took a further liberty, and invited the agent she had met at the old house in Kensington to view the Waterloo Street property. Only then did she write to Mrs Korechnya.

She could not pretend that the idea of leaving Waterloo Street had not occurred to her before she discovered that the house containing the master's old studio was for sale. As Martha saw it, Mrs Korechnya needed a quiet place, and a change, and it would be best to implement any such change while she was away, so that when she returned from her travels, she could begin her life afresh. She felt confident that the mistress would trust her judgement in this, since it was Martha who had taken control of the household affairs of necessity when the master died, and she had proved herself to be more than able.

Since receiving Lily's reply (via a remarkable contraption in the newspaper office which sent and received letters by wire) and her approval, for the mistress said she would sooner return to the house in which her husband had been so alive as a painter than the one in which he had died, Martha had moved swiftly. The repairs to the Kensington property would take until the end of March and even finding tradesmen to mend the roof in the winter months had been troublesome. But by now they were making fine progress and if all went well, the new house

147

would be ready long before her mistress returned in early summer.

The entire business had been keeping Martha so busy that she had enlisted the O'Reilly girls to help her with preparations for the move. The parlour was so full of crates and bundles, that one had to be cautious in entering the room so as not to topple a tower of hatboxes or tumble a portmanteau. Martha had set Sarah the task of packing all the books from the shelves in the library, since this was clearly her favourite place. It had taken the entire weekend and three evenings, since every time the housekeeper entered the room, she found Sarah seated on the floor with her nose buried in a book.

Martha always kept the little one by her side so she could keep an eye on her. She was no expert on the ways of children, since she'd never had her own, but she knew there was something not right with little Ellen, and she didn't think it was just the loss of her parents, or her missing layer of skin. Perhaps it was as Barbara Bodichon had said; that the murder of the Hindu, followed by the hanging of her friend Holy Joe, had all been too much for Ellen's bony little shoulders to carry.

Martha was certain now that Ellen saw the others; ever since they had taken down the curtains in the old bedroom together. In fact, the child had sensed the master's shadowy presence before she did, and when Martha turned to see why Ellen had not lifted the curtain hem from the floor as she'd asked, she saw the little one sitting on the bed staring into the corner of the room. And there was Franz, seated in a low armchair toying with a piece of jewellery. This took Martha by surprise as she had not seen his spirit for many months. At first the housekeeper thought he held some necklace from the satin box on the dresser, which Lily had not touched since his death. It contained many pieces that her husband had given her, and which she could not yet bring herself to wear. Then, as if to afford her a better view, the master held the chain up, and Martha saw that it was in fact the spectre of Lily's hairwork pendant. This was perplexing, and the housekeeper could only imagine that Mrs Korechnya must have lost it whilst in India.

After all the hot dinners and warm clothing and motherly attention Martha had given Ellen, the child seemed to be getting a little stronger, although she still had a nasty cough. The O'Reilly girls had resisted moving into Waterloo Street, but Martha had contrived to have them spend as many evenings and weekends there as possible. Martha had realised that Sarah was too proud to receive charity unless she was giving something in return, so she had been careful to put it to her that she needed the help; that the task of moving from Waterloo to Kensington was too great for her to undertake alone. She had further plans for the girls, but those would have to wait until the mistress returned.

In a break from all the packing, Martha saw Sarah standing by Lily's table in the library. Here, Mrs Korechnya had left her larger inkstand, taking with her only a small portable writing tray. Sarah was running her hand across the back of the leather chair, and looking longingly at the inkstand.

'You may sit down if you wish,' she said, and Sarah jumped.

'Oh no. I was just . . .' her cheeks warmed a little and Martha smiled kindly.

'The mistress would be pleased to have the room put to good use in her absence.'

She left then and, when she next had occasion to pass, she saw Sarah sitting at the table with paper and quill, studiously practising her letters. Martha could tell that she was suited to this industry, and decided to write another of her letters to Mr Harding – at least then one of the O'Reillys would benefit from the modern notion that girls could be educated. Ellen was no more devoted to this idea than she had been at the beginning, and had long since taken to arriving on the doorstep of Waterloo Street during school hours, having walked on her own from Westminster. When Martha sought the advice of Mrs Bodichon, they had decided that it would benefit Ellen's health as much to be in the company of the housekeeper as other children. Besides, Ellen was already so far behind that she would have to return to the same class the following year.

Sarah was another matter entirely; as sound as a pound with her boots firmly on the earth. Martha thought she would go a long way, that one, with her quick wits and hunger for learning. She was looking more like a girl too, ever since the day in January when she'd come to the housekeeper and informed her, in her matter-of-fact way, that she'd got the curse. She seemed proud of the fact, which made it all the easier for Martha to show her where to wash out her cloths, and how to make tea from dried raspberry leaf and lemon balm if she had the cramps. Sarah still insisted on her wool breeches and cap, but her hair wasn't shorn so short any more, and it curled a little around her freckled face. She'd stopped wearing men's shirts too, as Martha had sewn her some made of blue striped cotton, and a black velveteen waistcoat to match her new black boots.

All in all, this winter had passed much more favourably than the one preceding it, and Martha could hardly believe that it had been an entire year since they'd buried the master. The first year was always the worst, with its anniversaries and constant reminders of loss. The only shadow across this was the unease Martha felt about Mrs Korechnya. Perhaps it was just that she would be delayed in her return from India, or perhaps it was the distance, but the housekeeper could not see her clearly – it was almost as though a force were at work, clouding her vision. She shook the feeling away and returned to taking down the parlour curtains. At least now the mistress would not have to enter the rooms that contained memories and phantoms that would be better left to fade and become still.

⁘ 24 ⁘

My Dear Sarah,

I had every intention of sitting down to write you a long letter as soon as I set foot on terra firma. Now weeks have passed, and this is the very first moment I have had to sit quietly with only my thoughts for company.

I am fortunate to be stationed in a secluded and shady summer house, and as I write, the sultry air and the balm of jasmine and honeysuckle caress me. In the scriptures of the Hindu religion, it was in the gardens of Benares, also called the City of Light, that the world began. Indeed, the grounds of the palace of the Maharajah where I am a guest are the most magical place. There are pagodas – the small temples to the many gods and goddesses of Hindu – and peacocks, monkeys and exotic flowering trees. The Maharajah also has a pet tiger, and I cannot describe to you my terror upon first sighting the great cat, for it woke from its sleep when I came upon it, and roared in a most unfriendly manner! It is more sinuous in body than I might have imagined a tiger to be, and its coat is like gleaming bronze. Thankfully, I was accompanied by Govinda, and so both the tiger and I were soon calmed. When Govinda walked right up to the beast and stroked its fur, I was mesmerised, though I was later told that the animal has few teeth (they have been removed), and that its claws have been clipped.

Everywhere there are monkeys, darting about and looking for mischief. Why only this morning whilst I was in the bazaar my hat blew to the ground (yes, I have taken to wearing one, for here the sun blazes from rising to twilight) and immediately a monkey was upon it. When I fought back and retrieved my hat, a little furry hand tugged at the precious pendant about my neck!

There are a bewildering number of rooms and chambers in the

Maharajah's residence, and though I may roam freely, the prince's women may not do so without special permission. That is, with the exception of his favourite concubine, Sarasvati, an exquisite creature whom I am told is a girl from one of the villages. I am accommodated near the women's wing, which is the realm of wives, concubines, female servants and children only, except for the guards who wear voluminous trousers and carry sabres tucked into their brightly woven belts. I believe they are Arabs, although the Maharajah's personal guard is composed of a different type altogether. The royal guard is trained to kill to protect the prince and his treasures, so you can imagine my astonishment when I discovered that my travelling companion, Govinda, is the most senior guard of this order. I believe he is also a close advisor to the prince, and thus it is near impossible to persuade him to speak freely of anything!

The women's wing is called the zenana, and such a place you have never seen. Indeed, the prince keeps women as though they were very fine horses in a rarefied stable. Everywhere there is chatter and gossip, and children learning sitar and tabla; instruments which resemble the mandolin and drum. The Maharajah's women can spend hours bathing and dressing. They wash from bowls of scented water upon which float magnolia and frangipani petals, and they rub fragrant spices into their skin. They wear the finest silk saris and gold chains around their wrists, ankles and middles. I have seen some exceptional gemstones hanging from a gold headpiece and resting upon a dark forehead; stones as large as a fob watch and as luminous as stars. When all of the harem is dressed for the evening, it is like looking upon a band of bejewelled fairies, and I feel pale and plain, even in my finest gown.

I have begun a piece, which I hope to finish soon, about a most exceptional woman. She is the goddess Kali, a deity of the Hindu faith, and she inspires a terrible cult. Yet somehow, I am most taken with this goddess of death, for I cannot help but wonder if she has some connection to the strange and frightening events we witnessed in London last summer. You see, it is she who most covets the rare red diamond – the most extraordinary of all the nine diamonds that you and I saw at the Royal Academy. I am most perplexed that no one here has made mention of the diamonds, though I am certain that the prince must have demanded to know of their whereabouts. In Benares, I have perhaps found my peace with Kali, for here death is embraced, and is as much a part of life as the spiced food, jewels and palaces. I feel closer to Franz than I have since he departed, and it almost seems that the pendant upon which his hair is mounted, and which I wear always, brings me ever closer to him.

Sarah, I would urge you to take to heart any suggestion Mrs Vesper might make with regard to yours and Ellen's future. It is my greatest wish that you too will visit this remarkable land one day. I think often of you both, and I wonder if you are putting to use the parchment I gave you? I hope to write more anon, but must hurry to give this letter to the servant who takes the post to the railway, from where it will begin its long journey to London. London does seem a world, an aeon away, and it is hard to imagine that this day must be dark and cold there. I do hope Ellen is stronger, and that there is at least a little sunshine to light the heavens. Do not forget me, my dear Sarah!

Fondest regards always, to you and to Ellen,
Lily Korechnya

⁘ 25 ⁘

When the day dawned, thieves, low prostitutes, ruffians and vagabonds of every kind, flocked to the ground, with every variety of
foul and offensive behaviour. Fightings, faintings, whistlings, brutal
jokes, tumultuous demonstrations of indecent delight when swoon-
ing women were dragged out of the crowd by the police with their
dresses disordered, gave a new zest to the general entertainment.

Charles Dickens on hangings, *The Times*

Sarah got up from the table and went to look at Ellen again. She
supposed she wasn't much good at writing letters; she'd been up and
down every five seconds the past hour, and all she'd done was waste
precious paper. Now the tallow was burning low and the wan morning
light was beginning to creep in through the basement window. She
longed to return to her other, less troublesome early morning writing;
practising her hand by painstakingly copying passages from back issues
of the *London Mercury*.

Ellen was still asleep, and had been sleeping so soundly of late that
Sarah often became afraid and needed to reassure herself that the little
chest was moving up and down beneath the quilt. Ellen was just as
silent and far away as ever, though just maybe, Sarah thought, a glimmer
of her old, elfin boldness was slowly returning. She didn't like school
any better, but at least when she went off wandering, she was with Mrs
Vesper. The fact that Ellen was actually sleeping must be a good thing,
Sarah decided, even though sometimes she had bad dreams that she
never remembered by daylight. Perhaps that was just as well, Sarah
thought.

But for a tangle of pale hair, the Trub was almost entirely hidden by
their new, thick quilt, stitched with coloured squares and pretty patterns
and sewn by Mrs Vesper herself. The housekeeper had visited their
basement only once – Sarah had tried to prevent this, but she was a
stubborn one all right – and had since given them the quilt, new boots

and winter clothing. She was also making sure they got a hot meal at least twice a week and kept saying they should come and stay at the house in Kensington when it was ready. Sarah knew Mrs Vesper would have them at Waterloo Street every night if it were up to her, but she didn't want to be begging. Still, those two meals meant they could eat better the rest of the week, and her breeches weren't so loose this winter.

The letter from Lily was by far the best thing Mrs Vesper had given Sarah. It had been handed to her ceremoniously the evening before when they'd visited Waterloo Street, in a fat brown paper envelope with Miss Sarah O'Reilly written in fine copperplate on the front. The paper was crumpled and smelt familiar. It took her a minute to remember where she knew that smell from; it was the very same scent that clung to the beads Vikram had given to Ellen.

Sarah had read Lily's letter three times now. It was already close to the end of March and since the letter was dated mid-January, it had taken well over two months to arrive. This meant that Sarah would have to write her reply immediately and even then, if the ship encountered poor weather, it would not even arrive in time to reach Mrs Korechnya before her return voyage. Still it was worth trying. She could of course send a note down the wire at the newspaper office, but it wouldn't be the same as a real letter. The greater problem was that Sarah just couldn't find the words. It was the thought of someone, even Mrs Korechnya, reading her words that made her seize up and manage nothing more than foolish, prissy sentences such as:

Dear Lily Korechnya,
    It is queer in London without you, and the winter was awful cold.

Dear Lily Korechnya,
    The Maharajah's palace sounds grand, and I should like to see his pet tiger.

Dear Lily Korechnya,
    This is the very first letter I have written ever.

Sarah remembered what Lily had said in the carriage, the day they first went to Kensington; that she wrote things down to empty her mind. Well, it seemed to Sarah that letters were different and quite aside from the need to make them neat and legible, they made you want to write down what was in your heart. Sarah decided that she'd read Lily's letter one more time that evening. It was a peculiar letter in a way, and it would take a little more thinking before she knew how to reply to it. She thought about what Lily had said about the future, about listening to Mrs Vesper's advice for her and Ellen. She'd got used to not having to rely on anyone, but to tell the truth, it would surely be a good thing not to be so entirely on her own.

Sarah had already started thinking about her future, what kind of stories she might write if she were a penny-a-liner, and she fancied she could get Ellen to approach the queer folk she'd befriended for some tattle. That way, everyone would feel like they were doing something gainful. Ellen was just as good at getting people to like her as at finding her way about. Why, just the other day they'd been up around Cheap Street and Ellen had gone right into a tailor's shop and asked for a bit of ribbon to tie up her boot with. She'd come out wearing a wool shawl and eating an apple, since the kindly tailor thought her pinafore was too thin for the weather. If any of the other embankment mudlarks had tried a caper like that, they'd have felt the end of the tailor's boot.

The tallow was all but done, so Sarah took another piece of parchment and dipped the blackened nib into the pretty, china ink pot. She copied an item from the top of the metropolitan news column before the flame snuffed out. A fatal carriage accident had occurred at Ramsgate, she wrote, when a horse started off at a furious pace and the basket chaise driven by Mr Kelly of Sandwich was dashed against a fly and overturned. Mrs Kelly was so much hurt that she died in a few minutes. Sarah scanned the column for something less distressing to copy, and her attention was immediately drawn to another item. The Crystal Palace School of Art, Literature and Science, established to afford facilities for the acquisition of the highest branches of female education was about to embark upon its eleventh session. The advantages thus offered, were found to be appreciated by a large and increasing attendance . . .

Sarah put down her quill and closed her eyes. She imagined for a moment what it might be like to attend such a school. Surely, nothing could be better than that?

When Sarah opened her eyes, Ellen was sitting on the corner of the bed, staring at her. 'You look happy about it, Sarah.'

"Bout what, Trub?'

'Well, whatever you was thinking about. Was it something nice?'

Sarah shrugged. 'Aye, I was imagining being in a school, in a crystal palace.'

Ellen looked horrified. 'You can't have a school in a palace! Schools are horrid and palaces aren't.'

Sarah ignored her comment. 'How about you go get the kettle hot upstairs so we can have some tea.'

For a moment a shadow passed across Ellen's face, as though she had just remembered something unpleasant.

'Does it hurt, when you get hanged, Sarah?'

Even though several months had gone by, Ellen never stopped thinking about Holy Joe. The Sunday before the hanging, Mrs Vesper had asked Ellen where she'd like to go the following day, and Ellen had said she wanted to visit the garden at the old house in Kensington. Sarah was relieved, since she'd worried that Elly would choose the Rope-makers' fields, which would take them near the Old Bailey and Newgate Prison. Even going to Kensington meant that they'd come close enough to the festivity, since the roofs and balconies of buildings for a mile around the prison were crowded with spectators. Ellen had just stared out of the window and didn't say a word.

Mrs Vesper had not been to the old house before, and while Sarah helped Ellen look for a four-leaf clover, the housekeeper had walked around the outside, peering in dusty windows and shaking her head. When she returned, she was accompanied by a tall gentleman in a fine suit and top hat. He had an umbrella with a brass knob, and carried a large, flat leather wallet. Sarah couldn't hear what they were talking about, but the gentleman was pointing to the roof and then to the walls of the building with his umbrella.

When she'd turned around to check on Ellen, the Trub was nowhere to be seen. Sarah had looked all over for her, and finally found her sitting perfectly still at the bottom of the garden. Sarah wondered if maybe she'd seen a badger or a fox and made sure she tread slow and quiet, just in case. As she drew closer, and without turning around, Ellen spoke the first words she'd uttered all day. 'He's dead now, Joe's dead.' And she'd repeated it again and again, as though to make sure she remembered. Sarah bit her lip. 'Elly, come here' was all she could say. When Ellen came to her and buried her face in Sarah's chest she couldn't hold back her own tears any longer, and they both cried and cried; for Joe and for Mam and Pa, and for all of the troubles that their short lives had known. Sarah thought that was when Ellen had started improving – once she'd stopped holding in all the bad things.

Now, as they sat at the table in the early morning light, Ellen seemed to have clean forgotten the question she'd asked about hangings because she was looking in her ribbon tin and humming. That was a relief anyway. Devil's Acre hadn't had any cheer about it since Vikram's murder and Holy Joe's arrest and people had changed towards her and Ellen. Faces that had once been friendly turned away when they saw the O'Reilly girls, like they didn't know for certain that Holy Joe could never have been a murderer. Sarah didn't care about them, since trouble always showed you who your real friends were. Ruby had done her best to make them feel like the White Hart was still their home, bless her, and Sarah knew that she was making an effort to be all the more jolly when she saw Ellen. But in truth, having the companions of a murderer as lodgers was bad for business.

They had their breakfast and Sarah tied Ellen's hair back with a red ribbon. At the gate of the schoolhouse, she gave her sister a hug then set off for the office. Mr Harding had kept his promise about relieving Sarah from asthmatic balsams and miraculous cordials, but she still wasn't much looking forward to what she might find on her easel. She'd had a few weeks of rentals and lodgings; snuff-box makers and coachmakers wanted; elegant modern chariots and handsome brown ponies for sale; and numerous governesses 'of respectable connections and amiable disposition' looking for teaching situations. For the last week, it had been the comings and goings of visiting dignitaries and the social engagements of polite society that had been driving her mad. She couldn't give a fig that the Duke of Cambridge gave a dinner on Friday at his residence in Piccadilly, nor that the Countess Palmerston was recently honoured by the company of the Prince of Prussia and a baron by the name of Oberlitz.

When she got to the *Mercury* building, Sarah tipped her cap to Mr Parsimmons.

'Editor wants to see you, Sam,' he said without raising his head from his ledger. Mr Parsimmons liked to be mysterious, which Sarah guessed was how he got by, since you had to have something extra if you had a mug as ugly as Mr Parsimmons'.

It was not Septimus Harding, but Lark who stood by the fire in the editor's rooms.

'Good morning, Sarah. I expect you're looking for Mr Harding. He has summoned me also, but it seems that he has stepped out for a moment. Come, warm yourself by the fire, he'll be back directly.'

Lark resumed staring into the flames, and Sarah thought he looked weary. He'd been melancholy all winter, and she reckoned it must be because Mrs Korechnya was gone. She knew that he still felt bad about Holy Joe too, since he hadn't known what to say to her since that day they'd gone for a walk along the embankment. She wanted to let him know that she didn't blame him and searched for some way of telling Lark that she still liked him, since he looked like a man who needed a friend. Then it occurred to her precisely what might cheer him up.

'I've had a letter from Mrs Korechnya.' As she'd hoped, Lark's face softened at the sound of Lily's name.

'And is she keeping well?'

'I expect so. She has seen monkeys, and a tiger, and the prince keeps women like they were horses in a stable.' She had the satisfaction of seeing him smile. Sarah was busting to ask if he'd found out anything new about the missing jeweller's apprentice and the diamonds, since the paper boys had finally stopped bellowing about all their possible whereabouts. But just as she had roused the courage to ask him, Septimus Harding returned. He had a look about him Sarah had seen only once before, when he told her about Holy Joe's confession.

'Ah, Sarah. John. I have sad tidings indeed.' He sat down heavily then paused, searching for words; an uncommon handicap for the editor of the *London Mercury*. The room was so quiet as they waited, barely daring to breathe, that Sarah could hear the distant clackety-clack of the press in the basement. Mr Harding sighed, and the breath he exhaled was unsteady. Sarah gripped the back of a chair and she could tell that John Lark was just as tense.

'I have received, via the India Office and the telegraph service from Constantinople, some tragic news regarding Lily Korechnya. It took but five days to reach us – an extraordinary machine, quite extraordinary ...' Here, Mr Harding faltered again, and Lark sat down heavily on one of the green leather armchairs. Sarah wanted to press her hands to her ears and run from the room. Instead, she stood perfectly still, and waited until Septimus Harding uttered the words she could not bear to hear.

'She was taken ill quite suddenly, according to the British administration in Benares, but from what it is unclear. This happened on the 20th day of March ... only six days ago ... My dear friends, Lily is dead.'

Part II

I will paint her as I see her.
Ten times have the lilies blown,
Since she looked upon the sun.

And her face is lily clear,
Lily-shaped, and dropped in duty
To the law of its own beauty.

Quiet talk she liketh best,
In a bower of gentle looks,
Watering flowers, or reading books.

And her voice it murmurs lowly,
As a silver stream may run,
Which yet feels, you feel, the sun.

And her smile it seems half holy,
As if drawn from thoughts more far
Than our common jestings are.

And if any poet knew her,
he would sing of her with falls
Used in lovely madrigals.

And if any painter drew her,
He would paint her unaware
With a halo round her hair.

Elizabeth Barrett Browning

Benares, Uttar Pradesh, 1862

The Maharajah of Uttar Pradesh dreaded the incessant holy festivals of his Hindu subjects. As a Mohammedan and descendent of the noble Moghuls, he found the infidel pageantry largely unfathomable. Besides, it wearied him deeply. The Maharajah's public appearances called for a certain amount of formality and ceremony, and it was not only he, but also his poor elephant who had to suffer the discomfort of being decorated and constantly on display. There was no question that he liked jewels – indeed he loved them – but the princely costumes for state occasions were designed to inspire awe, not for ease of movement. Now, on the festival of Diwali, he was bejewelled from his diamond-encrusted Persian slippers to the enormous emerald and ruby sarpech that pierced the turban on his head. Were it not for the lights and the fact that the nautchnees would soon perform their Diwali dance, the Maharajah would just as soon be practising his polo swing or drinking gin.

The festival of Diwali, also known as the Festival of Lights, was to some degree worth all the commotion and ritual. During Diwali, the holy city of Benares was lit like a celestial candelabra, and from every rooftop, balustrade, ruin, temple, hovel and stone wall, there burned a galaxy of chiraugs. These small, earthenware oil lanterns created a spectacle the Maharajah never tired of, and from his lofty perch on the elevated howdah of his elephant, the effect was rather splendid, as though the city had indeed been transformed into the city of light, the dwelling place of the Hindu gods. The Prince of Uttar Pradesh was not entirely unaffected by Hindu superstition, and he knew it. There was one belief in particular he could not seem to dismiss: the mystery of navaratna. It haunted him, in spite of the probable futility of his quest for the ninth stone. Foolishly, his hopes were always raised during a holy festival, as though the presence of belief and ritual alone might bring him providence.

Now, the Maharajah sighed heavily and put it from his mind. He shifted his posture so that his jewel-studded cummerbund was not digging into his ribs, and watched the battalion of saffron and crimson-robed priests who were positioned along the banks of the Ganges. They were chanting and waving their feathered batons about, apparently attempting to dispel any ill-intentioned spirits who might prevent the safe passage of Lakshmi, goddess of fortune, into the city. It was in her honour that Diwali was celebrated and the chiraugs were lit – to illuminate her way and ensure her endowment of either a plentiful harvest, a new enterprise or a prosperous year.

When the nautchnees finally appeared before the Maharajah, he knew that all the discomfort and tedium was worthwhile. First came the musicians in their bright tunics and turbans and, behind them, in a snaking line and keeping time to the music, the dancing girls. A sigh of appreciation rose from the crowded streets and along the riverbanks and stone ghats, for the nautchnees' rare beauty lightened the drudgery of lives made ugly by poverty and ill health. The Maharajah cast his eye along the line, taking in the soft colours of the nautchnees' sequinned and diaphanous clothing; every graceful limb and glistening forehead; every kohl-lined and almond-shaped eye. Finally, his gaze fell upon a girl-woman towards the end of the line. The woman met his stare, which was forbidden, and he swore that there was an open invitation in those limpid eyes, that they were promising him something quite extraordinary. He wanted to drink in her every feature; the brown, honeyed glow of her skin, the delicate oval of her face, the shadow of a smile on her rose-petal lips.

The dancing began and the Maharajah could not take his eyes from her. She was costumed entirely in pale yellow and shone like the moon. When she again met his gaze, he felt more than mere desire. He was accustomed to beautiful women, indeed, he was even a little bored by them, for they were generally rather dull and seemed to think their fleshly charms were enough to sustain a man. It was perfectly clear that this creature had more than just grace of form and feature; she was spirited and she was intelligent, he was certain of it. Yet there was something else; something secretive about her, and it was this, above all else, that he found irresistible.

The purchase of nautchnees was a relatively straightforward process, and one which the Maharajah's secretary had executed many times.

The prince had often commissioned dancing girls to entertain him, but never before had he considered allowing one to join his harem. The ladies of the harem were Musalmani, which was not only a faith, but a privileged caste. He knew that bringing this girl into the harem would cause problems, but he did not care, and he knew that the Maharanee would not either, if she noticed at all. If only he had known, on that Diwali night, what else Lakshmi, goddess of fortune, was about to bestow on him.

⊹ 26 ⊹

A husband has a freehold estate in his wife's lands during the joint existence of himself and his wife, that is to say, he has absolute possession of them as long as they both live.

**From A Brief Summary in Plain Language of the Most Important
Laws Regarding Women, Barbara Bodichon, 1854**

On the evening of her coming of age, Sarah O'Reilly walked into the library of the Kensington house, dressed in breeches, boots and a waistcoat. She sat down at the table and lit a cheroot. 'I'm sorry to have missed luncheon, Martha. I've been out walking all day.' Sarah knew that Martha would have expected as much, considering the decision she had to make. Even Ellen, these days both Sarah's colleague and her consort on sallies around London, had unquestioningly let her walk out alone.

Sarah usually wore her breeches when she wanted to go unnoticed, for she could still pass as a young man if you didn't look too closely. With a hat pulled low over her mop of hair and her small, round spectacles, and given that she was still thin as a rail, she could easily be mistaken for a scholar. She carried an old satchel always, and the coat she wore with her breeches was long enough to cover any parts of her that might be questionably male. Nor had she the gait of a female, not having developed the careful, rigid movements dictated by the confines of a lady's costume.

The day had been unusual in many respects, for not only had Sarah passed it alone and brooding, but she had not given her work a passing thought. The letters she'd been handed earlier that day had set her thinking about how her life had evolved over the seven years since she had stood with Lily Korechnya, side by side at the attic window, on the day she had learnt Lily was to leave for India. Back then, Sarah had hoped that she might, in the future, become a little more like her erudite friend, and now, if only in a few small ways, she was. The changes in her had crept in slowly, and now here she was, a grown woman and a writer. She had even laid her breeches aside, at least for the purposes of everyday use, and if she was occasionally heard to be cursing, it was never in the company of anyone who might be offended by it.

The first significant change that had occurred, about a year after Lily died, had been the departure of the objectionable Mr Melville from the offices of the *Mercury*. He had gone to write for the cheap press and Sarah believed his talents were by far better suited to the tawdry penny magazines than to a daily newspaper. He alone was responsible for Sarah's fervent hope that impotence was caused, as the preachers warned, by wearing trousers that were too tight. Because his swift exit caused an immediate shortage of words, Septimus Harding had agreed to Sarah's proposal that she try her hand at the industry of the penny-a-liner. This was the very bottom of the heap in terms of reputable newspaper writing; penny-a-liners were not called grubbers for nothing. But Sarah had no intention of resorting to falsehood in order to have her copy in print, as she told Mr Harding right from the beginning.

As Sarah had always suspected, Ellen was an excellent consort to the profession, and threw herself heartily into foraging for news in London's dark corners. The Trub was as eager as a rat-catcher when it came to chasing after stories to sell to the paper. She had friends in the most peculiar places and knew the landlords and madams of establishments that would most certainly have Mam turning in her grave. Ellen had continued at school, reluctantly, until the previous year, when she'd announced that she had learnt everything she cared to learn and would just as soon be useful. Now she was happily occupied helping Sarah to earn a full-time wage, and was branching out into other areas of reconnoitring, since there were plenty of journalists at the *Mercury* who hadn't the time for leg work.

The other change in Sarah was, as Mr Harding had observed, purely cosmetic. As the grateful beneficiary of a scholarship provided by a patron of Barbara Bodichon, she had attended the Crystal Palace School of Art, Science and Literature. Here, she had struggled more with General Etiquette – an instruction on those decorous accomplishments that were considered a necessity for modern ladies – than with Latin, shorthand, science and French. General Etiquette provided rules of conduct for a lady in any given situation, and Sarah now knew that she must never wear gloves at table unless her hands were unfit to be seen or pick her teeth in company. Her use of profanities, vulgar terms and slang had been severely curtailed. Some of these rules she applied judiciously, but some she simply ignored, for they were impractical. She could not always avoid walking rapidly along the street, for instance, and ensuring the escort of a gentleman in the evening was ludicrous. She had made significant improvements to her vocabulary, and if she was proud of anything, it was this. She had come to see that there was an unexpected art to language, and that a pretty turn of phrase could prove more beneficial in certain circles than her former vernacular.

Sarah gazed into the beginnings of the fire and took a few drags on her cheroot. Normally, there was an easiness to the silence in the house, for all of its inhabitants were occupied enough with their own thoughts without the need for conversation, but Sarah knew that Martha was waiting for her to speak. She would be wanting to know if, after deliberating on the matter all day, Sarah had decided to carry out Lily's dying wish.

Sarah had received two gifts that morning, each, in its own way, plunging her back into the past. First there was the bank note that Martha had presented her with at breakfast. It was stamped with the bright scarlet seal of the Bank of England and inscribed with today's date: 18 March 1871. It was accompanied, and clarified, by an authoritative document, written by a British advocate in Benares. Together, the two documents confirmed that sufficient monies would, on Sarah O'Reilly's twenty-first birthday, be released to purchase her return passage to Bombay. The manner in which the money could be spent was not legally exclusive, should Miss O'Reilly choose to invest it in some other manner. The decision must be her own.

Over all the years since Lily's death, Martha had not spoken to Sarah of her bequest, nor had she spoken much of Lily, though the drawing room in Kensington was still maintained in the style that Lily had chosen for the Waterloo property. This, Sarah knew, was the mark of her love, for Martha Vesper was not one for bohemian and Oriental decor.

The very fact that Lily had taken the trouble to draft a Last Will and Testament, leaving the Kensington House and its contents jointly to

Martha Vesper, Sarah and Ellen, made it painfully clear that she had known her health was failing and she would not be returning to England. After Lily's demise, it had seemed entirely natural that Sarah and Ellen move into the old house with the housekeeper, and they were generously provided for, because the annuity left by Franz's Jewish family had been transferred to their household. The power of attorney had already been bestowed upon the housekeeper before Lily departed for India in 1864. That these endowments were even possible was a testament to Barbara Bodichon's dedicated campaigning towards the protection of women's property rights. In fact, as a widow, Lily had had more legal entitlement to both her own and her marital property than she had had as a wife.

It was clear to Sarah that Martha had been distinctly reluctant to hand over the banker's note that potentially heralded her departure for India; Martha had already lost Lily to that land, and was perhaps reluctant to trust it again. The housekeeper had been just as displeased by Sarah's second gift, this one from Barbara Bodichon, which was delivered by post shortly after breakfast. As Sarah unwrapped the thick brown paper, the housekeeper wrinkled her nose at the distinctly Oriental odour it exhaled. Sarah noticed Martha Vesper adjusting the pins that held her old-fashioned white linen cap in place and knew that she was having one of her feelings. The gift was a pretty camphor box, delicately inlaid with ivory, and containing two moderate-sized bundles of letters tied up with ribbon. The first bundle, which Sarah had spent the day reading, were letters written by Lily to Mrs Bodichon while she was still at Waterloo Street. The second bundle, which Sarah had not yet read, were from India.

In reading the chronicles of her beloved friend and her encounters with Lady Cynthia at Herbert House, Sarah had found herself puzzling again over the unknown fate of the nine diamonds that had once been the darlings of the London press. It seemed so long ago now, yet as she sat by her Mam's grave in the Ropemakers' Fields, reading and smoking, Sarah found herself thinking back to the case for it had never truly been resolved. The diamond jewel had never been found and neither Lark nor Gerard had ever really believed that Holy Joe was capable of killing his friend Vikram, let alone committing the other two murders. Sarah still saw Lark regularly in the editor's offices, and occasionally encountered Gerard when she had reason to call at the Westminster Police

Station. She knew that they had both found it difficult to let the case rest.

Now, as Martha Vesper silently left to prepare her a tray of supper, Sarah reflected upon the decision she had made and felt a little queasy. She resolved to book her passage directly, before she had occasion to change her mind, for the idea of sailing to an unknown land was already making her anxious. And just as soon as it was arranged, she must tell Septimus Harding, for otherwise he just might try to talk her out of it. But first she must tell Martha . . .

It was teatime as Sarah passed the most popular cocoa rooms and coffee houses between Pall Mall and Fleet Street on her way to Paternoster Row two days later. The establishments were full to the brim with young women in the new season's walking costumes, and dark brocade, velveteen and carmeline fancies lined every window like mannequins on display. Sarah herself was clad in a three-quarter length black cloak with an upturned collar and wide, loose sleeves. It was the next best thing to wearing breeches, since it made Sarah feel pleasingly inconspicuous.

The editor's office was its usual fusty confusion of pipe smoke, tea trays, stacks of old journals and new copy. Septimus Harding was nowhere to be seen. Instead, it was John Lark who greeted her, standing with his back to the grate and a faraway look on his face. Lark was in the throes of retiring but still visited his old friend to discuss the issues of the day. In the intervening years, the inspector had begun to turn his sharp mind to matters concerning the city's poor and destitute. More than once Sarah had seen him by the Thames, talking to bone grubbers and rag gatherers, or paupers collecting cigar butts and scraps of coal.

'Good day, Miss O'Reilly. The editor is attending to the afternoon edition – a crisis of several columns in excess, I believe, and another of grammar.'

'Business as usual!' Sarah smiled.

'Indeed. And how is business with you?'

'I seem to be filling my days and my head with a parade of stories.'

'Yours is not a mind that takes easily to quietude. Like you, I find the need to be ever in motion,' Lark replied.

At this moment, Septimus Harding puffed in with a deep sigh of exasperation. 'Then come and work for me, John, and you shall be! Good day to you, Sarah.'

'And to you, sir. We were discussing the need for occupation. It brings me to a matter I must discuss with you.'

The editor sat down and lit his pipe, eyeing Sarah suspiciously. 'Something tells me you are going to rattle me. You have that devilish look about you!'

'I am to travel to India. I have today booked my passage.'

She now had their undivided attention. Both men had aged somewhat over the last years, and betrayed a slight slowness of movement if not of mind. Septimus Harding had less hair, though what remained still managed to froth uncontrollably, and his hands were as gnarled as old wood. Lark was pole thin with a brooding, deeply etched face, and his whiskers were mostly grey. His boots still gleamed magnificently.

'Well, well, well.' John Lark was nodding his head slowly. 'And will you visit the palace of the Maharajah of Benares?'

'That is my intention, if he will have me.'

'By strange coincidence Gerard and I were talking recently of Cynthia Herbert and the '64 murders. He is investigating an attack in Hatton Garden, close to the address that was once Finkelstein's. There is a certain amount of superstition, even at Scotland Yard, with regard to the matter, since there have been an unusual number of violent crimes committed close to the sites of the three murders over the years. It has become something of a ghost tale, if you like, and there are some officers who will no longer patrol the alleyway where the Indian was killed.'

'How interesting. And what do you think of it all?' Sarah was immediately alert.

'I think that you should talk to Detective Inspector Gerard; he knows more of the matter than I. He is also an ardent reader of your Metropolitan News column. I believe he is at the courts today, but you may find him at the Westminster station any other day of the week.'

As they talked, Sarah thought that the mention of Benares had caused Lark to think about Lily, for there was a sudden sadness about him. She wished that she could tell Lark just how much respect Lily had had for him, but it would be impossible without embarrassing him. She did not know what had passed between Lily Korechnya and John Lark, but was certain that their rapport had never progressed beyond friendship. Instead, she confided a matter that was close to her heart.

'It was Lily's wish that I go to Benares. I think perhaps that it will help me to put her memory to rest.'

Lark nodded, addressing the flames in the hearth. 'Then you must go. I wish that I had some means of saying farewell myself. I did write to Lily, though my last letter must have arrived after she became too ill to reply.' He sighed deeply. 'I have regrets ... but she is at peace, and so we must be happy for her.' With this, Lark threw his half-smoked cigarillo into the fire. 'Now, Miss O'Reilly, I am keeping you from your business, and I must attend to my own. I look forward to hearing of your travels.' They parted with a lingering handshake which was as close to a show of affection as their years of acquaintance would allow.

Sarah usually encountered Detective Inspector Gerard only in the course of her investigations for the *Mercury*. The City of London Police Station was a sombre red brick building, the interior of which was a confusion of young men uniformed in navy blue amid disorderly towers of papers. The detective inspector was attired in the type of suit and waistcoat that one might see any professional gentleman wearing. He had not long since been promoted, and it was a relatively new innovation that the detective force dress in plain clothes rather than the dark serge, black helmets and white gloves of the beat policeman.

'Why, good morning, Miss O'Reilly. I hope no ill wind from the streets of London brings you here?' Gerard had grown neatly into the framework of a man, and was large without being brawny. He was fair-haired, with pleasing features if rather intense hazel eyes.

'Not precisely, Inspector, though I wonder if I might have a few moments of your time just the same?'

'As many as you wish. Perhaps you would prefer to converse in my office?'

This surprised Sarah, for normally they would discuss the business at hand across the busy front desk. She followed him up a flight of stairs and down a gloomy corridor to a narrow room that overlooked the northern aspect of Westminster Abbey.

'How fortunate you are to have such a view!' Sarah went immediately to the window, and turned back in time to see Gerard smile at her enthusiasm.

'Yes. It helps me to think, I believe, and I know the shadows and patterns on the stonework rather intimately as a result.' He looked at her searchingly for a moment. 'Might I also take this opportunity to wish you well on your coming of age.'

Sarah was surprised that he had taken note of it. 'You are kind. Let me waste no more of your time, for I am here to satisfy my curiosity as much as anything. Is it true that there is something of a phantom in the making in Devil's Acre? Inspector Lark has suggested that the locations of the '64 murders see more criminal activity than is usual, and that the constables have become superstitious and will no longer patrol there after dark.'

'It is true, although I do not believe the supernatural has any hand in this matter. Hatton Garden is a well-heeled area and therefore attracts both burglary and petty thieves. And Devil's Acre and Temple Pier have long been the haunts of the criminally inclined.'

'That sounds to me like a tidy explanation,' Sarah commented.

'I am a detective, Miss O'Reilly. I am duty bound to provide explanations.' Gerard looked at her quizzically before he continued. 'Particularly to one such as yourself.'

'You may disregard my profession, for I am here purely as a matter of personal interest. Then, you have no further observation to make upon the events which led to an innocent man being hanged?'

Gerard regarded her intently for a moment. 'I cannot comment upon the uncanny or the spectral, but it is true that there were some strange inconsistencies about the Finkelstein case and, of course, the disappearing diamonds have always puzzled me greatly. Finkelstein's apprentice, young Davey, simply vanished, although that is not a difficult feat in a city such as London. But I will admit that it was an entirely baffling case.'

Detective Inspector Gerard walked the length of the room and contemplated the view from his window. 'I understand you are soon to undertake the journey to India yourself.' Sarah thought that he looked displeased.

'I am. You are very thorough in your investigations, Detective Inspector.' When Gerard continued to frown, Sarah felt her indignation rise. 'I am a great deal more boldhearted than I might appear, sir, and it is a journey that rests closest to my heart.'

Sarah felt foolish as she uttered these words. She was growing intolerant of the constant measuring of her abilities against her gender yet she knew that her anger with Gerard was unprovoked, and was merely a product of her own misgivings. She was both grateful for and irritated by the detective's understanding smile.

'Indeed, Miss O'Reilly. They say that you hold a malcontent with my gender.'

'You have heard this, sir?'

'You must know that you are acquiring a reputation as a bluestocking and a liberal? But I for one believe that women such as Mrs Bodichon are fortunate to have your advocacy, for it is beyond time that we admitted that the better half of man has long been done a deplorable injustice!'

They both laughed, and a lively discussion ensued. Sarah had not been aware of her reputation, though she should not have been surprised by it. Her writings, though technically reportage for the Metropolitan News column, were inclined to be sympathetic to impoverished women who turned to prostitution and crime, and she was occasionally recognised as she strode through the streets in her breeches, smoking tobacco. These old ways still came more naturally to her than lifting her skirts above the mud and minding her colloquial.

Before she left the station, Gerard took a small, brown paper parcel from a drawer in his desk and presented to Sarah her third coming-of-age gift. She unwrapped a pretty pocket book of fine quality embossed leather.

'I was going to send this by messenger, but you have spared me the trouble. I thought perhaps you could put it to use, for I am certain a bluestocking and liberal such as yourself has more to commit to paper than the daily afflictions of the Metropolitan area.'

Sarah opened the pocket book, unable to keep the small smile of pleasure from her face. On the inside page of thick, ivory parchment, Gerard had scribed a verse by Charlotte Brontë in trim copperplate: 'If thou be in a lonely place, if one hour's calm be thine, as Evening bends her placid face, o'er this sweet day's decline'. She was certain that the verse was unfinished, and determined that she would find and read it in its entirety before departing London. She had not expected such a thing as a gift from the detective inspector, and it had surprised and confused her, though the gentleman himself appeared to think it unremarkable.

Before they parted on the steps of the Westminster station, he asked – keeping his voice pointedly low – that she might consider making 'discreet enquiries' whilst visiting the palace of the Maharajah of Uttar Pradesh. He did not need to say that he suspected Mr Govinda knew more about the nine-diamond jewel than he had ever divulged to the police. Sarah assured him that she would do so, and agreed to call on him upon her return from the Orient. It seemed, Sarah thought, as she walked her customary route along the embankment, that the young detective inspector still had every intention of solving the mystery.

At the herring docks, Sarah saw a familiar figure sitting on the rickety wharf, swinging her stockinged legs and waiting for her. She should not have been surprised, for Ellen always seemed to know where her sister was. She had grown into a pretty, if slightly unkempt, maid of fifteen, and always managed to look fetchingly dishevelled, even in a clean dress and shawl. Ellen was still small and could easily pass for one several years her junior, and although she had eventually benefited from the education she had so reluctantly received, she showed no sign of enjoying the pursuits common to her age. She would as soon have a game of marbles with the newspaper boys at the *Mercury* as sit still in a drawing room doing needlework or reading.

'Hello Sarah!' Her small face lit up when she saw her sister, but Sarah could tell that she was anxious. 'You've got your ticket, haven't you? You're really truly going then?'

'Yes, really truly. But you mustn't fret, Trub, I'll be back in no time. Please don't make a fuss, you'll only make me sad.'

Ellen's expression made it clear that she wanted to beg Sarah not to go to India, but realised it would be in vain. Instead, she unfastened the sandalwood beads she always wore and solemnly handed them over.

'You must promise to wear them always. For protection.'

'All right, I promise,' Sarah said as Ellen helped her to fasten the beads about her neck.

As they approached Temple Pier, she noticed that Ellen was frequently looking over her shoulder, paying undue attention to the crates and barrels and baskets sitting by the water's edge.

'What's the matter, Elly? You getting the dithers?' Ellen gave a little shudder but smiled up at Sarah and shook her head.

'No, it's nothing. I only thought . . . it's nothing really.'

They walked on a little, but now Sarah sensed it too; the unnerving, if indistinct, feeling of being watched. She wondered if it was just that they were both thinking about the past because of her imminent departure for India, her voyage in Lily's footsteps. Perhaps this was why, all of a sudden, she felt the same creeping sensation of danger which had marked those dark days.

❖ 27 ❖

No gift have I of jewels or flowers,
my room is poor and bare,
but all the silver sea is ours
and all the scented air.

Adela Florence Corey

The deck of the *Ranee* was the perfect place for Sarah to continue her reading of Lily's letters from India. On her lap was the pretty camphor box which Mrs Bodichon had presented to her and she rested her hands lightly on the smooth wood, running her fingers across its elegant ivory inlay, her gaze fixed on the endless ocean. When the sea was indigo and sequinned it made Sarah whimsical; when it was glittering cold steel she felt chilled by its menace and by the thought that a boat on the sea, no matter how large, was little more than a piece of drifting wood. Today, the water was serene and timeless.

Sarah had now been at sea for weeks and she had already read Lily's account of her own sea voyage. She opened the lid of the box gently and removed a folded piece of linen parchment. The correspondence from Benares appeared to consist of one very long letter divided into several entries, just as the letter at sea had been. It felt almost as if Lily were sitting beside her.

This evening it is the festival of Gangaur; a celebration of the marriage of the god Shiva to the goddess Parvati. I am soon to dine with the Maharanee, a benevolent but reclusive figure who, I am certain, must have spies through-out the palace and indeed the city, for she is unerringly well-informed.

Today, the zenana was in a frenzy of preparation. First the merchants visited, though they are not permitted to see the women, only to speak with them from behind a silk screen, and hand through their daintiest gold anklets and bracelets, and exotic perfumes. When purchases had been made, it was time for the most elaborate bathing ritual I have yet witnessed. I watched as servants filled three silver bowls, each with a different oil for the face, the body and the hair. Four copper vessels were then filled with four different herbal waters, each more fragrant than the last. First, the ladies had their hair washed with a pungent green paste made from crushing freshly picked thali leaves, and then smoothed with coconut oil. Next the body was washed with a sponge made from some peculiar fibrous bark; first with a pale powder of chickpea gram, and then again with water that was a luminous red, coloured, I am told, with the bark of forty trees. The face was then washed with oil containing saffron to prevent the growth of facial hair. Lastly, the hair was dried over fragrant smoke from a pot filed with hot coals and dried herbs. I was invited to partake in this extraordinary bathing ceremony, but I am content with my Pears' and rose water.

I have largely managed to stay clear of the society of my fellow countrymen and women, though I expect this will become increasingly difficult. Only yesterday I encountered one of the Marys in the bazaar, and was invited to take tea at the mission, which was as tedious an occasion as you might imagine. The orphans, dressed in threadbare English breeches, were learning Bible stories and prayers, and seemed as bored as I with the society of the missionaries. However, I took the opportunity to enquire after a certain temple to the goddess Kali, thinking that this was an item of gossip that might interest the women. The temple has been under grave threat of destruction, this time not by Moghul invaders but by the British officers who control the Municipal Board. There are plans to erect a pumping station in that very location, to improve upon the primitive sewage system. The matter of sewage does indeed need addressing, but the idea of demolishing a centuries-old shrine is a clear violation of and insult to the Hindu faith. The British officials have not the imagination to foresee what might happen should they continue in their acquisition of this sacred site. Already there have been demonstrations by the devotees of Kali which have turned violent. The undertaking is to be paid for by an increase in the water tax of the local people. This, one of the Marys acquiesced, was a shame, since the temple is situated in a poor area, but they were entirely in agreement about the destruction of the 'heathen shrine' itself. I asked if any of them had in fact entered the temple, and was not surprised to learn that they had not, for they were clearly horrified by the 'lewd engravings' to be found upon the walls of many Hindu temples. This particular shrine is at least four hundred years old and rather infamous, its mistress being considered a most fright-

ening and foreboding figure. I have since undertaken to write a piece on Kali, the most exceptional of women, for the London Mercury. *I find that there is some dark poetry encrypted within this affair; the patriarchal British administration destroying an ancient shrine to the most potent of goddesses.*

Sarah looked up from the letter to consider this. She wondered if Lily had ever managed to finish the piece for the *Mercury*, and if so, where was it now? The other deck chairs were empty, as usual, though she half expected to see Jonathan Elliot, since this was their usual meeting place. Perhaps he, like her, was not disposed to attend the revelry in the dining saloon. It was a costume ball this evening, if memory served her correctly.

It had been three weeks since the *Ranee* stopped for a day in the port of Valetta to take on coal. Those female passengers who were not too ill from the Mediterranean crossing had revived their spirits on the Strada Reale. Here, in the port's most famous shopping district, were boutiques selling Japanese ceramics, silver filigree and coral, curiosities and luxury textiles that could not be found in London. The Maltese lace was particularly popular, since this was what Queen Victoria preferred for her collars and mantles.

It was in the shop of an antiquarian bookseller on the Strada Reale that Sarah had first encountered Mr Jonathan Elliot, whom she recognised as a fellow passenger. Mr Elliot was easily identifiable, being exceedingly tall and lean, with the stoop of one who is accustomed to lowering his head to fit beneath a doorway. They merely nodded to each other on this occasion and he continued to browse the shelves dedicated to Oriental philosophies. Sarah was hoping to find works by Aphra Behn. The seventeenth-century playwright had been one of Lily's exceptional women, the first English woman to have earned a living from writing, having taken up the pen as a result of being widowed and finding herself in debtor's prison.

Since her meeting with Detective Inspector Gerard, Sarah been thinking over his words to her: 'I am certain a bluestocking and liberal such as yourself has more to commit to paper than the daily afflictions of the Metropolitan area.' She had once hardly dared hope that she might be even a newspaper writer, let alone pen something that required her to put her words to any greater use. And if she could, what would she write of? In the evenings, having no interest in deck quoits, Sarah often lingered by herself in the ship's small library, a cosy, dimly lit saloon upholstered in dark red velveteen. Here she could sit for hours, dipping into novels in which young heroines survived pitiless relatives, bigamous husbands and scheming maids. The sensation novel, as it had lately been called, was the surest way to secure both a publisher and the attention of the new female reader. The latter seemed to have an insatiable appetite for heroines who overcame all obstacles to attain the respectability, the gentleman or the fortune that was their birthright. Was this what Sarah must write of?

One evening she had discovered a slim volume published by the Theosophical Society, hidden away between two of the novels by Mrs Gaskell. It described how ancient wisdoms had been revealed to Madame Helena Blavatsky by two dead Tibetan mahatmas. When Jonathan Elliot entered the library, Sarah was absorbed in the work, and did not notice him until he cleared his throat.

'I hope I am not intruding?'

Sarah jumped in surprise. 'Oh. You startled me. I was reading . . .'

'About reincarnation, no doubt,' said Mr Elliot dryly, arching one eyebrow as he registered the title of her book. 'I believe we have encountered each other once before. It seems that we both favour the company of books.'

'Then you know of Theosophy?'

'Theosophia means knowledge of the divine. I know little of the Theosophical Society, but that some of its teachings appear to be merely the logic of nature.'

'Such as?'

'Such as the laws of compassion and brotherhood. Blavatsky holds that these basic principles are metaphysical, though morality is arguably an inherent human quality.' Madame Blavatsky, Mr Elliot then informed her, was attempting to bring Theosophy to India, and was proving to be immensely unpopular with the British in Calcutta. Sarah listened intently, for a woman such as Helena Blavatsky was clearly spirited enough to be a subject for her writings. As their conversation progressed, she assessed the young man who, she was not surprised to discover, was an Oxford scholar, and coincidentally also bound for Benares. Mr Elliot was about to undertake his third year at the Benares Hindu

University, where he was studying Sanskrit. He was pale and sombre, with grey eyes that hinted at the agility of his intelligence. His speech was cultivated – rather too highly, Sarah thought – and there was much about Mr Elliot which, on land, might have repelled her. At sea, however, the company of a scholar was nothing less than a blessing. She had no doubt that he too would not have dreamed of keeping company with one such as herself under normal circumstances.

The *Ranee* was little more than a confinement of all that Sarah and Ellen strived to avoid in London, though the ship's society was far more irritating for being inescapable. It seemed that the British community in India was small enough that many of the other passengers were already acquaintances, and even spoke to each other in a brand of Anglo-Indian which separated them from the uninitiated. Mr Elliot had become not only her unlikely travelling companion, but also an intermediary, explaining that a griffin (newcomer to India) such as herself was known as a *feringhi*, a foreigner, to the Indian. *Baba-logues* were the British children who ran from deck to deck chasing the ship's cat, and the ladies who sat wilting under pretty parasols, drinking endless cups of China tea, were *bebees*.

Sarah was aware that she had already stirred the disapproval of the bebees, not just through spending so much time alone in the company of a gentleman but – perhaps even worse – by taking little measure to restrain her boyish appearance. However, as the temperatures soared, her habitual costume became increasingly uncomfortable. The air grew as heavy with heat and moisture as the steam in a bathing house, and Sarah's clothing and hair clung to her and made her skin prickle. So, when the *Ranee* had docked in Port Said the week before, Sarah had taken the advice of her companion and bought some muslin at the bazaar. As she could find nothing plain enough for her taste, she was forced to buy a white cloth with a pretty woven pattern, which a local tailor had sewn into a loose fitting gown. This evening she was wearing it for the first time. She felt like an impostor, and Mr Elliot's observation when he suddenly appeared on the port deck confirmed it: 'I say, you look like Napoleon's Josephine.' She had also pinned her hair into an untidy chignon to cool her neck and shoulders, and her critical inspection of the looking glass had come as something of a shock. She looked feminine.

'It is the first time I have been ahead of the fashions then, or fashionable at all for that matter!' Sarah smiled.

'Your knowledge of worldly affairs continues to astonish me, Miss O'Reilly. You will thank me for advising you on such a personal matter as your costume when the heat becomes unbearable.'

'It is already unbearable, surely?' said Sarah, fanning herself with Madame Blavatsky. Mr Elliot was looking at her with an expression she did not recognise.

'Did I say something curious? You look puzzled.'

'Puzzled? Oh, no. I am just jolly unaccustomed to you looking ... Forgive me. Ah, I was telling you about the conventions of the memsahib last we met. Shall I continue?'

'With your permission, Mr Elliot, I should like to ask you a question regarding Hindu superstition. If, for instance, one were to wear a diamond as a charm, would the Hindu gods behave any differently?'

Mr Elliot looked surprised by this sudden deviation, but was too well mannered to remark on the fact. 'You are quite right, Miss O'Reilly. The diamond is a sacred and potentially dangerous stone in India. Have you not heard of Koh-i-noor?'

Sarah shook her head.

'It is believed that Koh-i-noor was given as a reward to a great king by the sun god Surya. It was stolen by the East India Company and presented to Queen Victoria. Some would say that the untimely death of Prince Albert was brought upon the royal family by Koh-i-noor.'

Sarah was silent for a moment, and resisted rubbing the gooseflesh that had appeared on her arm. 'I had not expected you to be super-stitious, Mr Elliot. It is only a stone after all!'

'There are many such stories. There was another famous diamond brought to Europe from India, by the French explorer Tavernier. It was violet blue and famed for its exceptional size and beauty, and some said Tavernier had stolen it from the eye of a statue of another god; Ram Sita. It was bought and worn by Louis XIV, who died wretchedly of smallpox. The next to wear it was Marie Antoinette who was guillotined. Disaster pursued whosoever possessed the stone. In Hindu lore, all gemstones have religious significance.'

'And do you think, that if I were to try to discover what had become of a ... lost diamond ... that something terrible might happen to me?'

Sarah could not help the note of disbelief that had crept into her voice.

Mr Elliot shrugged and stared out across the endless inky waves. 'Perhaps only if you were to try to possess it.'

'I think, sir, that you have become affected by the heat.'

'No, I am affected by the East, Miss O'Reilly.'

For the first time, Sarah glimpsed what lay beneath the veneer of respectability and stuffy intellect. She realised what it was that attracted the likes of Jonathan Elliot to India: an escape from the mundane.

When she was alone in her cabin that evening, Sarah opened the camphor box and shuffled through the letters. She was savouring each new entry slowly, for she did not want Lily's voice to be silenced, nor the precious closeness that she felt whilst she read them to end. She found what she was looking for and reread a particular passage:

After a short silence, Govinda quietly informed me that the charm was an 'astrological talisman' and that in its unorthodox composition; the jewel was potentially a danger to anyone who might seek to use it. I asked him to explain this to me, since I am quite baffled by the idea that a particular gemstone (or nine) could affect the very fibre of existence. All Govinda would tell me was that Lady Herbert believed that by being in possession of the charm she might make contact with the spirit world, and specifically with her dead husband.

Sarah gazed for a time at the grain of the dark mahogany panelling above the china wash bowl in her cabin. She was reminded of Inspector Gerard and the patterns and shadows in the stonework that helped him to think. She must certainly speak with Govinda, she decided, since he seemed to be present whenever the diamonds were mentioned and his belief in the power of the diamond charm was marked. Would he still feel like this, she wondered, or even remember after so many years?

When Sarah emerged from her cabin on to the deck the next morning, the *Ranee* was in sight of land. Throughout the morning the shadow on the horizon acquired form until a ribbon of white sand and then a verge of palm fronds were distinguishable. She could not take her eyes from the coastline. Ever since India had ceased to be a place of distant imagination, she had felt the resurgence of misgivings that she had thus far successfully ignored. Her fear was nameless; an intangible uncertainty that made her ache with longing for the familiar. She felt foolish, for had she not faced worse foes than a foreign land?

After the *Ranee* had docked, Sarah stepped into the commotion of the Custom House wharf with Mr Elliot at her elbow. Dressed in a suit of pale linen and a panama hat, and towering above the small, fine-boned Indians, he politely but firmly refused the help of the omnipresent coolies, side-stepped vendors touting pails filled with unidentifiable, curried foods, and disregarded even the most wretched of beggars. They passed a mountain of cotton bales awaiting exportation, and weaved their way through a crowd attired in an astonishing array of costumes. There were walnut-skinned sepoys in the olive green and crimson of the British army and swarthy, bearded men in conical turbans and voluminous turkish trousers; Jews in sweeping robes, memsahibs in white carrying lace parasols and Chinamen in short broad trousers with trailing moustaches and ponytails. Sarah was reminded of how she had felt when she and Ellen had arrived in London for the first time.

Sarah had agreed, gratefully, before leaving the sanctuary of the *Ranee*, to be accompanied by Mr Elliot both to a bungalow he knew of and then on the train journey to Benares.

'It is altogether a matter of appearing to have purpose, even if one has not,' Mr Elliot remarked as he helped Sarah into one of the brightly painted palanquins carried by four sinewed boys. She was appalled that they were to be transported in such a way, and said so. Jonathan Elliot nodded. 'But you must remember that it is a livelihood, and although they, the hummals, look frail, they are strong as oxen and might carry double our weight with ease.'

The bungalow was close to the central railway station, from whence they would depart for the holy city in two days' time. Sarah closed the palanquin's silken curtains against the jostling band of bare-chested young men shouting 'I master's servant! – I get master everything!' When she looked at her companion he was watching her with a concern she found mildly annoying. 'It can be a little overwhelming at first,' he said sympathetically. In response she straightened her back and peered back through the curtains, determined to appear undaunted. They travelled a distance along the esplanade and Sarah spied the sparkling bay and several British boating parties, looking for all the world as though they were on the Serpentine on a Sunday afternoon. Through the curtains on the other side she glimpsed what appeared to be a horse bazaar, for a great number of small Arab steeds as well as English coach horses were tethered in a square. They passed as many lofty chariots as ragged pedlars, for everywhere there seemed to be the same incongruous clash of poverty and wealth; of Oriental and Classical architecture; of the colonists in prim, colourless apparel and natives in brilliant, flowing robes.

Arriving at the bungalow, Sarah found her room adequate, if bare. There was a screen of fragrant grass called khus khus across the window which was kept wet to cool the air. Through this, she could hear and smell the city. The verandah was separated from the dusty road by a row of pomegranate trees and tuberose, the latter a heavily perfumed white flower, not unlike a lily. The air was choked with dust and the smell of fried oil, curry and overripe fruit, and there was constant shouting – a noisy riot of Chai tea sellers, merchants carrying vessels on their heads, children carousing around British soldiers, and chanting Parsee priests clad entirely in white. The noise which awed her most, amidst the din and clatter of a surprisingly industrialised city, was the wailing of the Mohammedans praying to their god.

That evening Sarah settled in to read Emma Roberts, who had travelled to India almost forty years earlier and become the editor of the *Oriental Observer*. And when she tired of Emma Roberts' descriptions of mosques and cupolas glittering in the sun, and the blank pages of her new pocketbook stared accusingly, she undid the latch on the camphor box which contained her most cherished of possessions.

⁕ 28 ⁕

When one knows the solitude of silence and feels the joy of quietness, one is then free from fear.

Buddha

There was measureless time for reflection on the last leg of the long journey to Benares. The days passed slowly as the train from Bombay crossed northern India and Sarah's gaze was often fixed upon the scenery beyond the carriage window: water beasts with long horns in mangrove swamps; women in bright saris walking through flaxen fields of grain. Occasionally she read a little more from Emma Roberts' writings, or a small part of a letter, still rationing her reading of them. It made Sarah feel strangely lonely, knowing that she was approaching the destination from which Lily had never returned. She hoped that she might learn a little more about the circumstances of her death, since all the official documentation had been sent to Lily's parents, Dr and Mrs Hall, whom Sarah had never met. Martha said that Lily's mother had called a few times since her death, but had clearly never acknowledged the bond between mistress and housekeeper. Perhaps the fact that Lily had given Martha power of attorney, not to mention the fact that their daughter had not done the respectable thing and returned home after her husband's death, was the final outrage.

The vividness of Lily's letter writing was beginning to build a picture for Sarah of what to expect when she arrived at the palace. Already she found India hypnotic. It flickered by in an endless, fleeting gallery of sun-blanched landscapes: a short train of camels, the burning amber sun sinking behind them; a coconut plantation and a wild pig with curved tusks, a crow perched on its back; a group of women sitting under a tree, weaving rushes together and gossiping. As they approached Benares, Sarah took another page from the camphor box:

186

Here there is no shame in walking barefoot, and the soles of my feet are delightfully cool against the smooth stone. Should I desire it, a servant would fan me with a large paddle made from rushes, but I have thus far declined this service, for I should feel too much like one of the English ladies I have seen in the bazaar. These women complain incessantly of the heat and the clamour, and refuse to take a step without a servant at each elbow.

I have now spent some weeks as a guest of the Maharajah of Benares, but I have yet to meet my host. At first I considered this peculiar, until I learned that the Prince was away in the northern mountains with his entourage, inspecting his tea and indigo plantations, and hunting tigers. He has been back for several days now, and I have still not had an audience, although I did have the pleasure of witnessing his return and it was a sight I shall never forget.

Firstly the household was notified of the event by the clashing of an enormous brass cymbal that reverberated throughout the many chambers of the palace. Immediately the entire zenana was in a frenzy, with women running hither and thither, combing and oiling hair, applying black kohl to their eyes, and dressing themselves and their children in finery. The Musalmani women are not permitted to leave the zenana except by permission of the Maharajah, and then only under escort, but there is a roof garden from which one can view the road leading to the palace gates. From here we watched a procession of more than a dozen elephants. The Maharajah's elephant was the greatest of all, and was bedecked with glittering harnesses and plumes. The Prince sat beneath a red silk umbrella and I could not see his features clearly from the distance, but by his bearing he may not be as elderly as I had imagined.

I have learnt more of the unusual young woman Sarasvati through passing long hours in the company of the inhabitants of the zenana. Being a village girl and also exceptionally beautiful, she is not popular amongst the Musalmani ladies of the harem, who are known as purdah nashin, *or* ranees. *These women pass their lives cloistered but, like the Maharanee, they have informants who apprise them of all that passes beyond their walls. My dear Barbara, there is intrigue and scandal such as you cannot imagine! The Maharanee herself is a figure of a ridicule, although this is most certainly the product of envy.*

I have noted that the Prince's number-one wife and his favoured concubine have become friends. Sarasvati is Hindu and she does not speak Urdu, the courtly language. I was thus surprised by her grasp of English, and have learnt that its use has spread quickly in any part of India that has seen envoys of the East India Company. As her village is famed for its alluvial diamonds, there has naturally been European interest in its commerce. Sarasvati is a creature more lovely than you can imagine, her eyes large and dark and elongated, her forehead high, and her nose delicately chiselled as though by a sculptor's hand. Her figure is part-girl, part-woman; long limbed and graceful. Unlike the Musalmani women, it seems that she may do as she pleases, even though she was a nautchnee, a dancing girl, before she became a concubine. She has told me that she still dances for the Prince, when he commands it.

But now I must rest my quill and my head, dear Barbara, for I am lately overcome with an unaccountable fatigue, as though the strength is slowly seeping from my bones. It can be no more than the heat, to which I am not yet accustomed. I shall write more anon.

Early in the evening of the sixth day, the train reached the outskirts of Benares – a stark contrast to the rural idyll of Uttar Pradesh. The bleak poverty of the outer slums was barely softened by the fading sky. Ragged children played by the railway tracks, and sat wide-eyed as the train passed, just as Sarah did, watching them through the Venetian shutters of the dining carriage. She suddenly felt immensely wealthy, for the carriages of the train were broad and comfortable, and her own compartment was thrice as large as her cabin on board the *Ranee*, with a dressing room, a wash basin and a small table.

There was a great deal that remained unknown about her destination, in spite of Lily's letters, and Sarah was thankful that Mr Elliot would soon join her here in the dining carriage, as had become their custom at meal times. Although he was unerringly genteel, Sarah had grown to anticipate their meetings more eagerly as the days passed. She was certain, however, that it was his exceptional knowledge she craved rather than the attentions of a gentleman. She had no wish to be courted, for she had had the experience twice already and both interludes had come to a regretful end. She had concluded that she simply wasn't the type for sweethearting in a tea garden, and certainly not for marrying.

When Jonathan Elliot arrived, it was with his usual grace and self-assurance. He made a small bow to Sarah before being seated opposite her. He possessed an improbable elegance for one of such proportions, and was always dressed in light-coloured linen, which he somehow managed to keep relatively free from creases and dust. Her curiosity as insatiable as ever, Sarah asked him to tell her what he knew of this holy city that seemed so stricken by overcrowding and poverty.

'According to Emma Roberts, Benares is the seat of Hindu superstition. Is it true, Mr Elliot?'

He nodded sagely. 'The city is expanding at a most alarming rate because the Hindus believe that if they die in the sacred city of Benares, then they will be freed from the endless cycle of reincarnation. But according to the American author Mark Twain, it is a place inhabited by the ghosts of a complex history. In fact, he called it "the Oxford of India" and I am inclined to agree. Benares was first settled in the second century by the Aryan peoples, and was, by the seventh century, famed for its ivory, gemstones and woven silks. You see, Miss O'Reilly, the Northern Road and the Ganges River were the two busiest trade routes in the whole of India, and they crossed in Benares, which therefore prospered enormously.'

As Sarah listened to Mr Elliot's history lesson, her eyes locked on to a pile of rubble where some dark-eyed urchins were rag picking, just as Holy Joe and Ellen had once done. For a moment she was back in Devil's Acre and her heart ached at the memory of the injustice that had sent poor Joe to the gallows.

The train began to slow, and Sarah expected that they would soon encounter mayhem akin to that of Bombay's central railway station. There, the coolies had seemed even more determined than those at the port, and loitered in groups eagerly awaiting the first traveller whose carpet bag or portmanteau might need carrying. Curiously, amidst all of this, Sarah had begun to understand Lily's love affair with India. Not for its pandemonium, nor its heartbreaking poverty, but for an altogether less conspicuous quality she had yet to identify.

As their carriage arrived beneath the awning of Benares central railway station, Sarah wondered if the telegraph she had dispatched on her arrival in India had reached the palace. Having seen the fracas in the telegraph office in Bombay, from where she had also sent word to Ellen of her safe arrival, she was concerned. Mr Elliot had since informed her that all of the palaces were situated on the River Ganges.

'But how many palaces are there?' Sarah asked, having presumed there would be only one.

'All the Maharajahs of India hold court in Benares during India's holy festivals, and each has a palace. But the palace of the Maharajah of Kashi is the most magnificent. You will see.'

'And what is Kashi?'

'Kashi means "city of light". It is another name for Benares, as is Varanasi.'

They escaped the station unscathed, except for the few rupees demanded by the porter before he would release their luggage. Although Mr Elliot was returning to bachelors' rooms somewhere near the university, he insisted on accompanying her to the palace. In spite of his thinly veiled confidence in his own superiority, Sarah suddenly felt a clammy dread at the thought of their imminent parting. A band of scrawny children tugged at his coat tails and at Sarah's muslin dress, which was rather the worse for wear after the long journey.

'Ignore them,' he said, and beckoned to a hummal to load their trunks on to the back of a palanquin.

It seemed that the entire roadside was a colourful market selling everything from bananas and mangoes to a freshly slaughtered sheep, its blood soaking into the sandy earth. The low, darkened doorway of a temple caught Sarah's eye, and as she passed, she was almost overcome by the pungent smoke drifting from it that mingled with the smells of cow dung and rotting vegetables. Sandalwood. She would know the smell anywhere and touched the beads at her neck which Ellen had given to her for protection, presumably against harmful spirits. Yet sandalwood was also the scent that had accompanied the appearance of Madame Blavatsky's dead Tibetan mahatmas. Perhaps it was associated with the deceased? As though in answer to her ponderings, a bier covered in red and gold cloth passed by, carried by chanting, white-robed mourners. They were on their way to the river, Mr Elliot explained, to one of the stone platforms called *ghauts*, where the body would be cremated.

Eventually, the crowds thinned as the leviathan stone archway of the entrance to the palace loomed closer, its burnished minarets radiant even in the twilight. Sarah's nervousness returned. She knew almost nothing of her hosts, although a telegraph from the prince's secretary, which had arrived just before she left London, had confirmed that they were expecting her. Everything that she had thus far read about the palace and its inhabitants seemed like a fairy story. She did not even know for certain if Govinda was still in the employ of the prince. She expelled a shaky breath as the sepoy guard at the gate stood aside and let them pass, then drew in another as the palanquin came to a standstill at the foot of some wide marble steps.

'I need not say that I hope you will be comfortable here, Miss O'Reilly,' Mr Elliot said as he shook her hand and cast a meaningful glance at her accommodation, 'but I do wish you well. Should you need a companion during your stay, there is a guest house at the central bazaar called Vaishya, with a small, terrace restaurant where I often take my breakfast and pass the morning reading.'

'I shall remember. Thank you for your kindness, Mr Elliot, I'm not certain that I would have survived the journey without you!'

'I am quite convinced that you would have, Miss O'Reilly, for you have the valour of a Celt.' He lifted his panama hat and bowed, then climbed back into the palanquin.

Sarah turned round and looked at the immense palace of glowing red granite and overwrought masonry, with balconies that appeared to be made of filigree ivory. The steps led to an immense door that was carved with creatures such as she had never before seen: a man with an elephant's head and another with the body of a monkey; a bejewelled woman with eight arms astride a tiger. The hummals reached the top of the steps with her portmanteau as the doors opened silently.

'Welcome, Miss Sarah,' said a deep voice from the shadows, and a moment later a figure in a white tunic and turban stepped forward and bowed. This was the *khansamah*, the head servant. 'I am honoured to meet a friend of Memsahib Lily. Please proceed to follow me this way, and I will show you.' Exactly what she was to be shown, Sarah did not know, but it seemed to her that she had entered the pages of a Persian tale as they passed endless corridors painted with mythical scenes and chambers where tigers' heads yawned down at her and ancient weaponry lined the walls. Even the silver door latches were engraved. Finally they stopped at one of the myriad delicately inlaid doors. Sarah felt acutely conscious of the condition of her travelling costume, but the Khansamah did not seem to notice.

'Memsahib Lily's rooms,' he said, bowing and stepping aside to allow her to enter. 'The Maharajah instructed that these rooms should preserve her memory, so we do not usually accommodate guests here.'

The room was vast, its tiled floor covered in a brightly woven rug that was almost the size of a tennis court. In the middle of the farthest wall was a door carved with oriental flowers, and to the left of it a low bed swathed in fine mosquito netting. On the wall above the bed was a hanging made from many bright squares of embroidered cloth and sewn with tiny mirrors. An ebony desk sat to one side of the room and on the other, an ornamental jade table. Long, shuttered doors opened on to a balcony, beyond which Sarah could distinguish the dark glint of the river Ganges.

It was night-time now and a gentle breeze cooled Sarah as she stood surveying the room that had once been Lily's. Was it possible that the faintest scent of rose water and Pears' soap lingered on the air after seven years? Surely not, yet something of Lily Korechnya remained in this room. With a shudder, Sarah suddenly felt certain that this was where Lily had died. It was an affecting reminder that she still did not know, after all this time, exactly what had caused the death of the woman who had become her dearest friend. From what Septimus Harding had managed to ascertain from a correspondent in Benares, Lily's health had weakened steadily during her stay at the palace, and she had not wished to travel to any other part of India. It had been Lily's express wish that her remains not be returned to England; in fact, she had requested a traditional Hindu funeral, though Sarah had no idea what this entailed. She presumed that Lily's belongings had either been returned to her parents, or remained here in Benares.

Sarah took the camphor box from her carpet bag and sat on the edge of the low, expansive bed. By travelling here she had hoped in some way to lay Lily's ghost to rest, for she needed to understand what it was that she had so loved about the city. Perhaps it was a place where Sarah also might find the inner quietude to muse. It seemed fitting, sitting in this room, to end the day with some of Lily's words.

Yesterday morning I was called to attend the Maharajah. I dressed with care and more modesty than usual, draping a fine muslin shawl over my short-sleeved bodice. I have had several new costumes sewn by a tailor at a place called Marnikarnika – less structured gowns that are more practical in this climate. Still, my dress is a source of some amusement to the servants as they are intrigued by the foreign items of clothing, and seem amazed that there is so much worn beneath the costume of an English lady.

I was escorted to the western wing of the palace, to a room that I had never seen before. The walls of this long, narrow chamber were covered almost entirely with paintings large and small. I was most taken with the gallery, for I had not expected to see so many works by renowned artists. I recognised Ingres and Delacroix, and the eerily lit landscapes of Caspar Friedrich, the German landscape painter Franz so admired. I had with me three of my husband's paintings, thinking that I would not show all at once, but gauge by the Maharajah's response if his interest was genuine.

I was therefore surprised when I was met by Govinda, and not the Maharajah after all. I have seen little of my travelling companion since my arrival in the palace, though occasionally we have encountered each other in the summer house, a tranquil place in the grounds where we both find solace. Govinda apologised on behalf of the prince, who he said had been delayed. He asked me then if I might show him the canvases, explaining that he often advises the Maharajah on purchases for his private collection. Some of Franz's canvases he has viewed already, for I took several with me to Herbert House. I watched his face as I unfurled each of the three. He nodded appreciatively but said nothing, yet I have come to read the nature of his silences, and could tell that he saw the hand of a true artist in Franz's brushstrokes. At his bidding, I had a servant fetch the other canvases that were stored in a drawer in my portmanteau.

When it came to the painting of the woman with a circlet of lilies in her hair, I felt a pang, for it was once my favourite. Now it only makes me sad, for I see in her eyes, so like mine, the love which was also mine. I wondered if Govinda sensed something in my mood, or has noted my lethargy, for he enquired after my strength, and my health in general. Then, quite without warning, he looked at me strangely and informed me in his quiet way that he was to leave the employ of the Maharajah and return to his village in the Himalayan kingdom of Kashmir. I did not ask why, as I have learned that Govinda will impart only what he wishes to. Instead, I asked that he say *goodbye before he leaves, for though I have passed little time in his presence, his company has been my most constant since I departed England.*

I walked the length of the gallery, and when I returned the Maharajah had arrived and stood talking quietly with Govinda. The Prince was flanked by two large Arabs and an orange-robed Sadhu. But for his sweeping and unashamed inspection of my shape, I might have higher regard for his character, though he was unerringly charming and enquired after my life in London. As I had imagined on the occasion that I watched his arrival home, he is not an old man; perhaps two and forty, though it is difficult to guess the age of the people of India, for their skin is smooth and their limbs supple and graceful even in old age. I attribute this to the practice of a discipline which they call yoga, an exercise not only of the body but also of the mind and spirit.

The Prince was delighted, he said, with all of Franz's paintings, and he clearly recognised my likeness in The Venus of Waterloo, *for he looked from it to me and seemed all the more pleased. He spoke highly of Cynthia Herbert, appearing genuinely regretful about her passing. I can only imagine that he has by now been informed of the fate of the jewel. The subject makes me uneasy, Barbara, for I cannot help but believe that her death and the murders in London were somehow connected to it, though perhaps I am a fool for giving any credence to what the papers print.*

I became aware that the Maharajah was again boldly examining my form, as though I had invited his gaze by not covering every inch of flesh as do the ladies of his harem. I did not flinch, but the uncomfortable silence gave me a moment to dwell upon the opulence of his own figure, for his fingers, cummerbund and turban were excessively bejewelled. The prince surprised me then by noticing my own simple pendant. He said it was a most unusual design, and asked if he might examine it. I undid the clasp reluctantly, for although it would have been impolite to refuse, I do not like to take it off. I explained that it was a tradition in England to wear the hair of the deceased as a memento of one's continuing affections. As I handed it to him, I smelt the sour odour of his breath, and was surprised, for drinking alcohol is unusual in Indians. I could not help but wonder if it was the loss of his precious diamonds that had driven him to take liquor in the morning.

Sarah folded the linen stationery carefully and replaced it in its box. She stepped on to the balcony, to the dusky odour of the river and a breath of jasmine, rustles and sighs from the darkened grounds below and moonlight on a glossy tree laden. When she returned to her room, she discovered that her trunk had been delivered along with a tray of food. It was clear that she would not meet her hosts this evening, Sarah decided, but she was grateful as she desired nothing more than to climb into the enormous bed. As she did so, she found herself wondering if Govinda had ever returned from the Himalayan kingdom of Kashmir.

⁙ 29 ⁙

The holy city of Benares stands upon the left bank of the Ganges. The confused masses of stone which crowd upon each other in this closely built city, sometimes present fronts so bare and lofty as to convey the idea of a prison or fortress. Others are interspersed with Gothic gateways, towers and arches, balconies, verandahs, battlements, mullioned windows, balustrades, turrets, cupolas and round and pointed domes, the fancies of all ages.

Emma Roberts

Sarah woke to the strain of Mohammedan wailing and the heady scent of oriental blossoms, each drifting in through the open balcony doors. As she gazed about the room, she imagined Lily sitting at the ebony desk by the shuttered doors, the old-fashioned quills she so liked to scribe with dusting the air as she wrote. A barefooted servant girl in a white sari entered silently with a tray, breaking her reverie. She smiled shyly, then retreated before Sarah could speak to her.

Her first outing, Sarah decided, must be to a tailor, for she would need more costumes like the white muslin in this soporific heat. The heavy, fragrant air was already cloying, and with the muslin currently unwearable, she had only her London shirts and waistcoats. She was reminded of being approached by one of the ladies from the Rational Dress Reform Movement some months earlier, who had hoped that Sarah might publish an account of their enterprise in the *Mercury*. Sarah had agreed to visit their exhibition rooms, even though she knew that Mr Harding was already wary of her bluestocking sympathies. She had taken Ellen with her, and here, rather than a display of practical and comfortable garments for the new woman, they had found an assortment which might have been cast offs from Drury Lane. Ellen had tried, unsuccessfully, to control her giggles when she saw the tartan skirts to the knee worn over narrow satin trousers, and a sleeveless

Ottoman coat paired with something which too closely resembled Amelia Bloomer's pantaloons.

After examining her bedraggled appearance in the glass in the dressing room, Sarah opened a wardrobe and was surprised to find an array of colourful gowns. These most certainly had been Lily's, Sarah realised with a pang. As she fingered the silken drapery, a honeyed voice made her start. 'Some of these were never worn by Memsahib Lily.'

Yet again, Sarah had failed to hear footsteps approaching, and when she turned she beheld a new, barefooted visitor. This was certainly not a servant though, for the woman was draped in a stunning sari of yellow and gold, and wore fine jewellery from ankle to forehead. She was also exceptionally beautiful.

'I am Sarasvati,' she announced grandiosely, and a memory stirred. Sarasvati was the Maharajah's favoured ranee. Sarah did not know if she was expected to curtsy or kiss one of her visitor's many Venetian gold rings, and she was acutely aware that she was not dressed. As she stood wondering, Sarasvati rifled unceremoniously through the gowns, choosing three or four. They were made of delicately patterned silk as light as lawn cotton and not unlike the white muslin in style, but here the similarity ended, for the silk shimmered and was trimmed with georgette ribbon and tiny pearl beads.

'These gowns were never worn. They will suit you,' Sarasvati stated.

'Oh, I could not wear such pretty things,' Sarah said, taking an involuntary step backwards. Sarasvati laughed prettily, like a child, making Sarah laugh also at her own tomboyish ways.

'They will not bite! Come.' She took Sarah's hand, pulling her back into the bed chamber, and threw her armful of whispering silks on to the bed.

Sarasvati then stood back and looked hard at Sarah, taking in the disorderly copper curls, her milk-white skin and the reed-like form beneath the crumpled calico. Sarah returned her gaze. Sarasvati was close to her own age, she thought, her smooth olive skin aglow with youthful cupidity. She was of a similar build, also, though more womanly in shape than Sarah. Her ankles and wrists were fine and both were accentuated by multitudes of gold bracelets. She was as dark as Sarah was pale, her almond-shaped eyes fringed with thick, black lashes, and between them, on her forehead, was a tear-shaped jewel.

'I think this one,' said Sarasvati, when her inspection was complete. She held one of the gowns against Sarah. It was fern green with bands of embroidered, ivory-coloured ribbon beneath the bust. As Sarah dressed, Sarasvati sat on the bed watching. 'You are just as Memsahib Lily described.'

'Oh?'

'She told me that you do not like to appear womanly. And that you are clever with words, like she. Now tell me what she said about me, for I know that she wrote to you.'

Sarah had not expected this and at first could think of nothing to say. More than anything she wanted to ask Sarasvati about what had happened to Lily, but realised she must first allow this exotic creature to preen. The woman before her was certainly nothing like the shy village girl Sarah had imagined from the letters.

'She said that you are very beautiful ... and that your English is exceptional.'

Sarasvati shrugged. 'The Maharanee had an English teacher for some time, and I asked to have lessons with her because the Maharajah likes to practise his English. The Maharanee likes the English words too because she says the language is well suited to storytelling. She loves telling stories. I think she wishes she were a writer, like you. What else did Memsahib Lily say?'

Sarah thought hard. 'That you ... are a distinguished dancer. Do you still dance?'

'I dance only when the Maharajah is bored. He has many women.'

'But they cannot all be as lovely as you!'

'No,' Sarasvati agreed, and looked pleased. Flattery was clearly the way to her heart. 'The other ranees are jealous, of course. Now, you will come with me today and I will show you Varanasi. I shall take you to the places where Memsahib Lily liked to go.'

Sarasvati was obviously accustomed to getting her own way, and since Sarah was aching to see the Gothic gateways, battlements and balustrades that Emma Roberts had described, she agreed. Her only request was that they visit the tailor in Marnikarnika, as she remembered that this was where Lily had had her costumes sewn.

Let me help you,' Sarasvati said as she saw Sarah struggling with the many tiny buttons that fastened the back of the bodice. As she came to the buttons that fastened at the neck, Sarah heard Sarasvati draw in her breath, and a moment later felt her touching Ellen's sandalwood beads.

'Where did this necklace come from?'

'From my sister. The beads were given to her when she was young.'

'It is unusual', Sarasvati said finally, 'there can not be many like it.'

'Yes, the carving of each tiny bead to resemble a rose is . . .'

'These are not roses, Miss Sarah, they are lotus flowers.'

Sarasvati said nothing more about the beads, but Sarah could tell that she was somehow displeased by them.

After she had breakfasted on papaya and mango in a fragrant syrup, Sarah was ready to accompany Sarasvati into the deepening morning haze. The streets of Benares steamed, the pre-monsoon humidity making even the light silk cling to her limbs. The palanquin in which she and Sarasvati were borne was quite unlike those the hummals carried, being much larger and made from ivory worked with an intricacy Sarah had only seen before in French lace. It was also flanked by half a dozen flat-turbaned Arabs, with long, curved swords hanging from their broad cummerbunds. Inside, it was upholstered in pink and yellow satin, with large velvet cushions and fine gauze curtains which allowed one to see out, but not in.

Through the gauze, Sarah had a fine view of the activity along the banks of the Ganges. The river was clearly the life blood of Benares, for here there were boatmen and bathers, the women fully clothed, their lime-green and cherry-pink saris floating on the currents of inky water; Sadhus with painted faces sitting cross-legged in their orange robes outside small temples; dobhi wallahs in loin cloths scrubbing their laundry against rocks by the water's edge; and children as young as five or six walking along the muddy banks with pots of chai, baskets of orange marigolds and small candles, calling to boatmen to row closer so that they might sell their wares to the passengers. They passed a young man with a basket of wooden flutes who was playing one of his instruments, but its clear note was soon drowned by a funeral procession, not unlike the one Sarah had witnessed the day before. The chant was the same: *Rama nama satya hai*. She asked Sarasvati what it meant.

'It means God's name is truth. For a Hindu, dying in Benares means taking the form of a god.'

'But why must it be in Benares?'

'It is here that creation began, of course!' Sarasvati said this as though everyone must know it, as if there could be no other belief. But then how would she, a village girl who had come to live in a palace, know that there were as many stories about creation as there were jewels in the palace vaults?

'It is here, within the holy city, that all of the gods and goddesses dwell. All but Yama,' Sarasrati continued.

'Who is Yama?' Again, Sarasvati looked surprised at Sarah's question.

'Yama is the god of death, and is not permitted to enter the city. That's why the Hindu people come here to die, because Yama cannot reach them, and so their journey between this world and the far shore is protected.'

'And is the far shore somewhere that you have seen?'

Sarasvati's laughter was not as pretty as it had been earlier, Sarah thought, and it seemed to contain an edge of something akin to despair. 'I have only seen it through a field of poppies.'

'Then you have no fear of death?'

'What is there to fear? In death I will be a goddess and will ride upon a great swan. The goddess Sarasvati is the consort of Brahma, king of the gods. I have nothing to fear, for the gods favour me.'

The petulance of the goddess-in-waiting entertained Sarah, but she felt it was time for a change of subject.

'When Lily first came to Benares she was accompanied by a man, Govinda. Is he still present at the palace?' She had wanted this remark to seem indifferent, but perhaps Sarasvati detected something else, because the look she returned was sharp. For the first time, Sarah saw the glint of her intelligence.

'He went long ago. To the mountains.'

'Did he ever return?'

Sarasvati shrugged, but then she turned and smiled coquettishly. 'Why do you ask about Govinda? I thought you had come here to see me! Afterwards, I will visit you in London, if the Maharajah permits it.'

Sarah bit her tongue. There was simply no polite way to say that she was here because Lily had wanted her to come. And as to this spoiled, if charming, young creature visiting London, the idea seemed fanciful rather than plausible.

The palanquin had now stopped, and the smoke from a large bonfire some distance away was coiling into the confined space. Sarasvati wrenched the gauze curtains aside and called out sharply in Hindi to one of the guards. In a moment there were men at either side of the palanquin, helping the two women to alight. As Sarah stepped out, a loud noise from the direction of the ghaut made her jump. One of the men grinned and mimed something, pressing his fists to either side of his head, then throwing them into the air. Sarah was baffled.

'It was the skull of a corpse exploding in the flames.' Sarasvati was beside her, holding her hand but watching her face closely; mischievously, Sarah thought, as the truth dawned. The burning pyre was a cremation, and as Sarah looked further south along the river and away from Dasaswamedh, the busy central ghaut, she could see at least two more such fires. Sarah walked past the pyre with as much composure as she could muster. She did not need to look at Sarasvati, who seemed delighted by her nervousness, to know that her fear was both irrational and foolish, but it suddenly seemed as if the certainty of death was everywhere, its presence never concealed.

Sarasvati pulled the draping tail of her sari over her head as they were propelled forward by the momentum of the bazaar, and the fierce-looking Arabs who had accompanied the palanquin drew in closer. One of the men walked beside Sarah holding a yellow silk umbrella above her head. Sarasvati took her hand again, smiling more kindly now at the wide-eyed awe with which Sarah was regarding the riotous colour and percussion of the street.

The workplace of the tailor was little more than a hessian awning stretched over a Turkish carpet. He was a stooped little man with a clay pipe clenched between his grinning, crimson teeth. The teeth were as much a mystery to Sarah as the odour of the tobacco he smoked. Sarasvati later explained that the tailor chewed a stimulating leaf called betel which stained his teeth, and that he smoked hashish in his clay pipe. This, Sarah supposed, accounted for his permanent smirk. By the time the tailor had been given Sarah's measurements and instructions to make three gowns from plain lawn cotton, the sun had climbed so high that even the silk umbrella was not enough to keep the baking heat from Sarah. It rose from the pale earth and seared through her thin, calfskin slippers, and she became unbearably thirsty. Sarasvati noticed her discomfort immediately and ordered a guard to bring the palanquin to them, telling him they would return to the palace. Whilst they waited, she pulled Sarah towards the market stall of a slipper maker. Here were all manner of glittering and sequinned fancies, and Sarasvati, after glancing at Sarah's feet, chose a pair in emerald green, sewn with tiny mirrors and beads.

'We do not wear shoes in the palace, but if you wish, you may wear these.'

On the way back, Sarah wondered about Sarasvati's past. Had Lily not said that Sarasvati came from a small village? How had a village girl and a Hindu come to be the Maharajah's number-one concubine?

'Your family must be proud of you,' she ventured.

Sarasvati shrugged. 'I have beauty and am a fine dancer, so my father would have sold me to a nobleman, if he could. I was of no other value to him. I came to Benares because I believed that the Maharajah would want me when he knew what I could give him.'

'And what was it, what could you give him?'

For the second time, Sarasvati looked at Sarah coldly. 'Something he longed for more than anything else; something only I could give him.' It was clear that she wished to divulge no more than this, but Sarah persisted, her curiosity roused.

'Will you not tell me his greatest desire?'

Sarasvati narrowed her eyes. 'Why do you ask so many questions, Miss Sarah?'

Sarah laughed. 'It is in my nature. And I admit that I am intrigued. You see, like Lily, it pleases me to write about unusual women. Perhaps I should write about you!'

Sarasvati's eyes lit up, and Sarah believed that she had found the way to convince her to talk.

'Then you should ask the Maharanee, for she alone understands me and knows my story,' she said mysteriously.

Sarasvati left Sarah at the door to her room, saying she should rest in the hottest part of the day, and later, when it was cool, she might come for her. She added that perhaps this evening Sarah would meet the Maharajah, if he was in residence. It seemed that the prince's mood and desires were as unknowable as his movements, and one simply waited to be called upon.

The gowns still lay where they had been on the bed, so Sarah gathered them up to hang them back in the dressing room. As she smoothed their folds, she noticed something achingly familiar nestled in the corner of the wardrobe and almost entirely hidden by the drapes of slippery silk. It was Lily's old blue hatbox. For a moment, Sarah was returned to Franz's studio in Kensington on the day she had first seen Lily there, writing by the French doors, the hatbox at her feet. She picked it up and carried it to the ebony desk.

As she lifted the lid, a fine swirl of dust danced in the rays of light that slanted through the open shutters. Resting on the very top was a sealed envelope addressed to John Lark. It looked as though it had been placed there in readiness for posting. Sarah thought back to her last meeting with Lark at the *Mercury*. He had told her that he had written to Lily but had received no reply. He seemed remorseful, as though there were some unfinished business between them. Had he said something he regretted? Sarah wondered.

Beneath the envelope with Lark's name on it, were several bundles; cuttings from newspapers, and what appeared to be letters, though without envelopes. There were also several piles of notebooks tied up with ribbon. The bundle of letters was puzzling, for Sarah could tell at a glance that they were in Lily's hand. But why had she not posted them? Unable to stop herself, Sarah untied the black ribbon, her fingers suddenly stiff and clumsy, fumbling with the bow.

14 February 1865

My Dearest Love,

Today I woke to feel your presence, and so I shall write to you, to tell you my secrets, as I once did. Today, as every day, I sit in the summer house amidst the glory of the Maharajah's gardens, and write a letter or two, fortified by a large pot of a fragrant tea which, I am told, comes from plantations in the northern hills of Assam. Around the summer house are a quantity of camellias, and a magnolia tree in flower, and a gentle breeze carries a sweet balm of honeysuckle and frangipani. To one side is a forest of bamboo from which, at any moment, the Maharajah's pet tiger might emerge, but I am less afraid of the beast now, and indeed have even stroked its fur.

I find that I am increasingly less hale in body, and have suffered from various ailments, which I am told by a local physician of Ayurveda are due to an excess of heat in my blood. Yet in spite of my weakness, I am more at peace than when last I wrote to you. Then I was but a shadow of the Lily you knew and loved. Who would have thought that grief could steal away not only one's wits, but the very marrow of one's bones? When last I visited your studio in London, it felt cold, and I knew that your spirit had left there. I must tell you now that I had hoped that I might find you here, in the place which the Hindus believe to be a doorway between worlds, but what I have found instead is an inner strength.

Now, let me confide to you what I shall tell no living soul. You will remember that I wrote of a charm, made from the Maharajah's nine diamonds, which Lady Cynthia Herbert was charged to have made? The same jewel disappeared mysteriously and, according to the London press, and even to Inspector Lark, was somehow connected to the three murders that took place in London last year. I have wondered, perhaps superstitiously, if Lady Herbert's death was also associated with the jewel in some way. Now, finally, I have discovered why this jewel was so special, although what became of it remains a riddle. After much pleading, Govinda agreed to tell me the story of the nine diamonds, about which he had hitherto remained silent. Perhaps he confided this to me because he is soon to return to his home in the Himalaya mountains.

The Maharajah of Benares had collected coloured diamonds over many years, hoping that one day he might have all of the nine colours needed to make a sacred Hindu talisman called navaratna. Those who knew of the Maharajah's intention worried, for there are very particular stones that must be used in a navaratna charm, and only one of these should be a diamond; a white diamond. No one had thought it possible that the Maharajah would find the ninth stone, crucial to the design of the charm, for this gem must be red: the central stone of the navaratna or 'sun stone' as Govinda called it. Red diamonds are known to be exceedingly rare, but then, mysteriously, the Maharajah found his ninth stone, the most powerful, and his collection was complete. Still the Maharajah could not have his navaratna jewel made, for no jeweller in Benares would touch such a dangerous constellation of diamonds. Envoys were sent to Delhi and Bombay and Calcutta, but with the same result.

When Lady Cynthia Herbert and her husband Charles visited Benares, the local diamond merchants soon came to know them, for they were often in the bazaar buying stones. As the Maharajah's guests, the Herberts were shown his jewels, including the coloured diamonds, and Lady Herbert became besotted with the idea of the diamond navaratna, for she had her own ideas about the power of diamonds. She believed that with such a charm in her possession, even for a short while, she might make contact with the otherworld. She therefore proposed that they take the diamonds with them to England and have the charm made by a London jeweller. The Maharajah agreed, but sent Govinda with them, both to guard the stones and to ensure the correct design of the charm.

I asked Govinda if Lord Herbert's macabre death might also have been connected to the diamonds, and he agreed that it had. 'Their desire for the stones was too great', he said, shaking his head sadly. It seems that Lord Herbert was killed when their party was attacked by bandits on a mountain trail. Govinda would tell me no more than this about the circumstances surrounding Lord Herbert's death. Still, I cannot help but think that it was simply the beauty of the diamonds, and not some curse or spell, which inspired these crimes, since I myself saw the stones and have never laid eyes upon anything more perfect in nature.

But how I miss you still, Franz! Watch over me and give me strength as you did in life.

Your Lily

Sarah replaced the letter with infinite care, noticing as she did that her forearms were covered in gooseflesh in spite of the sultry air. If Charles Herbert had been killed by the same person as the three men who were murdered in London, then surely Govinda was implicated in all four crimes?

❖ 30 ❖

One who renounces all desire, so that his longings cease, who never thinks that 'I am this' or 'this is mine' proceeds to peace.

Bhagavad Gita

The next morning Sarah sat at Lily's desk and watched the shifting diagonals of light strike through the venetian shutters and across the blue hatbox, as though inviting her to explore its contents further. She was not yet ready to do so, for she had been shaken by Lily's description of the jewel, though she could not say why. Clearly, Govinda had affected Lily – a woman not normally given to such beliefs – with his own superstition.

Something else had begun to bother Sarah. If the navaratna was as dangerous as Govinda seemed to think, then surely it could still work its dark magic on whosoever encountered it? Of course, after it had been stolen, either by the jeweller's apprentice or a murderous thief, it might have been dismantled so that the diamonds could be sold off separately. But what if the navaratna charm had not been dismantled? She shivered at the thought, and then immediately felt foolish. It was just as Mr Elliot had said – she was beginning to be affected by the East.

When Sarah looked up, a servant was waiting. She was to be escorted, finally, to meet the Maharajah and Maharanee. It would be necessary to wear another of Lily's costumes if she was to be presented to her hosts, and she chose a gown the colour of amber whose bodice was embroidered with chocolate-brown ribbon. She had taken to wearing her feet bare, as the silk carpets and cool marble floors felt smooth and pleasing underfoot. Still, to attend royalty, she could not bring herself to remain shoeless and so slipped her feet into the beaded Oriental slippers that Sarasvati had presented her with. Then, as though Lily were whispering in her ear, Sarah recalled her description of preparing to meet the prince. She must take care to cover her shoulders.

Instead of meeting the royal couple together, as she had expected, Sarah was first delivered to the apartments of the Maharanee in the west wing of the palace. Here she found a fleshy, opulently dressed woman reclining on a mountain of embroidered cushions. In attendance were several female servants, one of whom was oiling her hair from a silver bowl. Another was seated at her feet, and appeared to be fastening a gemmed anklet to a fat ankle already laden with gold. The room was thick with smoke, and Sarah recognised the sickly sweet odour immediately, for there were many opium dens in London.

The Maharanee examined Sarah carefully, taking in each detail of her form and costume in silence. When she spoke, her voice was smooth and drawling.

'So you are Memsahib Lily's beloved orphan? She spoke of you with great affection and we are happy to greet you. I should like to meet with you again, perhaps tomorrow. I will send for you. My husband will soon receive you in the throne room.'

The Maharajah was often called away, she told Sarah vaguely, and might soon be gone again. He needed to inspect his jute and cotton factories, and there was some problem with an indigo plantation near Lucknow . . . Sarah's impression, from the dismissive way in which the Maharanee spoke of her husband's activities, was that they led entirely separate lives.

The throne room was situated in the centre of the east wing of the palace and was the size of the entire ground floor of the Kensington house. Its walls were gold and the floor was covered with an enormous carpet of deep maroon, indigo and copper that shimmered in the light from hundreds of candles, since there were no windows. Upon the carpet sat a jewelled and enamelled throne. The chair itself rested upon the skin of a tiger, and on either side stood a guard; sinewy, dark-skinned men, quite unlike the Arabs in turbans and voluminous Turkish trousers who were to be seen in other parts of the palace. These must be members of the Prince's private guard, Sarah thought. At the foot of the throne sat an orange-robed fellow, whom Sarah took to be a priest, for his face was painted rather garishly, like the sadhus who sat by the river all day, meditating and chanting.

The prince was not on his throne, but standing with his back to the room, looking at some documents laid out on a narrow table against the far wall. He was slim and wore a silk turban and narrow trousers with a long embroidered tunic. He turned as Sarah entered. He must have been handsome once, she thought, but time, melancholy and alcohol had triumphed long ago. His eyes were dimmed and his nose was ablush with fine veins.

'Welcome to Varanasi, Miss Sarah. I am very happy to extend my welcome to any person who was a friend of Memsahib Lily. She was greatly admired here. I understand that you are also a scribe?'

'Yes, but I am merely a reporter of news, sir, while Lily Korechnya was a writer of substance. In fact, I did hear that she was employed in helping to save an ancient temple in Benares?'

'It would not surprise me, though I admit that my own affairs keep me so occupied that I am often not able to engage fully in the . . . greater world. But now that you mention it, yes, I believe Memsahib Lily was rather taken with the Hindu cause. You must ask the ranee Sarasvati about this temple, for she is of that faith.'

The Maharajah was perfectly charming and spoke highly, albeit sadly, of Lily, Sarah thought. It would not surprise her if the Prince had been a little in love with Lily Korechnya, for he would not be the first man thus affected by her grace and kindness. She was reminded of the letter to John Lark which sat in Lily's blue hatbox. She hoped that it contained the farewell which the Inspector felt he had been denied. She had wished many times in her youth that the two of them might become close, but, as she read Lily's letters, she understood. It was not only that Franz had been her one true love, but also that she valued her freedom.

Sarah made polite conversation with the Maharajah and when it looked as though she was about to be dismissed, she asked him if she might view his fine art collection at some point, for she was eager to see the paintings by Franz Korechnya. She also thought that if she had but a little more time in his company, she might find an opportune moment to ask about Govinda. The prince agreed and said he would send for her.

As Sarah was led back through the maze of mosaic walls and marble floors, she wondered if the Maharajah's gloom had indeed been caused by the disappearance of his beloved diamonds, or if he had always been this way. Perhaps he, like Cynthia Herbert, had believed that the diamond navaratna would somehow complete him. Yet surely, one whose very existence was defined by all the riches that presently surrounded her might simply purchase or command his heart's desire? What more could he want? She recalled Sarasvati's words from the previous day: 'Something he desired more than anything else; something only I could give him.'

As the sun climbed and the heat of the day intensified, Sarah retired to her room. She had intended to use this interlude in Benares to explore her own writing, but had achieved little since her arrival. She opened her pocketbook but in spite of her mood, could write nothing of consequence about Madam Blavatsky. She wondered if Aphra Behn had found it as difficult to mark her parchment to her own satisfaction. Perhaps it was just the oppressive atmosphere of the approaching monsoon? Sarah was delivered aromatic rice and a small bowl of a bright, fiery condiment for lunch, after which she lay on the bed and slept deep into the afternoon.

When she awoke, she rose and went directly to the hatbox, thinking that Lily's writings could perhaps provide the inspiration that eluded her. As she had hoped, there was a roll of parchment that contained some less personal writings, annotated drafts of essays, and notes on Lily's impressions of Benares. Amongst these, was the essay Sarah was hoping to find, but with it was an unfinished letter.

10 March 1865

My dear Barbara,

As whatever illness has beset me seeps into my bones, I have become aware of a stillness of the soul and feel somehow compelled away from the worries that harry the mind. Perhaps I have become one with the very fatalism of this land that I, at first, found impossible to fathom. It is a deeply personal thing that I shall attempt to explain, Barbara, and you must forgive me if I am clumsy.

I have sat for days in the marble summer house, oblivious to the occasional visits from servants who are still unaccustomed to seeing a woman write. It is some weeks now since I completed my essay on the fate of the

Kali temple, a copy of which I shall here enclose for your interest. When I did so, I was overwhelmed by a sense of relief. At first I believed it was relief from the task itself, for I have not before undertaken to report on the affairs of British India, nor of the pantheon of gods which inhabit Benares. I find that each aspect of the goddess Kali, from inspiration and creation, to betrayal and destruction, is mirrored in human history.

But in the weeks since completing this piece of writing, and having a greater understanding of the mystery of the dark goddess, I discover that I am possessed of a hitherto unknown serenity. I remain so within the frenzy of the bazaar and when beggar children tug at my hand; I am no longer awed by the grandeur of my luxurious surroundings. In truth, Barbara it is almost as though my attachment to the earthly plane has been severed . . .

Here the letter ended abruptly. Sarah unfolded the essay that accompanied it and read Lily Korechnya's last, and perhaps most daring, article on exceptional women.

THE MOST EXCEPTIONAL OF WOMEN by Mr Evans

In our age of industry and the achievements of men, of morality and sombre God-fearing Christians, it is easy to forget the great myths and legends upon which our civilisation was founded. It is perhaps a matter of discomfit to clergymen that the most enduring and powerful image, and one which appears in the history of almost every culture and religion, is that of a goddess: the great mother. Was it not, after all, the Virgin Mary, who gave birth to Jesus?

There is a curious legend about the most feared of Hindu deities, the mother goddess Kali. It is said that a king by the name of Ramaditya obtained the empire of the world from the goddess, but only until such time as a divine child born of a virgin would appear, whose father was to be a carpenter. After living for one thousand years, King Ramaditya recalled the prophesy and went to find the child so that he might put him to death and keep his empire. The king was defeated by a rival and slain, and so began the age of Kali.

There are yet more peculiar similarities in the doctrines of the Hindu and that of the Jew and Christian. There is a Hindu legislator by the name of Menu whom, in character and status, is very much like Noah, and if the letters of the great creator Brahma are slightly rearranged, he might be Abraham, and his consort Sarasvati, Abraham's wife Sarah. Christians and Jews would argue that their mythological personages have been stolen, but it may be wiser to consider the greater age and longer history of Hindu.

In my time in the holiest city of the Hindus, Benares, I have become most fascinated by the aforementioned goddess Kali, since she inspires both fear and devotion. It is said that temples to Kali should be built far from villages and towns, and near to cremation grounds, for this is Kali's dwelling place; a place where the physical elements are dissolved. In the Hindu tradition, cremation represents the dissolving of the attachments that bind the human; particularly anger, fear and desire. All limitations and ignorance are burnt away and replaced by the fire of knowledge, which Kali bestows.

There is a temple to Kali in the heart of Benares which was built long before the city became the crowded, bustling trade centre it is today. It is a place where the devout – both men and women – pay their respects to their great mother, and ask her for success in battle, both physical and of the spirit. Now a battle is being fought in Benares between the British municipal board, which has raised a loan to improve the sewage system, and its Hindu inhabitants. The debt must be repaid by increasing the taxes of citizens who are too poor to pay even the existing rates. Not only this, but the site chosen for the new pumping station is the very site of the temple to Kali; the oldest shrine in Benares. Those who are suspicious of the activities undertaken by the British officers of the municipal board say that this is a deliberate attack on Hindu, and a direct insult to Mother Kali. Thousands of appeals have been made to save the temple, but still the plans to destroy it advance.

One might even think that the temple is being demolished because the goddess Kali inspires fear in the British in India, for she dwells where the physical ceases to exist. Kali is the deity who laughs in the face of human frailties; attachment, fear and desire. These are the very qualities that drive forward the most powerful machines of industry.

❖ 31 ❖

Some Chinese gentlemen told me that they objected to the higher
education of women because if women were better educated they
would want to rule. That must be what Englishmen think, though
they do not say it. They say that our brains are lighter and that
therefore we must not be taught too much.

From *Ideala*, 1888, by Sarah Grand

When Sarah woke the following morning, she went looking for the
khansamah to enquire after the prince's number-one concubine. She
felt the need for company, even if it came in the somewhat truculent
form of Sarasvati. She found the servant by accident as she passed
through the doorway to a walled garden of palms. Here, under his
supervision, an army of white-turbaned gardeners was pruning and
weeding while others climbed the tallest of the palms, whose smooth
trunks had no foot hold, to cut away dead fronds. When Sarah asked if
he would direct her to Sarasvati's apartments, he hesitated for so long
that she thought he would refuse her. Finally, he spoke sharply in his
own tongue to one of the gardeners, who disappeared.

'Do you remember Mr Govinda?' Sarah asked the khansamah, whilst
they waited together in the burning sun.

'Yes, Miss Sarah. Of course.'

'When did he leave the palace?'

'After Memsahib Lily died.'

'And did he ever return?'

'I do not know, Miss Sarah.'

'How might I find out where he is now?'

The khansamah did not appear to like this question any more than
he liked directing her to Sarasvati's chambers, but eventually he sighed.
'Maybe the chaukidar, the head of the guard, will know.'

'Could you ask him? Please. It is very important that I speak with Mr
Govinda.'

'I will ask him.'

The gardener returned a moment later with the young serving girl who had been bringing Sarah her meals. She bowed and beckoned for Sarah to follow her.

The girl left Sarah outside the door to Sarasvati's rooms, but when she entered, Sarah felt disoriented as the room was in darkness, except for a ring of candles on the floor. It was immediately clear from the thickness of the air that Sarasvati, like the Maharanee, had been smoking opium, which Sarah was beginning to think was as commonplace here as tobacco was in England. The ranee was dancing as though to the rhythm of drums she alone could hear, and she was dressed only in some simple beads and a dopatta; a veil normally worn over the silk brocade pyjamas of the Musalmani women. The dopatta was entirely transparent and Saravati's naked limbs moved with the suppleness of willow fronds in the wind. Her eyes were unrecognisable and she looked for all the world as though she was inhabited by some arcane spirit. She was chanting something in a language which Sarah guessed must be Hindi, but the only words she could make out sounded like *'mera varga'*. Then, as her eyes became accustomed to the dim light, Sarah noticed two things; the beads which Sarasvati wore were identical to those around Sarah's own neck and, on the floor before the dancing ranee was a black statue, perhaps two feet high, of a macabre figure so hideous that Sarah felt icy fingers at her neck. As the candles cast both shadow and light upon the effigy, she saw that it had several arms and a long, protruding tongue which appeared to be dripping with crimson blood.

Sarah closed the door quickly and hurried away, the cool marble soothing beneath her bare feet. Suddenly, she wanted nothing more than to pass some time in the comparatively dull, very English company of Mr Jonathan Elliot.

As her palanquin jostled through the pandemonium of the river road to Dasaswamedh, Sarah could not help but dwell upon the scene she had just witnessed. She presumed that the statue had been one of Hindu's many gods or goddesses, though she could not say which. She was surprised by her own fearfulness, for she had seen many more terrible sights in the bawdy houses of St Giles. Once, she and the Trub had been in a brothel in that quarter looking for a certain masher who was sweet on Ellen, and who would tell her anything. The madam of the house was as close to an ogre as Sarah had ever known a woman to be, and as it happened she was a fine knife thrower as well. She had once been a circus performer, Ellen later discovered, which was just the kind of detail Mr Harding liked. Sarah and Ellen had been only a few feet away when a punter who was trying to dodge out before paying his dues felt the end of the madam's knife. Although he staggered a short distance with the blade between his shoulders, he was dead by the time he hit the floor. It was the first time Sarah had seen someone being murdered, and the first time she had reported on a crime she had actually witnessed.

With her mind thus occupied, it seemed to take no time at all before they reached the busy central marketplace. Here, the Vaishya guest house was situated on a broad, stone terrace overlooking the Ganges, with wicker chairs and tables arranged beneath an awning of brightly coloured cloth. It did not take long for Sarah to spot Mr Elliot. His panama hat was as unmistakable as his slightly hunched posture, and he was reading the broadsheet on the table before him with intense concentration. As Sarah approached, he looked up, surprised. She was secretly relieved when he smiled, for she had worried that he might no longer consider the company of a bluestocking such as herself appropriate, or even desirable.

'I say. Good morning, Miss O'Reilly. Do sit down. Will you have breakfast? Bannian! More tea! I can recommend the sweet chapatti, but don't touch the egg kidgeri; too much chilli by far. Do you know, I was just this minute thinking of you as I read the *Benares Observer*. It really is the best British broadsheet published here, should you wish to avail yourself of news of the empire. I was recalling our conversation about diamonds. It says here that they've been discovered in Africa!' Mr Elliot shook his head in wonder until his eyes lit upon another report. 'Good Lord! There is talk that they might one day allow Indian magistrates to try Europeans! Here, listen to this: " . . . at any moment we might be liable to be sentenced on a false charge by a copper-coloured pagan".' Mr Elliot shook his head again. 'Disgraceful.'

Sarah was not sure if it was the editorial or the idea of Indian magistrates which Mr Elliot found disgraceful, but she decided it would be better not to enquire. If she was to enjoy Jonathan Elliot's seemingly vast knowledge of Hindu lore, then she would have to put up with the less attractive aspects of his character.

'Do you know of a very old temple to the Hindu goddess Kali? I understand it is the oldest shrine in the city,' she asked, once they had discussed the weather, Sarah's impressions of Benares and Mr Elliot's lumbago.

'Indeed. It is famous, for the holy city is Kali's tract in a sense. She rules over the funeral pyre and the domain of death, and death is the central industry of Benares.' He said this rather dramatically, and Sarah suppressed a smile.

'You see, Miss O'Reilly, the gods are present in every aspect of life, for the Hindu is essentially a pagan and there is a god for positively everything. The old Kali temple is frightfully ancient and definitely worth paying a visit to, if you can find it in the medieval labyrinth of the Old City, of course.'

'I should very much like to visit the temple. I wondered if you might be my guide?'

'I would be delighted. I have lessons in the afternoon, but am free to spend the mornings as I please.'

After finishing their tea, they left the Vaishya, and Mr Elliot led Sarah into the maze of narrow alleyways that meandered through the ancient heart of the city. Here, it was possible to imagine how Benares had looked when it was the greatest trading city both on the River Ganges and on the Northern Road. The alleys twisted and turned between buildings hundreds of years old, whose crumbling stone walls were now barely upright. Even in the narrowest, darkest lanes there were tiny shops in which merchants sat cross-legged, and they beckoned as Sarah and Mr Eliott passed, insisting that their cloth, gemstones or silver candlesticks were the finest available. Silk merchants ran after Sarah, carrying armfuls of cloth so finely spun and delicate that she could not resist touching it, and in the end, she decided to purchase a swathe of sea green with silver brocade. Lily would have liked it, Sarah thought, and she wanted to bring something of Benares home to London. The merchant was convinced that she should also have a length of yellow, shot with pale rose. 'Yellow is very lucky; it is the colour of Sarasvati!' he persisted, trailing behind them.

'Do you know anything of the goddess Sarasvati?' Sarah asked Mr Elliot as they stepped to one side to allow a funeral procession to pass. It seemed commonplace now, the incense and garlands, the chanting mourners in their billowing white gowns.

'Indeed. Sarasvati is the deity most strongly associated with the sensual. She likes to wear gems and jewels, fine cloth and perfumes – sandalwood in particular – to protect her carefree nature against demons and evil spirits. She is the vainest, but perhaps also the most likeable, of all the Hindu goddesses.'

Sarah could only nod, for Mr Elliot might have been describing Sarasvati the woman. She was amazed by the degree to which the ranee had become like her namesake. Was it deliberate?

They passed through a quarter dedicated almost entirely to gem merchants, before finally coming to a low, innocuous doorway in a ruined stone facade. Inside was the original, colonnaded portico of a temple, its vibrant frescoes now almost entirely faded. Through another even lower doorway, carved from black granite, was the shrine to Kali. The shrine was dark and pagan, more like a cave than a temple, and around the walls were low-relief stone carvings of gods and goddesses fornicating, dancing, feasting and dismembering each other. These were eroded and broken in places, but there was evidence of the brilliant pigments that had once adorned the stone. On the floor, around the circular walls, a legion of candles provided the only light, flickering across the images and causing moving shadows that all but brought them to life.

Sarah and Mr Elliot walked slowly around the shrine until they came to its focal point: the altar to the deity. Towering above the low stone platform, the effigy of the goddess was over twelve foot high, with wild eyes and a protruding tongue from which there dripped crimson blood. About her neck, Kali wore a string of what looked like tiny human skulls. It was the very same deity that Sarah had seen Sarasvati dancing before. She felt a wave of nausea at the realisation, and without thinking she took hold of the sleeve of Mr Elliot's linen coat to steady herself.

'Monkey skulls,' Mr Elliot assured her, patting her hand. 'Kali is believed to wear a necklace of the heads of slain warriors, infant's skulls for earrings, and a belt hung with severed arms. There are stories about her bandit followers, the thugs or thuggees, chopping off their victims' arms and heads as an offering to their mistress, but first they strangled them in such an artful way that it left no mark. Crushing the larynx, I believe.'

Sarah shuddered and a distant memory stirred. Had she not once eavesdropped on an argument between Inspector Lark and Melville, in which the latter had speculated that the London murders had been the work of a thuggee? Lark had brushed the idea off as nonsense, saying that the bandits had been wiped out in the 1830s.

'I did not think there were any more thuggees?'

Mr Elliot laughed mirthlessly. 'That depends greatly on whom one speaks to. Why, the Maharajahs themselves traditionally recruit trained thugs into their personal guard. They are apparently most efficient, as killers go.'

Sarah's mind was spinning. Was Govinda a thuggee? Was it he who had killed the three men in London, and possibly dismembered Lord Herbert? It was almost unthinkable, but Lily's letters had implied that the death of Lord Herbert was so gruesome that Cynthia Herbert could not even speak of it.

'She seems an unlikely image of womanhood to worship,' Mr Elliot was saying, as he gazed upon the goddess. 'But it is Kali's strength and vitality that are seen as her transforming qualities – she alone conquered Shiva, most powerful of all the male deities, in battle.'

Sarah recalled Lily's essay: Kali bestowed the fire of knowledge. What did this mean? Mr Elliot was still talking, but she had to make a concerted effort to listen to him as her thoughts were racing.

'It is no accident that the gem bazaar should be situated so close to the temple. Kali is mistress of the diamond, which is considered to be an immortal stone. Indeed temples to Kali are often found in villages that mine diamonds, as the goddess protects her own. Legend has it that she is always searching for that rarest of treasures, a diamond the colour of blood. Miss O'Reilly, are you quite well? You've changed colour rather drastically. Here, come along with me.' He took her elbow firmly. 'It's terribly stuffy in here, you probably need some air.'

Once outside in the blessed cool of the alleyway, Sarah leaned against the cold stone wall, fanning herself with the panama hat kindly provided by Mr Elliot.

'I'm perfectly well now, thank you,' she said, after a moment. 'I don't know what came over me.'

As they returned through the labyrinth to Dasawamedh, Sarah allowed Mr Elliot to air his knowledge of Hinduism without interruption, while she regained her composure. The mention of the red diamond had been uncanny, she thought, but she was determined not to let fear get the better of her. A diamond was just a precious stone, after all, and if Sarasvati wanted to dance around in front of a bloodthirsty goddess, then so be it.

'It is, of course, the nature of paganism to be polytheistic. Every deity represents an aspect of humanity, so to worship the goddess Kali, for instance, means that you accept both the dark and the light aspects of yourself.'

'How convenient,' Sarah managed. 'I imagine that validates all manner of bad behaviour.'

At Dasaswamedh they parted with a firm handshake and the exchange of pleasantries and well wishes, and with a promise to meet again before Sarah returned to London. She climbed back into the Maharajah's palanquin and leaned into the velvet cushions with a deep sigh of relief. By the time she arrived at the palace gates, Sarah had decided that she must simply ask Sarasvati why she chose to worship the dark goddess, when her faith was populated by so many more attractive and benevolent deities.

⁜ 32 ⁜

I ask of thee love, nothing, but relief.
Thou canst not bring the old days back again;
For I was happy then,
Not knowing heavenly joy, not knowing grief.

Mary Elizabeth Coleridge

When she returned to the palace, Sarah was met by the khansamah, who had a rather eerie ability to sense the presence of a visitor at the gates.

'The Maharanee is wanting to receive you, Miss Sarah. Please follow me.'

'Have you spoken with the chaukidar about Mr Govinda?' Sarah asked as she was delivered to the Maharanee's apartments.

'Yes, Miss Sarah,' but he was gone before she could ask him what the outcome had been.

The Maharanee was seated on the floor cushions, toying with a small casket of gold and gemstones by her side.

'Gold from Venice is more yellow than Indian gold, and infinitely more desirable, if one can afford it,' she said as Sarah entered, though she had not looked up. The Maharanee was wearing voluminous kincaub trousers, tight at the ankle, a short bodice called a cholah, from which rolls of flesh cascaded, and a long gauze veil; all of the palest green.

'Sit down,' she instructed, and when Sarah did so, she could see more closely the creased and weary face and noticed that the thick black kohl that lined the Maharanee's watery eyes was smeared. She had perhaps been eating opium, for although the air was not smoke-filled, she had about her the stuporous lethargy of the drug. After a lengthy silence, she spoke again.

'I hear that you and Sarasvati have met?'

'Yes. She is a . . . unique person. Is it true that she came from a small village?'

The Maharanee looked at her suspiciously. 'Why do you want to know about my Sarasvati?' Sarah was surprised at the sudden sharpness of her tone.

'Only because I am curious to know more about her.'

'No one knows more about her than I.'

'Then perhaps you might share her story, your Highness?' Sarah replied, remembering the Maharanee's supposed love of storytelling. There was no immediate response. The Maharanee only examined the egg-sized rings on her plump fingers, whilst Sarah stared at the mirrors embroidered into the cushions. She wondered whether it would be productive to flatter or to coax her hostess into telling her about the younger woman – she could see that the Maharanee wanted to trust her, or perhaps she only wanted an audience, Sarah could not be sure which.

'If I tell you about Sarasvati, Miss Sarah, you must not to speak of it to her, for she is sensitive to certain things . . . to the past.'

'Of course . . .' Sarah began, but the Maharanee had already begun to speak. Her eyes became bright and her voice was possessed of a new vibrancy as she began to tell – to narrate – a story.

Sarasvati was named after a river and its goddess. The villagers thought that the river's alluvial diamonds were proof that the river goddess dwelt here; for she was adorned with jewels when she sprang from the mouth of Brahma. The baby was born on the riverbank, taking her mother by surprise whilst she squatted, pounding cloth against the stones. Sarasvati slid from her mother into the water and swam there quite happily until the other women came.

As a child, Sarasvati would watch the river wallahs from the high land above the river's snaking course. From a distance, they looked like swarms of water wasps; their thin doti cloths and turbans like white stripes on skin burnt black by the sun. A hundred men, diving and rummaging in the mud on the floor of the river until their bony knees and elbows were hatched with cuts. Sarasvati did not want to be the wife of a river wallah; she had dreams of joining the legendary and ferocious army of women; the Zuffar Plutun. She'd seen them once, for they rode through the village, their hair hidden beneath white turbans, and the glinting blades of sabres at their belts.

However her father had other plans. When she danced for her first Diwali and was praised for the fluid motion of her wrists, and the way her limbs moved like water to the drum beat, he decided that she must take lessons. Dancers often married well, or were sold as concubines to rich admirers. She was thirteen now; old enough to marry.

As she waded out into the river, Sarasvati longed to feel the sharp edge of a crystal beneath her foot. She often bathed at night but always when Venus was rising, for this was the most propitious time to find diamonds. She knew that one small stone could make a poor family rich, if they dared to keep it. She had imagined how it might be possible to hide a crystal, then take it to Benares and sell it to a gem merchant. Then Sarasvati and her family would eat their rice from golden bowls and she would wear perfumed oils, and marry whomever she pleased. It was but another dream, however, for she would never dare to steal one of the Maharajah's diamonds. This would be punishable by death, and besides, the stones were under the protection of the goddess Kali, the most fearsome and bloodthirsty of deities.

Under her feet, beneath the soft alluvial, were stones. The soles of Sarasvati's feet were as sensitive as the skin on her fingertips to their texture, but pebbles did not interest her. She knew what the rough skin of a crystal felt like; she had run her fingers across more than one in her father's diving basket, his dripping brow beaming with pride, for the villagers believed the diamond itself was a deity and therefore chose its custodian.

Sarasvati had never dared to bathe naked before, but tonight she felt bold. The current pulled against her hips and belly and swirled between her thighs, tugging at the yellow cloth she held in her hand so that she had to tie it around her waist to prevent the river goddess from carrying it away. Suddenly, there was a sharp edge beneath Sarasvati's foot, and she dived. When she surfaced, the crust of the rock looked black against the pale skin of her palm. She closed her fist around the object and swam until her knees grazed the river bed close to the shore. On the bank, she untied the heavy cloth from her waist and laid it on the grass to dry. She sat, and uncurled her fingers, opening her palm to the moonlight. She had been clutching the stone so tightly that it had cut into her hand.

At first she thought that her blood had spilt on the small crystal protruding from the rock's dark surface, for even in the bleached moonlight, its true colour blazed: a luminous red.

The priest's wife roused the old man from where he slept on his mat when Sarasvati's father visited with the red crystal. The priest was the oldest man in the village, and the most wise. There had been disagreement amongst Sarasvati's father and his river neighbours about the stone. One said it was ruby, another that it was a garnet. Sarasvati's father insisted that the stone could only be a diamond. The priest took the stone, and walked out of his hut, followed by Sarasvati's father. Sarasvati and neighbours were waiting outside and watched as the old man looked at the stars. They noticed how still he had become, and how he was holding the stone in the flat of his hand, with his arm outstretched. They did not know that he was thinking how this, the ninth stone, would complete the Maharajah's navaratna collection. It must never be.

Finally the priest nodded his head, and beckoned to one of the river wallahs. 'Bring me a diamond from the temple.' This is where the other stones were kept until they were fetched by the Maharajah's collectors. When the man returned, the priest took the second stone. 'Only a diamond will cut a diamond,' said the priest. He ran the sharpest ridge of the red stone across a flat surface of the clear crystal, etching a fine line into its glassy skin. 'You see?' he said, and then he laughed like an infant because a red diamond was the most rare, the most desired and potent of all stones, and he could not believe that it had offered itself up to a woman.

When the red diamond was taken by the village priest to the Kali temple, Sarasvati could not sleep. She wanted to behold it once more before it was transported to the palace. Everyone knew that the Maharajah had long sought a diamond of this colour – a gem so rare that some did not believe it could exist – although few knew the real motives behind his search. When she was certain that everyone was sleeping, she crept from her mat and along the path to the temple.

Outside the temple both guards were asleep. Within, the monstrous Kali, carved from black granite, towered above the offerings which had been made to her that day: a slain goat surrounded by flowers, rice, and a small pile of uncut river diamonds. The red stone was not amongst them, which could mean only that the priest had hidden it. This was not the custom, for the stones were to be watched over by Kali until the Maharajah's men came for them. Sarasvati wondered if the priest meant to keep the red diamond for himself. Surely he would not dare?

She stayed in the temple until sunrise. She had searched everywhere for the diamond, but it was not to be found. As the sun climbed above the river, a blade of light slanted through the open door and across Kali, illuminating her fearsome face. Between her hooded eyes, in the position called the third eye, was always a jewel, for it was believed that this would give the goddess clarity and keep her sweet-tempered. But in place of the usual white diamond there was now a red stone. So, the priest had intended to keep this stone from the Maharajah. It could not be. She must inform her prince that she, Sarasvati, knew where it was hidden. The gods had answered her prayer.

If the resin from the poppy made the body weak, then it lent great stamina to the mind, for the Maharanee had clearly taken enormous pleasure in escaping into her peculiar narrative. Sarah was intrigued by the poetic way in which she spoke of her subject as much as by the unusual nature of the story.

'You must indeed know Sarasvati well?' she commented.

'She has no other friend here. We are, each of us, like butterflies in a net.'

'But what happened then? Did Sarasvati send a messenger to the Prince?'

The Maharanee waved a hand lethargically. 'I am overtaxed. Let me rest.' As though this were a signal, a servant stepped forward with the hookah, and lit the silver pipe with a taper. Sarah watched as the drug took dominion, smoothing the creases on the Maharanee's forehead as her eyelids drooped in some private ecstasy. Sarah felt that she was now intruding, but when she stood to leave, the Maharanee's eyes flew open, black and glassy as obsidian.

'Sit!' The command was sharp, and Sarah obeyed, hoping it meant she would hear more about the red diamond, for surely this was the very same stone which she had seen in the Royal Academy seven years ago. She was not disappointed.

And so Sarasvati began her journey to the City of Light. It is uncommon for a young girl to travel alone, but in her innocence Sarasvati expected no harm to befall her, and so none did. It is the custom in this part of India to feed the traveller and to offer shelter to the stranger, so everywhere she went she was given chapatti, yaks' meat and goats' milk. If anyone asked her destination, she would tell them with confidence that she was bound for the famed school for nautchnees in Benares.

As she travelled, Sarasvati could think of little else but the diamond. She wondered if a red diamond, like other red stones, was ruled by the god of the sun, Surya. Surya himself was red, with three eyes and four arms, and he rode a chariot drawn by four mares. He was the deity capable of healing the sick, so wearing any red stone was considered to be beneficial to the health. Perhaps a red diamond was even more powerful than other red stones, and so the priest intended it for his own use?

Finally, she arrived in Benares, but the City of Light was not as she had imagined it. In her mind, its streets were wide and paved with gleaming white stone, its inhabitants were tall and strong limbed, there were no paupers, and the Mother Ganges flowed as clear and as fair as a mountain stream. When Sarasvati saw the reality, she wondered how the Maharajah, whom she imagined to be a kind and noble man, could allow beggars and filth to blemish the streets of this holy city. Surely, with all his riches, he might do something to help his people?

With this last remark, Sarah heard a trace of bitterness, and was not surprised when the story continued no further. She was waved away, and could see that the Maharanee's ruined body could function no longer without either sleep or more opium.

As she walked the long, ornamented corridors to her own room she puzzled over the household of the Maharajah. What was it that had caused so many or its members to numb their senses with alcohol and opiates? She could still hardly believe that diamonds alone would have such jurisdiction over the soul. Suddenly, an entirely irrational fear clutched at her and her heart felt as cold and as a stone. Had the diamonds somehow fixed their poisonous gaze upon Lily Korechnya?

⁑ 33 ⁑

Gold am I, and for me, ever men curse and pray,
Selling their souls and each other, by night and day.
A sordid colour, and yet, I make things fair,
Dying sunsets, fields of corn and a maiden's hair.

Adela Florence Corey

A week passed almost imperceptibly. Each morning, Sarah removed one or two items from the hatbox and pored over various writings and cuttings from Oriental newspapers that Lily had seen fit to preserve. In the languid afternoons she slept, deeply and inexplicably fatigued by the building humidity. Occasionally she found something to make a note of in her pocketbook and slowly, she believed, she was forming the beginnings of an essay, or even two. It seemed that there were, perhaps unbeknownst to Mr Elliot, a great many unconventional British women in India.

Sarah was building her own profile on the women of the Raj. Much of the journalism she had appraised appeared to exist in order to celebrate such things as the Christian charity of one memsahib who had opened a school for Hindu girls, or vilify the uncomely enthusiasms of another who had opposed child marriage too vociferously. To Sarah, the cuttings provided a reminder that being unorthodox in the bosom of Raj society was a crime, not only against her gender, but also against the empire. One of her favourite editorials was from an old copy of a Punjab newspaper. The lady journalist, one Flora Annie Steel, was clearly not the standard memsahib. She was given to entertaining both Hindu and Mussalmani notables in her garden, feeding them on plum pudding whilst chastising them for selling degrees at the Punjab University. The irreverent Mrs Steel delighted in criticising the inappropriateness of imposing British etiquette in India, and she took particular pleasure in mocking the behaviour of the memsahibs, who insisted that gentlemen should call between twelve and two in the afternoon, even though this was the hottest part of the day.

Sarah had made only one further outing to the bazaar since her meeting with Mr Elliot, yet the hours and days had not lingered. She had seen nothing of her hosts, and was beginning to think that they had forgotten her and that Sarasvati must be displeased with her, until a servant arrived one morning to inform her that she was to accompany the prince's favoured concubine to the zenana for lunch.

She found Sarasvati in her rooms, reclining on a large, ornamental swing that was suspended by chains from the high ceiling, and smoking a silver hookah. She was dressed in petticoat and veil of fine Dacca muslin over kincaub trousers and chola; yellow embroidered with gold flowers – yellow being the only colour worn by the goddess Sarasvati, of course. Her glossy black hair was knotted at the back and dressed with rows of pearls, which also fell across her forehead and supported a jewel called a tika. She had obviously taken a great deal of care with her costume, and Sarah could only surmise that it was intended to impress the other ranees.

Sarasvati inhaled deeply from her opium pipe, and then gave it to the servant who was pushing her swing. 'Hello, Miss Sarah.' She hurried to explain herself. 'I have been unwell. It is the custom here, you see. The resin of the poppy is given even to young children to stop them from taking cold.' Sarasvati sighed, and in a rare moment of insight, she added: 'But I have come to rely too much on the pipe, just as the Maharanee does, for it alleviates my boredom. I hope you have been enjoying your visit?'

'Very much.'

'Come.' Sarasvati held out her hand and they left her chamber through a lattice-work door that led into a walled garden. The enclosure was protected from the surrounding grounds and was obviously part of the zenana. The gardeners here were female, and they tended potted roses and delicate jasmine, glossy camellia bushes and small palms. In the centre of the pale marble paving was a fountain in the shape of a large water lily, its petals carved from rose quartz.

Sarasvati led Sarah through a gate into another, larger walled garden, though this was embraced on only three sides by masonry, its fourth 'wall' being a dense bamboo jungle. On a soft lawn of camomile grass was laid out a crimson carpet, upon which sat perhaps two dozen ranees. The ranees were as Lily had described them, like dark-skinned bejewelled fairies. Fairies with no purpose, Sarah thought, for the greater part of each day in the harem was dedicated only to bathing, grooming and gossip. In Sarah's company the women seemed both shy and insatiably curious, casting sideways glances at the white cotton gown that the Marnikarnika tailor had made for her. Even if she knew English, a Mussalmani lady was normally not permitted to speak freely to a feringhi. Sarasvati ignored the other ranees, as they did her, and this in itself was clearly a form of entertainment.

A meal of fragrant rice with pulses and chapatti bread was laid out, and now and then a small monkey would venture from the bamboo thicket to the edges of the carpet, only to be scolded and shooed away. As she ate, Sarah could not help but wonder nervously if the Maharajah's tiger was still alive.

They had just finished eating when a servant girl appeared by Sarasvati's side and whispered to her, then bowed and left. Sarasvati took Sarah's hand and pulled her to her feet. 'Come, Miss Sarah, we are called to the Maharajah's apartments.'

As they approached the east wing, Sarasvati stopped beside a graceful statue of Shiva, the lord of the dance. She turned and looked at Sarah with such wide, imploring eyes, that she knew immediately she was about to be asked a favour.

'We are friends, are we not?' Sarasvati began, and Sarah could only nod. 'You see, the Maharajah no longer goes to London as often as he used to. He is too old and tired, and he takes too much alcohol. But I, Miss Sarah, have always longed to visit, and I thought that you could speak with him for me.'

'I, speak with the Maharajah?'

Sarasvati nodded eagerly. 'Yes. You.'

'But, we have met only once.'

'And you shall meet again now, and then you can tell him that I should visit London, and that you will be my friend there.'

Because she could think of nothing to say, Sarah merely nodded, bemused. At first, she had thought that she might come to know Sarasvati, for she had liked her in spite of her peculiarities. But seeing her dance before Kali had surprised her out of her complacency, as had the knowledge that she had been instrumental in the Maharajah obtaining the red diamond. At least now there seemed to be more reason behind Sarasvati's hurried ascent from village girl to ranee. Quite simply, here was a young woman with a shadow, in whom ambition triumphed over friendship. Sarah could not help but wonder to what lengths Sarasvati might go to have her way. As to asking Sarasvati about her strange choice of deity, Sarah now felt strangely reluctant. There was an undercurrent of secrecy in this place that seemed to prohibit plain speaking.

The chamber in which the Prince received them was a long, narrow smoking room with an elegant, round table and several embossed leather chairs. They were served black tea, from the Maharajah's plantation in Gorakpur, and sugary rose water sweetmeats.

The Prince asked again about Sarah's work at the *Mercury* and then listened politely, though she sensed his disapproval when she told him about much of her subject matter. Sarasvati stood silently by, her eyes downcast in the presence of the Maharajah. It was not the custom, she later told Sarah, for women to either sit or speak in the company of men, unless they were alone with their husbands.

'But what if they have something to say!' Sarah exclaimed, shocked by the very idea.

Sarasvati shrugged. 'Then we speak to other women.'

'And to whom do you speak?' Sarah queried, though she already knew the answer. She longed to ask Sarasvati about the red diamond but she could not, of course, for she had given her word to the Maharanee. Sarasvati did not reply, and Sarah could only surmise that the pervading climate of silence and melancholy originated with the Maharajah, and filtered down to all who attended him.

After tea, Sarah was shown the prince's paintings, a collection which quite astounded her. As she walked the length of the rather gaudily baroque gallery, she suddenly stopped and drew in her breath sharply. There, amongst the works of Dutch masters, portraits of Moghul nobles and German landscapes, was the painting of Lily by Franz Korechnya; *The Venus of Waterloo*. As soon as she saw the portrait, Sarah longed to have it, for here was Lily as she truly was: whimsical, intelligent, and graceful, with a hint of laughter in her eyes.

Sarasvati was watching her closely when Sarah finally turned away, and Sarah took her hard stare to be accusatory, for she had said nothing to the Maharajah about London. But as they went out to walk in the grounds, Sarasvati said quietly. 'I can see that you would like to own the painting of Memsahib Lily. Perhaps I could speak with the Maharajah and see if he will make a gift of it to you?'

Sarah understood immediately that this offer was conditional. If she would invite Sarasvati to London, then Sarasvati would secure the painting of Lily for her.

It seemed that Sarasvati was quick at her work, for the Prince called for Sarah the very next morning. When she entered the smoking room, she could see that *The Venus of Waterloo* had been brought from the gallery, and was resting against the table.

'Sarasvati has told me that you would like to have this portrait of Memsahib Lily. I cannot refuse a request from a guest, and a friend of the woman herself.'

'Oh, but I did not request it, Your Highness, I merely ... I admired this painting. Greatly.'

'I see. Then the ranee was mistaken?'

Sarah sighed, unable to pretend. 'I'm afraid it is rather more complicated than that. I believe I am now beholden to ask a favour of you, on behalf of Sarasvati. She would like to visit London, and I have agreed to chaperone her. I am to depart from Benares in a little over two weeks.'

'I assure you, Miss Sarah, she would need more than a small woman such as yourself as her chaperone. I have not guards whom I trust well enough to attend Sarasvati.' For the first time, Sarah caught a flicker of something she had not detected before when the prince spoke of his favourite concubine. It was more than the instinct of a man who jealously guarded his harem, and more than a fatherly fondness for a woman less than half his age.

'There was one such guard, some years ago, was there not? A man by the name of Govinda?'

There was no mistaking the prince's displeasure at the mention of his name. 'He tired of the palace and its earthly concerns. I do not know where he is now.'

She wondered if she dared raise the subject of the navaratna with the Maharajah. She had little time left and was concerned he might disappear on one of his trips, so she took a deep breath. 'You will remember Lady Cynthia Herbert, Your Highness?' Sarah thought that his pallor lightened.

'Indeed. Her husband was killed by bandits near Ayodhya. It was a tragedy.'

'But, why was he killed? Were they thieves, the bandits?'

'Yes. The worst type of thieves. They are called thuggees; mercenaries who kill in the name of Kali. The thuggees believed that he was carrying a great treasure, something that belonged to me.'

Sarah's heart was drumming. 'But, if I am not being too inquisitive, how would they have known?'

The prince did not want to answer, and Sarah sensed that here lay the source of his unhappiness: someone in his own household must have betrayed him.

'It was a long time ago. I cannot remember all of the details.' He sighed deeply and his shoulders seemed to stoop. 'It no longer matters. The treasure is lost to me.'

Sarah almost felt sorry for the Maharajah as she left the room, but now she could be certain that the navaratna had not been returned to the palace. At least she could report this much to Inspector Gerard, if nothing else.

Later, when she retired for the evening, Sarah gazed at the portrait, as though expecting Lily to speak. What would she say if she could? Perhaps, she might tell Sarah what had happened to her, or if Govinda had returned to Benares? Sarah lay back on the great, curtained bed and closed her eyes. Soon, she thought sleepily, she must look for the summer house where Lily had liked to write . . .

It was still dark, though almost dawn, when Sarah awoke, disturbed by voices that pierced through the veil of sleep. At first, she thought them to be fragments of a dream, or simply a gust of wind sounding the bamboo chimes, for she always kept the doors to the balcony open. Now wholly awake, she huddled amidst a tangle of silk sheets. Beside the bed was the little table upon which she kept her inkstand and pocketbook from Gerard and beside it was a silver dish containing Ellen's sandalwood beads. She had been unable to wear them since she had seen Sarasvati dancing before Kâli, adorned with little else but an identical necklace. She thought that she would rather risk being overcome by evil spirits. Then, just as she thought she must have imagined the voices, she heard them again: one male and one female, at first low and even, and then raised. Sarah recognised the woman's voice: it belonged to Sarasvati.

Sarah crept from her bed and stood in the shadow by the window, but she could not see Sarasvati and her companion. They spoke in Hindi, but there were two words which Sarasvati kept repeating and which Sarah recognised; '*mera varga*'.

In the morning, Sarah asked the khansamah to direct her to the summer house, and requested that she might be served her breakfast there. As she made her way along one of the many shaded paths, she tried to gauge where the voices she had heard during the night might have originated from, but could not. She realised, as she walked, that she was growing accustomed to the splendour, and wondered if she would miss the otherworldliness of palace life. She would soon leave for London, and she was determined to make the most of the little time she had left.

The summer house was to be found in the far reaches of the grounds, beneath a tangle of honeysuckle. Inside was a polished stone table, a bench and the rustle of fallen leaves. Breakfast arrived only moments later, delivered by the usual shy servant girl in a white cotton sari. Her English was very good, Sarah had discovered, but she would not speak unless spoken to and usually forgot some item – today it was the sweet mango preserve which was customarily eaten with fried bread in the morning.

Sarah concentrated on her reading. After a time, a shadow fell across her, and she looked up, expecting to see the girl returning with the preserve. She was by now accustomed to the barefooted soundlessness with which the inhabitants of the palace approached and departed. However it was not the girl, but a man who had appeared whilst Sarah was occupied with her thoughts. Someone she had not seen before, either in the palace or the grounds. There was nothing alarming about his appearance: he was smooth of skin, and lithe, though clearly some-where in his fifth decade. He wore a neat turban of fine-quality unbleached cotton, and a tunic and trousers of the same plain cloth. He bowed.

'Good morning, Miss Sarah. I thought I might find you here. I am Govinda.'

Sarah was momentarily rendered speechless, for the man before her had come to seem no more than a character in the pages of Lily's letters.

'I am very pleased to meet you, Mr Govinda. I had wondered if I might find you before leaving Benares.'

He bowed his head graciously. 'I was pleased to hear that a friend to Memsahib Lily had arrived here. She was a most enlightened woman and I felt honoured to have made her acquaintance. I heard that you were asking for me,' he said.

It was curious; over the past few weeks, Sarah had thought a great deal about Govinda, yet in spite of the arcane events that preceded him, he had the air of one who had found peace in his life. In his presence, she had the oddest feeling that time had slowed, and even more peculiarly, that all was as it should be. His eyes were extraordinarily clear, Sarah thought, though not so much that one might guess what he was thinking. Sarah's immediate instinct was that she had no business asking him about the diamonds; something about Govinda prohibited it. After all, it was a long time ago, locating the charm would change nothing, and she was not going to insult Govinda merely to satisfy Inspector Gerard's curiosity. Yet, even as these thoughts fluttered away, another more detached part of her was disconcerted; did he hold some unknowable power to affect her in this way? Sarah heard her own voice, as though from a great distance.

'I heard that you had departed Benares some years ago. Have you travelled far since your time in London, Mr Govinda?'

'I like to travel.' Govinda's face remained unreadable.

Finally, she plucked up the courage to ask the most painful of questions. 'Were you with Lily when she died?'

The ensuing silence was not expectant, and she felt no need to mark it. Nor, it seemed, did Govinda, and it was only after a lengthy interval that he spoke.

'I was with Memsahib Lily, and she died gently in her bed. She was cremated at Marnikarnika ghaut, as she had requested. She was not unhappy in the end. Benares is the gateway to the other world, and she was eagerly anticipating the reunion with her beloved. I am glad that you have come here, for I know it was a request that Memsahib held close to her heart.'

Then, seeing Sarah's silent tears, Govinda smoothly changed the subject: 'The Maharajah has consulted me on the subject of allowing the ranee Sarasvati to visit London. I understand that it was your wish that she visit, so I am sorry that I must disappoint you.'

Sarah wiped her tears with a handkerchief and took a deep breath. 'It was not my wish, but hers.' She felt relieved, rather than disappointed, that Sarasvati would not be visiting London, and was surprised that the Prince had thought to reconsider.

'Indeed?' For the first time, Sarah thought that she saw an identifiable expression, displeasure, alter the supine quality of Govinda's face, but it was gone so quickly that she could not be sure. Something else was bothering her, something about his voice, which seemed strangely familiar. At that moment the serving girl returned, carrying a tiny silver pot on a large, lacquered tray. Govinda inclined his head to Sarah, and took his leave without another word. Then, in the ensuing silence, Sarah knew why she had recognised his voice: Govinda had been the person arguing with Sarasvati late last night in the palace grounds.

As the girl was leaving, Sarah called after her. 'Wait, I have another question for you. Do you know the words in English for *mera varga*?'

'Yes, Miss Sarah. *Mera varga* means "my diamond".'

⁜ 34 ⁜

Thou flowest still, O river,
Thou flowest 'neath the moon!
Thy lily hath not changed a leaf,
Thy charmed lute a tune!
He mixed his voice with thine – and his
Was all I heard around;
But now, beside his chosen bride,
I hear the river's sound!

The river floweth on.

Elizabeth Barrett Browning

As the sultry aura of the monsoon descended, Sarah rose ever earlier and became used to watching the sunrise from her lofty ivory balcony. From here she could see the dark waters of the Ganges turn amber and bronze as the sun spilled across the city's rooftops. With the first light, fishermen would push their longboats up on to the riverbanks, their night's work done, and Hindus would wade into the Ganges' holy waters to bathe and scatter petals before their gods.

In the hour after sunrise, Sarah often sat at the ebony desk. Her gaze would fall occasionally on the camphor box that contained Lily's letters, only one of which now remained unread. She could not yet bring herself to read this final note, for finishing it would mean severing the intimacy with Lily she had felt as she read her words. Instead, she perused her own writings, occasionally annotating, crossing through or adding a line. She was beginning to think that the art of composition, as opposed to reporting, required many shades of endeavour. At first, the undertaking was much as it had been when she'd fretted over writing a letter to Lily from the White Hart. Then, as now, the words glared from the page accusingly. Writing with one's inventiveness engaged required an unexpected quality of concentration. It was as though she must put herself under a spell, and afterwards, depending on how deeply she had managed to become enchanted, she felt either charged with renewed strength, or so fatigued that she feared she might lose the power of speech.

Still, now that she had begun, Sarah's overwhelming feeling was that writing with her imagination was as close as she had ever come to escaping from a world which often troubled and perplexed her. Much as she still loved the unpredictability and the thrill of the newspaper business, and was passionate about the issues of equality that she had discussed over tea with Inspector Gerard, she had always been a dreamer. It was how she had survived the early days, after Mam had died, and it had seen her through the acute loneliness of losing Lily too; the ability she had to detach herself from the often painful confusion of reality.

This morning Sarah resisted the urge to pick up her pen, for the Maharanee had finally called for her again; this time to take breakfast with her in her apartments. Sarah had not laid eyes on Govinda in the intervening days, and she did not know where to seek him out. Since their encounter in the summer house, she had wondered if he knew that she would be visiting Benares at this very time, since he had clearly known of Lily's bequest. Sarah had wondered much more besides. Why had the Maharajah consulted Govinda about allowing Sarasvati to visit London? Had he forgiven him for allowing the navaratna charm to be stolen? And why had Sarasvati repeated the same two words 'my diamond' both before Kali and in her argument with Govinda?

Sarah felt oddly deflated, for in one more week she must depart, and it was looking as though she would return to London with nothing but unanswered questions. She had hoped to discover something about the diamonds, other than the knowledge that the Maharanee had imparted about Sarasvati's role in the discovery of the red stone. Sarah recalled with some trepidation the legend that this was the stone that Kali also sought.

She bathed and dressed in her white muslin, then sat for a long time on the bed, waiting to be summoned. She looked about her, taking in the room she must soon prepare to leave. Her eyes fell upon *The Venus of Waterloo*, as they had done so very many times since she had hung Lily's portrait in her room. It would be impractical to transport it as it was, and she had already decided that she must remove the canvas from the extravagant gold frame which the Maharajah had chosen. She had examined the manner in which it was mounted, and discovered that a thin board had been tacked on to the back of the frame. She would dismantle it soon, Sarah decided, as she did not want to leave it until the last, only to discover that it was not as easy as she had foreseen.

When Sarah was finally taken to the Maharanee's rooms, she found the woman reclining in the very same position on her mountain of cushions, as though she had not moved since Sarah's previous visit. Today she wore lapis lazuli blue, embossed with silver, and was eating syrupy Turkish sweets from a pretty glass bowl. She beckoned Sarah over and patted the cushions beside her, then took the silver hookah pipe which another servant proffered.

The Maharanee was clearly not one to bother with parlour talk or social niceties, perhaps because there was now an unspoken under-standing between them that Sarah was here to hear Sarasvati's story. Yet, in the days since she had last sat beside this fleshy and enigmatic woman, Sarah had given as much thought to the Maharanee's own story. She was unsure of the protocol of asking personal questions of the prince's consort, so braced herself to be chastised. 'You are a natural storyteller, Your Highness. Sarasvati tells me you would like to be a writer?'

'I am a writer, child!' Her eyes had narrowed suspiciously – or was it jealously? 'What else has she told you about me?' The Maharanee scowled. 'Such disrespect, when it was I who cared for her and loved her when she was lonely and rejected by the other ranees.'

She rearranged herself slowly, painfully, on the cushions, and her faraway eyes seemed to have softened. It also seemed that breakfast had been forgotten, unless the sugary sweets which the pudgy hand now proffered were intended as the meal. Having drawn from her pipe and tilting back her head to blow the smoke into curling tendrils above, the Maharanee commenced her recital.

Sarasvati decided that the best way to get close to the prince was to use the talent the gods had given her. The school for nautchnees was easily found, for it was surrounded by a high wall, in the centre of which was an imposing gate. Behind the gate was a courtyard, and here Sarasvati sat all day beneath oleander and rose trees, waiting to be seen. Just before dusk the head of the establishment, Sainah Bebee, sent for her.

All of the nautchnees were pretty. Some, like Sarasvati, were beautiful. They were of all complexions, from the darkest ebony to the palest olive, and most of them had been sold to the school by their families. If they attracted the attention of an admirer who could afford them, then they were sold again, and both their families and the school profited.

The nautchnees rose at dawn to eat rice and bananas, and then the exercises began. The exercise room was made of bamboo, like the dormitory, but it was trellised to allow in the light and air. From a thick pole across its high ceiling hung ropes of different lengths, some knotted and others looped, and the nautchnees swung from these like pretty monkeys. It was not long before Sarasvati could perform on the ropes as quickly and smoothly as the most nimble of the nautchnees, and Sainah Bebee, who was difficult to please, praised her for the grace and poise of her dancing. She was chosen to dance at the wedding of a wealthy Hindu grain merchant, and then at the blessing of a temple to Shiva. Finally, more than one year after entering the gates of the school, she was to dance at the festival of Diwali. This was the biggest and most important of all the Hindu celebrations, and the Maharajah would be in attendance.

To Sarasvati, the Maharajah was the embodiment of perfection. He had always been thus, even before she laid eyes upon him, for he was prince of Uttar Pradesh and of the holy city of Benares. She had seen him only once, the day that he had visited her village to inspect the work of the river wallahs, but that moment was forever etched into her heart. The Maharajah had ridden an Arab warhorse, as white as river sand and as tall as a small elephant. He looked a man as much as a prince, and it was clear that he knew how to fight, for hanging from his broad belt was a beaten gold scabbard that had once hung from the belts of his Mughal ancestors. From that day, she had dreamed of no other man.

All eyes turned to the nautchnees as they entered the streets of the city, dressed in costumes which sparkled with thousands of tiny glass beads. An organza veil floated across their hair and their faces, and another fell from their hips. Delicately embroidered bodices exposed their smooth bellies, and they dazzled with ornaments from their fore-heads, noses, ears, wrists, ankles and toes. As they moved, they were brighter than all the lights of Diwali.

The Maharajah watched, seated upon a decorated elephant, and it seemed to Sarasvati that he only had eyes for her. She knew that she was the most beautiful of all the nautchnees, for she had often heard it said. She also knew that it was not uncommon for the prince to buy a dancing girl. Sarasvati had no doubt that the Maharajah would want her; she believed that it was her destiny, just as it had been her destiny to be born in the sacred river. Her most cherished wish was to join the palace zenana, for as the concubine of a prince, she would wear jewels and fine cloth, and eat only sweet halwa. And surely, she would have his love once she had informed the Maharajah how it was that she, Sarasvati, who could give him his heart's desire.

The Maharanee was snoring by the time Sarah left her, having quite abruptly ceased her narration soon after issuing an enormous yawn and lying back into her cushions. Since she had not yet breakfasted and it was now time for luncheon, Sarah asked the hovering khansamah if she might take a light meal in the summer house.

As she walked, Sarah puzzled over the story. The Maharanee's candid admission that one of her husband's concubines was in love with him did not seem to bother her in the least, and it was almost as if she needed to believe in this romance herself, since her own life was little more than an opium dream. Perhaps Sarasvati was no longer infatuated with her prince, for Sarah had seen no sign of it, and on the one occasion that she had seen them together, she had been submissive and silent. As to the Maharanee's vicarious existence, it was nothing less than a tragedy. Sarah thought that she had heard, in the telling of Sarasvati's story, the high regard the Maharanee had once held for her consort, but her husband's despondency and her cloistered life had since robbed her both of her attraction to him and her pleasure in it.

As she approached the summer house, Sarah heard a noise in the bamboo behind her, and quite suddenly Sarasvati appeared, dishevelled and with a ruinous look about her. She appeared thinner than she had only a week before, and was holding something limp in her arms, which

Sarah at first thought was a child. When she came closer, she realised it was, in fact, a small monkey. It was dead, and not only dead but dismembered. The fine yellow georgette of Sarasvati's sari was soaked with the animal's blood, and Sarah realised with horror that the head and arms of the monkey had been severed.

When she saw Sarah, Sarasvati fell on to her knees, wailing, though she showed no signs of recognition. The animal had been slain – was all Sarah managed to extract from the confused ramblings of the ranee – presumably by Hindu servants, as a sacrifice.

'Why does the goddess demand such things?' Sarasvati sobbed. For a terrible moment Sarah wondered if the woman on her knees could have done this appalling deed, but she put it from her mind. In a moment, two of the swarthy Arab guards appeared, seemingly from nowhere, and while one pried the gory remains of the monkey from Sarasvati's bloodied grasp, the other lifted her and carried her away. The guards discharged their respective duties gently, but with an air of sad resignation, as though it was not the first time they had seen such a drama unfold. Sickened, Sarah turned away and, unable to face luncheon after all, she returned to her room. Sarasvati was clearly unhinged by her habit, and perhaps something else.

As soon as she closed the door of her room, Sarah leaned against it and collapsed gradually to the floor, her legs no longer able to hold her erect. As she sat, dazed and also weakened by hunger, her thoughts turned to Mr Elliot. Again, his was the friendly face she envisaged when the shadowy otherworld of the palace became too much. He was probably no longer at the Vaishya, however, for his classes began in the afternoon, and she was reluctant to venture again from her room. She needed something to keep both her mind and hands occupied. It was time, she decided, to dismantle *The Venus of Waterloo*.

With the aid of a silver letter opener, Sarah removed the board, and found thick brown paper across the back of a wooden structure, on to which the canvas was fastened. She removed the brown paper easily, exposing a great number of tiny nails securing the work. And something else. Nestled in the corner of the simple wooden frame was a small object wrapped in a scarlet silk handkerchief. Intrigued, Sarah removed it and gently unravelled its swaddling. She gasped in disbelief at what slid into the palm of her hand. It did not seem possible, nor did it make any sense, but there was no mistaking that it was Lily's hairwork pendant that lay in the hollow of her trembling hand.

❖ 35 ❖

Maya maya thagini ham jani
(Illusion is like the female thuggee)

Kabir, poet of Benares

Sarah had never before held Lily's pendant, nor examined it so closely. The gold disc upon which the jet was mounted was clearly of a high carat, for it was heavy, and the tiny, perfect lilies were intricately moulded from the pale hair of Franz Korechnya. A central lily was surrounded by a wreath of smaller flowers, all fastened to the jet and covered in glass. There was something strangely alluring about it, though she had never before been moved by the English sentimentality of mourning jewellery. The rather complicated formalities of mourning were sternly observed by all who wished to appear respectable in London, encouraged by Queen Victoria's perseverance in wearing black more than a decade after the death of Prince Albert.

Sarah had presumed that the piece had been sent to Lily's parents, although in truth very few of her possessions had been shipped back to England. Now here it was, carefully hidden behind the portrait. Sarah laid the linen canvas flat on the desktop to judge its size. It would fit neatly into the drawer of her portmanteau. As she looked more closely at the image which Franz Korechnya had so lovingly painted, each brushstroke in accord with the lightness of Lily's spirit, she puzzled over the question: who had put the pendant there, and why? She supposed that Lily had wanted it to be kept with the painting which most represented her devotion to Franz, rather than hidden away in a box full of yellowing parchment.

She felt drawn to the pendant, perhaps because it had been so precious to Lily, and slipped it around her neck. It somehow seemed the perfect prelude to reading the last letter.

Dear Barbara

Today, as always, I write from the summer house, a pavilion made entirely of white marble, which does not absorb the heat like other stone, and when it catches the light it calls to mind the sunlit sea of my passage to Bombay. Here I find that I am always at peace with my thoughts, and may reflect upon all manner of things.

I have not yet described to you my good fortune in viewing the jewellery collection of the Maharanee. She is the prince's number-one wife and does not appear to associate with the other ranees, with the exception of Sarasvati. These two have a curious bond, and I can only guess that it is because each of them is, in a different way, favoured, and they are therefore not part of the society of the harem. The Maharanee is reclusive and keeps to her private apartments where she is fed all day on sago laced with rice syrup and opium.

Sarasvati is also permitted into the vaults, or so she told me, and it was in her company that I visited this place not long after I arrived at the palace. She led me deep into the maze of corridors and stairways, and I watched as she spoke to the guards at the door, two fearsome looking men who, I can by now tell, were part of the Maharajah's special guard. Although I could not understand what was being said, it was clear that the guards were being cajoled into allowing us to enter. Indeed I observed here coquetry of the highest order; each of them looked altogether smitten, for not only is this child-woman profoundly beautiful, but also she knows how to use her charms.

The small room in which the jewellery is kept is a windowless ante-chamber, accessible only through a low door that is hidden in an alcove behind a hanging. And here, such treasures! I was almost blinded by the radiance of so many gems, all contained in golden caskets encrusted with semi-precious stones. It was as I imagine a dragon's lair might look. I am informed that some of the bounty is the personal collection of the Maharajah, and some, jewels that belong to the state and are worn by his women on formal occasions.

Whilst I stood, rendered quite speechless by the treasures before me, Sarasvati seemed agitated, and went from one casket to another, taking great handfuls of precious stones and flinging them back as though they were pebbles on the shore. I asked her if she was quite well, and she said that she had hoped that Govinda would have returned the diamonds by now; why had he not? Were these the nine diamonds which had been taken to London to be made into a navaratna charm, I enquired, yet as soon as I had spoken I knew that I had made a mistake. Although Sarasvati clearly knew of the nine, and that they had been sent to London under Govinda's guardianship, I believe that she knew nothing of the charm. 'So this is why he wanted Kali's stone,' was all that she said and then became cold and sullen, and would speak no more on that subject.

When later we went to the bazaar by palanquin, she seemed recovered a little. As we were close to the old quarter of the city, I asked if we might visit the ancient Kali temple which I have come to feel a certain affinity with, not least because it is one of the oldest temples in Benares. (I have learnt that it was built before the Moghul princes brought the religion of Islam to India in the fifteenth century.) I am certain that Sarasvati quivered at the mention of the shrine to the goddess. She began to whisper under her breath as though in prayer, and I felt that I must ask what it was that perturbed her so. It was the red diamond, she said. Kali's diamond, she called it. It must not be used in a navaratna charm, for all of the gods would be displeased, and Kali most of all. The Maharajah was not Hindu and so did not understand what a foolish thing it was to make such a dangerous charm.

The day seemed hotter by several degrees than any I had yet endured, and I felt quite lightheaded by the time we arrived at the temple. Sarasvati would not step into the shrine with me, but remained at the door and I am certain that it was because she was afraid of the wrath of Kali. Just as I was about to enter, we encountered the wife of one of the municipality officers, who immediately introduced herself to me but ignored my companion. The memsahib proceeded to glorify the proposed new development, without pausing to note that I was not in its favour. I was relieved to leave her and the terrible heat, for I would choose even the company of Kali above one who has not the courage to face her own shadow.

There was an old woman inside the shrine, with a red mark painted between her eyes, and though I have seen this marking on many, with her dark robes and bent form, she almost frightened me. I suddenly felt cold, and while I stood there motionless, something occurred which I can barely bring myself to tell, for you will think it merely a delusion. Yet I must, for only then will you understand why it is I have become ill. Through the open doorway came the figure of a man in the very image of my dead husband. The light from the doorway was behind him, so I could not yet see his face, but by the shape of his shoulders and his gait, and the silvery halo of his hair, I knew it was him. When he reached me, he touched my neck and his fingers closed about the pendant I wear always. In another breath, he was gone.

Since that day, Barbara, I have realised that I am not ill, but dying. It is as though Franz keeps his promise to me, for here am I in the city of light, one of the few doorways between the worlds, and he is beckoning to me. Do not feel saddened, for I am at peace, my friend.

Ever yours,
Lily

A hot tear rolled from Sarah's cheek and stained the silk pillow as she slid the pendant beneath it and closed her eyes. Almost immediately she began to dream of a nine-armed goddess dressed in a mantle of mourning black and with serpentine bracelets, leading a band of thieves and murderers.

When she woke the room had darkened, and there was an unfamiliar quality to the light and the air. From the balcony, she could see that it was the approaching rains, for the greens of the foliage were heightened and the distant rooftops were softened by mist. Soon the city would be awash, but the monsoon was welcomed here, for it fertilised and nourished, and thus sustained life. The coolness of the air was revitalising and, curious to walk the palace grounds in the eerie, green light, Sarah pulled a paisley shawl across her shoulders and fastened Lily's pendant about her neck. It must not become lost again.

It seemed that she was not alone in her desire to enjoy the gardens, for as she came out from an arbour not far from the summer house, she thought that she saw Sarasvati again, or rather, a streak of filmy yellow organza. Nor was the summer house deserted, for Govinda was there, standing with his back to her, his gaze directed towards the skies.

As she approached, he turned and bowed. 'Good evening, Miss Sarah.'
'Good evening. It seems that we both favour this place.'
'I have always liked it here. It is peaceful.'
'Will the rains come very soon?'

'Yes, soon. In three or maybe four days.' Govinda again looked at the sky. 'There is a legend concerning a great drought which resulted in a terrible famine. Mahadevi, the earth goddess who has many eyes, was approached by the people, who begged her for relief. Seeing the wretchedness of her creatures, she wept. She wept from her many eyes for nine days and nights causing the rains to fall, the rivers to fill and life to return. Now, when the rains come, Mahadevi is worshipped and offerings are brought to her temples.'

'It seems that in your faith there are gods and stories to explain all things in nature,' Sarah commented.

'It is important to have something to believe in, Miss Sarah,' although he said this as though he felt burdened by his own faith, she thought.

'For example, the pendant you wear now,' Govinda continued, looking pointedly at the mourning jewellery she wore about her neck, 'that is also a symbol of faith.'

Sarah touched the glass self-consciously. 'Yes. I discovered the pendant in an unexpected place and now I find that I am loath to let it out of my sight.'

Govinda's expression was unfathomable. 'Such things should not be taken lightly. It is now a piece of jewellery that has its own memory, as all metals do, for it has known the pains of love and grief.'

'Surely it is but a piece of jewellery ... Tell me, was Lily wearing it when she died?'

'I could not say.'

'No, for she often wore it beneath her clothing and against her heart,' said Sarah, almost to herself.

They were both silent for a time, watching the sky billow and darken. Govinda's next words took Sarah entirely by surprise. 'It seems that I will travel to London after all. There is some business that I must take care of for the Maharajah.'

As she met his eye, Sarah wondered what it was that had made him agree to go to London, for surely the city could have no allure to one such as himself. She also hoped that this did not mean the Maharajah had decided to allow Sarasvati to visit after all. Govinda bowed and would have left, but Sarah hurried to find some topic of conversation to make him tarry. If only she could muster the courage to speak of the diamonds, for Lily's last letter had raised yet more questions.

'I have visited the temple to Kali, of which Lily wrote, and should very much like to go there once more before I leave the city.'

'It is no place for one such as yourself.' Govinda's words were sharp and cold, and beneath his composure, Sarah glimpsed his steely purposefulness.

'What do you mean "one such as myself"?' Sarah felt her indignation rise like a flame.

'I mean, it is a place for the many who worship the dark side of Kali, and could be . . . dangerous.'

Sarah laughed. 'I am not afraid of Kali, Mr Govinda.'

'Then you should be, Miss Sarah.' With this, he bowed again and was gone.

Sarah stayed long enough only to watch two monkeys squabbling over a coconut, and when one hit the other on the head with the shell, thus resolving the argument, she made her way back through the gardens. As she passed the part of the path where she had encountered Sarasvati, and thought that she saw the dark stain of blood still on the grass, she felt her heart flutter with the very fear she had moments before denied. But it would not do to become fearful and avoid Sarasvati, she told herself. Despite the shadow that sometimes took hold of her, Sarah could not help but feel a certain fondness for the zenana's outcast and she resolved to call immediately on the ranee in her apartments.

Sarasvati was on her swing, rocking back and forth woefully, like a depressed canary.

'I am forbidden to go to London,' she said mournfully as soon as she saw Sarah. 'The Maharajah will not allow it.'

'Perhaps it is a mark of his affection that he will not.' Sarah did not know what else to say.

Sarasvati shrugged. 'He does not care for me any more, and now I shall never see my friend.'

'Your friend?'

'My friend in London.'

'I am sorry,' said Sarah.

'No, you are not.'

Sarah did not refute it. As a means of changing the subject she unhooked the clasp which fastened the pendant about her neck and took a step closer to the mournful ranee. 'I found this, hidden behind the painting which the Maharajah gave me.'

Sarasvati took the pendant with a great show of disinterest, turning it over in her hand before nonchalantly dropping it back into Sarah's.

'Do you know how it came to be there?' Sarah pressed.

'It was the Maharajah who had the painting framed,' Sarasvati said, looking thoroughly bored. Sarah frowned, perplexed. Then was it the prince who had stowed the pendant there, for had he not once shown an interest in it? Perhaps he, like Govinda, thought it unwise to wear a piece of jewellery which was a memento of love and loss. Perhaps it had even been Lily's dying wish that no one disturb it from its resting place in her special painting. For a terrible moment Sarah worried that she had somehow violated Lily's memory by removing it.

As for Sarasvati, her reasons for doing anything were largely a mystery, for at times she seemed to exist in another realm entirely. Sarah wondered if one particular manifestation still had the power to frighten her.

'I should like to visit the old temple to Kali before I return to London.' Sarah said, feeling treacherous, for not only was she deliberately baiting the ranee, but she was also keeping from her the fact that this would not be her first visit to the ancient shrine.

Sarasvati looked up at her quickly. 'You want to go there! Why?'

'Because Lily . . . liked it.'

Sarasvati was silent for a time, as if she were grappling with something. 'I can not let you go alone.'

'But why not?'

'You might get lost. We will need guards. Tomorrow I will call for you.'

The ranee then abruptly returned to her swinging. Thus dismissed, Sarah fastened Lily's pendant at her neck and left without another word. By the time she reached the sanctuary of her own chamber, Sarah felt weighted with a torpor unlike any she had experienced. It must be the weight of the very air about her, she thought.

⁜ 36 ⁜

Blessed are those who seek her with pure hands and do not pursue
her with a treacherous heart.

The Beatitudes, Anon, first century BCE

In an unaccountably altered state, Sarah woke in the night believing
there was someone in her chamber. Frozen by fear, she thought she saw
a pale sweep of cloth slipping through the curtains on to her balcony. It
was impossible to know for certain, for the fine mosquito netting which
hung around her bed was billowing gently in the breeze, and through it
the shapes and shadows of the room were ill-defined. Sarah lay awake
and fretted, inventing new horrors, for there were trees that might allow
an agile body to climb up to her room and thereby reach her. What
reason anyone might have to harm her though, she could not say. She
fell into an uneasy sleep, feeling feverish in the sultry closeness of the
air.

In the morning, she awoke to find Sarasvati sitting by her bedside.

'I thought that we might walk in the garden, Miss Sarah, before the
sun is too high.'

'I would still like to go to the Kali temple.'

Sarasvati did not look pleased to hear it; she had clearly had a change
of heart about the outing she had reluctantly agreed to. 'It is not wise.
The temple is old and damp. There are rats.'

'I should like to go all the same. Do not feel that you must chaperone
me if you would prefer not to.'

Sarasvati frowned. 'I will go to the chaukidar and make certain that
we have sufficient guards,' she said, resignedly.

On the way there, Sarah asked Sarasvati if she could make a quick
stop at the Vaishya guesthouse. Sarasvati shrugged in response, and
only reclined further on her velveteen cushions.

Mr Elliot was seated at the same table, in much the same posture

248

and was dressed in his usual costume of pale linen and a panama hat. He looked up as Sarah approached and was unmistakably pleased to see her.

'Why, good morning Miss O'Reilly! What a jolly nice surprise. Will you have some tea?'

'I cannot stay long for one of the Maharajah's ranees is waiting for me. I wanted to say goodbye as I leave for London this week.'

'I am sorry to hear it. Do sit for a moment, won't you?' Sarah did. 'Now tell me,' Mr Elliot continued, 'where are you off to in such a hurry this morning.' He sipped his tea elegantly and looked at her over the rim of his cup, as though he expected she was up to some mischief.

'I am returning to the shrine of Kali.'

'Whatever for? Why, when we were last there I almost had to carry you away!'

'That is precisely why I am going back. There is something . . .' Sarah stopped herself and looked at her companion. Was he equal to the truth? 'There is some occult presence there that intrigues me, if you must know.'

'But of course there is, my dear Miss O'Reilly.'

'What do you mean?'

'Well, at the risk of sounding Delphian, according to Hinduism, actions without desire have no destiny, but where desire meets obstruction it becomes anger. Such as in the case of Kali. She is desirous of all our earthly offerings, she devours indiscriminately, but when her appetites are frustrated, her wrath is unequalled. What you feel in her temple is quite simply her divine anger, her thwarted desire.'

'But for what?'

'Who can say? For blood, for flesh, omnipotence, the eternal fire of the legendary red diamond . . . who can say?'

'And what if she were to acquire the red diamond?'

'I imagine she might be satisfied for a time, but then, is it not the character of desire to long for the unattainable? Think of the grail, Miss O'Reilly, or the search for true love? The quest for such treasures is in our nature, but we do not look beyond the immediate goal of acquisition.'

'Then, you do not believe, as do the Christian missionaries, that desire itself is wicked?'

'Ah, an interesting proposition. I have no moral dilemma myself, for

I find that it interferes with my own quest – for knowledge – but I am inclined to think that it is the nature of one's desire that is important.'

The philosophy struck a familiar chord with Sarah. 'It calls to mind something I have been meaning to ask you. Do you know of the Hindu jewel called navaratna?'

'An astrological charm, I believe. According to some, the power of the navaratna is that it is capable of granting one's wish or desire, if one is pure of heart. However, it might just as easily work in the reverse.'

'What if the stones were mixed up, or replaced with the wrong gems?'

'That is a most peculiar question. I am not a Hindu priest, but I would guess that it might very well anger the gods and cause all sorts of planetary disturbances. Are you sure you won't have tea?'

'Thank you, no. I must not leave the ranee waiting any longer.' Sarah held out her hand. 'It has been a pleasure to make your acquaintance, Mr Elliot.'

'And I yours, Miss O'Reilly. Do be wary in the temple, for you seem a trifle wan today, and one needs to greet the dark goddess with one's sword at the ready and one's armour in place!'

He shook her hand and their eyes met for a fleeting moment. Sarah wondered if it might be enough to take pleasure in a man's mind alone, aside from his other characteristics. If, of course, one were the type to consider such things ... She had long assumed that she was simply beyond the reach of romantic love, for she was unable to be either demure or deferential in the company of a gentleman. This, according to General Etiquette, was what was expected of a lady. In truth, lately, Sarah had wondered whether there might, after all, be another kind of love, for had Franz Korechnya not fallen in love with Lily for her mind as much as for her other graces? And what must it be like, falling in love? She could not imagine, but was curious.

'I hope I shall see you again, before you depart these shores, Miss O'Reilly. Perhaps you might permit me to escort you to your train?'

'Of course. I would be thankful for your company.'

When Sarah returned to the palanquin, she found Sarasvati was asleep, or pretending to be, which conveniently redressed the need for an apology or explanation. In addition to the hummals there were six guards, stationed around the palanquin, all of them dressed in turbans and the same flowing, colourless clothing which Sarah had seen

Govinda wear. They were intentionally devoid of identity, she realised, so that one did not even feel the urge to look upon their faces. Yet, she guessed that should they be required, theirs was a presence that would be felt, and not lightly.

Outside the low doorway to the temple, Sarah hesitated to alight. Sarasvati would not be roused, and Sarah was certain that this was her means of avoiding an audience with the goddess. The guards had now turned so that their backs were to the palanquin and they were facing in each direction along the intersection of narrow alleys. As Sarah turned to enter the shrine, she felt the gaze of one of them and looked up to meet it. It was Govinda. He looked away immediately, and Sarah felt unnerved by his unexpected presence.

It seemed that there were a greater number of candles burning in the shrine, more than she remembered, for she had not noticed before that the cave-like chamber was vaulted, the hoary timbers of its ceiling appearing like the carcass of a beast. At the altar, too, were many tiny flames, but no sign of anyone to tend them. The goddess herself was grinning lewdly, her long tongue bright with blood and the garland of skulls that adorned her neck glowing ghostly white. Sarah touched the pendant at her neck, and tried to recall Lily's final encounter with Kali. What had it meant, the vision Lily had here?

As she stepped closer to the goddess, Sarah instantly felt the same oppressive weight which had crept over her the previous day. It was as though all of her darkest imaginings were present; her struggle to be something more than an impoverished urchin; the burden of being Ellen's protector; the loneliness of her unconventional pursuit of a profession . . . And somehow, all of these fears seemed to be embodied in the figure before her. As she stared at the face of Kali, the goddess's hooded, bloodshot eyes seemed to gaze back into her heart and Sarah knew that she was falling into the abyss of her own shadow. As she fell, she saw a thousand splinters of light, for all the world like the refractions of a fiery red diamond.

Her head hit something hard, and she might have been lying there for any length of time before she thought she saw a luminous drama unfolding. A film of smoke now replaced the crystal shards of light, the altar became a pyre, and through its flames she saw the ebony figure of Kali burning. Before her was Sarasvati, dancing like a nymph as she had the day Sarah came upon her in her chamber. She held a candle in each hand and her translucent yellow veil could not hide the expression of triumph she wore. As the heat ascended and the smoke thickened, another figure appeared, though Sarah could not say who it was. Someone tall and dressed in pale trousers collected her in his arms and carried her away.

It was two days before Sarah felt well enough to venture from her bed, and still a spiritless languor slowed her limbs and clouded her mind. Twice Sarasvati came to her bedside and sat with her, though Sarah could not remember what they spoke of. Finally, on the third day Sarah sat up and took a glass of chai from the kind serving girl who had waited on her throughout her stay. Almost immediately, Sarasvati appeared, and Sarah could only assume that she had instructed that she be notified as soon as the invalid was recovered.

'You look better,' Sarasvati said, inspecting Sarah's complexion. 'The Maharanee would like to see you when you feel well enough.'

'I am well enough now, but for an aching head.'

'You hit your head in the temple.'

'Yes, I dimly remember . . . you were there too, were you not?'

'No, Miss Sarah, I'm sorry, but I was asleep.'

'But I am certain that I saw you! You were dancing . . .'

'You are mistaken,' Sarasvati's voice had turned brittle.

'Who was it that carried me out of the shrine? Was it an Englishman?'

'I do not know. Come, I will help you dress.'

As Sarah allowed Sarasvati to fasten the buttons at the back of her gown, she recollected her experience in the shrine. 'But, the temple – the statue of Kali was on fire!'

'Yes, but Kali is made stronger by the flames, for they bestow the fire of knowledge.' Sarasvati imparted this wisdom as if it were of no consequence, then smoothly changed the subject. 'I see that you no longer wear the sandalwood about your neck. I know that he gave them to you.'

'Who gave them to me – whatever do you mean?'

'If you know where he is, then you must ask him . . .' Sarasvati trailed off, as if she'd suddenly thought better of pursuing the matter. 'Come, Miss Sarah, the Maharanee is waiting.'

Sarasvati did not enter the apartments of the prince's number-one wife. At the door, she said, 'Maybe I will not see you again, Miss Sarah, for I sometimes lose track of time, and soon you will be gone. The Maharanee has told me that Govinda will visit London, and I shall instruct him to convey a message to my friend.' With this rather puzzling disclosure, Sarasvati disappeared without another word.

As before, the Maharanee was reclining slothfully and eating. She patted the cushion as though she were beckoning to a pet, and Sarah sat down obediently and made herself comfortable.

'Do you remember what I told you, when last you were here?'

'Yes, Sarasvati had danced before the Maharajah . . .'

'Yes, yes,' said the Maharanee, holding up her hand in a gesture of silence.

The zenana was not as Sarasvati had expected, for the other women were Mussalmani and were not pleased to have a beautiful Hindu in their midst. Once she had as many veils and cholas and gold bracelets as she could wish, Sarasvati became bored. If she was called to the Maharajah's rooms, it was only to dance for him, and for no other reason. He did not speak to her, nor did he even come near her, and it was unthinkable that one such as she would approach the prince. Nothing was as she had expected.

The Maharajah, though he wore his scabbard and rode upon a war-horse, was melancholic for the days of battle and glory. His ancestors had conquered cities and ruled as heroes, whilst he had only polo rivals and British society to contend with. Sarasvati did not yet know that the Maharajah sought the coloured diamonds in order to make his navaratna. He believed that with such a powerful charm, he might attract the sympathy of the divinities.

The Maharajah was accompanied at all times by guards; and always by one particular guard, who was quite unlike the others. He was paler of complexion, and his features were fine and strong. Sarasvati recognised that he was one of the Himalayan people, whom she had seen in the high country. She had been struck by their grace, not just of form, but of spirit. On mountain paths the Himalayan people would always greet another traveller with 'namaste', a greeting that was offered from the heart. It made her happy and sad at once, for it both lightened her spirit and reminded her of the destiny she sought. She would not, in her life, walk the mountain trails in a dusty cloak and woven boots. Not for her the heavy necklaces of coral and turquoise that the mountain people wore, but silk and gold and jewels.

A tear coursed down the Mahranee's soft, plump cheek, and Sarah felt certain that she was crying for herself, for neither would she walk the mountain trails, or be freed from her opulent prison and her addiction.

The Himalayan guard was called Govinda, and he had the Maharajah's confidence. There was another order of guards who were not Arab, and who protected the prince when he toured his estates. These were trained killers, even though they were often of slighter of build. They guarded the palace vault, and always accompanied the Maharajah when he was inspecting his opium fields; at times a dangerous undertaking. The prince's opium is a source of great income, as are alluvial diamonds from Sarasvati's village, but opium is easier to steal. Amongst this special guard, Sarasvati soon made a friend. He was weakened by her beauty, as men often are, and women too, and she realised she could have him do whatever she wanted. She decided that he should tell the Maharajah about the red diamond, since as a warrior of Kali, he was duty bound to serve the goddess. The prince sent immediately for Sarasvati, who assured him that it was true; the stone had been hidden by the village priest in Kali's third eye.

When he returned from her village, the opium guard told Sarasvati what had happened. He had watched as the priest was put to death, and the villagers wept. Sarasvati was shocked. She had not stopped to consider what might become of the priest, nor how the villagers would fare without him. She did not yet understand that the diamond could take lives.

On the day that the opium guard returned from Sarasvati's village with the stone, she sat waiting for the prince to call her to his chamber. She had dressed in the palest of yellow organza trousers and a chola bodice embroidered in gold. Across her hair and face she wore a shimmering veil. Once the Maharajah had the diamond, he paid a good deal more attention to Sarasvati. She became his lover that night, and thereafter when he called for her. She had given him the greatest of gifts, and he would always be grateful. Whether or not he also thought that she, Sarasvati, was worthy of his care, she did not know. He was always generous of purse, and it was in this way that he bestowed his attentions. He was otherwise remote, for although he had acquired the ninth stone, there was still no jeweller who would make his longed-for diamond navaratna.

Every day, Sarasvati went to look at the diamonds, though she dared not hold the red diamond again in her hand, for it had been touched by Kali. On some occasions she felt that only to look upon it gave her strength; that Kali smiled upon her servant; on others it soothed her loneliness and encouraged her vanity. Always, she tried to forget that she had caused the death of the priest.

There were many visitors to the palace, for the Maharajah liked to entertain Britishers and he particularly enjoyed the company of English ladies. When Lady Cynthia Herbert arrived in Benares and started buying diamonds, the Maharajah was, of course, apprised. She and her husband, Lord Charles Herbert, were invited to be guests at the palace. Lady Herbert and the Maharajah shared a devotion to diamonds, and it was not long before the Maharajah showed her his collection, explaining to her his desire that they be made into the astrological talisman called navaratna. Sadly, he said, no jeweller in India would accept the commission. They were too frightened, and no amount of gold could purchase their skill.

Sarasvati could not have foreseen what happened next, for she still did not know the Maharajah's secret. Two days after Lord and Lady Herbert had departed Benares, she went to visit the golden casket in the vault as usual. Only when she saw that the diamonds were gone did she understand. Sarasvati had seen the covetous look on Cynthia Herbert's face upon first viewing the stones, and she had observed the hushed conversations between Lady Herbert and the Maharajah. The Maharajah had allowed the blanched Britisher and her polite, insipid husband to take his beloved diamonds!

Immediately, Sarasvati summoned her opium guard, and instructed him to retrieve the red diamond, for she knew that the Herberts were travelling slowly with many porters and much baggage. When he returned without the diamond, she was consumed with rage. She lay awake at night, bereft. Without the stone, she felt that she was nothing. It seemed to her that when the diamond gave her substance; made her desirable and complete. How could the Maharajah ever love her now? It mattered little that she still had the prince's riches, that she might eat sweet halwa all day if she pleased. She went to the Kali shrine and made offerings; she promised the goddess that she would serve her for her entire life, if only she would bring back the red diamond. Finally, she told the opium guard that he must go to London; that she would give him gold and he could take opium and sandalwood to sell there. If he returned with the diamond, she told him, then she would be his servant.

When the Maharanee roused herself from the reverie into which she fell each time she told the story, she looked at Sarah with an air of satisfaction. 'You see, Miss Sarah, one does not have to commit a story to the page to be a clever writer.' She tapped her head. 'It is all here. And to be a good storyteller, one must have a subject one is devoted to. In my subject, I see everything that I once was, for I, too, came from humble beginnings. I wish for Sarasvati everything that I have lost, for if she finds happiness then there is still love in the world. And if there is love in the world, then all is well.'

❖ 37 ❖

A man is in general better pleased when he has a good dinner on his table than when his wife talks Greek.

Samuel Johnson

Sarah woke feeling disorientated, for instead of the tinkle of silver anklets and gentle shushing of the breeze she could hear the harsh cry of a street vendor. It took her another moment to remember that she was back in London, and that Benares was now a memory. For a second she imagined that Lily was here with her in the attic of the Kensington house, for there was a lightness to the air that had always accompanied her presence. The thought soothed Sarah as she lay in her bed, listening to the robins in the branches of the apple tree.

The most unexpected thing about having returned, only a little more than a week ago, was the sensation that one's travels had occurred in a dream. It came as a great surprise to Sarah that the scents of spice and blossom, the luminous sights and sounds of the palace, all seemed little more than fancy. In their place were the familiar smells of Martha's housekeeping – bread baking in the kitchen, linseed oil on the stair, and a bowl of rose petals scenting the water closet.

Sarah's homecoming had held a sweetness she could not have imagined. Not only was Ellen at St Margaret's Wharf to greet her, but also Martha. Considering that Ellen didn't like carriages and Martha rarely came 'into the town', as she put it, preferring to do her shopping at the Kensington Market, this was a special occasion indeed. Ellen threw herself at Sarah as soon as she came down the creaking stair from the deck, and did not let go of her hand for the entire journey home.

Leaving Benares had been just as fraught with unexpected emotion. She had taken her leave of both the Maharajah and the Maharanee, but when it came time for her to board the palanquin to the railway station, Sarasvati was nowhere to be seen. She still felt a wonderment over all the Maharanee had told her of the golden-robed ranee, and the fact that it had been she who had discovered the red diamond. It cast quite a different light upon Sarasvati's many peculiarities, not least on the translation of the Hindu words *mera varga*. My diamond. On top of that, when Mr Elliot had accompanied her to her train, he held her hand a little longer than was necessary as he helped her into her carriage.

'I have enjoyed your society tremendously, Miss O'Reilly. Should ever you return to Benares, I hope that you will remember me.'

'And will you return to London, Mr Elliot?'

'I believe I have forsaken that damp and dreary place. I prefer the peculiarities of the Orient, it seems.'

'Then I wish you well, sir. I shall always remember your kindness.' Sarah had turned away, confused by the emotion this leave-taking aroused in her. It was not love, surely?

There was a halcyon quality to the first stirrings of the day, the moments after waking but before awakeness, which seemed unnatural even more than one week after Sarah had stepped from the perpetual motion of the *Ranee*. It caused her to wonder if she was entirely sentient. She lay perfectly still, waiting for her bustling mind to begin its usual whirring and pondering. This took rather longer than normal, for she still did not feel as energetic as she ought. She was obviously not yet fully recovered from the journey, for the wrath of the deep had pursued them, first in the Indian Ocean and then in the South Atlantic. Tempests of crashing waves and squalls of ferocious winds had thrown the *Ranee* about as if she were no more than a leaf in a storm drain, and it was to this that Sarah attributed her continuing languor.

She threw the quilt from her and hastened to find a shawl to put about her shoulders. She would not let Martha build the fire in the attic room, for she found that the chill in the eaves in late summer invigorated her. It also reminded her of another time. She was thankful every day for all that fate had bestowed upon her, and would not allow herself to forget how it felt to be cold, huddled over the vents above the basements of Paternoster Row.

Sarah stood by the slanting window for a moment, looking down upon the lawn. There was Mrs Vesper, approaching her kitchen door from the back of the garden with her shallow basket full of herb cuttings.

She had the vigour of a much younger woman, and Sarah wondered if it was the housekeeper's capacity to be in constant motion that kept her so hale and youthful. Perhaps age simply could not catch up with Martha Vesper.

Sarah was tempted to dress in her breeches and boots, but she must go to the *Mercury* today and speak with Mr Harding about her essays. It wasn't that he minded her being dressed in this manner, since she had passed the greater number of her years at the *Mercury* thus. No, today, she wanted to make a point of not masquerading, for she intended to do business: the business of a female journalist. So instead of her beloved breeches, Sarah chose a plain brown carmeline skirt and a white cambric shirt. At least the fashions now allowed for less frivolity, perhaps because more women were looking for an alternative to marriage as a career, and therefore needed a more practical and less alluring costume.

Martha had laid the table in the library, as she did every morning, and was pouring Sarah's coffee from the pot as if she knew that it was just the right moment to do so. This uncanny knack of Martha's for knowing most things was something it had taken Sarah a very long time to get used to, but now it just seemed as normal as her other peculiarities. Just like the way she had recently hung a sprig of sage on the door of the studio, and how she always took certain cuttings from her kitchen garden when the moon was full.

Ellen was already at the table with the papers spread out before her, her cloud of golden tresses escaping from their pins and her narrow shoulders draped in a powder-blue shawl. Her smile was incandescent as Sarah entered, as though she had not seen her sister every morning for the past nine days.

'Good morning, Sarah!'

'Good morning yourself, Ellen. I'm not about to disappear, you know.'

'I know.' Ellen beamed. 'I know.' She chewed on her lip for a minute. 'I've something to tell you, Sarah.'

Sarah tensed immediately at the confessional tone, bracing herself for 'Ellen trouble' as she'd come to call it.

'Give me a moment to take a glass of coffee and freshen my wits a little.' Sarah sat down alongside a mound of warm breakfast rolls wrapped in white linen and a cut glass pot containing Martha's ginger marmalade. After a few sips of Mrs Vesper's fine, strong coffee and a bite or two of a buttered roll, she could no longer ignore Ellen's impatient gaze.

'All right Elly, what is it?'

'Well, it's only that I'm always trying to find a new gaff for the paper, and that's how I came by it . . .'

'What is it, Elly?'

'I give a farthing to Lou sometimes, the watercress girl at Farringdon Market whose Mam's got a barrow at Billingsgate and knows all sorts. One of her customers is all secretive, so Lou's Mam has been trying to get to the bottom of it. It happens that this woman has a son called Davey who works down the underground railway and almost never comes up on the street. Too scared, Lou's Mam reckons, so he's just been down there laying the tracks for years. They sleep underground too, just like moles – imagine that, Sarah! And you wouldn't recognise the track layers even if you knew them because they get all blacked-up and don't like to pay even a penny for a cold bath when they're just going to get all soot-covered again.'

'So, you think we should do a story about the track layers?'

'No, Sarah. I think Davey is Davey Simons, the jeweller's apprentice who went missing after those diamonds were robbed. I've known it since before you went off to India, but I didn't know how to tell you. You see, it's as though there's something wants all this out in the open now. Ever since you got those letters from Lily, and started getting interested in the diamonds again after so long, that something has been about.'

'Whatever do you mean, Ellen? What something has been about?' At that moment Martha Vesper entered the room, and Sarah had the feeling she'd been listening in.

'Martha knows it too, don't you Martha?' Ellen looked at her imploringly and Martha had the good grace not to pretend she hadn't heard them. She nodded her head sagely.

'Aye, there's something about all right.'

It was then that the housekeeper admitted what had been going on in Sarah's absence. A few days after Sarah's arrival in Benares, Martha had opened the door of the Kensington house to Detective Inspector Gerard, from the Westminster Police. 'A young man with a good tailor and eyes as sharp as a needle,' she told Sarah. Martha's immediate concern had been for Ellen, for neither of the O'Reilly girls had a respect for danger and the housekeeper would never admit to how many long and worrisome hours she'd passed, waiting for the two of them to come in late at night.

In her matter-of-fact way, Martha related how, after she had made Gerard comfortable in the parlour, she had busied herself preparing coffee, believing that the long hours of the policeman's profession would surely benefit from its particular properties. Sarah had observed how particular the housekeeper was about the Arabian coffee she bought from the swarthy roaster at Kensington market. She called it the Abyssinian bean, which, Sarah thought, always made it sound exotic.

When Martha had returned to the parlour, Ellen was sitting opposite their visitor, and she had about her the guarded look that told Martha something was amiss. Although Ellen was always busy chasing after stories for her sister to pursue, it had become clear to the housekeeper that the girl had been chasing the past too. Martha had sensed a shadowy presence ever since Sarah had left. Upon admitting to this, as though it were as common as dust, Sarah saw a glance being exchanged between Martha Vesper and Ellen.

Ellen looked at her sister imploringly. 'You see Sarah, I *had* to tell that detective that Davey is alive and that I knew where he lived, but I couldn't tell him exactly where, because what if the same thing happened to him as happened to Joe? I just know that he's no more a murderer than Holy Joe was.'

'There's been something afoot ever since,' Martha added, and as though this statement were self-explanatory, she cleared away the breakfast things and left the room without another word. Sarah sighed with exasperation, feeling, as she often did, that she was missing something that was as plain as day to Ellen and Martha Vesper.

'It wasn't him that committed the murders, Sarah,' Ellen insisted, 'I just know it. I think we should go and see him and get his side of the story. You see, that detective's been trying to find him, but if we were to talk to him first then . . .'

Sarah put down her glass in surprise. 'Wait just a minute, Trub. We don't know that it *wasn't* him who committed the murders. And even if he just stole the diamonds and isn't a killer, then he may still be witless.

Why, I hope Lou has the good sense not to tell her mam just who was asking after him. He could be dangerous!'

'Oh, but I'm certain he isn't, Sarah.'

'Elly, you can't possibly know that. Honestly, you do get the queerest ideas in your lovely head at times!'

Sarah took a second glass of coffee and walked slowly down the hallway to the room that had once been Franz's studio, puzzling some more over Ellen's 'idea'. Whatever had possessed her to go out looking for Davey? And, if she was right and this man was indeed the missing jeweller's apprentice, then it was almost certain that Gerard had discovered his whereabouts. She couldn't quite believe that Ellen was a better sleuth than the bright young inspector.

At the closed door to the studio, Sarah stopped and took a deep breath. The sense of Lily's presence was distinctly stronger in this room than anywhere else in the house, and it was especially noticeable today. She was surprised at the potency of her feeling, for generally speaking, she was the only member of the household who did not sense the presence of the others. But this premonition did not unsettle her. Now as she crossed the threshold, Sarah felt only calm, and she knew that she was stronger for having travelled to India and confronted the reality of Lily's death. It was good to know that she had been at peace during her final days.

Sarah crossed to her writing table, positioned as Lily's had once been by the long French windows. For an interval, she stood sipping her coffee and looking out through the spotless glass into the garden. Droplets from Martha's watering can sat like pearls on crimson camellia petals and Sarah was reminded of the glossy blossoms that had flowered around the summer house in the grounds of the Maharajah's palace. She wondered how long it would be before Govinda arrived in London. It was likely that he was not far behind her, for the passenger services between Bombay and London were now frequent. After a moment she roused herself and retrieved the papers she would need to bring with her to the *Mercury*.

There was a disorderly congregation of newspaper boys on the footpath outside the *Mercury* building, as this was the usual place for them to gossip and smoke while they waited for their papers. Aged twelve years and upwards, the news hawkers liked nothing more than to compare notes on the best stories of the day, trying to impress each other with their agile knowledge of politics or an important criminal trial. If she wanted to know the story of the moment, Sarah needed only to stop for a while and listen to their banter. Once she had smoked a fag with them, and took a devilish delight in the startled and disapproving looks she had received from passing ladies. Talking to the newspaper boys always reminded her of being out and about on the streets when she was the same age.

The offices of the *London Mercury* seemed somehow different to Sarah, and it took her some time to realise that it was not Mr Parsimmons' old-fashioned cravat, nor the editor's firm, dry handshake and twinkling mind that had altered. Nor was it the particular smell of esparato grass, wood pulp and coal tar from which paper and ink were derived. It was she, Sarah O'Reilly, who had changed. She was changed in a way she herself could not have described, but which John Lark noticed as soon as he walked into Septimus Harding's office.

'Why, Miss O'Reilly, you are glowing like a carriage lamp in the fog!'

'I hope you aren't likening the state of my rooms to the London fog, John,' quipped the editor, looking up from the copy he was scrutinising.

'That would be to do the fog a disservice, Septimus. And is it not so, that your finest journalist has blossomed whilst in the Orient?'

'Hmff.' Septimus looked up briefly. 'I hope you're not in love, Sarah. Bad for business, being in love.'

Neither Septimus nor John Lark remarked upon the fact that Sarah's blouse was less boyish than her usual pinstripe, or that her brown skirt was made of soft carmeline rather than stiff polished cotton. They probably did not notice that her hair had turned a more golden russet, and that her skin was no longer fashionably pallid but the palest olive. It was not only her outward appearance to which John Lark was referring, but the quality of her interior. It charged the air about her with a different kind of confidence; a kind of self-knowledge. If only he knew, Sarah thought, that although her travels had certainly lent her a new assurance, she also felt an unearthly weariness. If this was what it took just to write the two essays she carried with her in her satchel, then she was not at all sure that she was equal to the task.

Septimus Harding took little convincing to read the essays. He was quick to see that they could easily be the first of many, there being more female adventuresses, infidels and explorers than there were Wednesday editions of the *Mercury*. Wednesday was the day that the paper now printed a supplement for its new female readership.

As he accepted the sheaf of parchment which Sarah had rolled neatly into a scroll, the editor said, 'You might remember, Sarah, that some time ago I urged you to improve your grasp of the written word!'

Sarah left Septimus to his reading and climbed to the turn in the back stairs, just as she used to do. Here she waited, smoking. After a time, Inspector Lark left. As Sarah watched his lean form retreating, Sarah found herself recalling the day that she had seen Lily Korechnya pass him in the corridor. She remembered how Lily had been dressed, and the way John Lark had looked at her, as though the ghost of this moment still hung in the air of the old building. It was only then that Sarah remembered Lily's letter to him, sitting in the hatbox under her bed at Kensington.

Sarah finished smoking her cheroot, and went back downstairs, bracing herself for Septimus's response. She was so nervous that she could barely lift her eyes from the swamp of pipe dishes, teacups and inkwells on the editor's desk. She expected him to be harsh about her attempts at more serious writing, and prepared herself for an 'utter twaddle, Sarah' or a 'load of blatherskite and windbaggery', these being phrases commonly used by the editor. Instead, his eyes were gleaming.

'When you put it to me that you might try your hand at selling a line for a penny, I agreed because I felt that it was about time you started using your wits. You didn't immediately conclude that I wanted you to have a try at writing something of more substance for the paper, but perhaps I should have told you then, outright, that I want to see your name in print before I lay down dead, and would you please hurry it along!' He gave a little shake to the parchment which he still held in his hand. 'Splendid! Wonderful writing Sarah, and just what every bored and housebound woman in London wants to read. I knew you had it in you. I'll have these proofed and set for Wednesday's paper.'

Sarah felt like kissing him on his whiskery cheek, but instead, she simply thanked him and all but danced from the room.

As she walked from Amen Corner along the docks to the Strand, where she intended to celebrate with the purchase of some books,

Sarah barely noticed the busy trade of the wharves. Normally, a Chinese junk or the arrival of a clipper from the Pacific would cause her to pause and imagine the land from whence the vessel came, but today she was oblivious, basking as she was in the warm glow of Septimus Harding's approval. But when she took the path which led from Temple Pier to Strand Lane, and gradually felt her feet once more touching the earth beneath, she had the oddest feeling that someone was keeping pace behind her. She stopped for a moment and looked back, but saw only a rather pathetic figure leaning against a ruined wall, who looked more like a rag gatherer than a purse snatcher.

She continued on her way, but as the noisome motion of the pier faded, the eerie sensation that she was not walking alone up the deserted alleyway gripped Sarah once more. She turned in time to see that the rag collector had left his post and was now but a few steps behind her. His stride was purposeful and, Sarah believed, ill-intentioned. He was a much younger man than she had at first supposed, though it was difficult to tell as he wore a rather too-long and very tatty black frock coat. His face was narrow and troubled and, she realised as he approached, dark as pitch. She felt her heart lurch and quickened her step, still watching over her shoulder. Just then, two brawny sailors turned into Strand Lane. The shadowy form slipped into the crevice between two dilapidated storehouses and disappeared.

Sarah all but ran the remaining distance to the Strand, almost falling in her haste to reach the noise and crowds of the street. In the fleeting moment that she had seen her pursuer advance, she had also remembered that it was here, in Strand Lane, that the shipping clerk Herbert Peasey had been murdered.

⸭ 38 ⸭

As with the commander of an army, or the leader of any enterprise, so it is with the mistress of a house. Her spirit will be seen through the whole establishment; and just in proportion as she performs her duties intelligently and thoroughly, so will her domestics follow her path.

Mrs Isabella Beeton

Since Sarah had returned, Martha had caught many a shadowy glimpse of Lily in the master's studio. She had rarely entered this room in Sarah's absence, and then only to dust and to open the doors onto the garden once a week in order to give the room a good airing. Mystifyingly, Martha thought she'd recently seen Lily's shadow in the coal cellar, but her sight was not what it had once been, and she soon realised that this apparition was of a female whose garments could not possibly have belonged to Mrs Korechnya. The spectre in the coal cellar was from another time entirely, her gown high-waisted and of some stiff cloth. Still, in the two weeks since Sarah's return from India, the breath of rose and particular sigh of Lily Korechnya's silk costumes had become more evident. This, combined with Sarah's unaccountable fatigue was surely a sign that something was amiss. It was all that Martha could do to remember that it was not her place to interfere. There was a force at work here which she could neither understand nor identify. She had felt its malign presence all those years ago, and wondered if she had been a fool to believe that it had simply gone away.

Sarah had been rising almost as early as Martha and Ellen in recent weeks, and had been writing so furiously that Martha could often hear her sharp steel nib scratching away as she approached the library. Martha knew that she was finally putting her wits to something gainful, and was pleased. Otherwise, Sarah and Ellen had fallen back into their old rhythm of leaving the house after breakfast and spending the day, goodness knows where, in search of tattle, hearsay and, oft times,

Martha suspected, downright scuttlebutt. She had always thought the tawdry business of the penny-a-liner unequal to the superior mind of Sarah O'Reilly, though in many ways it suited both of the girls, since they were well used to mingling with the disenfranchised and lawless. Ellen especially liked having a hand in Sarah's industry, for hadn't her sister gone out working when she was but a child in order to feed and clothe the two of them?

If Sarah was already in the library when she started her morning's cleaning, Martha would had leave the hearth rug and the grates and the dusting in that room and start her work in the front hall. Here she polished the floor and the brass knobs, rubbed the hall table and ledges and, once a week, whitened the steps. When the sound of Sarah's fountain pen marking the parchment quietened, Martha would bring breakfast to the library, and then Ellen would come down from whatever it was she got up to amongst her whatnots and bibelots. Martha often wondered if Ellen had noticed that the rag of red silk was no longer in its tin. If she had, she showed no sign, but then she wouldn't. Martha had come across the scrap quite by accident, in the days when she still bothered to tidy the small one's room. She'd held it in her hand only for an instant before the entire room had all but disappeared, as if into the worst pea-soup fog. What she'd seen then had made her drop the old silk handkerchief in alarm and sit down quickly on Ellen's brass bed. Finally, Martha knew the secret that the little ragamuffin had carried around for all these years. Martha had taken the handkerchief and put it in the fire without another word.

The housekeeper had not realised just what manner of writing Sarah was up to in the library until Ellen showed her that morning's women's supplement of the *London Mercury*. As a rule, Martha found that she could get along better in the world without knowing certain things. However, what Sarah had written was not crime reportage, Ellen proudly pointed out to Martha Vesper, but an essay. It was right there, next to a long thin column which was the latest chapter of a lady's railway novel. Martha found herself wishing that Lily could have been there, for she would have been thrilled that Sarah had finally found her calling. Of course, Martha had had to read it; she felt that she must, although she knew next to nothing about the ways of an essay. Nevertheless, she recognised immediately that Sarah's scribing bore the mark of quality.

The doorbell sounded just as Martha was about to prepare afternoon tea. She was pleased to have cause to bake a cake in the afternoon, for it was a shame not to take a tray to the garden when the weather was fine. The making of tea was also, Martha found, a means of getting Sarah and Ellen to take the air on the days that they did not venture into the dark heart of London. Today Sarah had told the housekeeper that she would have a visitor. Martha untied her apron and patted her hair, and hurried along the hallway. The young man on the doorstep was dressed rather smartly, in a crisp white shirt and charcoal grey suit that might have been sewn by a Savile Row tailor it fit him so neatly. She wondered if Detective Inspector Gerard had dressed with particular care today, for she did not remember him looking quite so spruce on his former visit.

'Good afternoon, madam,' said Detective Inspector Gerard with his shining smile.

'Good afternoon, sir.'

'I am pleased to see you again, Mrs Vesper.'

'Please come in.' Martha stepped aside to allow the detective inspector to enter. 'Perhaps I might show you to the garden, Sir?'

When the inspector was settled, Martha hastened to the library. Sarah barely noticed the housekeeper enter, so intent was her focus on her work.

'Detective Inspector Gerard is waiting for you in the garden, miss.' Martha could not help but scrutinise Sarah's face, for she was most curious. Was this merely a social call, or some newspaper business or, was something else afoot? But Sarah's face was unreadable, except for the initial flash of annoyance at having to interrupt her work.

She put down her pen and removed her spectacles, rubbing her eyes. She straightened her pretty, embroidered waistcoat and rolled down the sleeves of her ivory linen blouse. She still wore plain dark skirts, but Martha had noted a subtle change in Sarah's dress since her return. It had softened, and once or twice, on the occasional balmy days that were peculiar to August, she wore an Indian cotton gown. The first time she had seen her thus attired, Martha had been unable to stop herself from remarking on how well she looked in the particular shade of indigo, for it made her eyes appear quite the prettiest shade of blue. This had embarrassed Sarah, who was unused to compliments.

Whilst Sarah went through to the garden, Martha busied herself with tea, and sliced the savoy cake which was still warm from the oven. She left the brew to seep into the pot and toasted yesterday's teacakes, spreading them with butter and marmalade. When she emerged into the garden, Sarah and Detective Inspector Gerard were seated at the table in such a way that it was immediately clear to the housekeeper that neither was indifferent to the other. As she approached, she could hear what it was they were talking of so intently.

'So you did not have the opportunity to ask Govinda about the diamonds?'

'I decided against it. It seemed rather impertinent, and not a little peculiar, to enquire after something which has not only been missing for seven years, but which might also have cost him his position with the Maharajah. Does it not strike you so?'

'Perhaps. Yet the case was never officially closed, so one might say the investigation, at least from the position of the police, is ongoing. You spoke with him then?'

'I did. We talked of Lily and of some matters pertaining to Hinduism.'

'Govinda is Hindu?'

'I believe so. Is it relevant?'

'Perhaps.'

'Inspector Gerard, do you remember what we spoke of before I departed London – about the areas where the '64 murders took place?'

'Of course.'

'I am certain that I was followed along Strand Lane from Temple Pier a few days ago. I am not easily frightened in deserted alleyways, for I once lived in Devil's Acre, yet ...'

Gerard was immediately alert, and Martha saw in him the very instinct for danger that justified the title detective inspector in one so young. She was shocked to hear Sarah's admission, for she knew that fear did not come easily to one as plucky as she. Martha gave a shudder: it was just as she feared: some Oriental sorcery had pursued Sarah from the East.

'Did you see this man?'

'Only briefly. Young, unkempt, dark-skinned – perhaps an Indian – and thin.' Sarah quickly changed the subject, as though she suddenly felt foolish. 'There is little I can tell you of India, for almost everything that occurred whilst I was a guest of the Maharajah was ... of a profound nature, you might say.'

'Indeed?'

'Yes, you see, I found out that the stolen jewel which Finkelstein was commissioned to craft was a type of charm with which a Hindu might petition the gods, and its loss has affected several people adversely.'

Detective Gerard was lost in his own thoughts for a moment. Martha placed the tray on the table and the conversation lapsed whilst she poured. When Gerard took a sip of tea his face lit up. 'What an excellent cup of tea you make, Mrs Vesper. It is an art that few take earnestly. Am I right in thinking that it is souchong?'

Martha was pleased. She was one for a strong cup of tea, and one unadulterated with willow herb or sweet briar. It was a crime, the blending of pure China tea with the dried leaves of British plants, and she, for one, could smell the offending foreign matter before the tea even wetted her lips.

'It is. I would brew no other. It is true, Inspector Gerard, that in many households little care is taken in the proper making of tea.'

The tea poured, Martha Vesper busied herself in her kitchen garden, allowing enough distance that the conversation at the garden table might resume, but not so much that she could not overhear it. She felt justified in her eavesdropping, for she needed to know exactly what was afoot so that she might be prepared.

'I believe Mr Govinda was sent to London to guard the diamonds, Inspector,' Sarah was saying.

'It interests me.'

'What is it that you find interesting, Sir?'

'The business of the stones having a guardian. What is your feeling about this, Miss O'Reilly, having met the man? Why would you say that he was given the job of protecting the diamonds?'

'Firstly, I believe that he was the finest of the Maharajah's personal guard, and was therefore the natural choice. I understand the coloured diamonds were the most cherished of all of the prince's treasures and this must not be taken lightly, for I could never have imagined the immensity of his wealth. Secondly, I think that Govinda is a man who might take it upon himself to do whatever he must to fulfil his duty, and that might make a lesser man afraid. I almost felt that he had a secret knowledge . . . oh, how might I describe it to you?'

'I believe I understand,' said the detective quietly. 'It was many years ago that I met the man, for I was present when Lark interviewed him after the death of Lady Herbert. I was never quite certain that he was telling us the whole truth. I must say also, that I felt he would be capable of murder, if he deemed it necessary. Had we but a scrap of evidence, I might have arrested him on suspicion of the fact.'

'Then I have some other news which might be of interest to you, Inspector Gerard. Mr Govinda will very shortly arrive in London, for he is to attend to some business here for the Maharajah. '

'That is of interest indeed. Indeed . . . I should very much like to meet Govinda again. Perhaps you will let me know when he has arrived in London, Miss O'Reilly?'

'Of course. I believe he will be staying at the Maharajah's residence on Hyde Park. We very narrowly escaped having another visitor from the palace, for the prince's favourite concubine, Sarasvati, was determined to come to London. She is a most intriguing person.'

'If you will permit me to say so, Miss O'Reilly, I wonder if she could be any more intriguing than your good self.'

To this, for once, Sarah O'Reilly had no answer, and Martha bustled into the wash house with a smile on her lips. Here, the fires were lit under her two coppers, and the linen had been boiling in soda and lime for the last hour. Here also, by the open window, she encountered Ellen, who almost certainly had been listening to the conversation in the garden as well.

One did commend to me a wife both fair and young. That had
French, Spanish and Italian tongue. I thanked him kindly and told
him that I loved none such, For I thought one tongue for a wife too
much. 'What, love ye not a scholar?' Yes, as my life, A learned
scholar, but not a learned wife.

Quoted in *A History of Women's
Education in the United States*, 1929

Sarah laid down her pen and sat for a long time at the French window
in Franz's studio. She had a yearning to ask of Lily's ghost her opinion
on the next essay she had scribed for the 'Pair of Bluestockings' column
she wrote for Septimus Harding. Had the realm of words delighted Lily
as much as it did her? To Sarah it seemed measureless, and even if she
knew every single word ever written, she could still spend the rest
of her days discovering their peculiarities; the way some were spelt
differently to how they sounded, and how one word with the same
spelling could mysteriously have so many meanings, and she loved the
way the rules of grammar seemed to have been made to be broken.
Exceptions to the rule had always been Sarah's speciality – she was one
herself.

Sarah stood, rolled the parchment into a scroll, and slipped it into
her satchel. As she prepared to leave the house she realised that she
had forgotten something, and took the two flights of stairs to the attic.
This room was smaller and colder than any other in the house, but
Sarah had always wanted to look upon a view that made her feel like all
of the world was spread before her. In the corner was her bed with the
white linen and old quilt which Martha had made for her and Ellen.
The housekeeper had wanted to replace it with a new one, but Sarah
would not hear of it, for she and her sister had slept under it together
and she knew every square and triangle of printed cotton intimately. On
the little wicker table beside her bed was Lily's pendant, where she

placed it each night before she went to sleep. Even though she still had not warmed to the notion of mourning jewellery, she liked the smooth feel of it and the comfort it gave her, and Sarah now felt its absence if she did not have it on her person. She fastened it at her neck as she came down the steep attic stairs, her mind occupied with new ideas for 'A Pair of Bluestockings'. Thus, she was startled to encounter Martha Vesper, her arms full of dried lavender for the airing closet. Martha's eye was drawn immediately to the pendant, Sarah noticed. She had never liked it, that was clear. Martha said nothing, but pursed her lips and bustled past with a brisk nod of her head.

Even after seven years, Sarah habitually went out of her way to skirt around Devil's Acre when she was in the vicinity of Westminster. This was not because she felt in any way endangered in her old haunts, but because the very stonework of the tenements held memories that clung like the persistent odour of the earth. Yet today, inexplicably, she felt compelled to turn into the alleyway where Holy Joe's old doss had once been, and which had once been her regular route home to the White Hart. Ruby had long since sold up the gin shop and gone off to live in Cheapside with the rabbit catcher, since the Acre was now little more than an extension of the Haymarket. You couldn't go two steps into any of the alleys without finding a brothel or gambling rooms, and even the ramshackle doss house was now a shadowy establishment whose true nature Sarah could only guess at. She had seen a group of small-time thieves at the front, gambling for coppers, and there was rickety furniture for sale and a placard announcing the prices one might obtain within for old glass, pewter, brass and lead. There was also a box of tattered penny dreadfuls for sale on the dusty step, and the shop girl seemed so brazen that Sarah was certain she was selling more than reading matter.

Sarah passed by, keeping her eyes cast down in order to avoid the muddy potholes. She fixed her mind on how lucky she was not to have to pick her way through these dingy alleyways every day. How fortunate, indeed, to be on her way to the *Mercury*, not with a few lines of tattle in her satchel but something she could be proud of. Lily would be proud of her, she was certain, and for the second time that day, Sarah wished that she could tell her friend the workings of her heart, just as Lily had confided hers through her letters. What if she were to write to Lily? Sarah smiled to herself at the thought.

As she skirted around the press of hovels that backed onto the White Hart and took the narrow pathway to the herring wharves, Sarah became more aware of her surroundings, and the peculiar lack of activity. She had seen only a three-legged dog and a skinny urchin, who darted away as soon as she saw him. Perhaps it was too early in the day for Devil's Acre to be showing signs of life, for most of the establishments here thrived nocturnally.

Just as she was wondering if she was the greatest lackwit on God's earth, coming alone into Devil's Acre, Sarah suddenly found her path blocked by the same dark-faced young man who had followed her in Strand Lane. She could not say where he had come from, for his gait was as silent as it was swift. He took a step towards her and she realised that he was not, after all, dark-skinned, but blackened by oily soot.

'I have only three shillings and some coppers in my purse, but you are welcome to it . . .' she stammered, terrified by his wild, staring eyes.

'It's not your money I want, Sarah O'Reilly.'

'Then, what? And how do you know my name?'

'I make it me business to know who's asking after me; I 'spect it was you who put the little one up to it. I know that you write for them papers. London in't such a grand old town that a man can't keep track of his . . . persecutors.'

The blackened, tortured face seemed pleased with this statement, but then the man's eyes lit on Sarah's neck. In a swift reflex, her hand flew to her throat and closed over Lily's pendant. She said a silent prayer. In a second, her assailant had taken a step closer, and his hand was at her neck. He had barely touched her when he was suddenly wrenched backwards by two constables in shiny black helmets.

'O'right young Davey, that'll be as far as you gad from the bowels of the earth today,' said one of the uniformed men, while the other hauled his arms behind him, and strapped his black wrists tight with a leather leash and buckle. Behind them stood Detective Inspector Gerard, a thunderous look upon his normally personable face.

By now Sarah was sitting on the closest doorstep and taking one deep breath after another in an attempt to steady her nerves. In a moment, Gerard was at her side, examining her face gravely and placing a reassuring hand beneath her elbow as she rose shakily to her feet.

'Are you unharmed, Miss O'Reilly?'

'I believe so. Thank you. But, how did you know . . .'

'I am a very good detective,' he replied with a wry smile. 'My office is but a few streets away, and my constables have been looking out for you.'

Gerard took an authoritative step towards his captive, who stood flanked by the constables. 'Davey Simons, I am arresting you on suspicion of murder and theft.' He gave a curt nod to the policemen and Davey was marched off towards Westminster Police Station, neither resisting nor uttering a word in protest. It was almost as though he had been expected this to occur.

'Might I say, Miss O'Reilly, that I am not certain if I am more amazed by your bravery or your foolhardiness in entering such a treacherous area unaccompanied.'

Sarah noted that she had recovered sufficiently to feel her indignation rise.

'And might I say, Inspector, that I refuse to be afraid to walk alone in the streets I once called my home. In fact, it seems to me that a woman is not entirely safe anywhere in this city of men.'

To Sarah's great surprise, Gerard made no attempt to defend his gender, but bowed his head in accord.

'Would that I might remedy that sad truth. I can only do my job.' His gaze met hers rather quizzically for a moment before he continued. 'And if that means I must keep an extra watch on reckless, crusading journalists, then so be it.' As Sarah opened her mouth to retort, she noticed the glimmer of humour in Detective Inspector Gerard's eye.

'Now, Miss O'Reilly, perhaps you will allow me to chaperone you to your destination.'

'You are kind, but It is rather a long walk, for I am on my way to Amen Corner.'

'Then may I at least accompany you as far as the embankment?'

'Of course.'

The day was fine and the river a florid procession of painted steamboats and barges with cargoes of all kind. Three-masted clippers somehow negotiated their way beneath London Bridge, and dozens of wherries paddled from one shore to the other, narrowly avoiding collision. Now that the shock was beginning to ease, Sarah felt only bewilderment.

'How is it, sir, that you came to be in the very place that you were needed?'

'I have been keeping a watch on you, Miss O'Reilly, since you told me what happened in Strand Lane. Today, I had intelligence that both you and Davey Simons were converging on Devil's Acre. It took little imagination to project the outcome of such an encounter.'

'I am grateful. I hope I did not seem otherwise ...'

Gerard only smiled, and they walked on in silence until Sarah felt that she should say something to ease the undefined tension that seemed to be gathering in the air around them.

'I have put the pocketbook to good use.'

'I can see that you have, for I read your new column in last Wednesday's *Mercury* and was most enlightened. I trust you are intending to write more in the same vein?'

Sarah patted her satchel. 'I am. I do hope that my readership will not be entirely female.'

'There are men who appreciate the difficulties ... we are not all entirely insensitive to the grievous imbalance of ... ascendancy, Miss O'Reilly,' Gerard sighed.

They walked as far as the stone foundations of Blackfriars Bridge, each lost in their own thoughts, and content to allow the bustling activity of the Thames and its banks to fill the lull in conversation. It was an easier silence than that which had fallen earlier. Sarah stopped at White Lion Hill on the eastern side of the bridge, where she always turned off to walk through to Paternoster Row. She extended her hand to her companion.

'I am most grateful for your company.'

Gerard bowed in response. 'Please call at Westminster Police Station at your earliest convenience, Miss O'Reilly, for I will need an official statement from you with regard to what happened today.'

'Then I will call tomorrow, Detective Inspector.'

For a moment she thought that he would say something else, bu he changed his mind and only nodded his head, before turning to walk back along the embankment. Sarah watched his trim, broad shouldered figure depart, still shaken from her narrow escape, and also perhaps by the confusion of emotions a simple walk along the Thames could bring.

⁘ 40 ⁘

Men's letters are proverbially uninteresting and uncommunicative.
Arthur says such letters as mine never ought to be kept – they are
dangerous as lucifer matches.

Charlotte Brontë

Sarah emerged slowly from the crisp linen of her bed clothing, testing
the air to see how she might fare, for she still felt uncommonly weary
in the mornings. Perhaps it was only because in her dreams, she revisited
the land where women dried their hair in perfumed smoke and where
a dark goddess guarded a temple filled with images of violence. Something was bothering her, increasingly, about the connection between
the Maharajah's palace and London, and the incomplete picture she
had formed of the past. It was almost as though she had all of the
information she needed to solve the riddle of the missing diamonds,
and perhaps even the murders, yet the order of the pieces eluded her.
As she dressed, Sarah caught sight of the blue hatbox beneath her bed
and remembered John Lark's letter. If she was to visit Westminster
Police Station today, then she must deliver it to him.

The Westminster Station was a hive of industry. She noticed that, in
addition to the army of constables quietly writing reports and attending
to members of the public, there were a small group of more official-
looking gentlemen. Amongst them were both Inspector Lark and
Inspector Gerard.

When he saw Sarah, Gerard immediately excused himself and came
to greet her.

'Good-day, Miss O'Reilly. You do seem to have a talent for arriving
just when I am most desperately in need of a cup of tea.' He lowered
his tone and raised an eyebrow, 'We have had an inspection this afternoon,' which made Sarah smile.

'I do hope Inspector Lark has been kind.'

'Oh, it isn't Lark that we need worry about.'

'He is a good man.'

'The finest.'

'I have something to deliver to him. Perhaps you would take it on his behalf?'

'You can speak with him yourself if you prefer. He will be occupied only for a short while longer. The gentlemen are discussing the deficiencies inherent in the writing of police reports. Meanwhile, would you care to inspect the view of Westminster Cathedral, Miss O'Reilly? I have news which might be of interest to you.'

In the tidy office of the detective inspector, Sarah found herself paying more attention to her surroundings than she had on her former visit. She was searching for anything which might tell her more about the man who was presently pouring her a cup of tea. Her eyes fell upon a small stack of books almost secreted in the lower shelf of a book cupboard. She longed to inspect them more closely. When Sarah turned back, Inspector Gerard was looking at her.

'I have it from a colleague at the Port Authority that a tall, light-skinned Indian by the name of Govinda recently arrived at St Katherine's.'

'I thought that he must be arriving soon.'

'I have a feeling that the tale of the Maharajah's diamonds might soon be told in its entirety.'

'And I think it is unlikely, Inspector Gerard. In fact, I believe it will require great delicacy to extract any information from that gentleman. I myself am intending to call upon Govinda, for I would like to have news of the palace.'

'I should prefer to accompany you when you do. Perhaps you will call at the police station again tomorrow and ride with me to Hyde Park?'

'I would be happy to have your company. Tomorrow then.'

Much as the offer had been lightly made, and in a gentlemanly fashion, it was clear that Inspector Gerard thought that she required his protection rather more than his company. Could he really believe that she was still in some kind of danger?

When Gerard had completed his report of Sarah's encounter with Davey Simons, she asked him if he had conducted an interview with his suspect.

'I have, but he insists on his own innocence, on both counts, and says that there was a drawing of the jewel which was not left with the jeweller, but retained in Lady Herbert's possession.'

'But why would such a thing not be left with Finkelstein? Surely he would have preferred to consult it whilst he undertook the commission?'

'That is another question I should like to put to Mr Govinda.' Gerard looked at Sarah then a quizzical expression. 'Miss O'Reilly, I believe our suspect was rattled by his encounter with you yesterday. Can you think of any reason why he might have been disturbed to see you? With the exception of the day in Strand Lane, have you ever encountered him before?'

Sarah frowned. 'No. It is true that he seemed disturbed, but I gathered that he sees me as an advocate of the newspaper, and therefore one of his "persecutors", for this was the word he used. My guess is that he has become deranged by his years in hiding. I thought that he would seize my throat.' She put a hand to her neck in remembrance, and again touched Lily's pendant, which today rested beneath her blouse and out of view. 'Unless he was drawn to Lily's hairwork pendant, for it was also crafted by Finkelstein. Perhaps he recognised it . . .'

'No, it could not be something as commonplace as that, although I am sure he was surprised to see the piece.' He paused strategically before he posed his next question. 'Whilst you were away I paid a visit to Kensington and spoke with your sister Ellen. It was she who acquainted me with the fact that Davey Simons was both alive and living in the city of London. Do you know of any reason why your sister might have made enquiries about him?'

Sarah felt her heart lurch at the thought that Ellen might be brought into the murder enquiry all over again. She could not bring herself to tell the detective inspector that Ellen had deliberately sought Davey's whereabouts, and that she believed him to be innocent.

'That is a simple matter to answer, sir, for Ellen has long been discharging odd jobs for several of the journalists at the *Mercury* including myself. She is unnervingly good at finding things out, whether it means taking the railway out to the records department at Richmond or stopping at the war office to learn how Paris fares. I would not hesitate to give her a greater portion of the credit for the continuance of my career as a penny-a-liner. She prefers to walk everywhere, as do, since it encourages one's curiosity. We often walk as far as the Ropemakers' Fields, where our family is buried ...'

'I would be happy to accompany you there, one fine day, for it is a rare quiet place amidst the pell-mell of the city. '

Their meeting concluded, Gerard escorted Sarah back to the ground floor, where Inspector Lark was now putting on his outdoor coat and preparing to leave. He bowed when he saw Sarah.

'Miss O'Reilly. This is an unexpected pleasure. Will you walk with me?'

'Certainly.' Sarah turned to catch Gerard's eye, but a legion of constables had already closed ranks about him. When she looked back, Lark was smiling a little and she felt her cheeks warm. 'If you have the time to take lunch, sir, there is a very good chop house close by on Vincent Street.'

The Vincent Street chop house was cosy and refreshingly indifferent to both the class and gender of its clientele. There were few diners as it was early, so Sarah and Lark had their choice of position and settled in a comfortable snug by the glowing hearth. Once seated, Sarah enquired of John Lark whether he had formed an impression of Davey Simons and if he believed him to be capable of murder.

'I honestly cannot say, for the young man has been driven half mad by his fugitive existence. It is still a baffling case, I cannot pretend otherwise. He must be released this evening unless we can find further reason to detain him.' Lark sighed. 'It is my intention to pursue the missing drawing, for it is the only new lead we have. I wonder if it might still be amongst Lady Herbert's personal effects at Herbert House? I believe her sister-in-law now lives there.'

They spoke a little of India, though Inspector Lark was careful to avoid the subject of Lily Korechnya, and Sarah was faintly relieved when their lunch of potatoes, oysters and buttered bread was served. Afterwards, finding courage in the dregs of a glass of port wine, she could delay no longer.

'I have something for you.'

Lark raised an eyebrow when she produced the letter. She watched his expression as he recognised the delicate copperplate in which his name was written. He reached for the linen envelope slowly and rose to stand by the hearth. He read with his back to Sarah, and when he had finished, he did not refold the parchment, but placed it on the table in front of her.

'You were Lily's close friend . . .'

'You would like me to read the letter Lily wrote to you?' Sarah wondered if she had misunderstood. John Lark had always appeared such a column of strength and endurance, that she was moved by his vulnerability.

Lark nodded. 'There is information here which will be of interest to you, with regard to the character of Govinda, though I must tell you that I am still not convinced of his innocence.' He exhaled audibly as though to gather his wits. 'It is also the reply I awaited. It was thoughtful, for she was ill . . .'

'She was considerate always.' Sarah replied.

'Yes, she was. I think I will take a measure of brandy with water . . .' and wearing a rather dazed expression, he left her to read.

> Benares,
> 27 February, 1865

Dear John,

I was delighted to receive your letter, though distressed to hear that headaches plague you still. Perhaps, as you say it is but a susceptibility to the dank odour of certain regions, though I agree with you that this is a condition which is entirely inappropriate for a policeman. Might I suggest that you try coarse brown paper wet with strong cider vinegar, or a cloth soaked in a distillation of marigold flowers? Do call on Mrs Vesper in Kensington, for she has a household book passed down from her grandmother containing many recipes for compresses and remedies, and she would be delighted to see you. She always spoke very highly of you.

You ask after my own health, and I will be candid. I can but recall the haleness of my former existence with some nostalgia. Yet in spite of m worsening and mysterious condition, I feel ever more calmed by this place I cannot in truth understand it myself, but that there is some verity in th local truth that Benares is the home of the gods.

There is something which has been harrying my conscience a little, an though it is not of great consequence, my memory of your petitioning o behalf of Holy Joe has decided that I must speak of it. My friend Govinda is soon to begin a journey north into Kashmir. His destination, he tells me, is a monastery high upon the mountain plains. Hence, he has lately confided to me something. You may recall that he was custodian of the diamonds, which might seem a peculiar way to describe his association with some relatively small, coloured stones. Strangely, it seems that Govinda was also philosophically opposed to the navaratna charm being crafted from diamonds, and tried to persuade the Maharajah not to pursue his search. I wonder, John, if he still feels that he is duty-bound to ensure that neither the diamonds nor any person associated with them comes to harm. I even wonder if he visited Finkelstein's workshop some time before the jeweller was murdered and collected the charm? You must not under-estimate the belief he had in its power, and I believe he feared that the desire to possess it might take hold of him, as it did so many others. I am unable to consider him a suspect in any other way, just as I am certain that you will already have considered these possibilities. I write only to defend the character of one whom I have come to respect.

I must here end this letter, for though it is not long, I am already worn. Yet I must say this: I did not take lightly your offer John, and often recall that night before my departure, in the drawing room at Waterloo Street. Part of me still wishes that I had been able to accept. The greater part of me has retreated, however, and remains beyond recall. I hope in earnest that we do meet again, but if we do not, believe that I have always been,

Yours In Fondest Friendship,
Lily Korechnya.

·· 41 ··

Kensington,
18 September 1871

My Dearest Lily,

It does not seem at all strange, writing to you, and now I wish that I had done so many years ago. When I discovered the letters you had written to Franz after his death, I thought it at first peculiar, but I have come to understand that those who have died are neither lost nor unreachable, if they are alive in one's heart. I think that I first understood this whilst residing in your room in the palace. I felt that you were there, especially when I retrieved The Venus of Waterloo from the Maharajah. I suppose that I have, in the past, done the same, in visiting the Ropemakers' Fields. There I have sat by Mam's grave and talked to her, yet I have not done so for some time now.

I am seated at the window in the attic, and I look out across the land as the light of day fades. Not many trees have yet lost their leaves, and here and there is an oak tree with its branches brimful and coppery like a purse full of shiny new pennies.

London has not been the same without you, and I know that Mrs Vesper misses you just as much as I, though she would never say. She did not attend her circle throughout the summer months after you passed, and one of the ladies came to call, begging that she return for the spirits would not descend without Martha Vesper there.

I am pleased to tell you that lately Martha has washed the parlour curtains twice, once last Wednesday and again this Wednesday, without realising. This might be because Mr Smythe, the gardener from the mansion house, has been to visit both laundry days, and I heard him ask Martha to walk out with him. It is peculiar to see Martha Vesper with a certain smile on her face – though only when she thinks I do not notice!

I have become acquainted with a detective by the name of Gerard who, you might remember, came calling at Waterloo Street just after the Maharajah's diamonds were stolen. I believe him to be as good and as honest a man as Inspector Lark, though I am not in the least interested in acquiring a husband, never fear, for I do not forget easily that it was a husband who caused my mam to cry all night and for our family to be so hungry. Still, I find that I am warmed by his company, for there is no other way to describe the feeling that washes over me when I am with him. He is alert of mind, as one in his profession must be, and this I find invigorating. But he is also kind, and I would venture to say that he is a man who might allow me to be myself. In truth, there is no greater regard that a man can show to a woman; indeed, that a person of any gender might show to another.

And now I come to the reason that I have taken up my pen to write to you, for you alone will understand. You see, Lily, Govinda has returned to London at the same time that Finkelstein's apprentice, Davey, has rather prodigiously reappeared, and quite suddenly it seems that the murder investigation of '64 has been reopened. How would I ever have guessed, that I myself might be in danger? But I am ahead of myself, and there is much to tell.

Earlier today, Inspector Gerard and I visited the Maharajah's residence in Hyde Park, for he was eager to conduct an informal interview with Govinda. When we arrived, we were shown by an elderly khansamah to a rather magnificent drawing room and served spiced chai tea. This, as you will know, is made with warmed milk, cinnamon, cloves and ginger, and I must confess that I watched Inspector Gerard's face closely as he took his first sip. He is rather a fusspot about his tea and, as I expected, he would drink no more once he had tasted it. From where we sat we had a rather fine view of a statue of the elephant-headed god, Ganesh, and some of the Maharajah's purchases from the London auction rooms. It is quite impossible to identify a disposition with regard to the Prince's taste in painting, for, as in Benares, here was the most astonishing array of artist and form that I have ever seen. You will not know the work of the French painters who have begun to call themselves Impressionists, but I am certain that your Franz would have appreciated the illusion of light and atmosphere they create.

After a short time, Govinda entered the room, clothed in his customary tunic, narrow trousers and soft leather slippers. He also wore an accessory

I do not remember noticing in Benares, for about his middle was a wide leather belt, and from it was slung a long, curved and ornately stitched scabbard. From this protruded the carved hilt of a knife or sword. I could not tell if he recognised Inspector Gerard, for his face remained inscrutable, but he bowed and welcomed us. Gerard did not waste any time with pleasantries or parlour talk. I shall do my best to recall here their conversation.

'You many not remember that we have met once before, Mr Govinda, after the sad event of Lady Cynthia Herbert's death,' Gerard began. Govinda did not say whether he remembered or not, but inclined his head slightly. I watched Gerard's face carefully, but like Govinda, he was giving nothing away. 'At that time, we were investigating the disappearance of a jewel made from coloured diamonds, which I understand was the property of the Maharajah of Benares.' Still, Govinda revealed nothing.

'Is it true, Sir, that you were assigned to guard the Maharajah's diamonds, and that you also assisted Lady Herbert in fulfilling the prince's wish that a diamond charm be made?'

Govinda nodded almost imperceptibly. 'It is true.'

'Then I must ask you, were you in any way an accomplice to the deaths of Herbert Peasey, Joshua Finkelstein and your own countryman, whom we know of only as Vikram?'

His face was utterly placid as he replied. 'I am sorry that I can be of no more assistance to you in your investigation.'

If Gerard was becoming frustrated by his unresponsive interviewee, he did not show it, but repeated the question again. In turn, Govinda repeated his answer verbatim. The silence which followed might have been comical, were the situation not so grave. Each man stood facing the other as though in silent combat, until finally, Gerard realised that he must leave, for this was Govinda's territory and there was nothing more to be gained. Of course, the detective inspector assumed that I would accompany him. I suggested instead that we meet at teatime at the cocoa rooms in Paddington Station, for I wanted to take the opportunity to enquire after the Maharajah, his wife and Sarasvati. I could see that Gerard was extremely reluctant to leave me alone with his suspect, and was almost certain that he would keep watch on the house. Gerard confirmed that he was at liberty to meet me and then left politely and professionally, as I would expect of him.

I suggested to Govinda that he and I take a turn about Hyde Park, for

here a visitor to London might see the more decorative English creature
in her preferred habitat. I must admit that I also felt a little anxious about
being alone with him, when everyone but I believed Govinda capable of
murder.

I have always enjoyed Hyde Park, for one might almost be walking in
the countryside, since horticultural and ornithological societies contrive to
make it so, as do the herds of goats, sheep and cows which are often and
inexplicably to be seen there. I still find it amusing that I may buy a glass
of milk, warm and fresh from the cow in the middle of London city. I
wondered, as we strolled through the pretty gardens and saw the ladies of
Belgravia in their trim habits, what Govinda might think of it all. He
appeared oblivious even to the heads which turned as we passed. I asked
after the Maharajah and Maharanee and heard that they sent me their best
regards, and that Sarasvati was still sulking.

Finally, when we had walked almost the entire pathway around the
Serpentine, I stopped, quite close to the water's edge.

'Mr Govinda . . .' I began, and then could not immediately proceed.

'Yes, Miss Sarah,' said he.

'Mr Govinda, did you know that the police have discovered the where-
bouts of the jeweller Finkelstein's apprentice, and have interviewed him?'

'I did not.'

I was certain that I saw him let his guard down for a fleeting moment,
or his eyes narrowed shrewdly. Now that I had begun, I knew that I must
proceed. 'Sir, do you in fact know where the Maharajah's diamonds are?'

'Do you, Miss Sarah?' And the look he cast at me was such I can barely
describe it. I thought in that instant, that Gerard and Lark were right
about him.

Later, as Inspector Gerard and I sat in the cocoa rooms, I tried to recall
the sequence of what had happened next. One moment I was standing by
the Serpentine, and the next I was falling backwards into the water
and Govinda's hand was at my breastbone, though whether he had been
instrumental in my fall or was reaching to help me I still cannot say. What
came of it was this: I got to my feet, now soaked through and waist deep in
muddy water, and Govinda held out his hand to me. I admit that I hesitated
before I gave him mine. As I stood, dripping and shivering beside him, I
realised that he was holding your pendant, which had broken from its
chain when he grabbed for me. I managed to thank him for at least rescuing

287

the hairwork. He looked at it with distaste, I thought, and I suddenl
realised that to the Hindu, whose earthly remains are normally cremated
a tiny shrine containing the hair of the dead must seem deeply repellant.

'Perhaps you will allow me to have this repaired for you,' he said after
moment.

'I would prefer not to be without it. I have another chain upon which
can hang it.'

'But I believe the clasp is now loose, so the pendant itself might not b
secure.'

'Thank you,' I said, 'but I will have it seen to myself.'

I held out my hand and he gave it to me. It struck me, as this exchang
took place, that Govinda might be more forthcoming on another puzzlin
matter.

'Do you think, Sir, that it was the Maharajah who hid this in th
painting?'

Govinda frowned, and was as usual reluctant to furnish a direct answe
'I can only say, Miss Sarah, that the Maharajah was . . . very taken with it

'I thought so!' I said, yet I wonder as I write this, Lily, if you yourse
knew . . .

By now, I wanted nothing more than to hasten, as much as my w
costume would allow, through Kensington Gardens so that I might chang
my clothes and still be in time to meet with Gerard.

As I bade the mysterious Govinda farewell, he said: 'Miss Sarah, you a
in grave danger, more than you can know.'

Now I wonder if Detective Inspector Gerard is right after all abo
Govinda, for later, in the cocoa rooms he expressed his own concern f
my safety. Though in his estimation, the danger rests with Govinda himsel

With all my hear
Sara

⁜ 42 ⁜

The miracle that you should come to me, Whom the whole world seeing can but desire, It is as though some white star stooped to be . . .

Adela Florence Corey

On the morning following her encounter with the Serpentine, Sarah woke to find that the pendant had disappeared. Her first thought was that Lily did not approve of her wearing it. The oval of jet and gold was no longer on the wicker table by her bed where she was certain that she had left it the night before. Thinking that it must have fallen to the floor, she searched on her hands and knees, crawling underneath the bed, and then beneath the washstand and dresser. She inspected the bedclothes, and then emptied every drawer and every waistcoat pocket. When she was certain that it was gone, Sarah sat down heavily on the tousled bedclothes, bewildered and distraught.

Someone must have taken it. The more she considered it, the more she thought that person might be Davey. She had noted the way he had looked at her neck in Devil's Acre, and perhaps he wanted some memento of his former existence. Besides, the pendant, complete with its heavy gold chain, was valuable.

Sarah found her breeches, a clean white shirt, and a waistcoat of moss green velvet. Then she sat down on her bed again to gather her thoughts, for her dousing in the Serpentine had done her little good and she felt weaker than ever. When she discovered that she had too few thoughts to gather, she decided that perhaps some of Martha's robust coffee was what was needed.

In the library, Ellen was in her usual station at the table, her gaze fixed intently on the front page of one of the broadsheets. She did not look up as Sarah reached the table, which was the first sign that all was not well. Martha was nowhere to be seen, which was also unusual.

Sarah's first thought was that they must indeed have been robbed in the night.

'Morning Trub.'

'Oh Sarah! It's Davey. They've found him in the Thames.'

'In the Thames? When?'

'Yesterday evening.'

Sarah gripped the edge of the table to steady herself. 'Dead, then?'

'Completely dead. And they're saying it might have been murder.'

Suddenly, Sarah knew who had taken the pendant, for surely it could not have been Davey. 'Tell Martha I shan't be needing any breakfast Trub.'

Ellen nodded, wide-eyed. 'But, where are you going, Sarah?'

'I'm not telling you because you can't come.'

The cabriolet which Sarah hailed on Kensington High Street smelt of the hay which was strewn on its floor. It was a sure sign that the driver thought it might rain, and preferred his passengers to wipe their muddy boots on something other than his varnished floor boards. She looked through the shutters at the sky, which indeed foretold a gathering tempest. It suited her mood.

As the carriage passed the grandiose mansions and stately homes Sarah was reminded that Inspector Lark's intended visit to Herbert House was due to take place today.

The khansamah at Hyde Park, a rather frail Hindu gentleman, showed her into the parlour and once more brought her chai. If he thought it strange that she was dressed in breeches and boots, then he did not show it. The tea tray and everything on it was silver and, whilst he poured, the dappled colours of the Impressionist paintings that hung on the walls were reflected in its sheen. Sarah became quite mesmerised by the effect, and found herself wondering what might have induced the aged khansamah to come to London. Had he once been a member of the Maharajah's Benares household? Perhaps he had come here when he was a young man, or even been born in the city? It was peculiar she thought, that the former lives of servants and attendants became insignificant, paling beside the lordly pretensions of their masters.

Govinda entered the parlour whilst Sarah's mind was thus occupied and waited silently until she noticed him. He inclined his head almost imperceptibly when she looked up and their eyes met.

'I imagine that you know why I am here, Mr Govinda?'

'Indeed I cannot guess, Miss Sarah.'

'I must insist that you return the pendant immediately.' Sarah saw a trace of artful surprise on Govinda's features. Did she see also the twitch of an eyebrow, or the shadow of deceit? It was gone so quickly that she could not be certain.

'Return it? Then, it is no longer in your possession?' Govinda met her gaze without flinching. Artful indeed, she thought.

'I presume it is the Maharajah who wants it – that is why he hid it in *The Venus of Waterloo*, isn't it?'

Govinda only shook his head, though whether in denial or weariness, Sarah could not say. Sarah wondered if John Lark was yet at Herbert House. She recalled his warning to her and was surprised by how calm she felt. If Govinda posed a threat to her safety, then there was nothing to be done about it. She felt peculiarly light-headed.

'Do you know, Mr Govinda, who was Sarasvati's "friend" in London?'

'Yes, Miss Sarah, I do.'

'And was that same person the opium guard whom she sent to retrieve the red diamond?'

Finally, Govinda nodded. 'It was.'

'Is that why you are here – to find him and to retrieve the diamonds?'

'He is dead, Miss Sarah, and the diamonds have done nothing but cause wretchedness to everyone who encounters them.'

So Vikram was indeed the opium guard, the man who would have done anything to gain favour with the capricious ranee.

'But then why was the Maharajah so desperate to have the diamond navaratna charm made?' Sarah asked.

Govinda shrugged. 'The Maharajah is unhappy. Since the British have been governing India, the sovereignty of the princes has been gradually fading. They no longer have an important role and there will come a day when they will be redundant. The Maharajah is therefore willing to try anything. He needs a greater purpose than the accumulation of wealth.'

'Do you think that the Maharajah loves Sarasvati?' Sarah could not say why she asked, yet it seemed important.

'Yes.'

'So, if you were to find the charm, would you return it to the Maharajah, even though you believe it to be dangerous?'

'You ask many questions, Miss Sarah.'

'Would you?' she insisted.

'The diamonds belong to him.' Govinda crossed the room so that he stood beside the vast statue of Ganesh; elephant-headed son of Parvati and Shiva. Sarah recalled the story of Ganesh from her train journey with Mr Elliot; he was considered to be the god of wisdom and also to be a skilled scribe. In India, writers often invoked his name and asked for his blessing. As was the way with much Hindu mythology, there were many stories about how the deity lost his human head. Sarah wondered how many variations there were on the legends of Kali.

'Do you know the tale of Kali and the red diamond, Mr Govinda?'

'It is a story only.'

'Yet I know that you believe in the magical properties of diamonds.'

'There is no magic. Gemstones are but a concentration of the energies which create life itself, and should therefore be treated with as much respect as other entities. If they are imbued with lust rather than the desire for good, they become corrupted.'

'Do you think the red diamond is corrupted?'

'It is infused with the . . . unpredictable energies of Kali. The diamond has touched her third eye, a place of power even in a mortal being, and therefore of unimaginable possibility in an immortal. Now she wants it back. It must therefore be returned.'

'To the statue of Kali in Sarasvati's village?'

'To any statue, for the deity is incarnate in the effigy.'

At that moment the khansamah entered, and held the door open for Detective Inspector Gerard, who was followed by two large constables. When he saw Sarah, Gerard looked surprised. That she was also dressed in the clothing of a man did nothing to assist him in comprehending the unexpected scene.

'Miss O'Reilly, what on earth are you doing here?'

'I am drinking tea.'

'I can see that, but . . . never mind.' Gerard turned his attention to Govinda. 'Sir, I am here to arrest you for the murder of Davey Simons. I have it from several witnesses that you visited him yesterday evening. Is this correct?'

'It is.' Govinda stayed where he was, standing calmly beside Ganesh. In the silence that followed, Sarah's feeling of light-headedness increased until it seemed that she had lost all the strength in her limbs, and her cup and saucer slipped from her hands. By the time the clatter of breaking china broke the hush in the room, Sarah was lying motionless on the polished floor.

As the drawing room took on the cave-like proportions of the old Kali temple in Benares, Sarah thought that she could hear Sarasvati's tinkling laugh. It seemed that the air shimmered about her, and in place of the icon of the goddess was a statue of Sarasvati. As Sarah watched, the statue came to life and began to sway, slowly at first; the rhythm of each slender limb evoking the beat of a distant tabla. Somehow, the silent drum beat quickened, and Sarasvati's body became fluid and graceful, her arms twisting and her balance shifting so quickly that her clothing floated and swirled about her. And then she was beside Sarah, her dopatta veil in her hands. Her face was glowing with perspiration, and her scent was sweet and woody, like sandalwood.

'I think you must tell me where the diamonds are, Miss Sarah, for you have them, don't you? Did I not tell you that I know the art of thagini? I know how the thagini kill by strangulation,' she said as she looped the dopatta loosely about Sarah's neck. 'When they have killed, they make an offering to Kali, and she grants them favours. You know who the opium guard is, and you know where the diamonds are, Miss Sarah. Think, think.'

As the dopatta tightened around her neck, it seemed that the temple filled with light, and for a moment Sarah thought that she could see Lily, beckoning to her.

⸙ 43 ⸙

Coins in the hand
Can be stolen
But who can rob this body of its own treasure?
Fools, while I dress

In the Jasmine Lord's morning light
I cannot be shamed —
What would you have me hide under silk
And the glitter of jewels?

Mahadeviyakka (12th century)

'I am not normally one to swoon,' Sarah said as she lay on the brocade divan, surrounded by indistinct forms. As her vision cleared, she identified five people: Detective Inspector Gerard, the khansamah and Govinda flanked by the two constables. The khansamah was holding an earthenware bowl full of brown liquid, and Gerard was bending over her with a wet linen cloth.

'Oriental smelling salts,' said Gerard, in response to Sarah's wrinkled nose at the pungent odour of the brew. 'I have no doubt that it could wake the dead.'

'Now, Miss O'Reilly, perhaps you could slowly attempt an upright position? I do not wish to rush you, but I understand that John Lark will shortly be arriving at Kensington. We agreed to meet there so that you might share in any news from Herbert House.'

He turned to Govinda, who had already been divested of his belt and weapon.

'I would like you to be present at the meeting with Inspector Lark, Mr Govinda, for there is some unravelling to be done. From there you will be taken to Westminster Police Station for questioning.'

Govinda merely inclined his head, and were she not so befuddled by her fainting and the vividness of her dream, Sarah could have sworn that she saw the hint of a smile.

Gerard indicated to the constables that they should escort their prisoner outside, and then turned to Sarah: 'Shall we? My carriage is waiting.' He turned to the khansamah with outstretched hand. 'Thank you for your kindness in preparing the herbs, sir. I am most grateful.' The old man looked momentarily confused to be acknowledged, but as they departed, Sarah thought that she heard him humming to himself.

The storm had passed and the cobbles were shining in patches where the sun had not yet dried them. Sarah sat opposite Inspector Gerard, in the shining black police coach and Govinda rode aft with the constables. She thought that the young detective seemed more puzzled by something in the region of her knees than by the latest twist in the case of the stolen diamonds. She had entirely forgotten that she was wearing breeches.

'I have always thought a man's costume more practical and comfortable,' he eventually said, before directing his gaze out of the window.

Martha Vesper merely raised her eyebrows when she saw the unusual assembly on her doorstep.

'Inspector Lark is in the garden,' she said, as though this kind of gathering occurred every day.

Sarah led Inspector Gerard, the constables and Govinda to the garden while Martha hastened to the kitchen to prepare refreshments. They found John Lark sitting, smoking a cheroot, and reading the paper. On the table beside the broadsheet was a black leather document wallet. When Lark saw Govinda he nodded politely, and then he and Gerard walked to the bottom of the garden to consult quietly.

Sarah left to bathe her face with camomile in the downstairs washroom. Her reflection in the looking glass above the washstand was a rather startled one. The delicate skin beneath her eyes was darkened and her face was as white as her shirt. But she quickly gave up on any attempt to improve her appearance, as she was too impatient to discover what, if anything, John Lark had discovered.

It had begun to rain by the time Sarah returned to the garden, so she showed the visitors in through the kitchen door. It was always warmer here than elsewhere in the old house and, to her astonishment, Inspector Gerard suggested that they take tea at Martha's large pinewood table.

'It is important that you do not catch cold,' he said to Sarah firmly.

Martha spread a starched white cloth on the table, all the while wearing a bemused expression on her face.

'Where is Ellen?' Sarah asked, keeping her voice low as she helped Martha with the tea things.

'She went out after Inspector Lark arrived. I think the little one knew there was going to be a commotion and wanted no part in it.'

Sarah was relieved and could see that Mrs Vesper was too.

When they were seated, she realised that Gerard had carried in one extra chair, and wondered if he thought that Martha would sit with them. She knew beyond doubt that the housekeeper would no sooner join visitors at the table than fly on a broomstick, but she thanked the Detective Inspector politely all the same. Just as Mrs Vesper was removing a tray of baking from the oven, the doorbell sounded.

Everyone looked surprised. 'Allow me, Mrs Vesper,' Gerard said, as Martha looked vaguely flustered, her hands being occupied with a tray of hot scones. When the inspector returned in the company of another constable, he looked entirely baffled and was holding a swatch of coarse brown paper, of the variety used for wrapping up food by street vendors. This he handed to Lark, who read it. The silence in the kitchen deepened momentarily so that the light rain could be heard pattering on the roof.

Gerard cleared his throat and addressed Govinda. 'I am informed that the body of Davey Simons has been examined under the new Anatomy Act, and it has been verified that he was not yet dead when he fell into the Thames.' Gerard paused and glanced at Lark, who met his gaze evenly. 'Further,' said Gerard, 'and to prove that Davey Simons was not pushed or otherwise forced into the water where he drowned, a letter has been found amongst his belongings. Inspector Lark, sir, would you please read it?'

Lark nodded. 'Dear Mam, It don't matter what they all think, it was never me and I'm good as dead anyway, like the rest of 'em that touched those evil sparklers, whether I tell where they are or no. I can't be doing with any more of this dark filthy work so am taking it on meself to have done with it. Your Davey.'

Gerard was watching Govinda throughout, as though he couldn't quite believe that he could have been so wrong. When Lark finished, Gerard sighed heavily. 'I owe you an apology, Mr Govinda. You are free to go, but I hope that you will stay a while and help us with this confounded enquiry.' He addressed one of the constables, 'Please unhand him and return his weapon.' As Govinda's sabre was ceremoniously returned and he attached his belt and scabbard, Gerard's composure buckled. 'So,' he said tersely, as much to himself as to the gathered company, 'if it was not Govinda who killed Peasey, Finkelstein and Vikram, then who in tarnation was it?'

As though startled out of her own daze, Sarah suddenly remembered the clue that had been presented to her in her dream. 'The opium guard!' Everyone turned to her, and she realised that the statement probably appeared quite witless, but she did not care. She addressed Govinda. 'It was Vikram, wasn't it? Sarasvati sent him, and he killed the shipping clerk and the jeweller in an attempt to retrieve the red diamond for her?'

Govinda inclined his head. 'Yes, Miss Sarah, it is so.'

Lark was also nodding his head, for now it was all beginning to fit together. 'But there must have been an accomplice, for the victims were all stunned before their larynxes were crushed. Vikram was a small man and would not easily have been able to overpower his victims before killing them. And it was Holy Joe's slingshot that was found next to his own body. Like the other victims, he had a bruise on his forehead. Perhaps whoever his accomplice was, turned against him in the end? Is there anything you can contribute to enlighten us further, Mr Govinda?'

'There is not.'

Gerard was drumming his fingers on the table and frowning. 'Well then, where are the blessed diamonds?'

'Ah,' said Lark, and at this, he untied the black ribbons that fastened the document wallet. A hush fell as Inspector Lark withdrew a slightly flattened scroll of rice paper parchment, unfurled it, and laid it on the table.

'By Jupiter!' exclaimed Inspector Gerard, who was the first to realise exactly what the drawing signified. Sarah leaned in closer, momentarily baffled. What was a drawing of Lily's pendant doing on the same draft sheet as a sketch of what could only be the navaratna charm? And why did it seem that the two were related, for the drawing was rendered in such a way as to demonstrate how these two similarly shaped pieces might interlock and become one. And then it struck her. This was exactly what they were: one. She drew in her breath sharply and stood up so abruptly that her chair fell backwards to the floor. She looked around the table and noticed that Martha had disappeared into the scullery. Lark was looking as smug as a cat and Gerard was still shaking his head. Govinda sat perfectly still, but, if anything, he looked relieved rather than guilty. When she glared at him pointedly, he shrugged.

'I do not have the pendant, Miss Sarah.'

'Do you mean,' said Inspector Gerard incredulously, 'How on earth . . . .?' He was clearly too astonished to complete his sentence .

'We must not jump to conclusions,' Lark cautioned, 'for remember, the drawings were made seven years ago, and no one has ever seen this mysterious navaratna charm, apart from those who have died. It is just as likely that the diamonds are elsewhere. Now, Miss O'Reilly, am I to understand that you are no longer in possession of the pendant?'

As Sarah was about to recount how she had discovered that the pendant was missing, Martha Vesper returned from the scullery. There was something expectant in the housekeeper's bearing and the way she approached the table. She was carrying one of the stoneware jars in which she kept her dried herbs. She stood for a moment without speaking, though the attention of everyone was upon her, for it was clear that she had something of importance to say. She put the pot on the table in front of Sarah, and busied herself clearing away all the tea things.

'What is it, Martha?' Sarah uncorked the jar and recognised the bitter odour of dried sage, the herb which Martha used to discourage .unwelcome spirits. Yet it appeared that there was nothing in the jar but a wad of cheese cloth, dusty with the powdered dregs of the herb. As soon as her hand closed around the cloth, Sarah knew what was wrapped inside it. She unwound the cheese cloth and placed the pendant on the table. No one spoke, and Sarah could only think that it was peculiar how knowing what might be hidden inside altered the very nature of the pendant. Finally, she looked at Martha Vesper.

'You took it Martha?'

The housekeeper nodded but showed no remorse. 'It bore ill tidings and I was more than sorry to see it in this house again. I did not want you to be harmed by it, for it was plain as day that you were sickening whilst you wore it.'

Long ago, Sarah would have asked how on earth a piece of jewellery could possibly cause her harm, but now she did not. Instead, she watched as Martha Vesper busied herself lighting the gas lanterns on the table as the rain continued to fall, making the day seem grey and leaden.

It was Inspector Gerard who dared to pick up the pendant. He turned it over in his hand, examining how it was made.

'An ingenious design,' he said, glancing at Govinda. 'Am I right in thinking that the hairwork was designed for the express purpose of disguising the navaratna, so that it might secretly be returned to India?'

Govinda nodded. 'Lady Herbert knew that she would not live long enough to return to Benares, and she also knew that I would not carry the diamonds. We agreed that this was the solution.'

'But, why transport it in such a way? And why give it to Lily to carry?'

'Memsahib Lily would not be corrupted, in the event that she dis-covered the hidden diamonds. It is the traditional character of navaratna to reflect the nature of desire. Should one wish for things beyond the realm of goodness, or be ... I think your English word is narcissistic, then its power becomes destructive. But a navaratna jewel made entirely from diamonds has unpredictable energies.' Govinda looked down sadly. 'I believe that this was what fatally weakened Memsahib Lily.'

Sarah's mind was in turmoil. 'It was you who took the pendant from Lily when she died, then?'

'I'm afraid it is so. It was impossible to persuade her to remove it while she was alive.'

'But then why did you hide it in the portrait?'

'It seemed the appropriate place. I could not simply dispose of the diamonds as they did not belong to me, but I did not want either the Maharajah or Sarasvati to have the finished charm in their possession. The hairwork part of the jewel was special to Memsahib Lily, so by hiding it in the portrait, the pendant was still with her and the diamonds remained in the palace.'

'Extraordinary,' said Gerard. 'Then it was both the mourning piece and the navaratna that Finkelstein was working on the night he died, which is why we found the pendant on his table. By law, the pendant belongs to you, Miss O'Reilly. The fact that the diamonds might be concealed within it makes it a rather more complicated matter, of course. Still, do you agree that it might be taken away and dismantled? Of course, there is no knowing whether or not the diamonds are still inside . . .' All eyes were now on the pendant, which lay in the centre of the bare table, the white of the hairwork startling against the smooth jet.

Sarah did not hesitate. 'Yes, it must be, for the diamonds belong to the Maharajah.'

'Then I propose that we take it to a jeweller and have him remove the glass casing and the jet . . .' but Gerard did not finish his sentence, for Govinda was now standing behind the detective inspector, his arms raised high above his head, grasping the hilt of his sabre. As the blade of the sabre came down, someone screamed, and afterwards Sarah was chagrined to realise that it had been herself. But the glinting, razor sharp sword had done no one harm. It had, in fact, landed precisely and with the force intended on the pendant, forcing open the hidden hinge. Now, lying on the table beside the two pieces of the cleaved pendant was an exquisite disc of wrought gold containing coloured diamonds, nine in total.

'Mercy me!' said Martha Vesper, her hand flying to her mouth, and she spoke for every person around the table as they gazed at the magnificence of the jewel. The coloured diamonds, with the inauspicious red jewel flaring in the central position, were set in a ring around the edge of the solid-gold disc; each corresponding to a compass point, or a planetary one. Around each was an engraving of tiny sanskrit characters.

Nothing could have prepared Sarah for the astonishing beauty of the navaratna charm, for even though the sky outside was darkened by ill weather, still the diamonds beamed as though each were illuminated from within. But it was the red diamond, the sun stone, which was the most radiant and commanding. The silence which had fallen was almost reverent, or perhaps fearful, in its incandescent presence.

'It would be a shame to destroy an object of such beauty,' breathed Sarah, finally.

'It is no shame,' said Govinda sharply, and the strain in his normally calm voice reflected the tension in the room. In a second he had brought his weapon down once more; again his aim was terrifyingly precise, for part of the soft gold bezel around the red diamond was peeled away as if it were nothing more than paper. Govinda stepped forward and seized the scarlet diamond from the amulet then dropped it on the white table cloth as though it had burnt his fingers. There it lay like a drop of blood, for no one attempted to pick it up or examine it more closely. Sarah suddenly felt weak with relief. It was over.

The rain had ceased, and through the kitchen windows the sky was a warm rose. Martha, as pragmatic as ever, roused herself from where she sat and set about making more of her strong souchong tea.

For a time no one spoke. The quality of the silence had altered; as though all spirits were at peace, be they incarnate or not. Inspector Gerard finally pushed back his chair, and Lark followed suit. 'I take it you still consider yourself custodian of the stones, Mr Govinda?'

The Indian bowed his head in affirmation. 'I must ensure that they are safely delivered to the Maharajah.'

'I should very much like to have spoken to you again, with regard to the death of Vikram, Mr Govinda, but perhaps we will not have the opportunity?'

'No, perhaps not, Inspector.' Govinda looked at Sarah and it seemed to her that he had returned to his former self. 'I am sorry to have dismantled the mourning piece, Miss Sarah. I think that it held special meaning for you. I'm afraid I am not skilled enough to replace the facing.'

'I shall take it to the Gold and Silversmiths' Company on Regent Street,' Inspector Gerard assured him. 'Now, please allow me to deliver you to Hyde Park in my carriage.'

Whilst Martha found a clean silk handkerchief in which to wrap the dismantled charm, Inspector Lark took a sheet of parchment from his wallet and wrote upon it. He handed it to Govinda. 'A receipt, Sir, which states that one navaratna charm containing eight coloured diamonds, and one red diamond, being the property of the Maharajah of Uttar Pradesh, shall be held in the safety of the police vault at the Westminster Station, and that it may only be collected by his representative, Mr Govinda.'

Govinda bowed in agreement and placed the folded parchment in his pocket before taking his leave. At the kitchen door, he turned to Sarah, 'I hope that we shall meet before I depart.'

Sarah nodded. 'I too, but I want no further encounters with the mistress Kali!' She saw Govinda smile as he turned away.

Martha departed to light the lamps in the carriageway, and Lark bade Sarah farewell. As he gripped her hand his smile sparkled with pleasure, then he and the three constables left her alone in the kitchen with Inspector Gerard.

'You will need rest,' said Gerard, with no attempt to disguise the concern in his clear hazel eyes. 'Will you allow me to call on you, to ensure that you are recovered, Miss O'Reilly?' He held her gaze for longer than was polite.

'I am accustomed to looking after myself,' Sarah replied. 'But I hope that you will call on me, just the same.'

⁑ 44 ⁑

And a stranger, when he see her
In the street even – smileth stilly,
Just as you would at a lily.

And all fancies yearn to cover
The hard earth where on she passes
With the thymy scented grasses

Elizabeth Barrett Browning

The doorbell sounded just as Sarah had settled herself at the table in the library and was about to open her leather pocket book, the one she reserved for ideas. It was the first time she had attempted to work in the week since the discovery of the diamonds. The call could not be the morning post, for it had already arrived and had included a notelet from Detective Inspector Gerard. He was frustrated, he wrote, that he had not had time to call, but had seen Ellen at the *Mercury*, who had informed him that her sister was greatly improved. And, if it were so, would Sarah be well enough to take a curative walk in the autumn sunshine on the morrow? Perhaps, he suggested, they might walk part of the distance to the Ropemakers' Fields, and when she was weary, take a cabriolet the remainder. Sarah had replied, in agreement.

Having only a moment ago seen Martha upstairs filling lavender bags so that the linen in the airing closet might smell sweet, Sarah rose, still pondering the day's first sentence. In that moment, Mrs Vesper appeared. Her expression was odd.

'Mr Govinda is here to see you, Miss.'

'Thank you. I shall see him in the parlour, Martha.' The housekeeper did not look as though she thought it at all wise, and closed the door so quietly that she might just as well have slammed it shut.

The parlour was really Lily's room, although no one ever referred to it as such. Here were the more decorative pieces of furniture from

Waterloo Street; the bohemian chaise lounge with the carved feet; Franz's low, leather armchair; the piano. There were Kashmir shawls across the backs of chairs and the turquoise and silver brocade silk which Sarah had purchased in Benares was now draped across a divan. *The Venus of Waterloo* had pride of place on the wall above the hearth, in a new, plain mahogany frame. When Sarah entered, Govinda was standing, gazing at the painting.

'I have come to say goodbye, Miss Sarah. I have passage this evening to Bombay.'

'And will you be taking the diamonds with you, back to the Maharajah?'

'I will. I promptly wired him to advise him of their recovery, and yesterday received his reply. From his telegraph, I would say that he is pleased.' Govinda smiled a little to himself, as though this were rather an understatement.

'And what will happen to the diamonds when they have been returned to the prince?'

'I suggested, before I left Benares, that if I was able to recover the nine diamonds for him, the red stone must be returned to Kali.'

'And he is willing to relinquish it?'

'The Maharajah has, as you might say, come to his senses. He seemed greatly changed in his reply to me, and I think that for the first time he recognises the absolute devotion of Sarasvati, and that she would love him even if she did not have the jewels and finery which are the assets of her position. I believe he might find that there is a greater purpose after all, than the glory of victory in battle.'

'And what of Sarasvati?'

'She has had the opportunity to recognise the law of dharma; the way of higher truths, for her actions led to the deaths not only of her priest but also Charles Herbert and those who were murdered in London. She herself will return the red diamond to the eye of Kali in her village and then she will know that the cycle of destruction caused by the discordant navaratna has finally reached its conclusion.'

Sarah nodded slowly. But there were things that had not been resolved in this strange case. 'It was Vikram who killed Lord Herbert, was it not?'

'Yes.'

Sarah did not hesitate to continue, for if she did, she would falter in her resolve to know the truth. 'And it was you who killed Vikram?'

Govinda neither flinched nor hesitated in his reply. 'It was necessary. He would have continued to pursue the red diamond, killing anyone who came between him and his purpose.'

'But he did not carry out those killings on his own.'

Govinda looked long and hard at Sarah. 'The other party was an innocent, driven by quite a different desire. On the night that I was following Vikram in Devil's Acre, the stone from the slingshot which hit him was intended for me. It only missed its mark because it was fired at the precise moment that I accosted Vikram.'

'Then, whomever hit Vikram was trying to protect him?'

'Yes, and you yourself must know who that is.'

As the terrible truth of this dawned, Sarah felt numb.

'There is no crime in an intention which is true, Miss Sarah. We have all caused pain when it was not intended.' Within his fleeting expression of sorrow, Sarah finally understood why Govinda had retreated to the mountains, and why he always appeared so distant. He believed that he had been unforgivably neglectful; that he had failed, and in this, had been indirectly responsible not only for the murders of Peasey and Finkelstein, but also for Lily's death.

'But you have undertaken what a lesser man would not, Mr Govinda. You have twice travelled from your home and across the seas in order to protect innocent people.'

She met his steady gaze. 'And you have kept a secret to protect a child, at risk to your own liberty.'

'Thank you, Miss Sarah. But now I must leave you. It has been my great pleasure to know you, and I hope that, if you ever return to Benares, you will ask for me.'

'Will you be there?'

Govinda shrugged. 'Who can say?' He bowed graciously and showed himself out, closing the door behind him.

Sarah returned to the library, deep in thought and opened the leather pocket book which Gerard had given to her. Her gaze fell upon the unfinished verse by Charlotte Brontë, as it always did, yet she still had not investigated the remainder of the stanza. On a whim, she rose and found a book of verse which would most certainly contain it and leafed through its pages urgently, suddenly desperate to know. When she found what she was looking for, she sat and read, her heart pounding.

If thou be in a lonely place,
If one hour's calm be thine,
As evening bends her placid face,
O'er this sweet day's decline,
If all the earth and all the heavens,
Now look serene to thee,
As o'er them shouts the summer even,
One moment – think of me!

❖ Epilogue ❖

The next day, as arranged, the detective inspector was waiting for Sarah at the western wall of Westminster Cathedral. If he was surprised that she wanted to walk all the way to Limehouse Reach, rather than ride part of the way in his carriage, he did not show it. It was customary to walk, Sarah assured him, for once she and Ellen had had no other means by which to reach the fields from Devil's Acre.

Instead of skirting around the Acre, Sarah led the way directly through her old stamping ground, just to ensure that she was not needlessly frightened by a place which now contained almost as many dark memories as happy ones. She pointed out to Gerard Holy Joe's doss house, the White Hart and, when they reached the embankment, the herring docks from which her Pa had gone off fishing. They had walked this way on the day that Davey was arrested, but now it all felt different; today, Sarah wanted Gerard to understand that this was where she came from.

They followed the river pathway again, a route so familiar to Sarah that she knew every kink in the bank and each turn of the tide. At the Whitehall Stairs, Sarah remembered a day when she had seen Ellen, Holy Joe and Vikram sitting together on the steps. She stopped still, just at the spot where Ellen had been when Sarah saw her take a pot shot at a passing steamboat with Holy Joe's slingshot, knocking a gentleman's hat clean off his head. Gerard stopped with her and looked concerned.

'Are you weary, Miss O'Reilly, perhaps we should . . .'

Sarah interrupted before he could finish his sentence. 'No, no. But there is something I must tell you.'

She described to him what had happened that day on the Whitehall

Stairs, just as she remembered it. She told him neither what she thought about that event nor what she feared, nor did she explain why it was that Ellen had fallen into a world where a childish fantasy had become so necessary. Gerard only nodded his head, and although he did not say so, Sarah thought that he had already guessed who Vikram's associate was.

After Govinda's visit the previous day, Sarah and Ellen had taken their afternoon tea in the garden, for the air was temperate and dry. When Martha brought them teacakes, she looked at Sarah in the same odd way as she had when she announced Govinda's visit. Then Sarah understood that Martha knew. Of course the housekeeper must have guessed what unfinished business would be discussed in the drawing room. Martha's expression had not escaped Ellen's attention either. In only a moment, an unspoken agreement was made between the three women: a child could not be held responsible for something which she had done in innocence, and it would never be spoken of between them.

At Temple Pier, Sarah and Gerard watched a clipper docking. At London Bridge, they rested, and strayed as far as the coffee houses on Lombard Street, to take a glass of the Abyssinian bean with some pie. By the time they reached Limehouse, Sarah was glad she had worn her breeches, for they were far more practical for climbing over a fence into a field in the company of a gentleman.

Sarah sat down beside the row of wooden crosses; all three with the name O'Reilly carved into them. She watched Inspector Gerard, who was wandering thoughtfully towards the upper part of the field, his hands behind his back. Beyond, the distant chimneys of lime factories and paper mills smouldered, but the field, being overgrown and on the very edges of the East End, felt fittingly remote. Occasionally Gerard would stop to read the name on a cross, or examine the dappled colour on a burnished leaf. What she liked most about Detective Inspector Gerard, Sarah thought, was the way he always walked carefully upon the earth, as though he respected every part of it. Even Devil's Acre. In his presence, not only was her habitual aloneness altered, but also the empty place in her heart, created by the absence of so many loved.

When last she had sat here, Sarah recalled, the graves were still draped in the wreaths of summer. Now each cross was laid bare. Inspector Gerard returned and stood for a moment, respectfully, a short distance away. Sarah smiled up at him and patted the grass beside her. She did not need to tell him how special this place was to her and Ellen; he understood.

Gerard reached into his pocket and brought out something wrapped in brown paper. Beneath the wrapping was a small, black sateen box, embossed with the insignia of the Gold and Silversmith's Company.

'I collected it this morning. They have done a fine job, though the goldsmith was most curious to know how the pendant came to be broken in such a way.'

'And what did you tell him?'

'I told him that it had been cut with a sabre by a Hindu warrior, and he simply laughed.'

Sarah removed the lid from the box. The object, which rested in scarlet satin, was even more lovely than it had been its original form. A gold rim now embraced the gleaming oval of black jet, and beneath its smooth glass casing the delicate circlet of lilies had been repaired with infinite care. The workmanship was exquisite. The pendant now felt lighter, of course.

'I am overwhelmed,' she said, finally.

'It is improved,' he agreed, obviously pleased, then added drily, 'especially through not being a vessel for smuggled diamonds.'

Sarah smiled. 'I imagine that by now the stones will have passed through the Thames Estuary, and the fearsome Kali will soon be reunited with her beloved diamond.'

'Indeed, for I have had confirmation from St Katherine's Dock. The brave and mysterious gentleman from Uttar Pradesh has set sail for the Orient.'

'And Sarasvati has been reunited with her prince.'

'So each is returned to her beloved.' He looked at her quizzically, Sarah thought, as though he were wordlessly asking her a question, and waiting for her reply.

She allowed a moment's grace in order that she be certain of her feelings. 'Although I might be accustomed to caring for myself, that is not to say that I prefer it, always ...'

'Then, perhaps you might prefer to do so only sometimes?'

'Yes, perhaps.'

Sarah undid the clasp which fastened the chain of the pendant.

Gerard was watching her closely, his normally serious face much softened. She handed the pendant to him, allowing him to brush her hair to one side and fasten it about her neck, his fingers grazing her skin lightly.

The sun was low when they stood to leave, for it had taken the greater part of the day to walk to the fields from Westminster. Gerard offered Sarah his arm, and they turned together towards the city. She touched the smooth disc resting against her breast bone and felt Lily close to her heart. She felt something else also; it was an odd quietude, as though all of the events which had brought her to this moment had finally found their peace.

Those who scorn my powers, be wary, and look to the histories: to the tales of cursed diamonds for which kingdoms have fallen. There are many such stones, and such stories; it is believed that I have cast spells and maledictions, for wherever is Diamond's blinding light are also the deepest shadows. The matter from which I am formed illuminates the stars, and when I touch the human form the energies of the planets and their gods are set loose. With my great age, comes knowledge of the histories, and wisdom, for my aspect inflicts desire such as few can resist. I am impotent without this. Desire itself gives me life; its actions form my fate, for an action without desire has no destiny.

Acknowledgements:

THE NINTH STONE started to take shape over conversations with two family members – my sister, Kirsten, a jewellery designer, silversmith and gem fanatic, and my brother, Conan, who first told me about the navaratna and later accompanied me to India.

Several other people were also generous with their time and knowledge: Keith Penton, then a Departmental Director at Bonhams in London, introduced me to the traditions of mourning jewellery and hairwork, and Mallika Sagar at Christie's in Bombay helped with the research in India. Morag Irwin suggested to me that what, to some, appears as a superstition, is considered a science by others . . .

I would like to thank my German publishers, Ullstein Buchverlage: my editor, Monica Boese, for her work on the German edition of THE NINTH STONE (DER NEUNTE DIAMANT), and Siv Bublitz for her support and understanding. I would also like to thank June Badcock for championing my work.

Kirsty Dunseath at Weidenfeld & Nicolson inspired and encouraged me to revise THE NINTH STONE for publication in the UK. She worked very hard to make this happen, and I thank her for her support and for her cretive input.

I am most grateful to Richenda Todd, who asked questions, made suggestions and smoothed over the wrinkles.

My greatest thanks are to my wonderful agent, Kate Hordern, who was there from the beginning to the end and whose ideas, support and friendship always keep me going.